Running
with
Buffalo

No Frills
<<<>>>
Buffalo
Buffalo, NY

D1446064

No Frills Buffalo
119 Dorchester Road
Buffalo, NY 14213

For more information visit
Nofrillsbuffalo.com

For my supportive family and friends, Christina and
Dr. Richard Simpson.

Also, to proud Buffalonians in New York and elsewhere, thank you.
This second edition wouldn't exist without you.

Running with Buffalo

by Michael Farrell

<<<>>

1

The buffalo chase dreams started in college.

The chase wasn't across the wide-open plains or Montana ranches where these two-thousand pound animals would roam. The pursuit was down littered city streets and along rocky lakeshores. I'd smell its scent and run through its dust as it galloped over my neighbors' driveways and groomed lawns. Every time, its shaggy fur would be inches out of my reach. This was a dream I'd have often, and when I would wake from it, I'd routinely question its meaning.

Why the chase? And why buffalo?

The cover art of the U2 CD single "One" showed buffalo, one by one, running off of a stony cliff. On the back of the case, it explained how Indians used to hunt buffalo toward cliffs so the beasts would throw themselves over. Maybe the cover's image had slipped into my subconscious to symbolize something else as it sat stacked amid my many discs. What was I really chasing? Was I approaching a cliff? An end?

And that's what people do with their dreams: analyze. More appropriately, that's what people do when they decide to evaluate themselves. But all dreams aren't subliminal, intriguingly symbolic of elevated meaning. Some dreams are simply calculated wanderlust, completely void of buffalo, antelope or any lumbering animal. There were those times when I lay in my bed, hands behind my head, and stared into the ceiling to take myself where I wanted to be, doing what I wanted to do. I'd pass away hours with thoughts of actions or activities that may or may not ever happen. Some people gaze out of a car window as it cruises seaside, staring into the vacant sky like it may hold the answers to where they'll be when they find the satisfaction their dreams are searching for. It's a satisfaction that, in a head flooded with expectations, stands as an unimaginable representation of security.

Approaching adulthood, those dreams grow a bit more complex, sometimes an extension of our professional aspirations.

Maybe you're seated for a succulent seafood dinner at a scenic location overlooking the Atlantic Ocean, flanked by your gray-haired CEO and his promiscuous, buxom and perpetually flirtatious assistant who appreciates the amount of protein in a salmon filet. This chief executive's name is Mr. Gary Buford, and Mr. Buford's actually dim enough to think you don't know he's bedding this emerald-eyed assistant, whose name is Bethany. But this information is peripheral; it's your dream, and these philandering issues are not of your concern.

Because of the fifteen percent market share increase you secured for the drugs Saxisil, Bilotex and Quadrophox last quarter, you are the top pharmaceutical salesman on the East Coast under the watchful eye of Mr. Buford, and in his hands rest a crystal plaque with your name carved into its base. With that plaque will be a raise, and with that raise will come your own office. With that office will be your own assistant, and after the dinner, the boss asks that you call him "Gary." He looks forward to working with you closely, and when you're ready to hire an assistant, Gary says Bethany has a "special" friend who'd be perfect.

But maybe that's not your dream. It might still be a scene of professional success, but your vision projects a different image. Your type of achievement provides an internal satisfaction that Bethany's friend, regardless of her charm and grace, would never deliver. In your dream, maybe you're an elementary school teacher or a social worker at a homeless shelter in the heart of an urban death maze you embrace after college. Maybe you don't see the success in your wallet as much as you see it reflected on the young or weary faces that surround your daily toil. It's a soulful gratification that allows you to walk to the bathroom mirror every day, take a good look into your eyes, and realize you see a person of morals, decency and character. As you peer deep into those blues, browns or emeralds, you are a person who cares about the mind over money, the soul over stocks. Yeah, maybe that is you. I'd like to think it's me, too.

But this is our adulthood. It's a constant duel between right and wrong. Between relevance and responsibility; between what we want to do and what we have to do. It always takes place in our dreams because reality plays out too fast in front of our faces. We wake up in the morning to take a shower, grab a bowl of cereal, shove some buttered toast in our pocket, then slug down a mug of luke-warm coffee while we iron our shirts for another day at a job we might not want, but need if we want to keep the creditors from circling. Before we know it, the day is over, and we scurry through faceless crowds and fight our way to a dreary train platform or the tallest parking garage. Off to the nearest gin mill or gymnasium to work off stress from another day we never envisioned in any of our dreams. After a good hour split between the Stairmaster, exercise bike or two stiff cocktails, it's back home for another hot shower, a dinner consisting of angel hair pasta and wheat bread, and a night of whatever mind-numbing drivel the television networks are pushing. It might be a reality show featuring a team of midgets challenging a team of elephants to drag a seven forty-seven down a runway with their teeth, but we don't have the energy or time to care. It'll be bedtime soon, so we lean back and enjoy the brain drain. We'll do it all again tomorrow because we can't stop the cycle, and the cycle rolls on. Soon enough, responsibility will dwarf relevance, and the cycle will have hypnotized us into a mindset concluding, "This is the way it is, no matter how stupid, pointless, and soulless it all may seem."

This reality could not be further from the dreams we had as kids. Personally, I never dreamed of dreading a nine-to-five in a corporate tower when I was a kid. Not once. When I was a child, my dreams weren't about responsibility or relevance. They were my dreams, and could be about whatever I wanted.

Thoughts of playing professional football under the falling snow of January, marrying the saucer-eyed sass box from down the street, or dropping the biggest kid in my neighborhood with one punch before laughing over him as he'd cry for his mother. These were the thoughts the permeated my days and nights. These were my childhood dreams I dreamt about, lying in my backyard on a Tuesday night, with the smell of freshly cut grass battling an aroma of grilled hot dogs over charcoal that drifted under my nose until nightfall. I never had to classify these fantasies as whimsical because I was in a time of whimsy, basking in youthful optimism. No one was barking in my face about how each could never happen, because when I was a kid, nothing had been broken yet. No spirits had been shattered, no aspiration had been deemed fool-hearty. None.

I was a dreamer. A skinny, freckle-faced, brown-eyed, floppy-haired, fatheaded dreamer.

I was a kid who believed playing the piano someday for Bruce Springsteen & the E Street Band on "She's The One" was absolutely possible; an optimist who believed it was only a matter of time before Huey Lewis and the News would need a new guitarist. I was a dreamer who believed that being a short, Irish Catholic from south of downtown Buffalo, New York wouldn't be a hindrance toward my NFL draft status. I would be the hometown scrapper, and that would be a big plus in Manhattan on draft day when my Buffalo Bills would select me as a defensive back.

When I was a kid, who could have told me that Springsteen would never let Roy Bittan vacate his piano bench, even after The Boss broke up the rest of the E Street Band before recording *Human Touch* and *Lucky Town*? No one. If anyone would have told me Huey Lewis wouldn't take his red suit and black t-shirt combo much further than the "I Want A New Drug" video but would later show up in a movie about karaoke hustling with some skinny actress named Gwyneth, I wouldn't have listened. And as I worked on my footwork and upper body strength, if anyone warned that my weight would stagnate at one-fifty and my height at five-ten due to genetics, lack of sleep, cigarettes, and heavy coffee consumption starting at age fifteen, I would have called them insane. Not only would I be at least six-feet tall and weigh two-ten, I would never stay up late in high school talking to girls on the phone. Coffee? Disgusting. Cigarettes? Butts were for outlaw bikers and old bingo ladies, not me. I was going to play cornerback in Buffalo's open-air cathedral called Rich Stadium, with Bills owner Ralph Wilson looking down at me from the owner's box through his thick-rimmed glasses, giving me the thumbs up after my fourth down pass deflection secured another AFC title for our city of champions.

"You're alright, kid," he'd say behind a cocky smile and gleaming dentures.

If anyone predicted the Bills would experience a string of catastrophic Super Bowl losses, later rename the stadium after Wilson, and finally, have to bring New England folk hero Doug Flutie down from Canada to save the franchise from relocation, I'd have collapsed in laughter.

The beauty of our childhood dreams always shimmered with their limitless boundaries. But now? As days roll by, the idea of any dreaming seems more and more frivolous and wasteful. If a dream does slip through, it's thought to be intriguingly symbolic of some unseen problem to be worked out with medication and a therapist's black leather couch.

Our hectic lifestyles have advanced us past our designation as Generation X or Y and full steam into our classification as Generation What's Next, so suffocated by future plans and obligations that our opportunity to daydream has evaporated. Daydreams waste minutes we could be spending in a cubicle, making money for a new coupe and spacious condo, or making calls to connect with a key corporate contact. Time to get ahead, but when we sit for a minute and think about what our childhood dreams meant, what do these mean? What's the goal anymore?

A house? A family? A career? And then what? What's next for our generation? When those materialistic dreams are achieved, are we going to be happy? Are we going to feel that internal satisfaction, with the warmth in our chest and chill down our spine we felt on summer nights as children? When these items are secured, are we even going to know what satisfaction is anymore? Are you sick of asking yourself these questions about the dreams you used to enjoy as frivolous fantasizing?

I am.

I'm also sick of examining my dreams, trying to find underlying meaning to visions I used to attribute to eating chocolate or salsa before going to bed. Night eating bred weird visions, and I was fine with that excuse.

But now, what does it mean when I dream I'm an acrobat, wearing army fatigues and walking a tightrope with no net below? As I walk the tightrope, Kelly Ripa, Regis Philbin, and ex-Miami Dolphins' quarterback Dan Marino watch me, heckling me to take a fall. Sweat drips from my sideburns and eyebrows. When I look down, I feel dizzy. Then Marino yells some disparaging remark, like,

"Eat it, pal! Eat it!"

With hecklings in my ear, my right foot slips, and I start to fall to my death. I scream and yell as loud as I can,

"Help! Help!"

And just before I hit the ground, I wake up in a cold sweat that drenches my face, back and bed sheets.

It was all a dream, and a ridiculous one that made absolutely no sense; some dreams don't. Chances are that, before I went to bed, I flipped the television channels through a show about the circus, an ad for Regis and Kelly's next show, and then an ad for the U.S. Army. As for Marino, well, maybe I fucking despise Dan Marino. Blend that together with seven beers and a ninety-nine-cent bag of cheese puffs and you have the makings of one freaky, nonsensical nightmare.

But when I wake from chasing the buffalo, I know the scenario is a therapist's dream, one asking to be probed by some waiting professional. It's not a collage of images, but a continuous chase that always has me trailing. If I only woke up from this dream once or twice, I'd have shrugged it off. But, on many nights, in multiple cities, and at various ages, I, Joseph P. Cahan, have been running after this once proud lord of the prairie.

Standing at the entrance of my college graduation ceremony, I sincerely wondered if I'd ever catch it.

2

As twenty-two-year-old student of St. Francis University in Cuba, New York, I stood short of six feet, with a skinny frame and my fat, Irish Catholic head intact. The freckles were still there, and they multiplied on those southwestern New York days when the sun shone down upon my face.

My aspirations had matured a bit past the goals of my childhood by the morning of my graduation. I stashed my piano dreams for good when the E Street Band returned to touring at full strength. Before my junior year, I had to sell my guitar for beer money and my secondhand amp to pay for books and a dry turkey sandwich, so Huey and the boys would have to tour county fairs without me. No longer did I harbor any thoughts about making it to the NFL either; I couldn't even carry my dorm intramural team to a campus championship. With my legs cramped from college lounging and lungs corroded with Camel Light resin, I was lucky to get off the line of scrimmage to run a simple slant route.

But, through some coffee-fueled nights on the yellow pages of stray legal pads, I did develop a love for writing.

I was a straight-A journalism student, except for one Intro to Mass Communications class I bombed freshman year. Going into college, writing was the only occupation I could ever see myself performing for a career, even if most students find out later they don't know shit at age eighteen. I was able to effortlessly shape my opinions into relevant papers for classes, and my professors encouraged me to mold a style of writing as my own. I progressed and tried to incorporate journalistic structure when creating short stories and poems, but couldn't even get mainstream work published in our school paper. I stopped submitted pieces after they turned down my sophomore year concert review on the local Rolling Stones tribute band, Sticky Fingers. In proclaiming the lead singer's sexual energy as meteoric and the drummer's Charlie Watts homage transcendent, I was convinced I penned critical gold. *The Franciscan Weekly* didn't agree, but when I opened that issue, I found they did agree a two-page spread devoted to "St. Francis University's Favorite Campus Puppies" would wow the student populace. There were even pictures of the owners, with testimonials about what their little puppies meant to each one of them. After this, I found no reason to ever be involved in our school newspaper.

To me, the job of a writer was to live, then detail life's outcome in print. If I could get paid to live, I figured that was the way to go. Along with writing about the countless adventures I'd inevitably fall into for newspapers and magazines, maybe I could develop some manuscripts about teen angst, or some crap about the male quest to find love in a confused world. Kind of like the literary answer to John Hughes, but without Judd Nelson or Andrew McCarthy.

If I ever did land a job as a writer, I wondered if I would have the opportunity to work where I was raised. Growing up off the shores of Lake Erie in a section of the Buffalo region known as the Southtowns, I had a view of the water just down the street from my family's house. It wasn't the ocean, but as one of the Great Lakes, our neighbors treated it like one. Feeling the breeze roll off its subtle waves and up my street, or admiring how the sun set over its placid surface on a warm summer night made me appreciate its existence as much as any other body of water. Lake Erie was part of the neighborhood, and when I would come home from college over breaks and holidays, I'd always make my father drive by it. It made me feel alive, and ideally, I wanted to work by its side.

Problem was Buffalo wasn't a known haven for aspiring writers, being a one-newspaper town with few places to beg for stable creative work. They filmed parts of *The Natural* in the city in the early eighties, and portions of the bizarre, independent favorite *Buffalo 66* were shot on the edge of the Southtowns. But two major projects didn't highlight the city as fertile ground for future prospects. Realistically, I knew I'd have to leave at some point to start a career, but I always intended to come back. My desired future always had Buffalo as its backdrop.

Getting out of bed, I hoped to toss on a bathrobe and walk

over to my home office blinds. With a cup of coffee in my right hand, I'd slide them open to reveal a beautiful wide shot of the water crashing against the shore on a windy sun-soaked summer morning. I'd look at that scene, take a deep breath, and then sit down at my desk. With the view to my right, I'd start my day writing. My wife would approach for a good morning kiss, and if she so pleased, she'd head out to work. Sipping my expensive Costa Rican coffee, I'd probably be so wealthy that the wife would have this choice. "Leave the kids with me," I'd say of the three young children we'd have.

While typing my next eagerly anticipated novel, they'd play around their stay-at-home dad. I'd type all day with a wide smile, only to get up for phone calls from my literary agent. I'd tell him to continue negotiations with the publisher, but not to bother calling me with any news between three and five. That's when I'd be taking the kids to the Buffalo Zoo to see the giraffes before heading over to Delaware Park for an ice cream and a walk through the rose garden. After five o'clock, my phone would ring and he'd tell me the extent of the offer: enough money to buy more Costa Rican coffee, send the kids to Catholic elementary school, private high school, then off to the college or university of their choice. Enough left over for family to appreciate ancestral roots in Ireland every summer, and enough exposure to keep my established literary fame rolling for years.

I recalled those nights I spent detailing such plans as I stood in my black cap and gown on graduation day. When I sat on barstools and next to kegs earlier that year, this became my mantra. Typing toward fame and fortune sounded great to me, and as people stood around with red plastic cups in their hands and smokes hanging from their lips, their nodding heads agreed. I was certain my plan was better than others' to attend graduate or law school. "Avoiding the inevitable," I'd say about this safe path of extended education. They were afraid of leaving the classroom's safe cocoon, tilting their noses out of books and rolling up their sleeves to get humbled and humiliated for what they want. They were afraid of working for a living, pressing the flesh and putting in the hours necessary to rise through the ranks of employment like our fathers and grandfathers had done before us. John Lennon once said, "A working class hero is something to be." Since John Winston Lennon was one of my heroes, be it with the Beatles, the Plastic Ono Band or jamming in his pajamas with Yoko in a Montreal hotel room, I was fine with this line. Of course, if I were a smarter guy at the time, I would have paid attention to the complete lyrics instead of ripping out one line as an identification of his views, since the song doesn't symbolize my stance at all.

Mr. Lennon also went on to state that, "they hate when you're clever, and they despise the fool." "They" were the teeth of entry-level Corporate America, ready to chew up new recruits. "They" were the unforgiving claws of a selective school board, reluctant to give out full-time teaching jobs to grads who suffered through student teaching. Hell, "they" would even be the unemployment office grads would slip into if employers weren't as enthused about their introspective, albeit impractical, major. Maybe Art History wasn't such a good idea after all.

But not for me. I wasn't afraid of casting myself out into the abyss for a chance at success. Journalism degree be damned, negative thoughts were completely absent from my head on the morning of my graduation ceremony. Actually, as a hand tapped my right shoulder that morning, the only thing running through my head was the throbbing pain of a monumental hangover.

"Dude, how are you feeling? You still look and smell like shit."

Standing behind me was my senior year roommate, Eli Moorman. With his long curly hair still dripping from the shower and onto the vibrant colors of the tie-dyed Phish t-shirt collar that peeked from the neck of his satin robe, he'd rolled me off our condemned blue couch so we'd make it to the ceremony on time. The couch fumed of stale smoke and staler beer from a year's worth of celebrations, so when Eli found me sprawled out in the a.m., he optimistically hoped it was our furniture that smelt. Standing two feet away from me, he realized otherwise.

On a morning we'd waited our whole lives for, I wore the faded blue Buffalo Bisons t-shirt and dirty khakis I woke up in underneath my black robe. My brown hair was greasily matted underneath my cap, and when I licked the front of my teeth, they tasted like the inside of a minivan ashtray. After a night celebrating an event that had yet to be consummated, I felt like I had dropped a drinking contest to Keith Richards and a cigarette smoke-off to John Mellencamp. After paying over eighty grand for a collegiate education, I didn't have the time to take a shower on the morning of my departure from it. Swipes of antiperspirant under my arms and generous aftershave on my neck was all I could administer to hide the aroma of the previous night's bottles of Budweiser and generous shots of Southern Comfort. According to Eli, it wasn't masked enough.

But I wasn't alone. On my right stood a girl I sat behind in Marketing 101. Her eyes were bloodshot, her lips looked chapped, and her blonde hair flowed snarled out from underneath her graduation cap. A few rows over stood a tall Polish rugby player who lived a few doors down my freshman year, with bags under his eyes that could have held two sacks of pennies. When he saw me, he offered a "hello" nod, but it could have served as a thank you for the chilled shot of Jameson's whiskey I bought him the previous night. I remembered his squeamish face as he choked it down, so the nod would have to do.

Along the sides of a sallow hallway leading into the entrance of St. Francis' intimate Roderick Center stood every student I had spent the last four years with. My glazed eyes panned across them and considered the time we'd spent together in classes, on sports fields, in bars. For four years, we dreamt of the adulation we would feel walking down that runway to our seats in cap and gown, waving at our parents holding cameras and pointing at our crazy Uncle Sid or Gary or Larry, clad in a

Hawaiian shirt and white cross-trainers to film the event on a camcorder; as if we'd ever watch the tape. If we did, we would easily be able to decipher which students had a good night sleep in their parents' hotel room the night before, and which had slept at the bar, face down in a puddle of Pabst Blue Ribbon with a lit cigarette still dangling between their index and middle fingers.

Standing in line with students of my major, I awaited direction from Professor Jenkins, who taught my junior year Article Writing 201. She assured everyone was in attendance, then quickly explained instructions for the upcoming procession.

"When the music starts, you'll walk down the center aisle and then circle around the seats to enter on the left. You'll stay standing until all majors and staff have entered the auditorium, then when given the cue from the Dean, you'll take your seats."

From the dazed looks surrounding me, I surmised that everyone would be depending on the person in front of him or her to get it right. It was simple enough, but I could sense so much more going through their heads, like "I can't wait to get this thing over with," "I hope I look presentable for my parents," or "what the hell am I going to do with my life when this thing is over?"

I stared off into the distance. What would I be doing next year? Would I even have a job? Would I be living with my parents, or for that matter, back in or around Buffalo? Speaking of my parents, I hoped they don't notice the mud stains on my pants. Looking under my robe at those stains, I was greeted by

Jenkins, who remembered my face from Article Writing.

"Are you ready, Mr. Cahan?"

It was a question I had twelve answers to. But since Jenkins didn't have time for my philosophical pontifications, I looked up at her, rubbed the right side of my unshaven face and gave her the simple.

"You bet, Professor. You bet."

When the music began, we started walking toward adulation and achievement. Through those doors stood some six-thousand family and friends, and as we entered draped in gowns and donning caps, cameras flashed and hands clapped. After our first steps, we stopped concentrating on the walk and began surveying the crowd. On our right, a brown-haired mother wearing plastic-rimmed purple glasses covered her mouth and awaited her tears as her daughter walked passed. That daughter tossed the snarled locks from her weary eyes and gave a wave. On our left stood an old man, short, white-haired, and in his eighties. He propped himself up with a wooden cane on his right side, and as we approached, he turned from stoic to jubilant. When he saw his heaping grandson in a long, black gown, a smile came to his face. When he got his attention, he pointed at him, flashed a dentured smile, and winked. When the wink met the Polish rugger, he pointed back at his grandfather, right index finger extended with whiskey ills in his rearview.

I began to scan the seats for the Cahan family. My parents were out there somewhere, along with my two sisters and brother, seated patiently in the wooden bleachers. Also waiting was my grandfather, Michael Cahan, who had made the drive from South Buffalo to witness his grandson graduate from college.

Michael was a devout Catholic husband, father and grandfather first, a World War II vet second, and a retired mailman third. He liked his whiskey on ice, his football under snow, and would rather be buried six feet under Buffalo's frozen soil than ever leave the city. As he saw it, Buffalo's residents were his family, just as much as his son who fathered me. Delivering mail to every corner of South Buffalo, along with stints on the west and north ends of the city, gave him an opportunity to see many faces and greet many voices. In turn, it gave each a chance to enjoy a vagabond courtesy from a man who couldn't be more rooted. I looked down at him and his head of white hair by about three inches, and along with his fat Irish head and short, puny arms, a lot of who I was could be attributed to him. Whether it was his looks, will or perpetual penchant for bringing a smile to someone's face, I always saw glimpses of who I hoped to become in his presence.

Since my grandmother passed away from breast cancer during my freshman year at St. Francis, he'd felt like he was doing everything for two. Going to my graduation is something she wouldn't have let him miss, so with her concerns tucked so sincerely under his demeanor, he'd parked his Caprice Classic outside the Roderick Center to gather with the rest of the Cahans.

While searching for his face, I felt the girl behind me tap me on my shoulder.

"Hey, Cahan," she said. "It looks like you have a fan club."

When I looked into the bleachers, I coughed out a laugh. In the upper ring of the auditorium stood my two sisters, Molly and Claire, waving their arms wildly and holding an opened umbrella facing the procession with the rest of my family behind them. On the umbrella, my older sister, Claire, had taken masking tape and spelled out the message, "We love you, Cahan!"

Aside from the occasional crisis or death to mourn, genuine sincerity was usually extinct in the Cahan household. Following the Irish Catholic tradition, we weren't the most outwardly affectionate family, even if we did love each other. Most of the time, the only way we expressed ourselves was through ridicule, so if you wanted to show love, you'd better make it funny. The umbrella was funny.

The message wasn't meant to bother me as much as it would my mother. Most people I knew called me by my last name and ignored the baptismal name she'd chosen. She hated this. The practice hit its boiling point when girls started calling our house in high school and asked if "Cahan was home." With the phone to her ear, my mother would look into the receiver and rudely reply, "Which one?"

I followed the procession to my seat at the end of the aisle, fourteen rows from the acceptance stage. Once the seats were full, our venerable Dean Bailey approached the podium to begin the ceremony of numbing boredom. It couldn't have been more painful—even if the lights were lowered for an unplugged performance by Canadian rock virtuosos Rush. I grew up with their music transmitted from Canadian radio stations and often wondered if I had to choose between a knife to the thigh or a seat for one Rush performance, which would I pick? I was zoned out amid this familiar contemplation, mentally asleep and leaning back in my folding chair as I heard Dean Bailey's voice emanate from the podium.

"Will the students of the Johannson School of Journalism please stand."

It was like someone had cued up the echoing spirituality of an Edge guitar solo off *The Joshua Tree* or the omnipresent pulsating drum beat of Larry Mullen Jr. on *Achtung Baby*; it was invigorating. An immediate groove filled my legs as I joined my classmates in jumping from our seats. With the Dean's mention of our major, many of our class dopeheads and booze bags decided to properly represent the Johannson School with a collective scream of, "Yeeeaaauuuh!"

With these screams, we sauntered in a single file to the right of the stage. Up the stairs we skipped, and as the Dean called one name after another, I became closer and closer to receiving a diploma in my two eager hands. Michael Babson. Maureen Billick, Summa Cum Laude.
Jonathan Brunson, Cum Laude. Suddenly, there was no one between the Dean and myself. My stomach rumbled with a

combination of anxiety, anticipation and alcohol irritation. My name was next, and as the Dean's mouth approached the microphone, I went numb.

"Joseph P. Cahan."

I heard nothing but the name. Not a thing. Not my sisters' high-pitched screams; not my father screaming, "Way to go, son!" Nothing. Everything moved in slow motion, and as I approached the Dean, I found my eyes fixated on the brown, leather folder in his left hand. With my right hand extended to shake his in congratulations, I brought my eyes up to meet his. His mouth moved to spit out, "congratulations," but I heard silence until that paper hit my hands. The minute it rested in my palms, real time kicked back in and I heard the screams and cheers from my obnoxious crew of Cahans. I found them again and pointed my thanks.

When I emerged from the auditorium after the ceremony, I saw my family gathered out on the Roderick Center lawn, my sisters twirling around that ridiculous umbrella like a pinwheel. My mother spotted me and grabbed me for a hug.

"I'm so proud of you, hon."

My father pulled me in for the same before everyone else took their turns at congratulations. First up was my younger sister, Molly, a freshman at nearby SUNY Fredonia. She was always the most honest one with each of us, so if she thought something, she was never one to spare our feelings. When she saw my unshaven face and bloodshot eyes that morning, she didn't hesitate.

"Joey, you look like death, huh? What did you drink last night? Moonshine?"

"Go to hell, Mol."

"Yeah, leave the drunken grad alone, Mol," said Claire, giving the umbrella another twirl over her brown hair. "You're just jealous that your head's not swimming in booze."

Away from her job in advertising sales for Buffalo's number-one classic rock radio station, Claire welcomed the opportunity to toss jabs at her younger sister instead of pitching drive time advertising costs to Queen City chicken wing joints and RV dealers. She laughed at Molly's embarrassment, but her enjoyment was interrupted by my father, eager to continue a tradition he'd started with my brother Frank five years earlier.

"Are you ready for the toast?" he said.

My father made all willing parties take a shot of Irish whiskey when Frank graduated from college. At that time, my father toasted the graduation with Bushmills, but had since heard the brand didn't hire Catholics at their distillery in Ireland. Being a fervent Catholic like his father, he refused to ever touch the stuff again. For my graduation, we'd toast with Paddy's, a brand referred to as Ireland's "working man's whiskey."

My father reached into a brown paper bag he'd smuggled into the ceremony and pulled out a slender bottle of Paddy's, along with six newly purchased shot glasses. There was one glass for each of us, except for my mother, who was adamantly opposed to drinking whiskey without ice cubes, a juice glass and a generous amount of ginger ale. He passed out the glasses to each of us and, in the shining May sunlight, poured shots into each one. For the toast, my grandfather asked if he could address the group. With his glass raised, he looked over at me and spoke.

"Joseph, my boy, I want to congratulate you on your big day. I still remember it like it was yesterday when your mother told me she thought you'd never make it."

Wide-eyed, my mother slapped my grandfather on his left shoulder.

"I never said that!"

"Ann, stop it! Yes, you did. You never thought the kid would make it, and look at him today!" he said. "In a black gown, diploma in one hand and a shot of whiskey in the other. In four years, mind you!"

"Never doubted the whiskey," said my mother, smiling.

Raising his glass, my grandfather implored us to do the same.

"Raise your glasses for my grandson, Mr. Joseph P. Cahan: college graduate and future millionaire!"

Our arms raised and glasses connected; down our throats the tepid whiskey burned. Frank smacked me on the back as he exhaled the chest scorch from the harshest brown liquor I'd ever ingested. Down in the heating components factory where Frank worked nights, guys probably polished off booze that tasted of wet lumber and peroxide on their coffee break, so I tried to hide my disgust in front of him. I let it burn while my sisters jumped at me for a playful hug. When we separated, Claire held her camera from the wrist string and started to look around the crowd. I knew exactly who she was looking for.

"Can you go find Johanna? I want to get a picture of the two of you together."

"I don't think so," I said. "We broke up last week."

3

I first laid eyes on Johanna Darcy in the fall of my freshman year at St. Francis.

I walked into the chilled October breeze and saw a beautiful redhead smoking a cigarette with two other girls in my dorm's shaded courtyard. She stood about five-three, with a delicate build and fair, freckled skin. She looked stunning, holding a cigarette between her fingers, wearing faded jeans and a brown woolen crewneck sweater. What I intended to be a casual glance hypnotized into a dazed stare, one you have to shake your eyes out of. Thankfully, she didn't notice my admiring gape as she laughed in conversation. Though faint, it was uplifting; a laugh that's so delightful it makes you want to laugh, even though no joke has been told. Her voice sounded smoldering between cigarette drags, alternating between a sensual tone and smoke exhalations. But there she was, and for a few seconds, I was lost.

And that's the way it is when guys see *the* girl, right? Time stops, we admire, and simmering stomach anxiety acts as an ever-tightening grip with every move she makes. You remember moments like these when you know it's the girl, even before she's said a word. You remember the time, the place, the weather, what she was wearing, how she was standing, what she said to you, and what you said to yourself. Since she said nothing to me, I could only remember my own dialogue. As I stood in the courtyard on that October afternoon, I said to myself, "I have to meet that girl."

One of the girls smoking outside that day was Susan Kofler, who I knew from my Poetry 101 class on Tuesdays and Thursdays. On the Tuesday following that memorable afternoon, I caught up to Susan outside after class.

"Susan, wait up."

"Hey, Cahan. Do believe this E.E. Cummings garbage we have to go over before Thursday?" she said, fumbling through her purse to find cigarettes. "Why the hell does that guy use all lower-case letters for his name anyway?"

"Some sort of typographical experiment in simplicity, I read. But forget Cummings. I have a question for you," I said. "What's your friend's name with the red hair? The one I see you with all the time?"

"Oh, Johanna? Yeah, Johanna Darcy, that's her."

"Johanna? Good name."

It was a great name, with even greater possibilities. If her personality ended up being favorably comparable to her looks, I could serenade her with Bob Dylan's "Visions of Johanna" over brisk winter weekends. I hadn't even met her, and we already had a song.

"So what's the deal?" said Susan. "You like her?"

"I don't even know her," I said. "So what's her story? Cool? Crazy? Dating anyone?"

Susan turned her head to the left and exhaled a mouthful of smoke.

"Yeah, she's great. Real funny. And no, she's not dating anyone. Quite slick how you slipped that in there," she said, smirked. "So, do you want to meet her?"

"Sure. When?"

"Now."

"Now? Right now?"

"Sure. I have to meet her for lunch at the dining hall. You have to eat, right?"

I did, but I didn't care about eating anymore; I wanted to meet this girl. I had no idea what I would say to her. Not a clue. In those early weeks of college, I only had my high school encounters to draw from. When I rambled on about The Clash and cheap draft beer to swaying teenage girls at a moonlight kegger on Lake Erie, it never stood as intimidating of a task as talking to a Johanna Darcy. Someone like her wouldn't have been caught dead at one of those parties. But as a freshman in college, I wanted to be daring, ready for new experiences. In success or failure, going up to this girl completely void of planned dialogue would be one of these daunting tasks.

When we reached her table in the cavernous hall, she sat with her back turned to us, talking with two other girls as I felt like my heart had grown hands to clench and punch the inside of my chest. Of the six seats at the table, all were taken, so Susan and I approached chairs at the table directly behind her. Susan set her books down and tapped Johanna on the shoulder after we reached our seats. Her head swiveled around, tossing her scarlet locks left to reveal her eyes—and my flirting interest in Johanna Darcy accelerated to full-blown. One look at those eyes was all it took.

The vision pulled me back to early childhood, sitting on the couch with my father for our traditional viewing of *The Quiet Man* on St. Patrick's Day eve. Along with John Wayne, the movie starred the stunning Maureen O'Hara, her fiery red hair intensified by our outdated Technicolor cassette. But in my early youth, girls were no match for Bills football or a Clarence Clemons saxophone solo. Girls hadn't settled into their rightful and unrivaled priority spot yet, but I still knew what beauty was. I knew what is was to watch O'Hara and her shimmering blue eyes skip across the fields of rural Ireland. I was so mesmerized that my expectancies of women ascended as high as her screen presence would allow.

I felt similar to those viewings while standing in front of Johanna Darcy, with girls now a prime interest. Susan gave her greetings, then motioned Johanna's attention over to me.

"Johanna, this is Cahan, er, Joe."

"Cahan's fine," I said, then nervously extended my hand toward hers.

Her eyes looked up and glistened, sending a shiver down my arms.

"Nice to meet you, Cahan."

I stood over her and tried to quickly study her looks. I didn't want to stare like a stalker, but I couldn't help admiring. Her smile was radiant, and her presence wasn't as intimidating as I'd assumed. Absorbing this first impression, I returned a smile before I put my coat on the back of my dining chair, walked toward the cafeteria line, and caught up with Susan.

"She's nice," I said.

"Nice? What the hell does 'nice' mean? Nice is what you say about fat girls. You like her or not? I can put in a good word, maybe about your extensive knowledge of E.E. Cummings."

"Oh, shut up."

I didn't need any good words, even if I knew they would help. I could, nay would, do this myself. Now that I'd met Johanna, the hard part was out of the way. We would see each other again, and I'd continue to build off my charming introduction.

The problem was, during the multiple times I did see her again, nothing happened. Outside of class having a smoke, walking in and out of my dorm and even at off campus house parties, she'd forget who I was. I'd reintroduce myself, and we'd continue to cross paths daily. When I'd spot her approaching, I'd be rehearsing lines to say to her in my head.

"What's up, Johanna?" or "How's it going, Johanna?" or

"Hey, Johanna. Want to go back to my room and make out to the earth-rattling electricity of *Highway 61 Revisited*?"

In the end, I'd always spit out a "hey" between cigarette drags and walk on. She would reply the same way every other person at St. Francis would: "Hey, Cahan."

Insincere as it was to have a girl address me like we were Tuesday night pool hall buddies, I didn't mind; at least she was talking to me. Johanna recognized me more and more outside of the classroom as the semester rolled on. At parties, I'd see her talking to her girlfriends in the corner of the kitchen or living room. She'd always be clad in faded jeans and a wool sweater, holding clear plastic cups of keg beer and raising another Marlboro Light to her lips. In bars, I'd see her through thick clouds of cigarette smoke and under the sounds of the Allman Brothers and Stones. She'd sit at a table with her friends, talking and laughing loudly over the music as her crimson hair rest on the shoulders of her sweater.

In the first months of my freshman year at St. Francis, most everyone was inviting and nondiscriminatory, and so was Johanna. In time, it grew easy to jump into conversation with her and her friends, knowing they wouldn't condemn as long as I had something insightful to add about the E Street Band, the Grateful Dead or any other band that echoed throughout our surroundings. When I heard a Beatles song play, I brought up the "Paul Is Dead" theory that erupted among Berkeley potheads in the late sixties before claiming to have heard the infamous distorted voice at the end of "Strawberry Fields Forever" indeed mumble, "I buried Paul." When I wanted to weaken their knees, I exaggerated details of how I had played "Revolution 9" backwards on my father's turntable to hear the creepy subliminal message of "turn me on, dead man" emanate from his speakers. I never actually heard that cryptic phrase, but I did ruin my father's copy of the Beatles' *White Album* with a reverse rotation attempt.

Girls who could sit down to enjoy a beer and conversation were the ones I targeted, and Johanna was one of these girls. She would sit with a subtle, make-up-free while passionately delivering a list of her favorite rock albums between 1975 and 1990. The enthusiasm she exuded seemed to entrance patrons who sat within three barstools of our booth, so her effect on me was considerable. In the time I spent with Johanna, I found her to be a girl who exuded this infectious zeal from wherever she sat.

I'd stand in front of her pristine complexion and listen to how she wanted to become an elementary English teacher so she could help children appreciate the understated importance of some of her favorite books, like S.E. Hinton's *The Outsiders*. Outside of class, I'd bum a cigarette and listen to her intricately explain why she thought U2 deserved a spot within the five greatest bands of all time, and how a ticket to their Zoo TV Tour inside Jersey's Meadowlands changed her life.

"Before that," she said, "I never knew one concert could affect the way you think or feel about everything."

In an oak booth at our local college bar, the Moose Nose, I'd sit across from her with a pint, mesmerized by her knowledge of Notre Dame football.

"My father goes to a game every year. Once, he was in South Bend when Rocket Ismail returned a punt for a touchdown against Miami. He loves telling the story about how he was so excited during that return, he spilled his Coke all over an elderly priest's head in front of him."

During all of these conversations, my eyes were fixated on hers. They shined no matter the light or shadows, and both lured me in deeper with every word she said. Her smoky voice was endearing and enticing. When I'd reply to her, she looked and listened, not anxious to intervene. Every word was important to her, and in turn, every word she said to me was gently situating me in a euphoric state I'd never visited.

Unfortunately, that fall semester I roomed with one of love's biggest skeptics, Vincent Petrocelli. A tanned, affluent and well-dressed kid from Syracuse, he had dark hair and a sluggish build, like he'd been chasing cheeseburgers with a pair of cigarettes and a Budweiser after lunch and dinner for three months. Though Vince was opinionated, the only major rift he initiated was his insistence on playing his favorite band, the Doors, seven days-a-week. Vince thought Jim Morrison to be God; I thought the Lizard King to be an absolute piece of shit.

On one of our last nights before Christmas break, he packed his clothes for Syracuse as I studied diligently on our carpeted floor, with books and papers sprawled about for my Intro to Mass Communications final the next day. Since Vince had taken his last final at noon, he was free to throw together laundry, gather terrible Doors albums, and delicately pull his pressed Bill Blass suit out of the closet as I memorized descriptions. As Vince flipped through his many discs, he wanted to know where I stood with this girl I'd been chasing. Since I hadn't told him anything, maybe he thought there was time to save me.

"So what's the deal with the redhead I've seen you smoking butts outside class with? Does she have a name?"

"Johanna. Her name's Johanna."

"Yeah, yeah, Johanna. Whatever," he said. "You nail her yet or what?"

Vince wasn't exactly subtle. When he didn't like you, he told you. If he wanted to hook up with a girl, he went to work on her whether he had a shot or not. There was no game with him; just action. He was direct with everything, so as a courtesy, I gave him the same back.

"No. This isn't the kind of girl you pick up on the lawn of a kegger after you've had twelve beers. She's deeper than that, a little too layered, fortunately, for you. In fact, I haven't laid a hand on her. I haven't even kissed her yet."

Vince looked up toward our cracked plaster ceiling and exhaled in disgust.

"Cahan, you're such a fucking pussy. You gotta stop with the flirting shit and dial this chick in. They're all the same. Quit romanticizing everything you do."

Vince knew me pretty well after a semester of sleeping in the same room. When we came home from the bars at night, we didn't want to go to sleep, but had no solitary haven to escape to. We were stuck with the same closet refrigerator, pulling out beers at three o'clock and cracking them open while we detailed past experiences. Vince was introduced to my background, so he knew of my sky-high expectations about women. He knew how nauseating my selectivity could be, but he didn't know how this girl was achieving a place among it. He didn't know I wasn't romanticizing; this could actually be romance.

"Vince, I'm telling you, this girl is different. There's no bullshit."

"No bullshit? Just wait. There's always bullshit."

Over some of those late night beers, Vince told me how he dated a girl in high school for two and a half years before finding out she was nailing a cross-town football player on the side. He thought it was love, was crushed when he found out it wasn't, and hence, didn't have a lot of faith in women or the existence of love. I was fortunate enough to not be so cynical, and often felt compelled to restore his shattered faith with the abundance of my own. I explained Johanna, not diverting from that routine.

"Vince, have you ever met a girl with her own soundtrack?"

"A what?"

"A soundtrack. You know, a girl who you see or meet who immediately ignites a tune in your head as she walks toward you or sits across from you. It's almost like her intro music to a feeling she wields whenever she appears."

"Never."

"I think you're full of shit."

"Believe what you want, but I've never heard a tune in my head when I'm trying to pick up some girl to nail. And let me guess: the song you hear in your head when this chick shows up is 'Visions of Johanna' by Dylan?"

"Actually, I hear 'Trying To Throw Your Arms Around The World' by U2. But that's not a bad idea with Dylan," I said, smiling. "You sure you're not some closet romantic?"

"I'm a realist, dude, but good luck with your delusions. You should stash those and try to score with her tonight. Room's all yours to pull all this John Cryer, *Pretty in Pink* sissy romance shit you want."

I crumbled up the notepaper I was reading and threw it at his head.

"Fuck off, pal," I said. "I have my final to study for tonight, so I'm barricaded in here, solo. No romance; just studying, with some John Lennon for a soundtrack."

Vince exhaled next to his closet and offered another disappointed look while shaking his head. He picked up his bag full of laundry, slung a backpack over his shoulder, and with his free hand, took his suit off the wall hook. When I saw his hands full, I jumped up off the floor to get the door. Once out, he turned around for one last thought.

"You should give it a shot, dude. Tonight. Get her up here, and you could switch the soundtrack to Dylan. Dial her in with *Johanna*."

I compromised to send him on his way.

"We'll see, Vince. We'll see. Merry Christmas."

I lit a cigarette after the door closed. Across the room, I opened the window a crack to exhale the smoke out into the winter night. Vince walked down the sidewalk in view of that window, saw me exhaling and jokingly flipped me off.

"Merry Christmas, Cahan! Smoke butts!"

He continued to backpedal down the walk, and I sarcastically waved before stepping back from the breeze. After my cigarette was burned down to the filter, I extinguished it in my ashtray, pushing it into the ceramic clay before lying down on the floor to stare at the ceiling. The nicotine flowed through my veins, and I allowed myself to forget about Intro to Mass Communications for a bit. I forgot about the importance of media on the development of society and culture, wandering from the various liberal and conservative views concerning this Internet thing and the impact it would have on the way we acquire information. I stared at the ceiling's plaster cracks and thought about what Vince said, about dialing in this girl.

Maybe I could take a shot at approaching her deep blues. I'd connect with her waiting lips as I touched her fair skin with my fingertips. I'd feel a chill go down my spine and lifelessness consume my legs. The thumping anxiety in my chest would turn to elated enjoyment, but my heart would beat erratically like I'd had twelve cups of coffee.

I could run one of my free hands over my desktop and feel around for my stereo remote without breaking away from her lips. I'd pick it up, scale over the buttons like brail and find the triangle. I'd push it down for Dylan's "Visions of Johanna," wait for the intro acoustic strumming to emanate, then play it cool when she broke from the kiss.

"I love this song," she would say.

"Great," I'd say. "Let's listen."

And we would continue with the kissing and the touching with Dylan as the soundtrack. Sex wouldn't be the primary focus because anybody could have sex; monkeys and dogs and Doors fans had sex. Johanna and I would flow with a serendipitous chemistry. It would be so rhythmic, so much better than I'd ever anticipated.

I let out a small laugh as these thoughts rolled through my head. This could happen, so I decided to call her later. I wanted to get some studying done before casually inviting her over. We could have a beer, talk over a few smokes before she went home for Christmas. We could talk about S.E. Hinton, whether or not her favorite song on *Achtung Baby* was, coincidentally, "Trying to Throw Your Arms Around The World," and if she thought Notre Dame had any chance at recruiting a championship team while still requiring all incoming freshman to take calculus. Then I could ask her what she thought of me. I'd ask if she'd like to go out sometime to an Italian restaurant or for a walk down one of the forest trails surrounding our St. Francis campus. If she said yes, I was in, and I'd float in for that euphoric kiss.

I shook off those thoughts, picked myself up off the floor and went over to the stereo. When I found *The White Album* I pulled it out of the case and slid the first disc into the stereo. Skipping past "Back in the U.S.S.R.," I stopped on "Dear Prudence" and pressed the triangle. It was back to the Mass Communications books, with a highlighter clenched between my teeth and a black pen in my hand. I had to suppress thoughts of Johanna and concentrate on Edward R. Murrow's impact had on broadcast news. Or was it print journalism?

About thirty minutes later, I stopped investigating Murrow's impact on anything. Regardless of his historical influence, he just couldn't contend with Johanna Darcy.

She was busy packing her wool sweaters for break when I called. Earlier that day, she handed in her final paper for English Composition 101 to complete her first semester work. She had to write ten to fifteen pages on a historical figure who she deemed worthy, so Johanna chose Burton Cummings, the legendary frontman of Canadian rock legends, the Guess Who. I nearly proposed marriage. The chances of me ever again finding a girl who had *any* insight into the music of the Guess Who was nil, so I'm surprised I didn't go through with it. Instead of proposing, I invited her over for a goodbye beer.

Johanna told me she'd be over in an hour and a half. Forty-five minutes later, there was a knock at my door. Sitting in ripped jeans, my navy blue Bisons baseball t-shirt and flip-flops, I assumed the knock was a dorm neighbor. I removed my brown-rimmed reading glasses and yelled to check.

"Yeah?"

"Cahan? It's Johanna."

Not a dorm neighbor.

"Just a minute!"

I jumped up from the floor and kicked my books and notes to the side. I had planned to jump in the shower before she arrived, but with her outside, there was no time. I ran over to my sink, pulled the Bisons shirt off over my head, and splashed water on my face and into my ruffled brown hair. With my hands still cupped, I ran more water into them to throw under my arms before rolling on deodorant.

"Be there in one second!"

From the top shelf, I reached for a white t-shirt and pulled it down over my wet hair before adding my father's old faded green v-neck sweater over top. I left the ripped jeans and flops on, and walked back over to the sink to check myself in the mirror. I looked fine, felt fine, but needed to exhale. Johanna was outside my door. I didn't know how I wanted to greet her, and I didn't have any Dylan cued up on the stereo. I wasn't ready, but I had to go open the door before she thought about walking away. I gave myself a last look, took a deep breath, clapped my hands together, and walked away from the mirror to open the door.

"Hi," she said. "Everything okay?"

Her eyes were squinted inquisitively and her head was slightly tilted, allowing her red hair to rest more heavily on her left shoulder than her right. Her shoulders were covered with a corduroy camel-colored barn coat, which extended down to the tops of her kneecaps. Under the coat, she wore a thin, light blue sweater, with knotted patterns to evoke a homemade feel. Over her slender legs were faded blue jeans, which bell-bottomed out at the ankles to cover the laces of her brown hiking boots. Yes: everything was okay.

"Absolutely. I just had to get dressed."

She took a moment to deliberately study me, to see the ripped jeans, flops, and faded green v-neck.

"Well, don't feel like you need to get all dressed up for my benefit. Maybe next time you could have some cut-off jean shorts on, like I was picking you up for a Ted Nugent concert."

I appreciated the sarcasm, then moved aside to let her in before replying.

"Hey, these are the best jeans I own. And I wouldn't have figured you a fan of the Motor City Madman."

"Really?"

"Yeah, you look like more of a Bob Seger woman."

She let out a delightful, discreet laugh.

"Funny, Cahan. I heard Seger was like a bearded Elvis in

Michigan in the seventies. Guy couldn't go anywhere without getting his clothes torn off."

"Were you there in seventy-five, his shirttail in your hand?"

She laughed again.

"I wish. So where's this drink you promised me?"

I walked over to the mini fridge and grabbed two cold cans of Busch beer. I opened one for myself before walking over to Johanna, seated on the gray carpet with her legs crossed. Taking a seat across from her, I stretched forward to hand her the unopened can.

After she cracked hers open, we toasted the end of her first semester. We talked about her impending drive home to White Plains on Route 17 to I-87, and how the trip may be one of the more hazardous tasks in the Northeast. With no rest stops, streetlights, and the omnipresent threat of deer crossing in front of her gold Mazda 626, the route was pretty stressful. She described how the route's mountains were so engulfing, they made her claustrophobic. She wished she had someone to drive home with.

"I'll go with you," I said. "After my exam tomorrow."

She smiled, like she thought I was kidding.

"I'm sure your family in Buffalo would be thrilled with that proposal, especially at Christmas."

But a small part of me was sincere.

"They'll get over it. Besides, I'll see them at Easter."

She looked down and laughed, then looked up at me and

smiled again.

"You're funny."

"Is that a good thing?" I said. "Or is funny like cute?"

"What do you mean?"

"Every time a girl has called me cute, it means she thinks I'd be a good guy to drink beers with or take to a movie so she wouldn't have to go alone. Are you using 'funny' like that?"

"No, I mean *funny*," she said. "You make me laugh. I like to laugh. I like you."

Feeling a chill down my arms, I took a quick, thick swig of my beer and decided to continue with the inquiry.

"What do you mean 'like'? Do you mean 'like' as in, 'I like you, so let's get a Guinness and talk about whether Dylan should've gone electric at Newport in sixty-five' *like* or 'I like you, so let's go out to a nice Italian restaurant, catch a John Cusack flick, then come home for a kiss good night' *like*?"

Johanna tilted her head down and laughed again. When she collected herself, she took a sip of her beer, set it down. After a second of silence passed, it seemed like an hour. Finally, she calmly leaned toward me.

"I hate Italian food, but I'd love to catch a Cusack movie. As for the kiss?"

Her lips rested about a foot away from mine, close enough to smell her peppermint gum. Twelve inches away, she continued to look into my eyes, waiting for a response in a moment every couple has known. The guy looks at the girl, girl looks at the guy, but both of their eyes peek at each other's lips to see if they're getting closer. Her eyes are inviting and fixated on his, and she's not backing away. She sits there for two seconds, making slight moves forward, but still giving him a chance to make the move and tilt his head to the right. After about three seconds, it was my moment.

I set down my can of beer and reached toward Johanna's right cheek as she moved closer. Her eyes remained open until our lips delicately touched. Gently touching the sides of her face, I kept my mouth closed, as did she, and concentrated on subtle passion rather than detrimental movement. I figured working the tongue around too much might screw things up, so I tried to focus on replicating affection portrayed in forties cinema, absent the forcefulness. I didn't go Bogart on her, grabbing her shoulders and mashing my face into hers. I kept it light, and so did she.

I dictated the innocent action as we lay back on the floor together, kissing her lips softly as she massaged the back of my head while my right hand scanned the floor. I saw the stereo remote around earlier, couldn't remember where, but finally found it underneath a blanket resting next to Johanna's head.

I knew I didn't have "Visions of Johanna" cued up in the stereo, but I knew I had *Blonde on Blonde* in the six-disc changer. I had no clue which slot it was in, but with the way things were going, I hoped momentum would grant me some luck. I tried to be nonchalant with the remote, feeling around for the sideways triangle as we kissed. When I found the shape, I pressed down to send an unfortunate guitar riff blaring out of the stereo.

DER-NA-NER, CHICKA-CHICKA-DER-NER, DER- NA-NER, CHICKA-CHICKA-DER-NER.

Out of the speakers cranked Nirvana's "Smells Like Teen Spirit," one of Vince's few discs absent of Morrison wailing. Once Kurt Cobain's pick hit the first string, Johanna stopped kissing me to notice my embarrassed, sour reaction.

Her initial look was shock, but it soon relaxed into a wide grin, lips clenched together to trap what would follow. Lying underneath me on my gray-carpeted dorm room floor, this beautiful girl began convulsing in riotous laughter. With each laugh, I became increasingly mortified.

I sat there, wondering how to fake my own death—yet Johanna was still there. She shook her head and smiled. She wasn't appalled or running for the door. She didn't suspect I was some freak who wanted to engage in sadistic grunge-serenaded heavy petting. She was delighted to make light of a situation that was supposed to be romantic. To her, it was another obvious instance of my apparent hilarity.

"What were you trying to play there, slick?"

"Visions of Johanna, by Bob Dylan."

"Very nice," she said. "Maybe you can try that one later, Cahan."

"Later?"

"Sure. You definitely have to work on this romance thing, and I wouldn't want to stand in the way of progress. Dylan was renowned social progressive, right?"

I turned down the Nirvana.

"If that means you're staying the night, then I agree."

On my graduating transcripts from St. Francis University, the only grade tarnishing my otherwise perfect journalism average was the C I earned by bombing my Intro to Mass Communications final. Unfortunate, but in the winter of my freshman year, I gladly sacrificed that class for entrance into the first serious romantic relationship of my young life. Looking back on it, I just wish I'd done nearly as well with Johanna as I did on that final.

4

I was nursing a lukewarm cup of black coffee, relaxing on our couch in flannel pajama bottoms and a white t-shirt with, "Buffalo: Talking Proud!" in red across the chest. With my hands cupped my hands around the sides of the mug, I hoped the heat from the sides would seep through my hands and soothe my head, pounding after another long night of celebration.

On the morning following graduation, my parents and Molly pulled up outside my apartment to load the car for Buffalo. When I didn't immediately get up to answer their knock at the door, the remaining Cahans decided to walk in, each making reactionary faces in response to the putrid aroma surrounding them. I lived atop a local townie bar called the White Horse, so the smell in my living room was akin to a bar at ten in the morning, polluted by patrons spilling draft beer on the floor until three that same morning. The scent of stale beer and cigarettes was always obnoxiously palpable upon entry.

Adding to the ambiance was the bar's janitor, a local vagabond legend and habitual breakfast dope smoker named Black Jack. He'd burn a j or two every morning while he mopped the floors and blasted reruns of *Charles in Charge* at a screaming volume. The smoke would rise through the vents and floor in tandem with Scott Baio one-liners to dance above my raggedy furniture. Before my parents ever set foot in the apartment, I warned them so they wouldn't question whether I was exhaling the stench over Jerry Garcia vocals. After meeting Eli and his long, curly hair earlier in the semester, my father assumed I was covering for my roommate's habits. The old man stood inside the doorway and took a thorough sniff before glancing at me.

"Long night last night, son? You look like you haven't slept. Have you?"

"A bit," I said.

Born and raised in the Irish-American enclave of South Buffalo, Patrick Cahan bounced around between odd jobs until he became a high school history teacher in the Southtowns before I was born. To earn some extra cash for our family, he took a second job working as a deckhand on the Miss Buffalo, a small passenger cruise boat used for sight-seeing and social events along the city's waterfront. When school let out in June, he would work from four in the afternoon until after eleven at night, assisting on cruises down the Niagara River and under the Peace Bridge until he earned his captain's license before my ninth birthday. As captain, he kept the four to eleven weekday shift, but added weekend shifts from noon to midnight all summer long. My father was in his glory, driving wild singles parties and senior citizen groups along Buffalo's shores as he enjoyed the city's most underutilized resource every day with infectious passion. Working as the Queen City's unofficial spokesman for the city's virtues behind the wheel of that boat, he would have bagged the teaching gig years ago if he could drive the Miss Buffalo year-round.

To talk with my father for ten minutes was a chance to see who I might become in twenty-five years; his Cahan mannerisms, demeanor and expressions would eventually be mine. He was the same height as me, and as he stood before me in my living room, his once full head of curly black hair was now gray and receding in our classic ancestral fashion. My grandfather blamed the Irish hairline—the recession of the right and left hairline corners above the forehead—on the winds off the Atlantic Ocean and the Irish Sea. As our ancestors would tend to their dairy farms in Counties Clare and Meath, their hair would be ripped back by ocean winds, taking the peaks and leaving a crop down the middle for delicate styling. If this theory was true, it was the winds off Lake Erie and the Niagara River taming my father's mane.

Reality was slowly seeping through my headache as we began to carry packed boxes and bags down the stairs of my apartment. Leaving Black Jack, the stench of his breakfast dope, or the echoing details of another amicable Baio solution would be a welcomed change. But, moving out would signal an end to my expensive collegiate escape, ushering me into the harsh reality of, well, *reality*. Once I started toward Buffalo, going back to live with my parents full-time for the first time in four years, I wasn't going to be able to engage in the same ridiculousness I'd grown so accustomed to.

No more smoking in bed. No more all-nighters with Springsteen's *The River* or the Rolling Stones' *Exile on Main Street*, analyzing different chords and lyrics over keg beers, cheap smokes and bags of crushed tortilla chips. No more coming home at two in the morning to turn up a Clash or Ramones album to eardrum-rattling decibels in a fit of drunken recklessness. There'd be no such thing as "after hours" on a Wednesday night with work looming on a Thursday morning. No more choices between a seat in Historical Geology or a seat on my couch for a replay of the Buffalo Bills' 1992 AFC Wild Card comeback on ESPN Classic. This realization had father-son time written all over it, so when it came time to leave, I didn't even consider approaching the passenger door to my mother's rusted Mazda 323, which we called the Blue Bomber.

I carried a case of CDs with my navy blue car coat draped on top as I approached the rear of my father's white Buick Regal. I delicately slid the case into the trunk, next to crates full of books, videos and clothes, then firmly shut the hatch while my father waited behind the wheel.

"You all set?" he said.

"Just one more thing."

I ran up the stairs and back into the apartment. Once in, I

took one last look around the empty space to see walls bare of rock posters and Buffalo sports pennants, the rotted wooden floors as filthy as they were the morning I moved in. The torn and soiled couch was void of its covering bed sheet, now fully emanating the stench of spilled whiskey and keg beer absorbed over two semesters. Eli even left behind the broken coffee table he bought for two joints earlier that winter. I gave my apartment key one last look before placing it on that table for the landlord.

I walked into the bathroom and flicked on the light to look at my face in the mirror. I was unshaven, but clean and healthy; ready to start the next part of my life, to dive head first into the uncertainty that waited. I knew I'd miss St. Francis. I would miss the friends and freedom I had, but I'd try to keep the undeniable idealism college afforded me. Sweat ran down my forehead and into my brown eyebrows. I turned on the faucet to splash cold water on my face. I shook off the drops, gave my cheek a slap and reflection a wink, and switched off the light. One more whiff of Black Jack's breakfast dope and listened to another televised zinger echo through my cavernous living room. Maybe I'd miss the guy a little.

"Roll on, Black Jack," I said, then closed the door behind me. "Roll on."

Once in the car, my father and I motored away from the White Horse with my life in the trunk. Driving with one hand on the wheel and another on the radio dial, he flipped through local stations until he found his tune. When he heard the local Cuba classic rock station, he stopped scanning to offer a deal.

"I'll give you a buck if you can tell me who sings this and two for the name of the song."

This was a Patrick Cahan special. When I was growing up, my family drove everywhere, never able to afford flights for the six of us. Whether it was to my aunt's house outside New York City, or down to Florida on a trip to Disney World, my father always drove. During those drives, the music kept the four of us kids civil. My father would offer spare change if we knew the song on the radio, always set to an Oldies station. Songs by the Mamas and Papas or the Loving Spoonful, or some lame folk number by Peter, Paul & Mary like "Leaving On A Jet Plane" were always the subject of his challenges. We never listened to modern rock, no matter how much we begged to hear one of Claire's U2 tapes. To guess the name of the songs, we'd always listen for the most prominent or repeated lyrics. Whoever shouted out the title first would get the money, but there was always one sneaky song he tricked us with over and over. Though aged and experienced at twenty-two years old, I still had to deal with my father trying to fool me again with this old question. Fortunately, I had finally learned to appreciate his classic oldies.

"The song is sung by Mr. Bob Dylan, and the name of the song," I said before a dramatic pause, "is 'Positively 4th Street.'"

The old man played stunned, but no doubt accepted the fact

that by then, I'd heard of a musician named Dylan. After being fooled roughly fifty-seven times with that question, my correct answer might have even indicated the beginning of the end of my father's perpetual intellectual superiority. It was just one song, but maybe he wondered about the closing gap as he turned to speak.

"Looks like it's going to be harder to stump you, huh?"

"Not necessarily. But, if you plan on keeping your dollars, you better bring something less familiar than Dylan. Speaking of which, I believe you owe me three bucks."

He held onto the steering wheel, dug into his khaki pocket and passed the three singles to me. I took the bills, crunched them into my denim pocket and got comfortable in the Buick for the two-hour ride home.

"I'm not sure if your mother told you, but we'll be painting your bedroom this summer. Beige. We started to take some of the raggedy posters off your wall. Already tossed a few in the garbage."

"What about the Kelly poster? Tell me you didn't ditch the Jim Kelly poster. Machine Gun Kelly."

"The poster that was all ripped and frayed?"

"Just tell me you didn't get rid of it."

"What are you going to need it? Adults don't have posters in their bedrooms. If they do, they put them in frames. And, if you plan on maturing past the age of twelve in the near future, you don't intend to mount a framed picture of a retired quarterback over your bed, do you?"

I stared back at him for a moment.

"What are you talking about? He's a first-ballot Hall of Famer," I said, annoyed. "Look, did you throw it away or not?"

A smile crept onto his face. He knew he had me.

"Of course not," he said. "I just wanted to see how mad you'd get if I told you I'd ditched that bum's picture."

My father regularly pushed me to the limit for his sheer entertainment. He loved casting a contrasting opinion to whatever I found interesting, relevant or fact, even if he secretly felt the same way I did. He'd say things against all my interests, just to get me creased.

On music I liked: "John Lennon's a hippie drug addict. He never wrote one good song with the Beatles. Any reasonable individual will tell you Paul was the brains behind that operation."

My father owned multiple Beatles and solo John Lennon albums. The *Shaved Fish* compilation LP was a staple on our living room stereo. Also, according to my mother, he actually cried at the kitchen table on the morning of December 9th, 1980 when news came over the radio that Lennon had been shot the previous evening.

On films I liked: "I don't understand all the foul-mouthed language and violence in these movies. Is it really necessary? I can't stand all the shooting and continuous use of the 'f' word."

My father's favorite movie? *Good Fellas.*

On the Super Bowl losses sustained by our Buffalo Bills: "So the Bills lost the Super Bowl again, Joseph. It's no big deal; it's just a game. The sun is still going to come up, and it's not the end of the world."

Patrick Cahan seethed the same frustration as the rest of the city through those four Sundays, but still regurgitated that same therapist mantra to me the morning after each. On those Mondays, the intense screaming match that ensued between the two of us had to be broken up by my poor mother.

But that was my father. He knew how to push my buttons, but he also knew how to give useful advice about life, religion, and in an emergency, women. He and my mother made sure we grew up in a loving house, but not an overbearing one. They didn't continuously check on our emotional stability, but cared enough to notice if something was wrong. They didn't worry about the complicated social climate that modern parents worry about or whether our self-esteem was being damaged by high school bullies or insensitive teachers. "Preventive measures" wasn't a phrase in their vocabulary.

Growing up Catholic, we dealt with things as they happened, and truly believed the best would come out of every situation with effort and faith. When a sticky situation arose, they recommended solutions to problems as best they could, most times borrowing from the lessons of their own parents. If they didn't have the answers and we asked "why," they'd call on the old authority card used on them long ago.

"What do you mean, *why*? Because we're your parents, that's why!"

When they did have answers, though, they were good ones. Patrick Cahan was skilled at delivery on these occasions. On that car ride home, I hoped he would answer questions about my launch into reality. Instead, he began an inevitable inquiry.

"So what happened with Johanna? Claire told me you guys broke up for good and seemed to think it might be a good thing. You?"

I took a deep breath while staring out the window. Our father-son conversations usually weren't very complex, but we'd had our highlights. The only time I ever asked him about sex, he simply replied with, "Don't have it." I knew three words wouldn't explain the complexities involved with the Johanna situation. The details were too ridiculous. Instead, I decided to play it cool.

"Yeah, I guess. Had to end sometime, right? I mean, what was I supposed to do? Marry her?"

"Why not? Your mother and I were married when I was twenty-two. How old are you?"

"Twenty-two. I just graduated, remember?"

"Right; of course you are. But, at twenty-two, did you see yourself marrying her, or do you think it ran its course?"

I paused for a moment to think, or maybe to allow the truth to sit in my head a little longer.

"Yeah, I could've seen us getting married, but not this year. Getting married isn't really in my wheelhouse."

"Is it in hers?"

"It might be, yeah. But she seems to want answers I can't give her as a twenty-two-year-old guy who just finished college. What's going to happen with us? Where am I going to live? What am I going to do? I can't even answer these questions for myself, let alone for a girl like Johanna."

My father paused before turning to me, his hands gripped firmly on the wheel.

"Did you love her?"

"Of course," I said, very matter-of-factly. "Why do you think we've been dating all this time?"

"You just said it: you're twenty-two. You don't have a clue where you're headed or what you're doing, so how should I know? She seemed like a good girl to me, yet here we are waving her goodbye. Do you mind if I ask you something?"

"Sure."

"Do you even know what love is?"

I sat up for a challenge more daunting than our three-dollar trivia. I absolutely knew what love was. I'd seen it, felt it.

"Love is when you care about someone more than you care about yourself," I said, feeling confident in my textbook answer.

"Well, you cared more about her than you did about yourself, huh? That's why it's a better idea to be broken up? So you can find out what *you* want to do and where *you* want to go?"

I sat pensive, slowly absorbing the magnitude of that one sentence.

"You see, son, your mother and I have been married for twenty-nine years. During that time, there's been days of terrible uncertainty. Where we would live, work and what we would do. We didn't have all the answers, but we didn't need space to 'find ourselves' or time apart to gather some sort of self-assurance. We only needed to know the answer to one simple question. You know what that was?"

I knew the answer, but didn't feel the need to yell it out. I sat silent, like I was a ten-year-old kid again, seat belted into the backseat stumped by "Positively 4th Street."

"Did we love each other," he said. "The answer was yes, and we decided to let life sort out the rest. It's called faith, boy. Unfortunately, situations like this have to arise for you to realize you need to have some."

"In what?"

"In that everything will work out. You think you loved this girl, and she might have been the one you saw yourself one day marrying. But it didn't happen because neither of you wanted to sacrifice your uncertainty for a chance at finding out what true love is."

I had no choice but to nod as he continued.

"Look son, I've been there. Women are crazy, and they'll drive you insane. I know right now you're down on losing this one, but give it time and you'll see it was for the best. Besides, you know what your grandfather always says."

Wary of my Grandpa Cahan's poetic Irish theories, I waited for the latest beauty my father was about to bestow.

"What's that?"

"That in life, Cahan men need only three things to survive: a house to call home, a woman to call 'love', and a barman to call you by name."

Confused, I turned to him for more.

"And?"

A smirk came across my father's face as he navigated his Buick Regal. I knew he had more, and he turned for the delivery.

"After we stop at Fitzgerald's for a beer on our way home, you'll realize two out of three isn't so bad."

His grin was infectious. As I turned to look out the window, passing through the mountains of southern New York with another Cahan value in my head, I smiled. He was my father, and on that day, I couldn't argue with the advice. It was Irish wisdom at its finest, but with this valued acumen, I reached into my right pocket to feel only the few bills I'd won earlier.

"But you got the first round," I said. "This Cahan only has three bucks to his name."

5

Fitzgerald's Lakeside Pub stood on a stone cliff overlooking Lake Erie. As we entered, a warm May breeze followed us through its smoke-filled lobby. Fitzgerald's served as our neighborhood's social forum, with stout taps and fried fish as the lures for congregation. On one side of the oak bar was our local councilman, sipping a bottle of Bud while a landscaper petitioned for a speed limit reduction on his nursery's street. With dirt under his fingernails, the landscaper suggested drivers exceeding forty-five miles-per-hour don't hit the brakes for as many rose bushes as those crawling along at thirty. On the other side of the bar, the balding coach of nearby St. Auggie's High School basketball squad talked to the bartender about his proposed defensive plan for next season. With quick guards coming in, he thinks a two-three zone could be more stifling than the mediocre man-to-man his team played the previous four seasons. The bartender agreed; the team's past ability to slide picks on the high post was pathetic. The coach ordered up another pint of Genesee.

The bartender approached his line of taps and slung a soiled bar towel over his broad left shoulder. He offered a friendly nod to my father, and without asking, grabbed two pint glasses and set two coasters in front of the taps on the bar top. There were two open barstools, and Eddie the Bartender had saved them for us.

"Eddie, this is my son, Joseph. He graduated from college this weekend."

With a thick head of slicked back graying hair and a full beard to match, forty-three-year-old Eddie Fitzgerald stood tall and stout behind the bar. In his earlier years, he had been a star defensive end for St. Auggie's football team. His line prowess earned him a scholarship to play for Syracuse University, but a blown knee in his freshman training camp prevented him from ever playing a down for the Orange. Always clad in a white dress shirt, top button unbuttoned with the sleeves rolled up, he'd been pouring drinks for his family at Fitzgerald's since the early eighties. He was known as *the* bartender, a neighborhood staple. Before I took a seat, I extended my hand as if we'd never met before. He did the same.

"Joseph, congratulations. I'm assuming you're following the old man's lead with a pint," he said and gave a subtle wink.

In the previous four years, my friends and I downed our weight in Guinness while seated on Fitzgerald stools and chairs. Thanks to our drinking, Eddie had a Ford Explorer in the parking lot instead of a Ford Escort. Town councilmen, nursery owners or balding basketball coaches didn't tip or drink nearly as much as frivolous college students, ones who'll splurge on a round of Southern Comfort shots to impress younger women and the man pouring. In addition, we weren't a collection of vodka-swilling locals, there to throw fists before hugging the bathroom toilet with a pair of black eyes. We made our drinking mistakes at an earlier age, so by the time we found Eddie, we had become savvy drinkers, no longer shitheads who'd mix in Cuervo shots with pints of Genesee Cream Ale. We'd been there, learned our lesson, and he knew it. As long as we all had valid, albeit fake, identification, Eddie didn't care how old we were. Sitting with my father, I could finally flash my real driver's license—though I wasn't asked to.

After he set the pints down in front of us, my father held out a ten-dollar bill. Giving a brief glance at the money, Eddie threw up his hands in refusal.

"Patrick, the boy's graduated from college. It's a celebration, and I'm sure my family wouldn't mind if I put a round on the house for the Cahans."

"Eddie, take the money. You'll give the boy ideas that his diploma is a way to score free drinks all over the city."

Eddie then placed his forearms on the handles of the taps and leaned over.

"Patrick, Joseph is now a college grad. An educated man. Now, you know as well as I do that if he's intelligent enough to get a degree, he's smart enough to know what the three most important things in life are."

With the pint on my lips, I glanced up to see Eddie and my father looking at me. I lowered the pint to its coaster, removed the stout froth from my upper lip with my bottom lip, and gave a sigh. My father was out on the town spreading ancestral wisdom again, so I decided to recite the adage.

"A house to call home, a woman to call 'love', and a barman to call you by name?"

My father was satisfied, but Eddie twitched his head back before stepping away from the taps. He didn't seem aware of this Cahan ramble.

"Well, one out of three is better than nothing," he said. "From where I stand, at least you got the most important one."

"So what are the other two?" I said.

With a look of blatancy, he delivered.

"An honest mechanic and a skilled barber. Those are hard as hell to find, so when you do, you hold on tight. As for the ladies, if the woman who calls you 'love' can also do an oil change and fade up the sides and back of your hair with a one clip? Christ, you may have something."

"Funny," my father said, then politely laughed. "But, I'm not sure I follow."

Again, Eddie leaned his forearms on the tap handles and looked at us, concentrated but cordial. From across the bar, the councilman yelled over.

"Eddie, two more Buds over here!"

"Coming up, councilman." Eddie glanced across the bar,

then turned back to us to conclude his point.

"If Joseph's smart, he'll know the common thread that ties these things together is respect. You respect the things you appreciate. You hear the councilman over there?" he said, motioning over his right shoulder with his right thumb. "I don't like to be yelled at for drinks. I don't like to be called buddy or guy, chief or slugger or shooter. To yell at me like a servant is condescending, and if I don't know you, I may pour your pint of Guinness over a teaspoon to give you a straight, shitty pour, and I definitely won't let it settle in the well for three minutes like I'm supposed to. If you don't respect me, I won't respect you, and will want to get that shitty pint down your throat quick to get you the hell out of my bar and clear a stool for someone with respect. I know the councilman. He's a good man, and he's got a seat at the bar like you two. I know you both understand the mutual respect that comes from a bartender knowing your name, and those pints in front of you are a testament to that. With this clear, I doubt Joseph would ever disrespect my generosity downtown on Chippewa and Elmwood Avenue for free beers. If I ever found out he did, next time in here, he'd be getting the straight pour."

"With the teaspoon." I said.

"You got it, Joe," he said, smiling. "Enjoy the pints, Cahans, but I should get those Buds before the councilman starts calling me 'guy'."

And away he went to the cooler, grabbing two bottles of

Bud before flicking the caps off with the mounted opener attached below the bartop. I watched him set each down in front of the councilman before giving the man playful jabs in the arm as he waited for cash. I shook my head and took another sip of my pint. My father gave me a slap on the back before adding his own conclusion.

"Son, sometimes the most important lessons in life don't come in the classroom. They're taught through experience, and you'll see once you earn some."

I took this all in with another sip. Contrary to popular belief, true knowledge might not come from the findings of Sigmund Freud, the reporting of Dan Rather or the poetry of e.e. cummings. Would the advice of Eddie Fitzgerald trump the lessons taught by these trailblazers? Maybe. My father had a knack for delivering the right advice, but instead of thanks, I chose to respond with sarcasm. It wouldn't be a Cahan moment without some.

"So you think I should start hanging out in bars as much as possible then? Maybe ask Eddie for a job application?"

My father calmly sipped his Guinness, removed the froth from his upper lip and delivered.

"Sure. See if he's hiring. Also, with the application, ask him for a new place to live as well."

After another pint, we headed home. Too much time spent at Fitzgerald's did not make my mother a happy wife, so to keep

my father and his old afghan off the living room couch, we took
the short cruise along Lake Erie toward our house on Norton
Drive. When we arrived, my father parked and patted on the
back of my head.

"Welcome home, son."

Against the green siding of our two-story house leaned my
black mountain bike, rusted but still functional. I delivered the
Buffalo Gazette with that bike when I was twelve years old, and
at the base of the seat, I could see a yellow paper tie still
wrapped around it. Hanging from our fruitless pear tree in the
front yard was a tire swing football target, one that swayed back
and forth as I'd try to throw a perfect spiral through its center
under the rain and snow. Though the lake-effect weather had
frayed the knotted rope secured to the tree's branch, the worn tire
still swung ably. With an oversized red duffle bag slung over my
shoulder and a crate of CDs in my hands, I walked past all of it
and into my kitchen to smell hot dogs boiling in sauerkraut. My
mother sat at the kitchen table, peeling potatoes onto a paper
towel and cutting them into quarters to toss into a pot of boiling
water.

"I was going to bake a chicken, but your father thought you
wanted your favorite meal on your first night back home. Is this
really your favorite meal? Hot dogs, sauerkraut, and mashed
potatoes? Wouldn't you rather I make a chicken?"

Though a wonderful cook when she wanted to be, Ann
Cahan only served five dinners (aside from cereal) consistently:

baked chicken, boiled hot dogs with sauerkraut and mashed potatoes, creamed tuna on toast, fried hamburgers, and Irish spaghetti, which consisted of noodles and jar sauce with ground beef mixed in. I assumed my father's recommendation was based on the assumption that I never bought cans of processed sauerkraut at school. If so, he was right.

Before my mother was spinning her selective menu on Norton, she was Ann McNamara, living with her parents on the other side of the Southtowns and working as a local branch's bank teller when my father walked in. She never revealed what he said through her teller's window that day, but whatever it was proved good enough to get her out for a night with South Buffalo's Patrick Cahan. A year's worth of dates produced a moderately-priced engagement ring, bought with the cash my mother exchanged to my father through her teller window. Married soon after, my mother stayed home to take care of Frank first, then Claire, me, and Molly. She supplemented my father's income by babysitting other people's children, reasoning that she could make money, stay home with her children and provide us with playmates. Until Molly was twelve years old, she did, then took a job as the rectory receptionist for our neighborhood church, St. Theresa's. After watching my mother put four children through their elementary school and drag us into mass every Sunday morning, St. Theresa's felt the least they could do was hire her. It was too bad they never let her cook for them. The mere smell of those simmering franks would have given their clergymen some needed liturgical enthusiasm.

"You know why the potatoes are so good?" said my father, standing tall and proud next to my mother. "Hand masher and warm milk. No whipping. No beater. Just the heated milk, butter, salt, and your mother's elbow grease. My mother did the same, and her mother in Ireland before her. I passed it onto your mother when we were married. Probably the biggest perk of becoming a Cahan."

My mother smacked the back of my father's thigh with her right hand while holding the peeler in her left.

"I'll 'biggest perks of being a Cahan' you. If you two weren't sitting on your brains at Fitzgerald's for the past hour, maybe I could actually enjoy being a Cahan for a minute and stop feeling like I work for 'em. Patrick, sit and finish peeling these potatoes while I go change my clothes, will you?"

After my father reluctantly sat down, I continued across the tiled kitchen floor, through the dim living room and up the stairs to my bedroom. Climbing the green-carpeted steps, I could see the spot on the right side of the hallway from my brother's fist, who'd punched a hole through the dry wall after his old girlfriend dumped him for another guy. The hole had been plastered over, but I could still see where Frank fantasized about wrecking her new flame's face.

My bedroom door was still covered with rock band stickers, magazine covers, and now, my old poster of legendary Buffalo Bills quarterback Jim Kelly. Aside from the minimal paint-prepping, the room hadn't changed since high school, so the nostalgia was comfortable. After I walked in, I quickly found an empty space on the floor to drop my duffel bag and CDs before stepping over to my twin bed, still intact to the right. I lifted up the mattress to see my yellowed newspapers I kept atop the box spring. When I was younger, I saved Sports sections from days when the Bills won a big game between the mattress and box spring. As I held the mattress up, I could see those papers were still in good shape. To the left was the section from when the Bills beat the Raiders 51-3 for the 1990 AFC Championship. To the right rested the front page with the headline "Un-Bill-lievable" after the Bills overcame a 35-3 second half deficit to beat the Houston Oilers in the legendary 1992 AFC Wild Card game.

I grabbed that section, then set the mattress back down before settling on my bed to read the story like it had just happened. Aged between springs for eight years, the paper's print was faded and the pictures were less vibrant, but I could still transport myself back to that day. Sitting atop my childhood bed delivered me back to those younger times as well, days and nights in a bedroom plastered with pictures of The Clash, U2 and the E Street Band. Beatles album covers mounted on a wall flanked by John Lennon lyrics, tacked up as a statement I knew nothing about. I settled in to get more comfortable, adjusted the pillows and moved the blankets behind my back to prop me up. Engrossed in lines written years earlier, I was ultimately relaxed until my mother yelled up the stairs.

"Joseph, leave your unpacking for later and get down here," she said. "While you were at Fitzgerald's, Terry and Duff called. They're coming over and I don't have extra food for them, so get down here and eat before they get here. Those two always walk in while we're eating, so let's go!"

I set down the paper and darted down the stairs to join my parents at the six-seat table. With Frank and Claire now living in their own apartments downtown and Molly out for the night, I found my parents surrounded by empty seats. They were already holding hands, so I took my seat and joined hands with my mother. We bowed our heads, closed our eyes, and at the head of the table, my father began.

"Bless us, O Lord for these thy gifts which we are about to receive, from thy bounty, through Christ our Lord, Amen."

I raised my head, opened my eyes and tried to release my hand from my mother's—but my father continued.

"Also, tonight, Lord, we'd like to pray for all the suffering people on the streets of Buffalo, that they may find food and shelter. For all the Buffalonians who have left us in the past few years, we pray they may come home and reunite with their roots and families to be where they belong."

I opened my eyes to see my potatoes getting cold, but he proceeded.

"And, finally, Lord, thank you for bringing home our son, Joseph, from school, safe and sound. We pray that you bestow your guidance upon him in everything he does and everything we do in our daily lives so that we may become better people."

When I raised my head for the third time, I opened only my right eye in anticipation that the old man might continue. He had a habit of lengthy dinner prayers.

"Amen."

Our eyes finally opened in unison, our heads rose and our plates were full with helpings of one of my mother's five favorites. I immediately started cutting into one of my hot dogs, slicing it into five pieces and dipping the first piece into the potatoes and sauerkraut with my fork. I brought it to my mouth, but was interrupted by two clenched fists banging on the kitchen door behind me. Terry and Duff. Like my mother said, they always seemed to show up during dinner.

"Told you, Joseph," my mother whispered. "Let 'em in, but I didn't make enough food for the two of them. If they want to eat, they'll have to grab some cereal from the cabinet."

Fine: If you include the cereal, my mother had *six* salacious specialties. But, if she would have fed Terry and Duff more over the thirteen years we'd been friends, they both would have been as big of a hot dogs, sauerkraut and mashed potatoes fan as I was.

6

I met Terry Ford and Duffy Morris in the fourth grade at St. Theresa's elementary school.

At nine years old, Terry was a thin kid, with tanned skin, dark eyes, and a long, tall head, which inspired some of the older students at St. Theresa's to call him "Tall-Headed Terry." His hair on that head was thick and, with a spray bottle and large yellow comb, was slicked to the back with delicacy by his mother every weekday morning. Even outside our school hallways, the kid was always dressed fancy. When we dressed down from our school uniforms of white shirts and blue ties, he'd change into khakis and a crisp polo. His family was more affluent than either mine or Duff's, and though it showed in his clothes and primped hair, it didn't show up in his attitude. If it did, he would have had the shit kicked out of him more than once during our friendship. If he had any attitude, there wouldn't have been a friendship. But, when we were younger, he had his moments.

Duff had the size to pass for a sixth grader when he was in the fourth, but was never intimidating unless provoked. He was tall for his age, with some upper body mass as well. Though his Irish father was slender, his mother was a healthy-sized German woman. While I was at my family table fighting for the last of the creamed tuna on toast, he was stuffing down kielbasas and pot roasts with his two older brothers, both offensive linemen on St. Auggie's football team.

Terry laid the ground for our friendship with an ill-advised plan: He wanted to impress some sixth grade girls by making our class's biggest kid look clumsy on our lunch schedule's most anticipated day, Pizza Friday. Carrying a tray with three slices of pizza and two cartons of milk, Duff didn't like to look clumsy. He walked down the center aisle, holding his tray with one hand and brushing his sandy blonde hair out of his freckled face with the other. Terry stuck out his shined penny-loafer and caught Duff's shin. As Duff tripped, he lost his balance, his pizza, and as he hit the marble floor of St. Theresa's cafeteria, he lost his nine-year-old temper.

With Terry cackling in a wise guy, sinister laugh above him, Duff rose from the ground, grabbed the back of Terry's button-down collar, and in front of those unimpressed sixth grade girls, dragged him out of his aluminum chair. Holding Terry by his skinny neck, he picked up one of his slices of pizza from the floor and slapped Terry across his long face with it. When Terry wiped the red sauce from his eyes to see the whole room laughing, he had to counter. One of Duff's milks was still on the ground, so as Duff enjoyed the retribution, Terry picked up one of the milks, ripped off the top and threw it in Duff's face.

If I wanted Terry Ford to ever see the fifth grade, I knew I had to do something. On my tray sat a half-eaten slice, a side of corn niblets and a chocolate pudding cup. I stood on my chair, tray in hand and screamed, "Food fight!" That day's pizza tasted like cardboard, so I didn't mind wasting it. I flung it and the rest of the food over my shoulder and into the air; following my lead, the rest of the room did the same. Duff and Terry scattered from each other to seek cover and ammunition as the pizza slices, corn niblets, and pudding cups rained down. The firing became heavy. The lunch ladies called our principal, Sister Regis, down to quell the battle and reprimand those responsible for starting the melee. Within seconds of her entrance, Duff, Terry and I were pointed to her grasp by lousy squealers and led up to her office by our shirt collars. After she yelled at the three of us for twenty minutes, she called our parents, assigned us a month's detention and sent us to the bathrooms to clean the corn out of our hair.

When you spend a month writing essays and cleaning classrooms with only two other people, it tends to drag. In that time, we found out we had a lot more in common than our love for Pizza Friday. We loved the Buffalo Bills and, despite the amount of sloppy interceptions he was tossing, their star quarterback, Jim Kelly. Even at that young an age, we liked sifting through our fathers' old records, all mesmerized by the Rolling Stones and Beatles albums we'd play on ancient turntables. When we grew up, we all wanted to be professional athletes, and when we made our millions of dollars, we wanted to buy one of the mansions that lined Lake Erie not far from St. Theresa's. It seemed like a legitimate idea back then, but as Terry Ford and Duffy Morris entered my kitchen as adults, none of us had become professional athletes. St. Theresa's was still educating aspiring millionaires, and Sister Regis was still scolding kids for throwing vegetables. We hadn't earned our mansions yet, but after our time spent dreaming in detention, our four years of high school at St. Auggie's and another four apart at college, we were still friends.

"Mr. Cahan, Mrs. Cahan. How was the graduation?" said Terry. "Did you have to pinch yourselves to believe it, Joe getting a diploma from anywhere other than that Sally Struthers School?"

"Well, Terry, it was hard to accept. Almost as hard as accepting that some institution admitted *you* into their law program," said my father. "The legal system in this country must be going down the toilet if the University of Buffalo is encouraging loudmouth miscreants like you."

"Mr. Cahan, to uphold the law, one must first understand how one could break these laws and why."

My mother wanted in.

"Really, Ter? Why don't you tell us how you've been breaking these laws? Pull up a chair and grab some cereal."

Duff laughed as he walked to the corner of the kitchen to lean on the counter.

"You really buried yourself on that one, guy. Better start digging out."

Terry stood behind me in front of the kitchen door, tanned arms folded with a defeated smirk under his yellow baseball cap. He'd fallen into his own mess, so he rerouted the questioning to clean himself off.

"So how was the drive back? Mrs. Cahan said you guys already stopped at Fitzgerald's, so that kills our evening before it starts."

"That's where you wanted to go tonight?" I said, mouth stored full of potatoes.

"Yeah. I figured first night back, keep it simple with a few pitchers. Besides, on the first night back from school, there's bound to be fantastic talent out, hungry for redemption."

"Redemption?" said Duff. "For what?"

"For not going out with me all these years. I'm a college grad on my way to law school, and when that story gets around, it'll play well with the local girls. Some of them love guys with goals higher than a healthy pick-up truck and a union card."

"All right, besides the guys I've worked with at Ford for the last three summers, you just insulted my old man, his F-150, and his UAW card," said Duff. "Say that to his face and his highest goal will be kicking your ass. Also, if you plan on meeting any women tonight, you might want to start by losing your pretty hat. Stories will get around all right, and they'll have less to do with your legal aspirations, and more to do with your sexual aspirations. You look gay in that thing."

Once again, Terry looked defeated underneath his cute yellow hat, shaking his head after being trumped again. Even my father wanted to get some shots in.

"You're the best looking guy you know, aren't you, Terry? I saw some of those girls down at Fitzgerald's, and they all said your muscles were hard—hard to find."

He found his joke more hilarious than anyone else, and we laughed at his sheer enjoyment of Terry's belittlement. I had to bring order.

"Dad, would you knock it off? Look, guys, I don't feel like going back there tonight; maybe tomorrow. I was hoping to get downtown to Doherty's on Elmwood, snag a booth and monopolize the jukebox all night 'til they throw us out for playing the entire *Exile on Main Street* album four or five times."

"I could go for that," said Duff. "They have five-dollar pitchers of Bud tonight and, since I don't start work for another week, I wouldn't mind saving money under the Stones."

Terry surrendered to our two votes, pulled off his hat by the brim and ran his fingers through his thick mane. He gave a sigh of frustration and relented.

"Fine. We'll go downtown to Doherty's, but the only talent filling their stools will be chicks who drink Genny pounders, smoke Marb Reds and bring their own darts to bars."

"If that's the case, I may not spend much time in a booth," said Duff. He slapped his hands together with a mocking grin and approached Terry. "I'll be too busy at those stools getting phone numbers. If they're ripe for redemption, I'll send them over to you."

We had another laugh at Terry's expense, and as I sat finishing my dinner, I enjoyed a familiar scene. Though our ages had changed, the conversation and comfort between the three of us had not. We were older, yet not necessarily wiser, and shared a simple, unspoken truth: My home was their home, and their homes were mine. Extended family for a trio of idiots. Duff had a theory he stood behind, whether tailgating in the December cold before a Bills' home game or sitting on those rickety barstools at Fitzgerald's. His old man once told him that, in life, a man is fortunate to have one true friend. Numerous people were roaming the earth without a single companion, so if a man had one, he should be appreciative. Since Duff had two, he considered himself well-off. He usually broke out this reasoning after we each had a dozen beers, but he was right. I was lucky to have friends like Duff and Terry, and I always remembered that when struggles with school, work or even Johanna arose. Things could be low, but no matter how bad they got, I knew I'd always have at least two friends to call family.

With this view cemented, it made sense that we weren't too concerned with the undetermined outlook ahead. In my kitchen, we should have been shaken to the core, looking out at the uncertain future with no promise of success. But, we weren't worried about where we would end up. We were more concerned about getting down to Doherty's for a few pitchers, some laughs, and the sound of Mick and the boys wailing out the jukebox.

When we walked through the doors of Doherty's, it was busy, but spread out. Small groups mingled in sections of the barroom, every barstool was full, but there was still room for us to walk to an empty booth. When Duff and I spotted one, we staked our claim while Terry went for the first pitcher. Duff started the questioning once we settled into the booth.

"So Terry and I were talking about getting season tickets this year for the Bills," said Duff, lightly drumming his fingers on the table as he talked. "You think you're going to be around or what?"

"Not sure yet," I said. "You know the story."

"I know, but you should think about it. Terry's uncle in the box office said he could get us some nice ones. Thirty-five-yard-line, twenty rows up. I've never had seats so good before. My old man always gets the end zone tickets with rest of the blue-collar drunks."

"If I could get something going here, something at the Gazette doing anything, I'd probably stay." I leaned back into the booth and grabbed a smoke from my shirt pocket. "The three of us could get an apartment down here on Elmwood. Terry could take the train to classes, and if you stuck around the stamping plant for a while, it wouldn't be a bad drive."

"Yeah, it'd be nice. But I don't plan on staying at my summer job to get my UAW card. Since that newspaper has been laying people off for the past year, I'm guessing they won't have room for slims like you running coffee," he said, then reached across the booth to smack my left arm. "Still, you should think about sticking around. This could definitely be the Bills year. You're going to feel like a real asshole when you're sucking up at some random newspaper or magazine in the middle of nowhere while we're in Niagara Square, watching Ralph Wilson hold the Lombardi Trophy in his old, wrinkled hands."

"They were eight and eight last season," I said. "You're out of your fucking mind."

"Parity, my friend. In the NFL, any year can be *the* year."

"Someone should do a parody of you," I said. "You sound like a fucking idiot."

"Ha, ha; parity and parody. I get it, jag-off. But when you see our Bills in the Super Bowl this season, don't say Duffy Morris didn't tell you so."

Terry approached our booth with a shit-eating grin, as well as three empty pint glasses and a pitcher of Budweiser. Setting down the glasses and pitcher on the table, he balanced himself in prime air guitar position as he raised his imaginary pick and waited for the intro.

DER NA DER DER, DUR DUR DA DER!

Terry played Keith Richard's opening air guitar on "Rock's Off" as the lick blasted out of the juke, like he was auditioning for the Stones at our booth. He moved his fingers up and down imaginary frets before Mick Jagger's vocal opening "Ah, yeah" came over the speakers. Duff and I laughed at his enthusiasm while we did our own Charlie Watts impersonations on air drums. When the song kicked into full rhythm, Terry threw himself into the booth before laying his palms flat on the table top, alternating sinister looks between Duff and me as Duff poured the beers. His face suggested that he gathered some enticing information, and as he pulled his own pint glass close, the smile stayed as Duff filled it. After Duff and I looked at each other, both eager to know what the hell was so interesting, I spoke up.

"Yeah? Let's have it. What's so hilarious?"

Leaning over the table, he looked to his right and left before he spoke, like he was about to tell an ethnic joke but had to check that no one of that specific culture was present.

"Guess who's at the corner of the bar?"

"Who?" I said, intrigued.

"You have to field a guess. That's why I said 'guess.' It's a question, so give me a fucking answer and I'll tell you if it's right or not. And don't look."

"Jim Kelly?" said Duff. "My old man told me he tosses darts in here."

"You fucking idiot." Terry leaned back in his bench, frustrated. "It's somebody you know. Someone you've talked to."

"I've talked to Jimbo before."

"Yelling at your tube while he shuffles in the pocket doesn't count," I said. "Praying to him doesn't count either."

"Fine," said Duff. "Is it a girl or guy, Terry?"

"Girl."

"Cute or a slob?"

"Cute."

"Tall or short?"

"Short."

"Hair?"

"Brown."

"History with any of us?"

"Desired."

"Desired?" I said. "We desired one with her, or her with one of us."

"She with you, specifically."

With this, the game was over. I needed the answer, so I stood up to survey the barstools. Sorting through barflies in worn t-shirts and Buffalo Sabres hockey hats, panning past women in their mid-thirties styling hair clips and ordering pounders of Genesee, my eyes found the girl at the corner of the bar. With her arms extended over the bar top, a brown-eyed girl of medium height and thin build stood fiddling with cash while waiting for her drink. I watched as she brushed scattered locks from her face. I immediately recognized her.

"Maria Santoro."

"Get the fuck out!" said Duff. "St. Theresa's superstar, Maria Santoro? Is she still wearing those hoop earrings, or did the eighties ask for them back?"

"Let me check."

When I stood up to get another look, Maria was getting change back from the bartender before mouthing a "thank you." When she looked down to put the bills back in her purse, one ear peeked out from under her chocolate hair to reveal a golden shine.

"Still got 'em," I said.

She caught my glance amid Duff's laughter. She squinted in my direction and gave a small wave when she realized it was me. Holding a clear cocktail, she started over to our table, smiling and looking eager.

"She's coming over. Shut up."

I stayed standing to greet her with the standard hug, provoking Terry and Duff to put down their beers and follow. When we finished our hellos, we sat back down and she stood at the edge of the booth, resting her drink on the tabletop. Panning across the three of us with her inquisitive Italian eyes, she started with me.

"So, Joey, I saw your mother getting groceries last week and she said the family was going down for your graduation."

"They were there."

"And? How was it?"

"It was a graduation. I graduated."

"Joey, that's great. And the girl situation?" she said, not wasting any time. "What's going on with that?"

"We broke up," I said, not thrilled where the conversation was headed.

"Yeah, that's what your mother told me. Such a sweet woman your mom is, Joey."

"Well, why'd you ask me?"

"What? Whether you broke up?"

"Yeah."

She pulled a cigarette from her purse, put it to her lips and lit it with a pink lighter.

"Well, the last time I saw you, you said you weren't sure if it was going to last, but then I saw your mother and she said you were going strong. She said you never know what you want, so I wasn't sure what to believe. So?"

"Broken up, Maria; guarantee it. If anything changes, I'll tell my mother to give you an update next time she passes through your grocery line, okay?"

I brought in my beer in for a long, soothing drink. Terry intervened after a good three seconds of awkward silence.

"So, Maria, I'm starting law school in the fall over at UB. First year's supposed to be hell, so if any of your friends are interested, better tell them to inquire soon. I won't have any time come first semester."

"Inquire about what?" she said, holding her straw and sucking gin and tonic through the tip. Once again, Terry leaned back in his bench, frustrated.

"My availability for summer dating. I wouldn't be against taking some talent on a romantic walk along the waterfront, a cruise with Mr. Cahan on the Miss Buffalo or even a quiet night here at Doherty's. Right now, my summer is wide open."

Maria covered her mouth, spitting up her drink in a quick spurt of laughter.

"Oh, Ter," she said, batting her browns with sympathy. "If you want to start getting inquiries from *women*, you might want to start by ditching the yellow hat. This isn't California, sweetie; it's Buffalo. Most girls here would see that hat and assume you were gay."

"Thank you, Maria," said Duff as he clapped his hands in approval. "By the way, love the earrings."

"Thanks," she said, then revealed them for a better look.

"Well, I'll let you guys be. See you later."

Before she stepped completely away, she gently brushed her fingers down my left forearm. With a smile on her face and a pout in her eyes, she said,

"Bye, Joey."

I looked up at her coolly as her fingers ran down my skin—even as my body went numb. Her look was incredibly sexy; tight blue jeans and a sleeveless white top that accentuated her tanned skin. When she was gone, I took another long slug of my beer, drinking to the bottom to slow my racing heart. I reached for the pitcher to pour another as Terry and Duff's elbows were on the table, their eyes firmly fixed on me.

"What the fuck was that, Cahan?" said Terry. "Correct me if I'm wrong, but is your mom trying to get you laid? What kind of bullshit has Ann Cahan been feeding that girl?"

"Yeah, *Joey*," said Duff in a female voice. "What was that all about? I thought you two never hooked up. Is there something you want to share?"

The truth was there really wasn't anything to share. I'd known Maria since the second grade at St. Theresa's, and at seven years old, she'd flirt with me before I knew what flirting was. Tossing her hair around in a plaid Catholic jumper, she would turn around in her cramped wooden chair to give me winks most boys found gross. We didn't find girls gross anymore, and on that night at Doherty's, none of us found Maria full of cooties. She looked fantastic, so when she seductively stepped away from our booth, thoughts of the past immediately started bouncing through my frazzled head.

Why didn't we ever hook up? Not sure. I was always attracted to her, and since she grew up a few streets from my parents' house, we saw each other around. Through college, we ran in different circles, but I still saw her and her family at St. Theresa's on the Sundays I was home. Our families were familiar, so Maria always seemed to know what was going on with me. But, most of the time, there was just something else going on. Whether it was my inflated expectations toward women in high school or my college relationship with Johanna, something always halted my pursuit of Maria. That night at Doherty's, the chance was presenting itself with flashing lights and blaring sirens. She was pushing the issue with her enticing tone, and Terry and Duff wanted ringside seats for the action. Even my mother seemed to be seeking this union out at the local grocery store. Still, I played it off like I was oblivious to nearly fifteen years of sexual tension.

"What? We've never hooked up, I swear. I don't know what that was, but you know Maria; this isn't new. And I have no clue what my mother has told her. You know how she is with Frank and me."

"You mean how she promotes you guys to any local girl with ears in hopes of finding each of you your very own queens of the Queen City?" said Duff.

"Exactly. Ann probably told her about how her poor, loving son was stuck at college with a snobby redhead from White Plains who doesn't appreciate him for all his flower buying, poem writing and general Catholic pleasantness. 'He just needs a good, strong, beautiful Buffalo girl to take care of him and straighten him out.'"

Terry flashed me a squeamish look.

"You wrote Johanna poems?"

"My mom found a poem I'd written for one of my classes and assumed it was for her. Actually," I said, then stared into my beer's carbonation. "I'm not sure if I ever wrote anything for her."

Uncomfortable silence. When Johanna's name was mentioned, neither of them knew how to address it. Terry and Duff were like my brothers, not my sisters. Though we were close, it didn't emasculate us. When we had family problems or the rare serious relationship went to the can, we'd address it. But most of the time, we were guys who talked about the complexities of the Bills' defensive packages or the historical relevance of Jimi Hendrix's drummer, Mitch Mitchell. Just because I lost the love of my life, it didn't mean Terry or Duff had acquired the necessary feminine sensibilities to coax me through the heartache. They didn't have the words to make the situation better, but they had to say something. Terry decided to be the one to take the bullet.

"Yeah, uh, Cahan. Sorry about Johanna, man. When I called before, your mom told me, but I didn't want to force the issue. Since Maria broke the ice, um, do you?"

"Do I what? Want to discuss it?"

"Yeah," he said. "If you don't want to, we can say 'fuck it' and move on. I have other stuff to bring up about this summer, and I should probably get another pitcher too."

"I agree," said Duff. "If you don't want to discuss this shit, fine. But we know what this girl meant to you, so if you want to talk, we can fucking talk. If not, we can pretend the fucking bitch is dead and gone. Totally up to you."

That was another thing with us: We did care about serious life issues, but to preserve our presumed masculinity, we'd insert expletives into discussion to make it seem like we didn't. If we inserted the word 'fuck' as an adjective, noun and verb, it served as a good disguise when we wanted to be sincere without sounding like a "Very Special Episode" of some awful sitcom. But, despite the masked sincerity, I knew they cared. They wanted to know if my head was straight after losing who I referred to as *the* one. And, I could see they had their doubts after the mild emotion I showed toward Maria's seductive pass.

"Well, besides the girl completely ruining Bob Dylan for the rest of my life?"

"That's rough," said Duff.

"Sure it is, but what can I do? It's over, she's gone, and she's not coming back. I guess it's kind of like she *is* dead and gone."

"What do you mean?" said Terry.

I leaned back to prepare for my explanation, then delivered.

"The redhead with a fucking smile tattooed on her face? The one who finished my sentences while we lay together and listened to *The Joshua Tree*? She's gone. In her place is a girl who's emotionally void, always depressed and mentally unstable. She doesn't seem concerned with what she does to herself, and she's definitely not concerned with what she does to me. I wish I could understand what the fuck happened, but since she refused to cooperate, I broke up with her. I didn't see any other fucking solution; I still don't."

"So you really think this is it?" said Duff, obviously

skeptical. "Like Maria said, dude, this shit's happened before. Remember last summer? The arguments started, you thought about walking and here we are today talking about you actually doing it. What's different this time?"

"Communication and friendship," I said. "When our troubles started, we had chances at school to sit down, talk them out and make promises of change we knew deep down we'd never keep. When the promises were broken, the problems got worse and the communication died. We never talk anymore, and with her in White Plains, we probably won't again."

"And friendship?" said Terry.

I reached in my shirt pocket for a smoke and then pulled the booth's ashtray close. I lit the stick and took a long drag. After I exhaled, I answered,

"We no longer have one."

I inhaled, exhaled. Terry and Duff exchanged uncomfortable looks before tossing the ends of their beers down their throats. Terry grabbed his empty glass and slid out of the booth.

"I'm gonna grab another pitcher. And shots. You two want shots? I'll get 'em. Whiskey, chilled."

After Terry walked from the booth, Duff slapped me on the back, which offered more consolation than any words could have. It was rugged reassurance, more therapeutic than lines I had written and said to myself over the past few weeks and months. Every scenario, every solution and every euphemism had been scribbled or voiced.

"You know what the hardest part to accept is?" I said.

"What?"

"The goddamn friendship part of romance. When you're with someone romantically, there's so much more involved emotionally and sexually than with a simple friendship, but you still consider yourself *friends*. When it's done, you break up because you want the sexual relationship to end, but you end up losing a friend as well. Sometimes, it's a best friend. I think that's my biggest problem: I've fucking lost a best friend."

Duff folded his arms on the tabletop and offered up what he could.

"It sucks, but that's why girls are a goddamn catch twenty-two. It's like my old man told me once when we were in high school: you love it when you love 'em, and you lose it when you lose 'em."

I mashed my smoke into the tray and nodded in agreement.

"Romance and friendship is a wild fucking recipe when you combine the two, Cahan. You want to take those ingredients and bake it into your own cake to eat. With this situation, it sounds like you got a nice, tall layered one. Now, it's like that cake was tossed, stepped in and shoved right in your face, frosting and all. You had a girl you loved as a girlfriend *and* a best friend, and now, that's all gone. You had to break up with a friend, and you never have to break up with your friends."

"That's exactly it. If you and I weren't getting along, I

wouldn't have to break up with you, right? Wouldn't happen."

Duff flashed a wry smile and put his hand on my shoulder.

"Cahan, I hope there's a lot of shit you and Johanna did as friends that you and I wouldn't do, all right?"

"Hilarious," I said. "But you see my point?"

"Cahan, love and sex fuck friendships up; always have. When they go together with no turbulence, you know you've got something rolling. When they don't, you lose 'em both because they didn't mix. It's throwing the baby out with the bath water, but that's how it goes. Maybe to get over this, you need to find a few new babies, and forget about the bath water."

Duff's metaphors were making me dizzy.

"What?"

"I'll put it in music terms for you: Right now, you're listening to the Stones play 'Moonlight Mile' when you should be cranking up 'Loving Cup.' Like Mick says in the lyrics, 'just one drink and you'll fall down drunk.'"

"Just one drink?"

"Sex, Cahan. With some girl you're not fitting for a wedding dress in your head. Start looking here, tonight."

Back with another pitcher and three shots of whiskey cupped in his left hand, Terry's ears perked up when he heard the words "sex" and "tonight."

"Sex tonight? Who? What are you talking about?"

"Cahan," said Duff. "We have to get the fucking reclamation process rolling. It's the only way to get his head straight."

"Great idea, but I haven't had to put in pick-up time with a girl in almost four years. If I walked up to one right now, I have three questions for her, and one of them would undoubtedly come out as, 'So, do you come here often?' I'm booing myself thinking about it, so where am I supposed to start?"

Terry and Duff both looked at each other, smiling with sly grins and the obvious answer to my idiotic question.

"What about the Italian who just offered herself to you?" said Duff. "Running her fingers down your forearm with those hoops swinging from her ears, I don't think she was asking you for friendship tonight."

"C'mon, you guys. Maria? After all these years, you want me to call her in off the bench for a one-night stand?"

"This is the night she's been waiting her whole career for," said Terry.

It wasn't that I was hesitant toward one night with a beautiful girl with dark hair, dark eyes, seductive mannerisms and an inviting frame. This girl was no slouch, but she was still Maria Santoro. This was the same Maria who would see my mother at the grocery store after this went down and tell her, after only one night, she had found love with her son. My mother's prayers would be answered, overjoyed that her son had finally found a proper Catholic girl from Buffalo. Soon enough, it would be around the whole goddamn Southtowns that Maria and I were an item. Soon enough, we would walk into mass hand-in-hand to signify our true love in the face of the community. You always knew a couple was getting serious when they decided to start showing up to Saturday or Sunday mass together at St. Theresa's. When word reached my mother, she'd offer to drive us.

But why was I concerned about this peripheral crap? Guys walked into bars, said a few lines to vulnerable females and whisked them off into cars every weekend. They talked some more, approached each other for a kiss and progressed to some innocent action in that car. When the parking lot became a spectacle, they'd retreat to more private quarters, get to where they wanted to go, and it was over. The next morning, the sun would come up, and sometimes, they never spoke again. They didn't always start dating and calling each other on the phone four times-a-day. They didn't always advance to the right pews of St. Theresa's. They would have sex, and weren't thinking twelve steps ahead. I wasn't like this.

But I was sick of who I was.

I was sick of caring about practicality or consequences, and I started thinking about what could happen if I got up out of my booth to approach the attractive brunette across Doherty's. She still had the gin and tonic, but it was looking low. She might need another, and looking at the empty pint in front of me, I needed another one, too. The draft beer was fogging my head, and with the whiskey waiting in front of me, it was about to get foggier. After I glanced over at her again, I turned to the guys with a wry smile.

"Well, I don't want to keep her waiting, right?"

Terry smiled and raised his shot. With a grin still fixated from ear to ear, he offered his final assessment.

"Talent like that doesn't wait on the bench forever, Cahan."

Duff and I hoisted our shots and smiled before tossing the burn down our throats to light up our stomachs. When the liquor settled, I wormed my way out of the booth and up to the bar for two new drinks and a quick look in its mirror. The liquor bottles rested in front of the part I was facing, but I could still see my reflection between the Beams, Walkers and Bushmills. I waited for the bartender, caught sight of myself and collected my thoughts. I looked fine and felt fresh. The drinks loosened me up a bit, and that shot was a real cooler. I had to relax. This was just a girl, one I've known most of my life. There's no game here, and she knows everything. Stand and deliver, see where it goes. Great.

"Gin & tonic, whiskey on the rocks," I said to the bartender.

When I woke up the next morning, still in my clothes and shoes on a living room couch I'd never sat before, those words were my last taste of clarity.

7

When I opened my eyes, I was surrounded by windows with unfamiliar views. My heart and mind raced for recollection.

My God, I thought. Where am I and how did I get here?

Eddie the Bartender once told me a story about a drunk who walked home from Fitzgerald's, took a turn onto the wrong street, mistakenly walked into the wrong house, and slipped into bed. The woman already under the sheets woke up screaming and paused her cries long enough to knock his lights out with a porcelain lamp. After I slowly searched my head for lumps, I was happy I didn't have any.

My petrified eyes cautiously panned the scene. In a house I'd never seen before, I could only hear unfamiliar voices whispering in the background; I was terrified. My mind scanned frantically for answers. Why was I on this couch? Where's my wallet? Are my pants on? God, who are those people talking?

The voices continued as I closed my eyes tightly and pretended to sleep. I stayed motionless, giving no indication I was awake or alive. The enunciated words grew louder. I could understand a stern male voice talking to a female, both older and genuinely concerned.

"So, what's he doing here? Why is he on our couch?" he said.

"She said he came in and fell asleep, and I believe her. What can we do? Just let her wake him up and get him out of here."

She said? Who was *she?* Did I go home with someone the previous night? Where? God, if you get me out of this alive, I swear to you I will never miss Sunday mass or mass on any observed holy day for the rest of my life.

"So, we shouldn't talk to him or ask him why the hell he decided to come in and sleep on our couch?"

"We don't want to embarrass the kid, right? Besides, I can smell the booze on him from over here. Jesus, let's leave him be."

Finally, the male voice yelled up a stairwell before he walked out the front door.

"Maria, we're leaving. We'll be back later today."

Maria? Oh, thank you, God. See you on Sunday.

It slowly started to seep in. We had left Doherty's together, but I was still clueless as to where I lay. I'd been to Maria's house when we were kids, and it didn't resemble my surroundings. Huge bay windows surrounded me, with excessive sunlight shining onto a cream-colored throw rug on hardwood floors. To the right and left of a fireplace, there was a view of Lake Erie beyond a collection of newly planted trees in a sprawling green yard. The Santoro living room I remembered had wood paneling along the base, brown shag carpeting and a view of local railroad tracks through two screen windows.

The sunlight was killing my eyes as my head pounded harder than my chest. I heard footsteps down the staircase and toward the back of the couch. I closed my eyes tight. With the way my morning started, I feared there was still a remote chance I was in some stranger's house with a tenant named Maria.

"Joey. Joey. Are you awake?"

I opened my eyes.

"Maria? Where the hell are we?"

"It's my parents' new house. I told you last night how they moved into this one a while ago. Don't you remember?"

I sat up as she stood waiting for an answer. I suddenly remembered my mother telling me Maria's family had moved, but I didn't remember any ride home. Folding her arms and releasing a frustrated sigh, she walked around the couch to join me. Stretching my arms before massaging my temples, I looked toward her for the explanation.

"After Doherty's closed, you said you didn't want to go home yet, so we came here," she said. "When we walked in, we went to the couch, started to kiss, and then in mid-action, I felt you stop moving."

"Dammit, I'm sorry."

"I tried to revive you with a shake or two, but nothing. Whispering your name? Nothing. There was a point I thought you might be dead, but then you started mumbling about a buffalo or something, so I got up, grabbed you a blanket, and went to sleep. Alone."

"I don't know what to say. I'm so sorry. Must have been the whiskey. Knocks me out sometimes."

"I'll say," she said. "Do you remember anything about our talk on the way home?"

After a substantial pause, I questioned.

"Why?"

"Well, you may have let slip with some future intentions; intentions for the two of us. I never knew you felt any of these things."

My headache slipped into my stomach, rumbling and tossing the way a stomach does when you house a half a bottle of whiskey on a casual evening, then wake up to hear the regurgitation of ridiculous, drunken things said to a girl the night before. What the hell was she talking about? Future intentions?

"Maria, I really don't know how to say this, but after we left Doherty's, I don't remember a damn thing."

She slouched into the corner of the couch, bent her legs into her chest and wrapped her arms around them. She focused her sullen brown eyes in my direction.

"So, last night's *I've always thought you've had serious future Mrs. Cahan possibilities* was all bullshit?"

My headache intensified with her every word. Why did I listen to Terry and his football metaphors? Talent like that doesn't wait on the bench forever? This was the same guy who referred to girls as "talent." And why did I drink so much whiskey? My grandfather has always said that too much brown liquor serves as a mind eraser for the Cahans.

"Maria, look," I said, then reached out to touch her lower leg. "I just got out of this long relationship, and to be honest, I don't see anyone having future Mrs. Cahan possibilities anytime soon. I need some down time."

Maria stretched out her legs and put her feet on the floor. Still seated with her arms folded, she stared out the window at the lake for a few seconds, then looked at me.

"You know what, Joey? She's gone," she said. "I heard what happened with the two of you at school and it sounded nasty. Even if you did love her, the best thing to do is forget her and move on. Now."

I sat up straight, put my feet flat on the floor and leaned toward her.

"Right, Maria. I need to get over her. That's everyone's suggestion, but it's not that easy. I'll get over her, but not today. Not this soon, and not like this."

Then, we both sat silent for a minute. She was frustrated because she wanted to be with me for more than one night; I was frustrated I didn't wake up with amnesia. If I couldn't remember the past, I would have been on that couch with a beautiful woman who wanted everything to do with me, right at that moment. Sure, I still would have had an excruciating headache and a mouth tasting of ash. And, of course, the amnesia would have knocked any memory of Maria out of my head, causing me to worry whether this woman was preparing to rob or kill me. But, it would've freed me from the thoughts of Johanna, shackles that made me second-guess the past and long for it at the same time. I knew she was gone, but as Maria Santoro sat glaring at me, I knew I wasn't ready to accept it. Finally, she broke the silence.

"C'mon, I'll give you ride home. Ann's probably worried sick about why you didn't come home last night."

"Yeah, if we could keep this night between the two of us, I'd appreciate it. I wouldn't want anyone jumping to conclusions."

"Anyone? Like your mother?"

"Exactly. I'd appreciate it if we tried to keep this low. You don't think your parents will say anything, do you?"

"My mother said that since moving out of the neighborhood, the only time they bump into your parents is at St. Theresa's for Sunday mass. My hunch is that, 'by the way, I found your drunken son passed out on our couch last weekend after a night out with our daughter,' isn't a topic you bring up after mass. You should be safe."

"Thanks. Ready to get out of here?"

"Sure," she said, then slowly leaned toward me. "Just one favor to ask."

"Anything."

She reached out to touch my face and grazed my right cheek with her fingertips.

"When you do get over this Johanna, you'll call me, and we can do this again. Deal?"

She closed her browns and softly kissed my cheek. I closed my eyes as well, and when I opened them, what should have been a drunken debacle had become a truly sentimental moment. Instead of letting it exist as that, I opened my mouth.

"You got it. Soon as I'm over her, I promise to go out, guzzle whiskey and come back here to blackout on your parents' couch again," I said, grinned. "By the way, really comfortable couch you have here. Make sure you pass that on to the family, will you?"

Maria folded her arms again, shook her head and smirked.

"You're such an asshole, Joey."

Later that day, my parents' side door was left open, but I knew no one was home. Radios were silent, table lights were off and there was an air of emptiness as I entered the kitchen. Since we didn't live in a high crime area of the Southtowns, all the doors in our house could be found wide-open all day. Once in a while, there'd be a random hooligan who would steal my father's beer from our garage, but that was it. He had a lot of faith in the conscience of the neighborhood, and my mother had faith that God was watching over our house at all times.

"It's the best security system in the world," she'd say.

On that morning, her belief in the Almighty's watchful eye allowed me to waltz into our kitchen keyless. On the kitchen table, I saw a note from her set underneath the table lamp.

Joseph,

Called Terry this morning to see where you were, and he said you were sleeping on his couch. Next time you decide to stay out, please call and let us know. I almost sent your father out to search alleys. Anyways, please get your things in order and into your room at some point today. I'll be back later this afternoon, and make sure you're home for dinner. Your father's bringing home a fish fry from Fitzgerald's after work. Also, Johanna called you this morning. She said to call her back later today.
Love,
Mom

Johanna. The worst part about trying to get over a girl is how, no matter where they are in world, they always know the most opportune times to fertilize seeds of longing. After a night of binge drinking and attempted rebounding, of course I would be greeted with a phone message from Johanna Darcy. It was like she could sense my feelings from across the state, and unfortunately, they existed. There was longing, and I wouldn't be able to soothe it with shots of whiskey or power plays on amorous Italians.

I took my mother's note up the steps and into the bathroom. I chased three aspirin with a glass of water and limped into my bedroom. Eyeing my bed, I flopped in on my back, still clutching the message. Just looking at her name got the memories rolling, but instead of calling her back to deal with the present, I slipped toward the past. I lay back to recall when it all made sense.

Approaching winter break of our sophomore year, Johanna wasn't just a fling I tried to impress with the most appropriate Bob Dylan song. Besides existing as a girl who floored me with her smile, Johanna Darcy also became my best friend. College hosted a series of inaugural experiences, a period in which triumphs like love and professional direction were first realized. Walking the St. Francis campus that semester, I had Johanna and a collection of journalism classes that motivated me to fill my yellow legal pads. With things going so well, I wasn't prepared to deal with the death of my Grandma Cahan, who lost a struggle with cancer on the morning after Christmas. Johanna coaxed me through the shock, sharing stories of how, in high school, she got through her own grandmother's death. After hearing about her terrible time, it gave me hope for the future. When she spoke, I believed, and I was able to make it through with her beside me.

It always felt like love, and recalling the times we spent together, I could lay out the ones that accentuated that feeling. The nights spent holding her, listening to Allman Brothers albums on my stereo and exhaling cigarette smoke out my cracked window. The weekends isolated in a booth at the Moose

Nose, drinking pints of Guinness and trying to figure out who in the bar had the balls to waste quarters on "Pressure" by Billy Joel. Those cold winter mornings I awoke early to peek at her sleeping soundly in my dorm bunk. And isn't that what love's supposed to be? Events dripping with bliss and perfection, without a hint of disaster anywhere in sight?

Not always. That's why sophomore year was always the year that got me with Johanna Darcy. It wasn't just a year filled with lazy days of laughter and love to enhance the relationship. What solidified our relationship was a simple winter morning phone call.

"Cahan," she said. "I think I might be pregnant."

My body went numb.

"What?"

"Well, I'm usually not this late. I'm late sometimes, but not this late."

My heart was lodged in my throat while holding the receiver to my right ear. My hands were trembling, and I recall holding down dry heaves. I sat in silence, my mind racing over what she said. Pregnant. Johanna's pregnant. My life is over. School's over. My parents might disown me. I'll have to get married as soon as possible, and I should probably put a call in to Duffy as well. Maybe his dad can get me on nights at the Ford Stamping Plant, into the union and working overtime. We're going to need money for this baby. God, how could this happen? Please help me now.

"So, what should we do? Should we go buy a test? Go to a doctor? What?"

"We could go buy a test. I'll pick you up in five minutes."

I stood in the February cold, waiting outside my dorm for Johanna to pick me up. Since she was the one with the Mazda 626, we were in a bit of a role reversal: She seemed to be the one calm enough to drive, and I was the one in the passenger seat, trembling with fear. We went to the local pharmacy to buy a pregnancy test, and then sped back to Johanna's dorm room. As I waited for her to return from the bathroom, I lit a cigarette, took heavy drags, and paced along the side of her bed. The stick hung out of my mouth as I knelt next to her bed and clenched my hands together harder than ever before. Eyes closed tight, I didn't bother saying the prayers silently to myself; I said them out loud.

"Hail Mary, full of grace, the Lord is with thee. Blessed art thou amongst women, and blessed is the fruit of thy womb Jesus. Holy Mary, Mother of God, pray for us sinners now and at the hour of our death, Amen."

I said this prayer over and over again, taking deep breaths in between drags to calm myself down. The anxiety was unbearable, but the prayers temporarily soothed my mind. I even slipped in a few personal messages to God between prayers, just to mix things up.

"Dear God. Please help Johanna to not be pregnant. We're not ready for this, or at least I don't think we are. Please, spare us of this if you can. If not, I'll fully accept this responsibility. I love Johanna, and if it's in your will, I'll take care of her and our child for the rest of my life. Thank you, and Amen."

My heart jumped when I heard the door open behind me. Johanna walked in smiling, and then closed the door to stand above me. I could see tears forming in her eyes, but still smiling, she remained silent.

"Well?" I said. "Please say something. Anything."

"I'm not pregnant."

She sighed, but then took another deep breath to seemingly brace another emotion. I exhaled and let my body collapse on the floor. I took my cigarette, dumped it in an old bottle of peach iced tea on the floor, and then looked up at Johanna. Her tears were falling and I couldn't understand why.

"Why are you crying? I thought you said you weren't pregnant. That's a good thing, right?"

Still looking at me, she crouched down and reached across to grab my hand.

"I heard you praying outside the door," she said. "You're really ready to be with me for the rest of your life?"

I didn't always think when I prayed. In my lifetime, I had prayed for Bills victories, U2 tickets and to one day grow to be six-two. I was always taught to ask God for what I needed, not for the ability to understand the practicality of what I was asking for. At nineteen, maybe pledging to God that I was ready to be with my girlfriend for the rest of my life was nervous jibber. But when I looked at Johanna, peering into my eyes with her own shimmering, maybe it wasn't.

"There's nothing I wouldn't do for you," I said. "Of course I'm not ready to be married now, or even have little red-headed children running all over the place."

This paused her tears for a little laugh.

"But, I'll tell you this: I couldn't imagine a more beautiful thing than seeing one of those little redheads in my arms. I'd be there for you, no matter what the circumstances. I love you, Johanna Darcy. I really do."

With tears coming down again, she approached me for a kiss. When our lips separated, we exhaled, fell back to the floor and stared at the ceiling, my sentiments still dancing above us. As I stared at the ceiling in my own bedroom, I still believed the most critical measurement of love was how two people handled perilous situations together. If I had any doubts about my feelings for Johanna, the daunting responsibility I was once willing to accept quelled them.

Maybe my father was right; maybe I don't know what love is. But, as I lay waiting for my headache to subside after a night spent trying to forget the past, it sure felt like I did on one winter morning.

8

"Joseph! Joseph! Are you up there?" said my mother up the stairway. "Your father is home with the fish fry! Come down and eat!"

I rolled over and looked at the clock. I'd slept for the past three hours. My headache was gone, and the three aspirin I downed had me feeling fresh and hungry. I opened the door at the top of the stairs to the aroma of fried fish, grizzled batter and macaroni salad, which lured me through the doorway, down the steps and into the kitchen to find my mother, father and Molly at the table.

Placed at each setting was our cheap Irish china, stenciled around the edges with tangled vines and clovers. In the middle of the table sat an opened cardboard box full of five pieces of fish, golden brown atop the bag it came in. The box was saturated with grease, as was the bag underneath. With sides of crinkle-cut French fries and macaroni salad resting beside it, we all sat down in our seats, said grace, and then passed the helpings around the table. Molly passed me the fish and started in on me.

"Tough night at Doherty's, eh Joe? Seems like you enjoyed

your mid-afternoon sleep-off."

"Go to hell, Mol."

"Joseph Patrick Cahan, watch your mouth," said my mother. "And while we're at it, did you get the note this morning?"

"Yeah, mom. I got it. I'm sorry I didn't call last night. Won't happen again."

"You bet it won't," said my father. "Remember, you're living at home now. You don't live above some dope-smoking janitor, mopping and not giving a care in the world when your feet come banging on his ceiling. We care when you get home, so get home at a decent hour."

He paused for a minute to shovel some fish in his mouth, chewed and swallowed, then pointed to Molly.

"Also, you're setting a terrible example for your younger sister."

"Sure," I laughed. "Like she hasn't been at the beach every weekend since she was fifteen years old, sucking down sixers of Genny Light."

It didn't matter what I said. She was the youngest. She always got away with everything, appearing as the sweet daughter who could do no wrong. She knew this, loved this and played it to her advantage at every turn. No matter her age, she had to act the part to keep her perpetual innocence intact. She dropped her fork, let out an exaggerated sigh and punched me in the arm.

"I have not!"

"She probably learned it from watching you," my father said, shoveling more fish and macaroni salad in his mouth. He always ate like he was stealing it.

"Eeenough!" my mother intervened. "No more talk of this. Joseph, you go out at night, you come home at night. Simple as that, agreed?"

"Agreed."

"Now, Patrick. Do you have something to tell your son or not?"

"Yes," he said. "Actually, two things. One, your mother and I have decided, for your graduation present, we're going to sell you the Blue Bomber."

"Really? For how much?"

"A dollar."

"A dollar? Why don't you just give me the thing? You really need a dollar that bad?"

"Joseph, it's a tax thing. To be an official transaction, we have to charge you at least a dollar. Besides, you're lucky we're not charging you more."

I laughed.

"For the Bomber? Thing's the size of a matchbox car. Duffy picked up the back of it once."

"Hey, if you don't want it, I can start lining up prospective buyers at the drop of my hat," he said. "Just say the word."

"No, no, I want it, and thank you. Here's a dollar." I stood and passed the bill down the table. "So what's the second thing?"

"Well, I bumped into Paul Connors out at lunch today. You remember Mr. Connors?" he said, then leaned back in his chair and wiped his mouth with a napkin

"Yeah. He owns Connors Supply near downtown, right?"

"Yeah, that's him. We got to talking about our kids, and I told him you just graduated and were going to start looking for a job soon. In the meantime, I told him you didn't have anything immediately lined up for income."

"Okay. And then what?"

"Well, he mentioned he may need someone to work nights in packaging and shipping this summer, noon to ten. I figured you could get some hours in there while you set up interviews in the morning. What do you think?"

"Shipping and packaging?" I said, unenthusiastically. "I paid over eighty grand to go to college, and now, you want me to slog around with high school dropouts, shipping groceries across New York State?"

"Well, unless you have another plan on how to start earning a salary somewhere. Do you?"

"As of yet, no. But I don't think I'll be sticking around here for that long."

"Really? Where do you plan on heading, and how do you plan on paying for it?"

"I'm not sure yet, but we've had this conversation before. I don't want to get into it again."

"Fine; we won't. I know you're not sure if you want to stick around here right now, but why don't you try to give it a chance? Too many kids your age are leaving Buffalo. The flight's killing the city from the inside."

"Dad, you know I would stay if I could, but I don't think I can. Where are there any jobs? Connors Supply? Besides, if I want to write, it might be beneficial to inhabit some new surroundings. Haven't you ever wanted to live somewhere else, just for a change?"

He sat up straight and considered, briefly.

"No. Why would I want to live anywhere else? With family, friends, and a great community, we have everything we need right here. You'll see if you leave."

"I hope so. But you never wanted to leave? Ever?"

Leaning back in his chair again, he took a deep breath, considering.

"Son, I've had lots of chances to leave. When your mother and I were in our early thirties, I used to hear about teaching jobs in Florida, North Carolina, you name it. Better opportunities, more money, and warmer weather, but I never pursued any of them."

"Why?"

"Because that's not what life's about," he said. "It's about your roots, having respect for your community and appreciating the worth of your family and friends. Moving would have cost us all of those things. Would you have rather grown up in Florida, cheering for the Miami Dolphins instead of the Bills, with two blonde-haired friends named Lance instead of Terry and Duff, dreading a hurricane instead of a blizzard?"

"I hate the snow," said Molly. That comment drew my father's glare before he came back to me.

"Well?"

"I guess not."

"All I'm saying is give it a chance," he said. "If it doesn't work out, you can go do your exploring to find out your old man is right. You only have one home, and it's right here in Buffalo. Sooner or later, you'll realize this place is the most important thing you'll ever have in life."

Leaning back again as our resident dealer of Cahan wisdom, my father beamed before my mother walked over from rinsing the dishes.

"Honey," she said. "You've got ketchup on your mouth and macaroni salad on your shirt. Before you hand out any more life lessons to your children, you might want to learn how to eat properly."

My mother stood over him as he shamefully wiped his mouth and shirt. She gave us a wink before she smiled and strutted back to the sink. That scene was an exhibition of my father's point: No matter where I went or what I did, I'd only have one family and one place that was truly mine. I knew this, and it was drilled into me with every passing day.

9

Idealism is an "ism" that basks in censorship. It's not that the view endorses restriction; it's that when one subscribes to this frame of mind, it's pursued with blinders. With idealism, one generally ignores the negative. The view creates a mental utopia we would all like to regularly enjoy.

For example, take dating. When a man meets a woman, I would bet the first thing to usually pop in his head isn't, "I bet this woman hates children, endorses the death penalty and sleeps with her mouth open. What's the point of this date anyway?" Before any given date, the positive is prevalent and hope is at its highest. It's only after the first few dates that a man finds out that a woman has no intention of having children, has no sympathy for the wrongly accused on death row and, on the morning after an intoxicated third date, does snore with her mouth agape. Realistically, things don't always work out the way we want them to. Even if they eventually do, there are a multitude of potholes along the way. It's fine to have expectations, but it's insane to not accept that things aren't always going to go one's way. Relationships are a great example. The first job I took out of college is a better one.

My idealism was always anchored very loosely to reality. I knew I didn't want to work in an office for the rest of my life, but I accepted that time might be spent in one if I ever wanted a paycheck. Staring at cubicle walls for the security of medical insurance seemed exciting as colitis, but I could tolerate the pain while I waited for my break. I wanted to live the dream, writing on Lake Erie with the kids around, cup of coffee and the morning paper. But I knew it wasn't going to happen when I was twenty-two years old; or twenty-three. In the meantime, I wanted to be a paid employee who was competent and earning useful experience. These thoughts bounced through my head on a sunny June morning as I drove the Blue Bomber into downtown Buffalo for my first day at Connors Supply, which wouldn't take place in a cubicle.

That morning, I held the steering wheel tight while cruising over the Skyway. Opened in 1956, the elevated roadway was built as a two-lane overpass high above the Buffalo River, allowing cargo freighters to arrive at their lakeside destinations. Unfortunately, it has existed solely as a hazardous arching passage into downtown from the Southtowns since boat traffic diminished years ago. One quick move to the right would send you into the side barrier and over into your choice of catastrophe. When winter would hit, the perilous combination of fierce wind and lake-effect snow would force city officials to shut down the overpass completely. Thank God the sun was shining.

Over the Skyway and off at the Seneca Street exit, I headed

toward a small group of people at the Metro light rail stop across the street to the left. The Metro Rail was built when I was a student at St. Theresa's as an alternate mode of transportation through the shopping district on Main Street and toward the University of Buffalo campus. The small collection of men in suits stood waiting for the train's arrival as businesses on Main stood decimated or vacated because of the train's existence. Its trolley tracks closed the street for car travel so, ironically, the train made the street less accessible. Closed storefronts lined the street, and the suits were joined by others who looked like they slept at the stop. Wearing stained sweatshirts and tattered jeans, they raised small paper bags to their mouths as professionals idled.

A right on Washington Street took me past the gorgeous greens of the ballpark, built for the minor league Buffalo Bisons in hopes of luring a major league baseball expansion franchise to Buffalo. Despite daily sellouts, Florida got a team instead, and our hopes as a city were crushed. It's a shame we didn't get to the majors, but the park's red seats looked beautiful shining in the sun.

Up on my right was the vacated Memorial Auditorium, which was home to Buffalo Sabres hockey, as well as Buffalo Braves pro basketball in the seventies. When I was younger, my father told me stories of the classic games played under the Aud's roof, like the 1975 Stanley Cup Finals fog game against the Philadelphia Flyers, or the courageous playoff battles our

Braves staged against the mighty Boston Celtics. The interiors of the arena began to deteriorate long after the Braves moved to San Diego, an event that soured my father and many residents of the city toward pro basketball since. Thank God our Sabres only moved down the street.

I continued toward the entrance of their new hockey home on Perry Street, only two blocks further down. The sterling arena was supposed to launch our dynamic waterfront, luring businesses to set up shop on surrounding cobblestone streets, thus reviving what was once known as the aptly-named Cobblestone District. A left onto Perry took me past that still hollow historical district, now only home to the historic post-game drinking of Molson Canadian at the block's only watering hole, the Cobblestone Pub. The area sat vacant and dormant, with closed storefronts lining the street and debris strewn across parking lots that should be filled with employees of a bustling entertainment district.

A right onto Michigan Avenue brought an invasive aroma of chocolate and oats through my car windows, the General Mills factory fragrance that seduces the neighborhood. Past the Swannie House Tavern and a left on Miami Street brings a view of a factory row, one after the other, overwhelmed with weeds and surrounded by piles of rubble. I wondered how these buildings were functional, but smoke billowed out of every stack while functional cars occupy the nearby parking spaces. They're in business, and with a right turn onto Ohio Street, I started to look for Connors.

882. 884. 888.

Standing behind a rusted chain-link fence stood a red-brick warehouse, corroding on the façade from wind and snow damage. Aside the large metallic garage door hung a weathered wooden sign, seemingly crafted from driftwood fished out of Lake Erie. Swinging from one nail, the sign was suggestive rather than authoritative:

TRESPASSING STRONGLY DISCOURAGED.

Once in the gravel lot, I was surrounded by yellow forklifts and white delivery trucks. The lifts and trucks were proceeding to a loading dock next to the main entrance of 890 Ohio Street, Connors Supply. After shifting into park, I walked from my car and through a white door to find a time clock and employee cards attached to the wall. Third from the top, center row, I found mine: CAHAN, Joseph. Pulling the card from the slot, I slid it into the clock for the punch. Seven minutes before noon. I was early, so with a large coffee in one hand and a bag dinner in the other, I walked back to Mr. Connors's office to get started. I spotted an unshaven worker at an isolated packaging table, enjoying a smoke with a Bills cap turned backwards. He bopped to a small tape recorder playing Johnny Cash's "Rock Island Line" and gave me a head nod as I passed. I returned the nod, then continued back to Mr. Connors's office to knock on his opened door. He waved me in and pointed to a seat in front of his desk as he screamed into his phone.

"You want what to go to Utica and when? I can't do that! It's a three-hour drive if we haul ass, and besides, I think we're out of the thirty-six ouncers. Fine, Turk. Yeah, I'll get back to you!"

Mumbling under his breath, Mr. Connors slammed down the phone and gritted his teeth before matting back his thinning hair. Reaching into his shirt pocket, he pulled out a smoke, lit the tip, and took a heavy drag.

"Mr. Cahan, sir," he said. "Sorry you had to be in here for that. Prick in Utica thinks he's going to see a case of thirty-six ounce Clorox bleach bottles by breakfast tomorrow with the rest of his goddamn order. Not going to happen, but since I've had his family's business since my father opened the doors of this place, I have to dance for him. Anyways, here for your first day, right? Let's get you started."

We headed toward the packaging stations in the front of the warehouse. Aside from the isolated station I passed on the way in, there were ten up front, five running side by side. The whole staff had not shown up yet, so around noon, most tables were vacant of workers. At one of the tables stood a man of medium build, with floppy brown hair and tanned skin. He wore a torn red pocket t-shirt with blue slacks over brown steel-toed boots while placing bags of sugar in a cardboard box. There was one large radio booming a few tables away from him, and as we approached, he wasn't crazy about the music.

"Hey, Stretch!" he said a tall, spectacled co-worker. "Turn

the fucking station, will you? You know I can't stand Rush, and it's all they play on this one. If I hear those assholes whine about Tom Sawyer one more time, I may go on a fucking killing spree."

"Cool it with the killing spree talk, Hutch," said Mr. Connors. "Just pack the order and ignore the fucking radio."

"I'm sorry, Mr. C., but you don't understand how that band crawls under my skin," he said. "Bad experiences with them, man. I'll tell you that much."

"Whatever you say." Mr. Connors took a drag off his smoke. "Look, this is Joe Cahan. He's starting today on the packing and shipping line, and I need you to train him. Show him how to pick, pack and label by the end of the shift, all right? Shouldn't be too hard."

Extending his hand, he introduced himself to me.

"Joe? Mark Hutchinson. Just call me Hutch. Everyone does around here, and out there," he said, pointing to an exit. "I'll take care of him, Mr. C. But hey, any chance you can change the radio station? In place of training wages?"

"Yeah, fine." Mr. Connors turned the dial and Hutch heard his song coming through the static.

"Right there, right there!" said Hutch. "Leave it. Leave it on 'Cat Scratch Fever!' Got to love the Motor City Madman. You into Ted Nugent, Cahan?"

"Got to love the Nuge," I said. "But never understood why he played guitar for Damn Yankees. Bizarre."

This brought a sour look to Hutch's face. He placed his right hand on my shoulder, then left it there as he smiled and wiped the sweat off his forehead.

"Cahan, you and I will get along fine, just as long as you never mention Damn Yankees again. Deal?"

"Deal."

Hutch led me back to a wire bin adjacent to the time clock. In it rested a large stack of paper, each piece a typed, detailed order. I picked one off the top, and he walked me through the interpretation.

"All right," he said, holding an order sheet. "Each one of these is an order that needs to be picked and packed. On the left is the item and size, and on the right is the quantity needed. For instance, here: Corn Flakes. Twenty ounces. Six boxes. Get it?"

"Got it."

"Good," he said, then slapped me on the arm. "Here's a small order to start. Pick this one, and meet me back at the packing station so we can package the order and label it." He paused, then looked around to case for any eavesdroppers. "Also, you smoke?"

"Cigarettes?"

"Naw, naw. Weed. Marijuana."

"No, I'm all set with that. Why?"

"At first break, the guys usually meet behind a dumpster off the back loading dock to blow a j. If you change your mind, you're welcome to go back there for a toke."

128

"Sure, I'll let you know. And thanks."

Hutch went back to his table, and I took my cart down the first aisle of the warehouse. In six months, I'd receive my first student loan bill for the thirty-five grand I'd borrowed to attend a private Catholic university in the mountains of southern New York. For four years, I had yawned through classes about the importance of the Copyright Act of 1976 and the value of journalistic integrity. During my graduation ceremony, I vaguely remember remnants of a keynote speech about, "attacking the future with the power of my degree." On the desk in my bedroom rested the first copies of my crisp, new résumé. I hadn't sent them out that day, but they'd soon be in manila envelopes and into various offices of downtown Buffalo, including the *Buffalo Gazette*. After each reached its destination, my phone would ring and I'd don my only suit to wow some editor or executive with my professionalism, ambition and desire. They'd offer me an entry-level position, I'd accept, and I would thank Mr. Connors for the opportunity to earn a few bucks while I waited to start another job. A real job.

But, as I waited for that day, I would be working at Connors Supply on Ohio Street in downtown Buffalo. Picking and packing thirty-six-ounce bottles of Clorox bleach off shelves for Turk's Stop n' Shop of Utica, New York. Avoiding Hutch and the dumpster dope smokers, five days a week. With overtime available on Saturdays.

10

There wasn't a lot of motivation for me to pick and pack orders for Utica, Elmira and Owego once July rolled around. I wasn't climbing the Connors executive ladder to make warehouse foreman by age thirty, so my patience for an escape was waning.

I followed my father's suggestion and spent my mornings mailing résumés around Buffalo to banks and financial firms looking for entry-level employees to handle cashier work or even to train for mutual funds sales, but heard nothing back. I had no specific interest in these pursuits, but these were the area's nine-to-five jobs that would pay me a salary while I wrote on the side. It would be a steady income to pay my student loans and eventual rent while I sent out writing samples to small local papers like *Artvoice* and *Buffalo Beat*, or the main draw, the *Buffalo Gazette*. Sneaking in there for my first salaried gig was unrealistic, but I still sent each of their editors a manila envelope. Publication in one of the indie locals was more realistic, and would give me a chance to develop a portfolio to submit to the *Gazette*. If I wanted to pursue a career at home, I had to either travel that route or enjoy the spoils of packing orders at Connors.

But, on those mornings, I knew the only things Connors provided were back pain and beer money.

Student loan officers wouldn't start smelling blood for a few months, so the money from my meager paycheck was committed to nothing. I had no rent or grocery bills at the Hotel Cahan, and since I bought the Blue Bomber for the Blue Book value of one dollar, I had no car payment. I hadn't fallen into the tiger trap of credit card debt, so three tens were all I needed to meet Terry and Duff at Fitzgerald's after each shift.

The pints tasted better when I donned a filthy work t-shirt and ripped jeans. My degree was supposed to shield me from such menial manual labor, but with my hands on the bar top after a long shift at Connors, the warehouse dirt under my fingernails indicated an earned thirst. After busting my ass hauling carts and boxes across a dusty concrete floor, the taste of that first pint on my tongue every night was more quenching than water. Tired arms and a sore back were validation for a job well done, and I never imagined it would be. I still complained about it; everyone did. Hutch complained every morning at our packaging stations.

"I'll tell you what, man," he said. "One of these days, I'm packing one of these fucking boxes and launching it off the fucking loading dock, man, because I'm fucking out of here. Never fucking spitting on this fucking dirty floor again, man!"

Hutch would always launch into these tirades, about getting out and never coming back again loud enough for everyone to hear. That was Hutch, but from the first time I laid eyes on him, he looked out of place on the warehouse floor. He had the uniform and the crass lingo, but his appearance ignited my suspicion. He looked relaxed and affluent, with a tan complexion not usually found on a man strapped to a packaging station. But every morning, his actions were typical of the rest of the warehouse staff, like his lengthy bathroom breaks. We knew he was going to the can to read the paper, and occasionally, we would throw money down to bet on how long he'd be gone.

"I got ten bucks on seventeen minutes, dood," said Spanish Hector, a local high school dropout who slapped a tenner on his table. I dug into my jeans for money to match.

"I say twenty-two."

We watched the clock above our stations as seventeen minutes passed. Hector rolled his bill up in a ball and threw it at me.

"Eat it, pandejo!" he said, then walked back to his station.

Hutch came strolling back to his station after twenty-one minutes, and we all mockingly clapped. He put his hands up to settle us down, went back to his station and sipped his coffee.

I clapped before strolling back for my own turn in a stall. There was usually a discarded Lifestyles or Sports section of the *Buffalo Gazette* on the bathroom floor. Some days, we'd strike gold with a *Rolling Stone* or a *Maxim* next to the toilet. When Hutch would go in there, he left sections of *The Wall Street Journal* or *New York Times* behind. It seemed odd that someone working in a monotonous hole like Connors Supply would pass his time with such intelligent reading material, but he left behind their pages strewn on the floor every day.

At the packing stations, he talked about the radio's emanating music with the experience of hundreds of live shows and hours of educated listening in his ears. His knowledge flowed intricately and unapologetically once Pink Floyd came through our speakers.

"Here's the thing with Pink Floyd, brother. Even after Syd Barrett freaked on drugs, shaved his head and took supervised residence in his grandmother's attic following the release of *The Piper at the Gates of Dawn*, Floyd had another virtuoso ready to help continue their fucking arduous pilgrimage to the rock gods. Roger Waters righted the ship, and then cranked out transcendent shit like *Dark Side of the Moon* and *Wish You Were Here* before my favorite release, *Animals*. If you listen to the album on a quadraphonic sound stereo, dude, you can totally hear critters running back and forth from speaker to speaker. Waters was a fucking genius in audio manipulation."

"Hutch, you were probably tripping so hard you imagined that shit," said Hector.

"Shut up, you greasy Spaniard," said Hutch. "Go home tonight and play the fucking album, amigo. You'll see. Fucking genius."

Hutch was always presenting arguments about music, politics or religion that wouldn't add up to his vocational expertise. Their delivery could have been stolen directly from my St. Francis professors, but Hutch would always make sure to mix in enough slang to dumb them down. The last thing you ever wanted to do at our stations was let anyone know you had any education. Before I started, Mr. Connors told me not to let anyone know I'd just finished college. They'd look down on me for it, like I was trying to be better than the other pickers and packers. Hutch masked his intelligence with every 'dude' or a 'fucking, fuck' he added to his sentences.

I knew there was an explanation. When the dinner whistle hissed one Thursday night, Hutch went to find a seat on a pallet far away from the rest of the staff, with a book under one arm and a bag dinner under the other. When I saw him, I decided to join him away from everyone else; isolated, I thought I could get some answers. He looked up from his bag as I approached.

"You mind if I join you?"

"Suit yourself, but I'm doing some reading."

"What do you have?"

"The Way to Freedom: Core Teachings of Tibetan Buddhism, by this Bstan-Dzin-Rgya-Mtsho guy. Haven't a clue how to pronounce his fucking name."

To get some answers about Hutch's past, I was going to have to reveal some of my own.

"We covered some passages from that book in a theology class my sophomore year of college. It makes a lot of sense, Buddhism. If I wasn't raised Catholic, I'd consider subscribing."

"College? You drop out or what?"

"No," I said, "Just graduated."

"Well, what the fuck are you doing here? Are you training for management under Mr. C?"

I laughed.

"No, I'm just earning some cash while I send out résumés and decide whether or not I can stay in Buffalo. Keep that to yourself, will you?"

"Yeah, I won't squeal on you to the boys. If I did, they'd be calling you 'college queer' by quitting time."

"So you mind if I ask you a question?"

"Shoot."

"What the hell are you doing here? Guy reading *The Wall Street Journal* in the can, discussing the intricacies of Floyd albums at the packing stations, and reading The Way to Freedom on your dinner break? It doesn't add up. Did you go to school?"

"For a while, yeah. I went to Cornell on an academic scholarship. Big into English lit, but also had a nose for finance. Then, I didn't finish. Got into some shit."

"What kind of shit?"

"Well," he started, then paused. "Look, Cahan, you don't say a fucking word of this to anybody, you got it? Nobody."

"Hutch, you've got shit on me already. I won't say a word."

"Fine." He took a deep breath. "Back in my sophomore year, I was caught making acid in the school's chemistry lab. Made it worse by dealing, and the Dean threw me out on my ass. With that on my record, I had nowhere to go, and my parents were so disgraced with me they wouldn't try to buy me into anywhere. So I moved back home here and started working for my brother on the city's east side selling tires."

"But you kept reading a lot?"

"Sure I did, but working around those slums, I got really mixed up with coke and any other drug I could get my hands on. I would spend my day breaks reading Bukowski or Hemingway, but I'd spend my nights doing drugs like those guys drank. Soon enough, I started to get desperate, trading tires and auto parts for dope or coke on the streets. When my brother found out, we were already losing too much money. He lost his business, I lost my job, and I haven't talked to him or any member of my family since."

"So how did you end up here?"

"Mr. C's son was my best friend growing up. When I hit bottom, I called him and told him what happened. He called his father to get me something while I tried to clean myself up, and for a while, it wasn't going too well."

"Why?"

"Well, as I struggled to keep away from the coke and all the other shit, I became a vicious alcoholic. When I first started here, I'd usually use this dinner break to run down the street to the Petro station and buy a few forties of Silver Thunder."

"Malt liquor? That shit's nasty," I said.

"Sure it was, but I could get shithoused on four of those things for eight bucks. I'd slug 'em down in an hour, come back here to the stations and try to start all kinds of shit. I tried to start a fight with Hector once because I didn't like his little Spanish moustache."

"And now?"

"Well, Mr. C sat me down and told me if I didn't immediately check myself into rehab, I'd not only be out of a job, but would probably be dead in an alleyway within weeks. He was the first person to ever lay it on the table like that. Just looked straight into my fucking eyes and fed the brutal, bitter truth: life or death? Take your pick. With that, I decided to check myself into rehab, do the twelve steps and try to get back to where I once was long, long ago."

"Are you going back to school?"

"I'm taking morning courses over at Erie Community College right now. Not really sure what direction I'm going in, but I just love learning anything, man. Any day you learn something new is a good day."

"And you've had some good days?"

"Trying to, man," he said. "With a little diligence, maybe someday we can meet for lunch on the outside, at a table downtown on Elmwood Avenue in shirts and ties, away from these pallets and bagged dinners."

"Maybe by then, you can talk me into Buddhism."

Hutch gave a little head-toss laugh and placed his book on the floor. He slapped his hands together and looked back at me.

"I don't know there, *Cahan*. You never know where you'll

turn when it all hits the shit. Booze, drugs, religion? You never know where you'll turn."

"What about you?"

"I've seen 'em all, and I'll take this." He grabbed his book and shook it in front of me. "The pursuit of some sort of inner peace: costs you less, earns you more."

"And not having to scrape together eight bucks for Silver Thunder isn't bad either," I joked.

"Christ, that shit was terrible," he said, then grimaced as we laughed. His sense of humor about the topic was an indication that he accepted his mistakes, hopeful he wouldn't make them another day in his life. After he collected himself, he took another reflective breath, looking up to the warehouse ceiling before delivering his closing.

"When you get out there on the streets, Cahan, do me a favor."

"And what's that?"

"Focus on what's important to you. If I would've done that, I wouldn't be eating this shitty dinner out of this fucking bag and sitting on a pallet talking to some kid about what I should've done."

He said it with a sincerity only exchanged away from the packaging stations, where the rest of the staff wouldn't pay any concern to Hutch's words. No one took him seriously and, until recently, I doubt he took himself seriously. His life was soaked with regret, and as he handed off wisdom, he was trying to move on. Telling his story to someone who wanted to hear it was a way to vent, and at the same time, inform. His words were a live public service announcement, boldly broadcast in front of my face: *THIS IS WHAT WILL HAPPEN TO YOU IF YOU SCREW UP. THIS IS WHERE YOU'LL BE IF YOU DON'T TAKE ADVANTAGE OF WHAT YOU HAVE. STOP STALLING, AND GET GOING.*

After that conversation with Hutch, I knew I had to send out the rest of my résumés—

immediately. Almost two months of summer had passed, and I hadn't heard anything positive. When I followed up on a mailing, that business wasn't hiring for entry-level positions. If they were, they weren't interested in hiring me. Not enough business circulating around the downtown area to necessitate hiring a St. Francis grad with no applicable experience. I sent out assorted writing samples to every local indie, even to some that covered only community events in the Southtowns. I received rejections and apologies for my efforts. The *Gazette*? They didn't respond at all.

But I had to keep mailing and calling. I had to write more cover letters, print more résumés. I had to find more writing samples to dazzle local editors. I wouldn't go to Fitzgerald's that night, and I wasn't sure if I'd go there the next night, either. It was time to focus on the next step, and I wanted to start right away. I was out the door at the ten o'clock Connors whistle, into the Blue Bomber and back to my house. I ran to the side door, through the kitchen and into the living room, up the stairs and into my bedroom to find résumés and envelopes waiting on my desk. The envelopes needed to be addressed, so I kicked off my boots and got to work. The mail didn't go out until the next day, but I didn't want to wait any longer; I wanted to start my life that minute. I wanted the house on our lake, with the wife and the kids and a dog; I'd never had a dog. The sooner each was addressed, the sooner I could get out of Connors Supply and into an office on Main or Delaware in downtown Buffalo. I could get the interview, toss on my gray suit, get the job, and tell Mr. Connors the news. Ten envelopes would be addressed that night, not the next day or week.

Then my phone rang.

I walked into the front door at Fitzgerald's twenty minutes later, said hello to Eddie and sat down with Terry and Duff to three pints of Guinness. I stumbled out the same door after ten more rounds, my head flooded in stout while talking to some guy named DiFazio about how the lead-in to Bruce Springsteen and the E Street Band's "Candy's Room" is the most underrated drum intro in rock and roll history. In that same breath, I asserted that Jim Kelly was the most electrifying quarterback the AFC or AFL had ever seen, regardless of inferior statistics. Terry pulled into my driveway and shook me awake in the passenger seat at about four in the morning. It was back to Connors in eight hours, and after a brief drunken slumber, my mother yelled her customary call up the stairs to get me up and out by noon.

"Joseph! Joseph! C'mon, you're gonna be late for work!"

My résumés sat on the desk, their manila envelopes still unaddressed. Already in the shower, I let the water rain on the back of my head as I vomited stout into the bathtub drain and thought of ways to help myself. Leaning and heaving against the tile, I knew my nights were destroying my days.

And maybe that was how Hutch got going.

After he was thrown out of school for making acid, maybe he got caught up in the fun of partying. Then, he started working at his brother's garage to earn a few bucks. The next thing he knew, he was puking up Silver Thunder forties before a shift at Connors. I didn't wonder too much about his life's intricate progression until that moment; the picture he painted was vivid enough. He lost his focus and ambition in bars and back alleys, and now, he was relegated to warning others about screwing up their lives like he fucked up his own.

I knew of the word complacency. With the word's negative connotations, college wasn't a time to experience complacency. College was a utopia away from reality, and if I was complacent with that environment, fine. I expected to find responsibility in new challenges once I graduated, relationships aside from the ones that built me into the person I'd become. But, what if my residential contentment doomed these pursuits? Tossing up black into the drain that morning, I was suddenly scared to death of the potential personal complacency I could encounter within Buffalo and anywhere near it.

I loved going to Fitzgerald's with Terry & Duff, talking about Rolling Stones records, old times at St. Theresa's and St. Auggie's, or the state of Buffalo sports. I was comfortable sitting at the kitchen table with my parents, listening to jokes as we shoved down another night's helpings of hot dogs or fried fish. I looked forward to Sunday mass, turning around as I knelt during communion to see if anyone was bringing their new girlfriend or boyfriend with them down the aisle to indicate the most serious of serious Southtowns romance. Absolute serenity flowed when I drove the Blue Bomber along our lakefront, seeing the subtle skyline of downtown Buffalo and ignoring the industrial wasteland tainting the view.

I could walk into Terry and Duff's houses any day of the week, whether they were home or not. I could go out to a bar and see a girl who had a crush on me in elementary school, and then somehow cajole that girl into leaving with me. I relished the annual chance to feel an entire region exhale as Lake Erie began to thaw in March and let its thawing ice float down the Niagara River in early April. We all knew we wouldn't need to shovel snow again until maybe Thanksgiving, but likely Halloween. I appreciated how these comforts assured security, physically and mentally. That was Buffalo for me.

That was home, and it scared the shit out of me.

Later that day, I went into Mr. Connors's office and gave him my two-week notice. I thanked him for the job, but told him I planned on moving away in the next few weeks for another opportunity.

"So where are you moving?" he said.

"I have no idea."

"Well, where's this opportunity then?"

After a short pause, I inhaled and exhaled before answering.

"I don't know, but I know I have to find one away from here. Away from home."

11

The chase was on. I was wearing the same ripped jeans, old black Bills AFC championship t-shirt and steel-toed boots I wore to Connors. The hairy beast ran down my street and toward our lake, but as I clogged after it, it kept getting further from my grasp. It galloped ahead furiously; I quit and let it go. When I stopped to catch my breath at the corner of Norton Drive, slouched over with hands on knees while clutching my shirttail, I noticed a tall man in a suit, holding a suitcase and peering confusedly at me through wire-rimmed glasses.

"What the hell are you doing?" he said.

I looked back at him in disbelief.

"What am I doing? Did you happen to miss the big fucking beast rolling past here? I was chasing it."

The man stood there, puzzled. He looked down the street toward the tracks the buffalo made, looked back at me, and then looked down the street again.

"Why don't you take this bus? Downtown to Exchange Street, then take the train to New York City. You'll be sure to catch it there. You'll never catch that thing here. Never even sniff it by foot." After his suggestion, the bus pulled up and began repeatedly beeping its horn.

BEEP. BEEP. BEEP. BEEP.

I rolled over to furiously slap my alarm clock, once, twice and then again until I finally nailed the snooze. The clock read four o'clock, and there was no reason for me to be up at four o'clock. The chase was a dream, but a dream so vivid and startling that it would've woke me up even without my malfunctioning alarm clock. I lay staring at my ceiling and began to analyze the dream before I lost memory of it.

Another buffalo. Another chase in my own neighborhood. But why was I in my work clothes this time? Why the suggestion from the suit that I head across state to New York City? Was I supposed to move to Manhattan?

At least one member of my family would be against this plan. My father delivered dinner lectures throughout my childhood about how New York City was an enemy of Buffalo, stealing our tax dollars and disregarding our regional prominence while its residents condescendingly referred to us as upstaters. I'm not sure what was so bad about that designation, but in my house, it was understood as an insult to our once great Queen City of the Lakes. We were the City of Good Neighbors and the City of No Illusions. We were a national asset once labeled the Gateway to the Midwest.

Sitting four hundred thirty-nine miles from mid-town Manhattan, Buffalo changed New York State in 1825 as the commercial terminus of the Erie Canal. Years later, the city wowed the country as the host of the 1901 Pan American Exposition. A year later, the Buffalo Forge Company's Willis Halivand Carrier invented the first electrical air conditioner. The first chicken wing was served at the Anchor Bar on Main Street in 1964. We were the home of beef on weck and the back-to-back AFL champion Buffalo Bills. We had the Albright-Knox art gallery, rows of bars on Chippewa Street and Elmwood Avenue, the Buffalo Philharmonic Orchestra and the Frank Lloyd Wright-designed Darwin D. Martin estate. There are fifteen four-year colleges and universities in the Buffalo-Niagara area, and a short drive from any number of these campuses will get you a front row seat to one of the greatest natural wonders of the world, Niagara Falls. Hell, the famous list of Buffalonians included such names as thirteenth U.S. President Millard Fillmore, NBA Hall of Famer Bob Lanier and superstar superfreak Rick James. Who did New York City have? Lou Reed?

But, despite these highly-touted Buffalo attributes, New York was still the undisputable media capital of the world, providing professional opportunities I would never see at home. *Rolling Stone*, *Spin Magazine* and countless other pubs had headquarters in New York City, not Buffalo. For allies in the overwhelming metropolis, I had my old dorm roommate, Vince Petrocelli, who had moved there after graduation. He'd call me every once in a while to tell me how unbelievable all their girls were and that the money to be made there is more than I'll ever hope to see in Buffalo. I nodded and smiled during these calls, but as I lay in bed analyzing another dream, I knew it was good to have Vince already set up in New York. Knowing one person would get me what Duff always stressed we should all be lucky to have in life: one friend.

And then there was Johanna Darcy. A twenty-five-minute Metro North train ride from Manhattan to White Plains could unite me with what I left behind.

The Sunday morning moonlight shone through my blinds. My body was exhausted. In four hours, I'd need to roll over for eight-thirty mass with my entire family. We would pile into my father's Buick, drive to St. Theresa's, and all the while, I'd be obsessed with these New York City thoughts, staring off into nowhere on the car ride down Norton Drive. Molly would ask why I was acting so goofy, so that morning, I planned to come clean. I walked away from Connors, definitely leaving Buffalo, and possibly falling into the arms of our state's arrogant big brother.

I turned to my right to see our long church pew filled with my entire family, with me first in from the center aisle. At St. Theresa's, five fit into a pew comfortably, but you could squeeze in six. My mother made sure we inhaled and squished in on a day where all of us were together for once. Molly's elbow uncomfortably jammed into my rib cage for most of the mass as my mind wandered from prayer, the priest, and from the news I'd bring up at breakfast. I stared at a ceiling much nicer than the cracked and poster-covered ceiling in my bedroom. St. Theresa's interior peaks were painted the blue of the sky, lightly sprinkled with golden stars at the fingertips of angels bordering the perimeter. Above my head was the image of St. Michael the Archangel, pointing to one star with his right index finger. Michael appeared strong and sure. As an angel, confidence was one of the perks.

An angel has no worries for himself, but does carry the burden of anyone who takes forty-five seconds to get down on two knees and pray. Angels listen to the worries of a little boy in Rochester, his hands folded and eyes closed for his grandfather's Parkinson's disease. They hear the pleas of a little girl in Toronto who cries to the skies so her dog, Wilbur the Wondermutt, can recover from the fall he took from her daddy's Ford Ranger. They're even patient with a ten-year-old on Norton Drive, head bowed and hands clenched together on a Sunday afternoon. The Buffalo Bills have the ball at the Miami two-yard-line. The boy would like to know if an angel wouldn't mind giving a pursuing Dolphin linebacker a quick leg cramp so Jim Kelly could have the extra tenth of a second to dive into the end zone for a winning score. Please, angel? Thanks.

This is what I believed angels dealt with. And there was Michael, long hair flowing like a California biker, offering a look of assurance with the weight of the world on his shoulders.

His eyes peered into mine the way paintings usually do. It was strangely calming. This guy was responsible for looking out over all mankind, and he looked pretty relaxed. I was a twenty-two-year-old puke who needed to move to a different city, and I was needlessly stressed out in his boss's house. But, as I looked up at that painting, a star-scattered sky with only a confident angel pointing the way, I felt better. It seemed like a sign, with Michael's finger seemingly indicating a way out of town. I convinced myself it was a sign. St. Michael had formed an alliance with the galloping buffalo to nudge me toward a vacating conclusion. I was blinded by faith, certain.

The priest rose for his blessing. We all rose from our jammed pew, knees colliding and searching for arm room. Internal warmth ignited an aloof, yet confident, smirk across my face. I had faith I'd be fine—no matter what.

"May the Lord be with each and every one of you."

"And also with you."

"In the name of the Father, and of the Son, and of the Holy Spirit."

"Amen."

"The mass has ended. Let us go in peace to love and serve the Lord."

"Thanks be to God."

The Queen City Diner was bustling after mass. Our waitress ran feverishly in and out of the kitchen to serve eight of the restaurant's twenty seated tables. In her black slacks, white blouse, and pink apron, she slapped her black Reeboks on the linoleum toward each table with a steaming pot of coffee in one hand and a chilled tin pitcher of water in the other. When she finally came over, she was chewing her gum with such speed it made us as anxious as she appeared to be, standing behind my left shoulder, with black pen to paper.

"What do you say folks, ready to go? Good. Let's start with you, dear. What's it gonna be?"

"Three eggs scrambled, with home fries, ham, and rye toast, please," I said through the smell of cigarette smoke emanating off Judy's clothes. That's what her name-tag read: Judy.

"Please? Where's mom?" she said, casing the table with squinted eyes.

"Right here!" said my mother, waving excitedly like she had just won a contest.

"Good job, Mom," said Judy. "God bless you, sweetie. I can't even get my boys to say, 'excuse me,' after a burp at the dinner table. Father's fault. Guy's a total bum."

Without missing a beat, she moved down the table. Some French toast for Frank, some pancakes for Molly, and one order of eggs benedict for my father. At nine-thirty, there was coffee poured for each of us to keep our heads off of the table until our food arrived. The aroma of each cup provided the energy to engage in any sort of meaningful conversation we hoped to have. I was exhausted, and I should have told Judy to leave the pot.

Frank turned to me after his first sip of black coffee. We hadn't spoken much over the summer, with night shift hours at a heating components factory affecting his availability. He usually slept while I worked, but when he got word from my mother how I was over at Connors, he wanted some answers. Frank was laid off from his sales job months earlier, but with the connections of an old high school buddy, he reluctantly picked up shifts at the factory to make ends meet. He spent his evenings and early mornings carrying scalding heating duct casings from an assembly line toward an inventory rack, so he wasn't too pleased to hear of his younger brother toiling in similar grunt work by choice.

My sisters and parents preoccupied in their own conversation, so he could talk to me without the rest eavesdropping. If he talked low and directly, we could have a one-on-one while the others talked about Mrs. Fandetti, an Italian woman who lived in a large white house at the end of our street. They were sufficiently occupied, laughing about how Mrs. Fandetti once chased her balding and overweight husband between those pillars with a meat cleaver, swearing at him in Italian so the whole street could hear. Frank leaned over to me under this laughter.

"So, Joe, what the hell are you doing over at Connors packing boxes? Ma told me you're over there until two some nights and back doing it all over again at noon. I know pops isn't giving handouts, but are you serious? You should be spending your days writing and looking for a real job, not hauling boxes with high school drop-outs. You think I want to be hauling those casings when I could be sleeping or at my old sales job? I have rent and student loans to pay, kid. What's your excuse?"

Frank was right, but I didn't like getting talked down to, even if he knew better. With everyone else laughing about Mrs. Fandetti, I quietly tried to gain footing and deliver, not willing to submit to my older brother.

"Look, I quit there, okay? I quit on Friday, so settle down."

And just as I answered Frank, I heard the rest of my family enter the intermediary silence common in reunion conversations. A story is told, and there's a pause until someone else decides to chime in with another tale. This was their pause, and unfortunately, it had come at the one moment of breakfast I'd rather it didn't. Their ears were opened as I blurted out my state of affairs. My father's ears were opened. He folded his hands at his chest, elbows on the table. Eyebrows raised.

"You quit what?"

"I quit Connors this week. Friday," I said. "I quit on Friday."

"Why? Did you get another job?"

"No, not yet."

"Well, what are going to do for money? You know I'm not giving any to you." He leaned back in his chair, arms folded and blue eyes fixed in a glare. "What's your plan?"

"Well, I'm thinking of moving."

Enter a solid five seconds of silence: One. Two. Three. Four. Five.

"Out of our house?" said my mother.

"Yes," I said. "And out of Buffalo."

"And where do you plan on going?" said my father.

"Well," I said, tentative and ready to play defense, "I've been thinking about New York City."

One. Two. Three. Four. Five.

"New York?" he said. "Manhattan? You can't be serious."

"Well, I think that—"

"Just so you know," he said, cutting me off before I could continue, "the New Yorkers who occupy that supposed urban utopia don't know we exist as anything else but a punch-line for snow jokes and football losses. You know that, right?"

"Dad, that's not just New York City; it's the whole country," I said. "We're a punch-line everywhere, so I might as well stay in the state, right?"

"So now you think being from an honorable, blue-collar city is a joke too? Not high-class enough for you?"

"Of course I don't, but—"

"I told you about my experience there, didn't I? Years ago, I was still in our state, in Manhattan with your mother and your aunt when I needed to cash a check from Buffalo at a bank off 6th Avenue. When I got to the teller, she told me she couldn't cash the check. When I asked her why, do you know what she said? Do you?"

"No."

"She said she couldn't cash it because it was an out-of-state check. Out of state, Joe! This woman wasn't aware of the second-largest city in the state! You know why?"

"Why?"

"Because we don't exist to them. They think they're their own state, even though hard-working Buffalonians' tax dollars probably contributed to the roadways that teller drove over to get to her job that day, or the tracks of the train she takes out of work with friends to get Happy Hour martinis."

His voice echoed loud enough for surrounding patrons to notice. My mother calmly reached out for his hand to settle him down.

"Patrick Cahan, lower your voice." She looked around the table and tried to restore order. "We can talk about Joseph's plans when we get home. For now, let's just try to enjoy this breakfast. We so seldom get to see each other together, so can we relax and enjoy. Please?"

"Fine," he said. "We'll talk about this when we get home."

He took a sip of his coffee before offering one more point. He had to get one more in.

"But let me leave you with some truth as we wait for Judy to bring us our breakfast. We may live in the same state as New York City. We may all have the same driver's licenses, license plates and governor. But I'll tell you this: I've never waited for a New York Yankees World Series parade to roll down Delaware

Avenue, with pinstriped players waving and blowing kisses at me. I didn't feel conflicted during Super Bowl twenty-five when the Bills lost to the Giants, and I never chanted 'we want the Cup' with the Madison Square Garden faithful when the Rangers were gunning for Lord Stanley. And do you know why?"

"Why, Dad?"

"Because they're not crying for the Bills in Brooklyn, and the other four boroughs don't care if the Sabres get screwed out of another hockey championship because of crappy officiating. The New York Times didn't type one line in their Sunday edition about how a baseball team in Buffalo could spark a cross-state National League rivalry with the Mets, nor did the Post devote one story about how the NBA let a crooked, greedy owner steal a team from devoted fans who led the league in attendance two years prior. Manhattan doesn't care if Buffalo develops the waterfront, recovers from our Rust Belt image or rejuvenates our economic outlook to compete with other cities for bright, young employees. They don't. So don't expect me to be overjoyed about donating another Buffalonian to their workforce when they don't give a damn about us."

One. Two. Three. Four. Five.

"Now where's Judy?" he said. "I need another cup of coffee."

12

Almost a week had passed. My father and I still hadn't talked.

He would work all day and night on the boat, and I'd conveniently be nowhere to be found when he came home. I didn't want to talk to him as much as he didn't want to talk to me, so the avoidance seemed to suit us fine. Unfortunately, it was no such convenience for my mother. She was stuck in the middle, and as we got out of the Blue Bomber in our driveway on Friday, she was anxious to put an end to it.

"Your father called earlier today and said he's bringing home a fish fry tonight from Fitzgerald's, so don't even think of slipping out of the house with Duff and Terry before he gets home. You'll talk this out tonight and that's that. Got it, Joseph?"

"I got it."

After I relented, I walked through our side door to see the answering machine's red light blinking.

"Somebody's got a meh-sage," she said, with mocking enthusiasm.

She shuffled over to the machine and pressed the PLAY

button.

Cahan, it's Eli. Been up in Boston, Massachusetts for about a month now and wanted to see what you've been doing. I wanted to talk with you about a possible opportunity, so give me a call at 555-8631 when you get a chance. Later.

I hadn't talked with my senior year roommate Eli Moorman since we left St. Francis, but I heard he followed the band Phish around the country for almost two months before ending up on a national television news report about the tour. In the feature, he was shown naked, dancing with a group of stoned-out neo-hippies in front of the camera, his privates blurred for the national audience. After following Phish through June, he moved to Boston and got a job selling medical software to area hospitals and clinics in New England. My mother stood over the sink, fixated on a collection of dirty dishes as I recalled Eli's fifteen minutes of fame.

"An opportunity, huh?" she said, sifting through plates and bowls. "You should give him a call and see what he's got for you."

"Maybe later," I said, leaning against the table and staring blankly at the kitchen wall.

"Later? Did you forget about your father's breakfast lecture? My advice would be if you have a chance at an opportunity outside New York City, you should do it and do it fast for my sake and the sake of this family. Your father hasn't talked to you in a week, and I fear he's just getting started."

I agreed, and then headed up to my room to call Eli. When he answered, the first thing he asked was, "Cahan, dude, you still thinking about coming to Boston?"

Eli and I had college conversations considering future plans every evening on every barstool. On some nights, dropping out of school to drive cross-country seemed like a fantastic idea. Grab a copy of *On the Road* by Jack Kerouac, get a custodial job at a roadside motel and live out of someone's car for a few months? It had to be better than the Historical Geology class I was barely passing. On other nights, I was ready to move to Oregon and get a job at a lumberyard just to live in the Pacific Northwest for a year or two. Eli had vagabond aspirations that induced these thoughts of senseless wander, so in one of those conversations, I may have said I wanted to someday move to Boston.

"Cahan, you would love this place. Guinness-swigging pubs on every corner with little Irish girls running all over the place, plus great music every night in bars all over the city. I'm living in the west part of Boston with this kid I met on the Phish tour named Lou," he said. "Cool guy. Kind of eccentric, but you'd like him. He actually works over at Commonwealth College doing financial aid or something, and that's where you come in."

"Where I come in?"

"Well, since Lou works there, he can go to their film school really cheap when classes start this fall. Have you considered going back?"

"Back? Back to what?"

"School," he said. "Lou tells me that CC has a killer creative writing program. If you decided to move up here, he could get you a job working there so you could go back to school on the cheap."

"This all sounds great, Eli, but what's in this for you guys? Why are you recruiting me?"

"Honestly?"

"Yeah. Not that I don't appreciate the offer, but what's up?"

"All right, all right," he said. "This friend of Lou's named Sniff was living with us for the past month. All of the sudden, we wake up one morning and the dude's bedroom is empty with only a note saying he moved to Denver with some girl he met at a Widespread Panic show."

"And?"

"We need another roommate to pay rent, and I figured this opportunity might be right in your wheelhouse. You get a job, a chance to earn a cheap master's degree, and a chance to live in a city with, like, a hundred free papers and mags you could write for on the side. This place has your name all over it, Cahan."

"And you need a roommate?"

"Me and Lou, yeah."

"Can you give me a week?"

He laughed.

"Dude, take two if it'll get you here. Just let me know."

I tried to dismiss the timing of Eli's call after I hung up the phone. He just happened to call after my father's reaction to a Manhattan relocation had stomped my serendipitous and faith-fueled desires into the ground? I lay back on my bed and considered his proposal.

I'd only been to Boston once in my life, with my father to see the Bills play the Patriots at Foxboro Stadium during my sophomore year at St. Francis. The stadium was well outside the city, but since we stayed in the center of Boston, I was able to take in the surroundings Eli spoke of. The historical architecture accentuated the city's pristine urban layout, its highlights impressive enough to dwarf the perpetual construction going on everywhere. The residents seemed nice, always willing to give us directions, though suspicious the minute we said we were from New York. Most poignantly, I remembered walking down sidewalks and noticing the majority of individuals walking the city's streets were not my father's age, but were mine. Boston was overrun with youth, and with the enthusiasm Eli pitched the area with, I assumed it still was.

With students and young professionals swarming the streets, there had to be opportunities on every corner. Besides the Commonwealth College job, there would be chances to find an audience for my writing. Instead of a few art magazines and the *Buffalo Gazette* to beg for a byline, I could offer samples to the *Boston Globe*, the *Boston Herald*, or various sidewalk rags on every corner and campus stretching across the city and over into Cambridge near Harvard.

The possibility of "Master" and "Joseph P. Cahan" being printed together anywhere was intriguing. I remembered shaking my head at students with graduate aspirations, convinced they were too timid to face the real world. Each was a coward hiding behind a book. Now I was starting to realize the flaws of my ignorance and realize the truth: They were actually focused; I wasn't. Over the past week, moving to Boston, Massachusetts never seemed like a resolution to my proposed defection to our supposed enemies in New York City, but it did after Eli's desperate recruiting call. The idea was still fresh when I smelled the aroma of fried fish drift up the stairs toward my bedroom later that night.

I descended the stairs to see the fish grease had already saturated its box and the container of macaroni salad was already in Molly's hand as she scooped a helping onto her plate. My mother was seated and my father looked down the table to glare at me as I stepped to the table. He didn't say a word, so I pulled my chair out, took a seat and reached for the box of fish.

"So?" said my mother. "Did you call Eli back?"

"I did, and it sounds like he has a good opportunity."

"Would you care to share this news with your father?"

"Is he going to reply to what I say?"

"What is it?" he said, not even looking up from his plate. "Get a good deal on a U-Haul from Buffalo to Brooklyn?"

"Patrick Cahan, you will listen to what your son has to say!" she said, then took a deep breath. "Well? Go ahead, Joseph."

"Eli Moorman called me. He lives in Boston."

"Eli?" he said "That the hippie you used to live with at school? Kid's room smelled like dope."

"Well, he's looking for a roommate again, but he also said he can get me a job at Commonwealth College. School employees get a huge break on tuition, so if hired, I could work toward a master's degree."

"Since when do you want to go back to school? What happened to immersing yourself in the real world? Getting a job?"

"This is a way to do both. I get a paycheck and the chance to write, albeit on the side."

"If you want to go back to school so bad now, why not try to get a job at Buff State or UB? Why move to Boston?"

I stared down the table and exhaled a frustrating sigh.

"I thought you would be happy I was suggesting an alternative to New York. You just don't get what's going on, do you?"

"Do I get that you're abandoning your home and roots when they need you the most? Yeah, I get that."

My mother tried to intervene.

"Oh, c'mon. Stop it, you two. Stop it right now."

No use.

"Look outside the door!" I said to him. "Look around when you're down at the marina, when you're coasting along on the lake. Look at the waterfront district that doesn't exist. Look at the crumbling buildings downtown standing neglected. I'm not deserting this city; this city has deserted me and every other young person who wants to live here! All the ambition, all the potential every college kid comes home with? We have nowhere to direct it. There are legions of people my age who want the chance to contribute toward something they believe in, and this city doesn't get it. You know how many calls I've gotten back on resumes, dad? Do you?"

"How many?"

"Zero! Not one goddamn call or letter in the past two months since I've been back here!"

"Two months isn't a very long time. You know how long I had to wait to find a good job when I was your age?"

"I don't care, Dad. Honestly, there is no parallel to your experience and mine. None. You had a choice when you were my age. I don't. I have to leave, and that's all there is to it."

He looked down at his plate.

"Fine," he said. "When do you leave for Boston? Tomorrow? Next week? The sooner the better."

Molly fidgeted in her seat.

"Can I be excused?"

"Go," said my mother, then looked to the ceiling and sighed.

"I'm thinking about leaving next week. First of August. I'll load up the Bomber with whatever I can fit in it, and then take off. Is that okay?"

He didn't even look up.

"Great, but don't expect my help. I'll be working the whole day. You know, working for a city that's alienated all its young superstars like yourself."

I set my fork down as my heart beat furiously. I glared down the table at him, my stare burning into his scalp. I could see my mother's sad eyes staring at me, her agitation nearly matching mine. She thought Boston would quell the disappointment my father felt about me leaving Buffalo for New York City. It actually exacerbated it.

"Joseph, leave the kitchen and take your food out on the front porch," she said. "Now."

I continued to stare at my father, waiting for him to notice. He never did, so I walked out of the kitchen, through the living room and out the front door. I sat down at the far end of the porch, and my anger stirred before settling in my stomach, giving way to regret. I wished I could've made him understand the fear of complacency introduced through Hutch, or how I saw the guarantee I'd be mired in it with every new pint inhaled at Fitzgerald's. I wish he understood how I felt Buffalo had turned its back on me. When he met my mother, he had a choice of whether to stay or go. He'd never understand what it was like to be robbed of that decision.

That was a choice graduates in New York's five boroughs or students in Boston had that a large portion of young Buffalonians didn't. When we got home from school that summer and sat around at Fitzgerald's or Doherty's, our conversations didn't focus on what we were going to do for a job; we talked about where we would have to move to get one. For finance majors like Duff or aspiring lawyers like Terry, they could try to swing something in Buffalo. Though he was biding his summer at the Ford stamping plant with his father, Duffy could eventually satisfy his business degree at a local insurance agency or a bank with great benefits and long-term prospects. I couldn't, yet there were mornings I prayed for the strength to ignore my ambitions.

I'd quietly get up on those mornings before sunrise and sneak out of our side door. I'd slip into the Blue Bomber, drive down Route 5 along the shore and park at our neighborhood beach pier overlooking Lake Erie. I'd get out of my car, sit on the hood, and light a cigarette as I waited for the sun to rise. I'd rest against my windshield and the sun would rise behind me, over the trees and houses overlooking the lake, then shine onto the factory-lined shore and glisten off the weathered buildings of downtown Buffalo.

With the sun in the sky and the streets still vacant, I would continue down Route 5 and head over the Skyway. On a bright and sunny morning, the dazzling view of the lake compensated for the neglected waterfront. I'd see the arena on my right and the ballpark's light posts glistening in the distance behind it. I'd head toward Niagara Square and past City Hall, then drive slowly around the rotary and past the marble McKinley monument standing in the median. I'd continue up Delaware Avenue, past the unopened bars and coffee shops, and past the venerable Asbury Delaware United Methodist Church, blocked off with cement barricades and police tape for years. When I would reach Allen Street, I'd take a right and proceed to Main Street before taking another right. I'd drive down the dilapidated Main strip to see the most concentrated view of downtown, a frame of Buffalo's tallest and cleanest buildings condensed in the backdrop behind the Metro Rail trolley system and the shimmering theatre district arch. It was a view I wanted to see every day, representing an image many young Buffalonians bookmarked as their vision of the city: beautiful in our eyes, bursting with potential that none of us had the power or prominence to develop.

My father would never be able to relate to this discouragement. I was mired in it, so I'd have to leave my family and friends, and, as he put it, abandon Buffalo. I wasn't defecting to our enemy downstate anymore, but to him, it was still high treason to take my aspirations elsewhere.

A week later, I packed up the Blue Bomber for Boston. Every inch of the car was stuffed as it sat in my parents' driveway. When I was ready to leave, I greeted my mother and Molly outside my driver's side window. My old man was nowhere to be found.

"You know he loves you, Joseph," said my mother. "It's just going to take a while for him to adjust to this. You'll see when you're a parent. You won't like watching your children move away, either."

"Then why are you being so cool with this?"

"Because I know you'll be back."

"You do, do you?"

She reached into the right pocket of her khaki shorts and pulled out a set of baby blue rosary beads.

"I want you to put these in your glove compartment," she said, handing them through the window. "Your Grandpa Cahan gave those to me for guidance when I married your father. Keep them in there for the Blessed Mother to guide you safely, okay?"

"I will. Thanks."

"Say a prayer on those when you're looking for some help, okay?"

"Okay, Ma."

"I'll pray for you to have a safe trip on my other set inside, then may ask the Blessed Mother herself to guide you right back here. You'll see," she said with a smile.

She stuck her head in the window, gave me a kiss goodbye and patted the top of my head. Molly reached in after her to give me a hug before I headed toward Duff's house. Taking two steps back from the car, they both gave a wave as I backed out of the driveway and turned up The Clash cassette I had in the tape deck. I headed up Norton Drive, away from the house I grew up in. I could see my mother still waving in my rearview mirror until I went over the hill at the top of Norton.

I pulled into Duff's blacktopped driveway to find him and Terry sitting in green plastic patio chairs on the cement stoop outside his front door, sipping cans of Bud. Terry threw me a beer out of his cooler as I walked to meet the two of them. I caught it, nodded thanks, cracked it open to take a small sip and exhaled to enjoy the awkward silence. I still hadn't grasped that, when I left Buffalo, I'd be leaving Terry and Duff. I wasn't going into seclusion, but the simplicity of our daily interaction would be gone. I wasn't sure if Eli or Lou would know if I wanted a beer by the look on my face. Terry did, but since I made the decision for change, I wouldn't be able to enjoy this mundane certainty any longer.

"So you're seriously moving?" said Terry. "Just like that? It's only August, dude. Things could happen in the fall."

"If I don't go now, I'll never go. Just something I have to do, like you going to law school."

"Emphasize the words *have* and *to*," he said. "Unless I want to kiss ass and hold re-election signs, it's either law school or shifts at the stamping plant with our boy here."

Duff jokingly cocked his fist toward Terry.

"I have an interview with a bank this week, you prick," he said. "Cahan wants to write, and you know he can't do it here right now. Get something going in Boston, then make Terry and me famous in print when you get published. I won't even make you change my name if you decide to use it in stories."

"Me neither," Terry said. "That would play huge down at Fitzgerald's. Talent would be all over us."

I laughed, then took another small sip of my beer.

"Shut the fuck up," I said. "You two will come up soon, right? Maybe we can catch the Bills and Patriots at Foxboro this season. I think they play in late November."

"Sure, sure," they both mumbled before raising their beers to their lips.

"You think that shitbox is gonna make it all the way to Boston?" said Duff, motioning to the Bomber with his beer can. "Hate to get a call from you stranded off the ninety in Oneida with nowhere to go but the Boxing Hall Of Fame."

"I'll make it," I said. "But, if anything goes wrong, I'll call you. You gonna be around?"

He leaned back in his green plastic patio chair.

"Be right here," he said. "We're not going anywhere, Cahan. Born in Buffalo, live in Buffalo, die in Buffalo. Try to catch a break so you can come back and join us."

Duff stood up from his chair and raised his beer toward Terry and me.

"Good luck, and as the tired saying goes, know that you can always take the kid out of Buffalo, but you can never take the Buffalo out of the kid. Remember that when you're knocking back beers with Bostonians."

We clanked our beers together before I finished the end of mine, not wasting a drop. I set the can down on the stoop, gave Duff and Terry each handshake hugs before backing down the driveway and climbing into the Blue Bomber. I pulled out in front of the house and gave them a thumbs-up out my window as they raised their cans again. My body was numb of any emotion as Joe Strummer's vocals on "Capital Radio Two" stormed out of my speakers. It didn't feel like I was leaving; it felt like I was going on vacation. Seeing the looks on their faces as I left, I knew reality would seep in somewhere on Interstate 90.

Once I exited the neighborhood I grew up in, I felt the sun's rays on my left forearm as it hung out the driver side window. I took my sunglasses down from my visor and put them over my brown eyes as a buzz ran down my spine as I headed for the New York State Thruway. After I saw the first sign for it, I diverted back down a side street to take one more pass along Lake Erie. The sun glistened off the water on an August day that was Buffalo's secret. I rode along the lake's edge and gave its waves a wink. One more glance and I was gone, my life in the backseat.

13

I had to turn on my car's interior light to follow Eli's directions.

Getting to Boston from Buffalo was a straight drive east on the New York State Thruway to the Massachusetts Turnpike, but it got complicated once I crossed through the Brighton toll barrier before downtown Boston. After I passed the lights of Fenway Park and had a view of the Prudential Building in front of me, I was to get off at Exit 18 toward Jamaica Plain, my new neighborhood on the city's west side. According to Eli, its streets were full of college students, fledgling rock acts and struggling restaurant workers.

Eli said there was an Irish dive I'd love called the Jeanie Johnston that had a live rockabilly night every Friday. He mentioned a pastry shop called The Toaster that served the best coffee he'd ever tasted. Since lesbians ran the place, Eli called the place "Lesbian Coffee." I was due to pass both on the way to my new apartment. But, the closer I got to the address, the shadier the neighborhood became.

I drove past the Jeanie Johnston and The Toaster, but was still four turns from our place. The address on the directions read

3048 Washington Street, and when I approached the corner of Washington and Green Street, I saw a Boston Police station and a small beeper outlet across the street. Washington Street was scattered with trash and debris over the sidewalks of Juan Carlos' Hairstyling, Margarita's Hair & Nails and Sol de Manana convenience store. The triple-decker Victorian houses lining Washington looked old and rundown, and the dim streetlights showed shingles clinging to sides and boards across upper-level windows. A small brick apartment complex's archway entrance was blocked off with yellow police tape, stretched in front of a candlelight vigil and arranged flowers. 3138. 3122. 3082. Down a little further on the left was Sagliano's Liquor & Pizza, with a sign shining to advertise the week's delivery special: Two large pizzas and a six-pack of Budweiser, $14.99.

I saw a light in the front window of the second floor of 3048 Washington, right across the street from Sagliano's. I parked in front of the beige Victorian triple-decker and emerged to hear the streets dead and quiet. The smell in the air was of a fresh summer night, with hints of marijuana smoke intermixed. I closed my car door before my recognition was interrupted by a disheveled and delirious woman running toward me, arms flailing about as she shouted, "Oh, mistah! Can I trouble you for a minute?"

This woman had come out of nowhere, wearing a dirty and ripped purple t-shirt underneath an oversized green and blue flannel. I wasn't usually approached outside my parents' house by strange women in blue jeans, stained and draped tattered over bare feet; it didn't happen at St. Francis either. But I wasn't naïve. That's why I guarded my wallet as she began her inevitable questioning.

"Mistah, I got no way home, and I need to get back with my kids. They haven't eaten 'cause I got no money, so if you could, do you think you could lend me fifteen dollahs? I swear I'll come to pay you back. I'll leave you my driver's license or whatever you want!"

Fifteen dollars? This woman was bold.

"Lady, I wish I could help you, but I don't have a dime to my name," I said, clutching the thirty-four bucks in my right pocket. "That Sagliano's place looked open if you wanted to check in there, but I can't help you out."

"Ah-ite, ah-ite," she said, now slightly twitching with a defeated look on her face. "Have a nice night, then."

She walked feverishly down the street, and I turned to make sure all my car doors were locked. Five minutes in Boston and I had already encountered my first lunatic. The denial seemed natural, but as she continued down the street, I felt bad. I assumed she was a junkie as she twitched and talked. Then, the hint of Catholic guilt kicked in. What if she really did need it for her kids? What if these kids were starving and my lack of generosity would send them spiraling downward? I couldn't live with that on my conscience.

I reached into my pocket and pulled out a ten and a five before sprinting down Washington Street after the woman. When I caught up with her, she was startled. She swung around like I was about to rob her.

"Here's fifteen bucks," I said, then handed her the cash. "I forgot about the extra money I had in my shoe."

"Oh, uh, thank you sir. Thank you. You want me to leave my license with you?"

"Don't worry about it," I said. "And have a nice night."

I felt at ease walking back to the house. I helped someone in my new neighborhood, even if that woman didn't actually live in my new neighborhood. She'd get home, my money would feed her children and my conscience would be clean. Unfortunately I turned around at the front door of 3048 and saw the woman sprint into Sagliano's Liquors. As I stood on the steps of my new apartment, my Catholic guilt gave way to gullible hope. Maybe she'd use my money for that two large pizza deal.

The front door buzzed and unlocked after I rang the doorbell, so I pushed through to see Eli waiting at the top of the stairs.

"Cahan! You made it one piece, dude. How was the ride?"

"No problem. Good directions, but I was just outside giving some lady money. I think she went over to the liquor store to get booze with it."

"She ask you for fifteen dollars?"

"Yeah. How'd you know?"

"We call her Black Velvet," he said.

"Because she's black?"

"That, and because she uses the money she gets off suckers like you on a bottle of Black Velvet whiskey. She goes to the park down the street, drinks most of it, and then starts singing Etta James tunes on the park bench until she passes out. You'll hear her when it gets real quiet around here. Pretty good voice, actually."

"I feel like an idiot," I said. "But I felt guilty turning her away."

"Don't feel bad, dude. Getting taken by Black Velvet is like initiation into this neighborhood. Both Lou and I got bilked before. Hell, Lou gave her money one morning, and then gave her one of our travel mugs full of coffee, too. Told her she could borrow the mug, and he actually thought she'd bring it back. He still asks for it when he sees her."

"So where is this Lou?"

"In his room, I think. Sometimes he stays in there all night."

I walked into the apartment; it didn't look that bad. Two old couches and a nice leather recliner were arranged in the living room in front of a cheap entertainment center, the kind of build-it-yourself type made of woodchips and sawdust. They had a twenty-seven-inch television and a four-disc stereo in the entertainment center, and hanging on the wall were a panoramic of Fenway Park, two framed Phish play cards from recent concerts and a painting of Jerry Garcia Eli bought off a street corner in Cambridge. We walked down a narrow hallway and stopped at the bedroom door on the right. Eli gave three knocks.

"Lou, you in there?"

"Yeah."

"Can we come in? I got Cahan out here."

"No."

"Why?"

"Naked."

"Doing yoga?"

"Yup," said Lou. "Be done in a little while."

"Naked yoga?" I said. "Is he serious?"

"Lou's strange, but you'll like him," he said. "Good guy."

We continued down the hallway and into the kitchen to find a kitchen table with three wicker chairs in front of three windows overlooking the driveway. There was a small ashtray overflowing with cigarette butts on the window sill and a mound of dishes in the sink next to it. Empty Busch beer cans were scattered over the countertop, and a small white stove hosted spaghetti sauce stains splattered around its burners. The wood-paneled floor looked newly shined, but the luster wore thin once I noticed the mousetraps set up along the baseboards. Five in all, and they were all baited except for one.

"Mouse problem?" I said. "Looks like they snuck the cheese off that one."

"Slick bastards. If we don't catch any with the cheese, we're going with peanut butter and poison next. Guess that works pretty well."

"Call me crazy, but I'd go with the poison. You know, if the object is to kill and not feed."

I walked with Eli to the room vacated by Sniff with a paranoid eye to the floor. I opened the door and saw that Sniff left his bed, a small nightstand and a forest green lamp atop it.

"I assumed he couldn't fit this shit in his van to Denver, so I thought you might be able to use it. The mattress still smells a bit like patchouli, but I've had the window open for two days trying to air the thing out. Even put the dryer sheets on the back of a fan to freshen up the room."

"I appreciate the effort."

The bed still smelled of marijuana, too, but it was better than sleeping on the mouse-infested floor. Sniff left some Phish and Widespread Panic ticket stubs pinned to the wall, but as I approached the wall to look at them, screams came from above. The ceiling started to shake with the pounding of feet and what sounded like a lamp smashing on the floor. The stomping turned into louder thumps that dislodged plaster from the ceiling corner. Eli stood in the doorway, eyes peering toward the ceiling while shaking his head.

"I told her not to do it."

"Do what?"

"Girl upstairs is sleeping with her roommate's boyfriend, but since her roommate usually works nights, she's been getting away with it. Saw them making out in the hallway the other day and warned her she'd get caught. Sounds like she did."

"Oh."

"They tend to get into it quite a bit up there, but when Sniff was here, he'd give a few raps on the ceiling with a baseball bat. They'd tone it down after that. Feel free to use my lacrosse stick if you want."

"Thanks."

Eli left me to sit on the bed as the violent screams from above rained down. I'd moved from home to start a new chapter of my life, but with the scent emanating from the mattress under me, maybe I had subconsciously retreated back to the comforts of college to escape the reality Buffalo revealed. Maybe I was afraid to take the next step in my life. Being away from home was a way to hide eventual failure from family and friends who would actually care.

Or, maybe I was engaging in needless analysis when I should've been enjoying my first apartment as an adult. I had moved out of my parents' house, moved away from my hometown and onto the East Coast in Boston, Massachusetts. Soon, I'd have my first day at a salaried position, my first sizable paycheck, and an unexpected seat in a graduate course. Maturity was right around the corner, but as I waited for its arrival, I had things to do. Important, vital things. I had to go smoke a cigarette in the kitchen with Eli, avoid cheese-lusting mice, air the marijuana smell out of my new bedroom, hope the girls upstairs didn't crash through my ceiling, then meet my new roommate—as soon as he was done with his naked yoga.

14

It wasn't my faulty alarm clock that woke me up at six the next morning for my first day in Boston. The barking dog below my opened window startled me quicker than my clock ever did.

"AHRFF! AHRFF! AHRFF! AHRFF!"

I rolled out of bed and walked to the window to see a shaggy black dog, looking like it hadn't been clipped or bathed in years. He was chained to a stake, secured next to a makeshift doghouse made of driftwood and scrap metal. Painted in white on a piece of that metal was the dog's name: Rocky. I stood by the window and introduced myself.

"Shut up! Shut up! Shut up! Shut up!"

He looked up, tilted his head in confusion before retreating into his doghouse.

"That was easy," I said to myself, then shuffled back to dig in under the bed sheets. Moments later, an ungodly odor drifted under my nose. With my door opened a crack, it was coming from inside the house. It took nearly an entire bottle of Febreeze, Eli's lacrosse stick and a new set of sheets, but I'd beaten the marijuana and patchouli smell from Sniff's old bed. I'd made the room nearly tolerable with a nice vanilla-scented candle until another smell infiltrated my room.

I ripped off the covers, jumped up and walked out my door. I stormed down the hallway while the smell thickened toward the kitchen. When I turned the corner, I saw a tall guy with a shaved head and headphones on his ears, holding the handle of a frying pan over our little stove. He wore a ripped U2 shirt with "War" written on the back as he bopped his head, rhythmically simmering unidentified vile ingredients with a spatula as he shuffled his feet in gray running sneakers and khaki shorts. I could tell he didn't notice me. If he did, I'm still not sure whether he would've stopped dancing.

"Hey! Hey!" I said. "What the hell are you cooking?"

He took off his headphones.

"Breakfast. You Cahan?"

"Yeah. Who are you?"

"Lou. Lou Sperduti, your roommate," he said. "Sorry I didn't come out last night. After yoga, I put on some Willie Nelson and fell asleep on my floor. You ever listen to the Redheaded Stranger?"

"Not really, no. What the hell are you making? It smells awful."

"Six eggs scrambled with a can of sardines. Great source of protein, man. I try to eat at least this much for breakfast after a five-mile run."

"What time do you go running at?"

"Usually at five or five-thirty every morning. I kind of slacked off this morning and got out the door a little after five-thirty. It is Saturday, though."

"And you make the sardines every morning?"

"Naw. But always the eggs, and sometimes I throw some chicken or other fish in there, too. You should try it sometime."

"Maybe another day. For now, I'm going back to sleep. Nice meeting you, Lou. See you in a few hours."

"See you later, man, and nice meeting you too," he said, and I walked back to my room. I closed the door tightly, stuffed a towel at its base so the smell couldn't seep back into the room, and started to long for my bed's marijuana smell.

I awoke a few hours later to find Eli and Lou sitting on the couch, watching the replay of "Baseball Tonight" on ESPN. Eli pointed to the takeout coffee on the table he'd brought me from The Toaster. I popped off its plastic lid to take a sip, then smiled at him in affirmation; those lesbians made a good cup of coffee. I took a seat in the empty leather recliner and listened to Eli detail the day's agenda.

"So, we were thinking about going down to Fenway for the Sox-Twins game today at one o'clock. Bleacher seats are only sixteen bucks, and after the game, we can go down to this bar whose bartender looks like Lou Gossett Jr. Spitting image, Cahan."

"Guy will even shout out quotes from *An Officer and a Gentleman* and *Iron Eagle* if you ask nicely," said Lou. "Had to tip him extra for that 'steers and queers' line last time, but it was worth it."

"Sounds like a day," I said, enthusiastically. "Plus, Lou, I could talk to you about the job at Commonwealth College, right?"

"I handed your résumé to my supervisor last Tuesday, so you should be able to check on it this week. I'll tell you everything about the job as we wait in the bleachers for a Manny Ramirez blast to hit Ted Williams' red chair."

"Red chair?"

"You'll see," said Eli. "Get yourself together by eleven-thirty and we'll take the T down to the Fens."

We arrived at the Green Line's Kenmore Square stop around noon. We emerged from the station onto a sun-drenched Commonwealth Avenue to see Red Sox fans everywhere. They flooded the sidewalks and streets surrounding Fenway, dressed in blue baseball caps and white or gray jerseys with names like "Martinez" and "Garciaparra" on their backs. I'd never seen the ballpark in person. Constructed of aged and weathered red brick on the exterior, it looked like someone picked it out of the twenties and dropped it in front of us. The smell of peanuts, hot dogs and beer blew with the breeze and, at that moment, I wished hot dogs and beer had as much protein as sardines so Lou would be waking me up with that smell every morning.

I followed Eli and Lou as we walked past a man hawking game programs with a thick Boston accent.

"Red Sawx-Twins game programs, heah! Get yoah Sawx programs, heah!"

There was a tall thin man with glasses on our right. He didn't say a word in any accent, but advertised a simple message in bold, black lettering on a graphic painting draped around his neck: REPENT OR SUFFER ETERNAL DAMNATION. Blunt options. If the words didn't do it for the passers-by, the picture hanging from his neck of a large crucifix bridge stretching across a fiery cavernous gulf would have. The man in his "Jesus Saves" cap had made his point.

Lou eventually approached a guy wearing a shamrocked t-shirt, blue windpants and gleaming white cross-trainers.

"Got three bleachers for fifty?"

"Three for fifty?" said the scalper. "Do you see the weather out here? It's seventy-five degrees and sunny, ideal day to be in the bleachers to see the Sox. I could get eighty."

"And we could go up to the window and get 'em for forty-eight bucks," said Lou. "The game's not sold out, and we're not playing the Yankees. No one gives a shit about the Twinkies."

The scalper scanned from side to side, looking out for the cops. According to Lou, the cops didn't care, but every once in a while they'd intervene—just to be pricks. He countered again once the coast was deemed clear.

"Three for sixty."

"Forget it," said Lou. "We'll go to the window."

The scalper relented once he saw our backs.

"All right, all right," he said. "Fifty-five for three, then get out of my face."

"Deal," said Lou, then each of us dug the cash out of our pockets and handed it over in exchange for our three tickets. Section forty-two; row four; seats twelve, thirteen and fourteen, and away we walked toward Lansdowne Street and Gate C to get comfortable for the game.

When we squeezed into our decrepit emerald seats, we each held a beer in each hand, and I tucked a bag of peanuts under my right arm. The park was a sight on a sunny Saturday afternoon, as each section around us slowly filled. Red Sox outfielders played catch in front of us, and in the distance stood the Green Monster left field wall I'd seen so many times on television. Fenway Park felt like a Little League field, with fans right on top of the action and so close to each other. The three of us had to be careful with our elbows when we drank; if we raised each beer to our mouths too quickly, we'd knock each other in the jaw. I sipped mine slowly, elbows tucked in, and took it all in.

"See the red seat over there?" Lou nudged me and pointed over to our left at the empty red seat amidst all the green ones in our section. "That's the seat Ted Williams hit on the fly with a home run back in forty-six. It's supposed to be the longest-ever hit in Fenway. Five hundred feet or something like that."

"No shit?"

"Ramirez would have to go opposite field with one to hit his own chair, but maybe today's his day. I was here a few weeks ago when he launched one over the Monster that hit the Mass Pike on the fly. Had to be longer than Teddy's, but I don't think anyone felt like running into oncoming traffic to check."

I took another sip as Lou continued to bombard me and Eli with Red Sox moments and stats he knew from spending summers as a kid with his grandfather in Boston. Lou's outspoken Sox passion had hooked Eli in the short time they know each other. Lou grew up in Maine but spent his formative summers in Boston, watching Sox games on television or enduring the short drive to the park to grab tickets. Most of his memories were spent in the same bleachers we sat that day, so as he reminisced, he felt right at home.

Lou's three favorite players of all-time were Marty Barrett, Mike Greenwell and Mo Vaughn. His favorite plays at Fenway were Tom Brunansky's sliding catch in right field to clinch the American League East in 1990, and Roger Clemens' twenty-strikeout game against the Seattle Mariners in April of 1986. His favorite team was that '86 squad, so his heart was crushed when they dropped the seven-game World Series to the Mets.

"I was in this park for Game Five, and we all thought we had it. We thought it was all over, finally," he said. "When we lost the series, I cried for two days, man. No bullshit. Like, ten times worse than Wade Boggs was crying in the Shea dugout on television."

When I disclosed my deep torture from the Bills' missed field goal in Super Bowl twenty-five, he briefly empathized before slipping back to Game Six of that World Series. I thought he was going to start crying again, this time in his beer.

"Fuck Buckner. He should've never had to field that grounder in the first place. If Calvin Schiraldi could've gotten one more goddamn strike over the plate, just one, that would've been it. Dammit!" he said, head down to muffle the scream. After staring at his beer for a second, he inhaled a deep breath before chugging the entire cup. When he finished, he turned to me, exhaled and said, "But what are you gonna do, right?"

I related to his fan frustration and sensed I'd be on board with his Red Sox by the end of the afternoon. Misery loved company, and I seemed to have found my people. Now, I just needed to find a job, so I diverted the conversation away from baseball and asked Lou about my possible future with Commonwealth College.

"So, speaking of doing, what can you tell me about the Commonwealth job? I assume I'll be in a cubicle, but what's the job you submitted my résumé for?"

"Financial advisor in the Student Accounting department, but don't get freaked by the designation. The title's window dressing for the swarthy positions we actually occupy. We're, like, welcome mats for the goddamn school's instituted oppression, man. You'll see."

"So what do we actually do?"

"Our office handles all fees paid to the college. Since we're the ones sending out the enormous housing and tuition bills, we're an easy mark for aggression, man. You'll spend half your time deflecting parent and student complaints about the school's expenses."

"Why do they pick on us?"

"Because we take their money. People tend to get pissed off when they have to write thirty-five-thousand-dollar checks, so we're on the front lines to absorb their disenchantment, man."

"So, um, why do I want to do this?" I said, silently questioning why I didn't ask about this before I packed up the Blue Bomber.

"It's just a job, man; nothing more. You show up, do your work, get paid, and concentrate on your aspirations on the side. That's the price you pay for wanting to pursue careers like you and I do. I have film, you'll have creative writing, but we're going like Frost wrote, right? Taking the road less traveled."

"Right, I guess."

"Look, it's a first job, man. Problem is this country puts too much emphasis on the importance of what you do professionally. Like it has to define you, you know?"

"Well, it does," said Eli. "It's usually the second thing you tell people after your name. After you graduate, the question, 'What do you do?' replaces 'Where do you go to school?' at family reunions and bar pick-ups. In what country is this emphasis non-existent?"

"France," said Lou. "Most of Europe, actually. When I was traveling through there last year, people would leave work and go right to the bars or cafés to spend their money on letting loose. People over there work to live, man; they don't live to work. Work is for money, not status."

"That's prioritizing," I said. "Think you'll be able to reassure me with this belief if this job drives me insane?"

Lou grinned.

"I'll try, man. I'll try," he said. "If you get stressed, we can always head down for some drafts with Lou Gossett Jr. Few lines from Toy Soldiers will put a smile on your face, I assure you."

"And if not?"

"Then the twelve draft beers he pours you will. I don't think they've cleaned their taps in years, so their suds are like fucking moonshine, man."

We laughed in our bleacher seats of historic Fenway Park. Eli and I clicked our cups together and finished our beers as a loud crack of the bat echoed through the stands. We stood up, looked toward the Green Monster and could see the ball screaming over the wall, over the protective netting, and over Lansdowne Street toward the Mass Pike. It was a home run, but collective moans and groans of the crowd greeted the Minnesota player rounding the bases. Lou shook his head in disgust, and I turned to him for a quick question.

"Was Manny's blast crushed as far as that one?"

"Farther, man. Much farther," he said. "I'm going to need another beer if the Sox are going to be pitching like this all day. If you plan on following this team regularly, you'll need one, too. You in?"

"I'm in."

And I was in. For the beers; for the Red Sox; for Boston; and for my first salaried employment with Commonwealth College. Lou's supervisor called me the next day, and after a brief interview, they offered me a job as financial advisor in their Student Accounting department. I accepted, and there I was: Joseph P. Cahan from Buffalo, New York. Aspiring writer and soon-to-be financial advisor in Boston, Massachusetts. It would make perfect sense to family and inviting barroom singles in the upcoming months.

Sure it would—in France.

15

I herded off the Green Line with young professionals, old professionals, and obvious college students once the train stopped at Commonwealth West. I was able to differentiate between the young professionals and students not by their clothes or haircuts, but by their facial expressions. As a warm breeze swept down Commonwealth Avenue, workers walked to administration buildings with reluctant commitment, checking watches for their main motivation to scurry quicker. Students walked groggily and nonchalantly into the same building, knowing there was no boss to fear if they were two, three or four minutes late. Workers sighed and huffed, holding cups of coffee as they walked up the sidewalk toward their fate, enviously past students who heightened their disenchantment. I quickly deciphered their daily torture: In these students, each professional glimpsed the past they once reveled in on their way to a future they never anticipated.

Pretty deep, right? And it was only my first day.

I walked into our Student Accounting office wearing gray slacks, a blue dress shirt and maroon tie fastened tightly around my neck. Once inside, small beads of sweat dripped down my face as I found two rows of three light-gray cubicles to complement the gray walls and gray carpet I walked on. At quarter to nine, some of the cubicles were empty, but I could hear voices emanating out of one or two. I proceeded past the adjoined rows and back to my new supervisor Neil Davis's office. When I knocked on his door, he looked lost in his computer screen, his arms crossed to support the hypnotized concentration on his bearded face. He was so focused that my knock startled him as he swung his head up to see me.

"Mr. Cagan," he said. "Here for your first day, huh?"

"Yes sir," I said. "But, it's Cahan. Joe Cahan."

He walked out from behind his desk.

"What'd I say?"

"Cagan. With a 'G'."

"Aw, jeesh," he said, shaking his head in obvious embarrassment. "I'm sorry, Joe. I was totally engrossed in this news article. You know how hot the weather's going to be this week?"

"No."

"High eighties. That's pretty hot for you, huh?"

For me?

"Yeah, I guess."

"Have you ever seen weather this warm in your life, Joe?"

I stood confused.

"Sure. Every summer of my life."

"But Lou said you grew up in Buffalo, right?"

"Right."

"What's the warmest it usually gets there? Fifty or sixty degrees tops, right?"

I smiled. What a fucking moron.

"Buffalo has a higher average annual climate than Boston, Mr. Davis. Summers are very warm there, even in the nineties sometime."

"No kidding?" he said, sincerely surprised. I just stood there, trying to keep annoyance from creeping onto my face. "You learn something new every day, right? Let me show you to your desk, huh?"

Mr. Davis was mildly overweight in khakis, a navy tie, and a short-sleeve white dress shirt. With a slight limp, he walked slowly to show me to a corner cubicle void of any decorations or pictures. The others I passed were littered with photos of families and friends, along with promotional Red Sox calendars from a local coffee shop. Luckily for me, the previous occupant of my new cube had been nice enough to leave his calendar behind, laid on the empty desk for me to hang up.

"You get an hour for lunch every day, and you're also free to take two fifteen-minute breaks as well," he said. "Coffee's in the back kitchen down the hall, and put a quarter in the jar next to the pot when you grab a cup. We use that toward the coffee. Now, I'll let you get situated at your desk before I come back to start your training. Sound good? Great."

I tacked the Red Sox calendar up over my first desk once he left. It was initially thrilling, even if I hadn't even considered what I'd actually be doing at my first desk. Before I got up to grab a cup of the twenty-five-cent coffee, I found Lou, who walked in the door and slapped my cube's sidewall.

"Welcome man, welcome," he said, headphones wrapped around his neck and still emitting music. "Where you headed?"

"About to go grab a coffee. You want one?"

"No, I'm all set. I read in Newsweek that coffee causes prostate cancer and accelerates hair loss, so I've been trying to cut down."

I laughed in the face of prostate cancer and hair loss, and went to grab my coffee before Lou took me around to meet the three other employees occupying our office's cubicles.

There was Porsche Bennett, an oversized black woman in her early twenties who pushed aside an orange soda and a bag of Funyons so we could be introduced. She was smiling and friendly as she explained how her mother named her after the car, but as we were talking, her cell phone started ringing. It was her boyfriend, and as Lou and I left, she started yelling at him. Lou explained later that, between surfing the Internet and combing through celebrity gossip magazines, Porsche usually engaged in at least one such fight a day with her boyfriend, who she had a baby boy with named Tre a year earlier. Though she prided herself on being a strong Christian woman ever since Tre's birth, she was known to let the boyfriend have it on various issues during the course of a workday. Lou said her boyfriend's role in Porsche's pregnancy might have been the motivation for more than a few of those fights.

In the next cubicle sat a beautiful, petite yet curvaceous Hispanic woman, Sophia Garcia, who looked to be in her early to mid-twenties as well. Lou said Sophia had moved to Boston from Venezuela to attend Commonwealth, and started working in our office soon after her graduation. I figured she had only started working there recently, but was floored when Lou told me she was thirty-eight and had three children. A picture of these children hung on the wall behind her, along with one of her husband, who sported a wide grin. Lou said it was the opinion of every male employee at the college that Sophia's husband was one of the world's luckiest pricks. Sophia's smile, sensuality, and sultry, soothing voice gave every man enough reason to hate her husband's fortunate guts.

Finally, Lou introduced me to Natalie Burton, our office manager under Mr. Davis. Natalie was a tall, thin Connecticut native in her mid-thirties who was an eight-year CC veteran. When she shook my hand, she was jittery and uncomfortable, and her smile seemed forced and fake. It was all teeth and head nods. When she finished her sentences, she laughed nervously. Maybe it was the result of the large coffee on her desk. Maybe it was anxiety. We'd just met, so I didn't rush to final judgment.

Lou told me later how Natalie had a recent run of awful luck in her professional and personal life. When Lou was hired,

Natalie was supposed to be leaving for an internal promotion within the college, but was passed over and forced to stay on as office manager in the Student Accounting department. She had no interest in staying, but since her fiancé had left her, she had to. I'd noticed her hand was vacant of a wedding or engagement ring; apparently, she recently ditched the one she had. Her fiancé had cleaned out her bank account and maxed out her credit cards while they were together, and then decided to leave her for a Commonwealth student. She had taken the news understandably hard, and when I had the pleasure of meeting her, she was at her desk for the first time after a ten-day leave of absence.

This would be my environment from nine to five, Monday through Friday, and these were the people who'd filled it. I was now a financial advisor, and I'd take phone calls from parents and students regarding their financial status with the school. When I called Terry from my desk, he told me my professional title would play nicely with Fitzgerald's talent over Thanksgiving.

My cubicle was soon decorated with pictures of my family and a panoramic of Buffalo's downtown skyline to accompany my Red Sox calendar on one of the four beautiful gray walls. My nameplate was attached with Velcro on the outside of the cube. Every day, I would see that as an indicator that I'd reached adulthood. Supposedly.

On my morning calls, parents and students would use me as

the punching bag for their frustrations, just like Lou predicted. I got a call one day from a father in Chicago.

"Why do I pay thirty-six grand for my kid to go to your school? Do you know how expensive rent is in Boston? I could have her living in an apartment on Lake Michigan for four hundred-a-month!"

Another day, I took a call from a freshman who thought our office had the ability to give her more money for tuition. We weren't the financial aid department, but she continued to vent.

"I was an honor student in high school last year. Almost straight A's every quarter! So why won't this school give me more aid? I actually had to sell back all fourteen of my Beatles discs just so I could buy books today, and the prick at the record shop only gave me three dollars for *The White Album* because it didn't have the goddamn booklet inside. Three dollars!"

There were other days my adulthood consisted of eight hours of e-mail to friends or phone calls to my mother, sisters and brother. We talked about home, and I tried to give them each a description of my daily responsibilities. I delivered the most euphemistic explanation I could conjure, mentioning the opportunities I had to help students and parents with their financial questions and issues. At the end of the description, I reminded them how I'd be going to grad school real cheap. That momentarily quelled their confusion, but Frank still seemed disturbed that I was wasting my time in a customer service position, no matter what my bullshit title was. He knew I could be doing better; in the back of my head, maybe I did too. But, my doubts were squelched daily as I surfed the Internet to read fifteen or twenty publications and websites to pass the time between abusive and agitated phone calls concerning the hard-earned money pumped into CC.

I also made calls to Duff and Terry to hear about any news at Fitzgerald's or Doherty's. Duff told me he met this amazing brunette named Kiley Donlan at the jukebox of Doherty's. I talked to Terry later and he confirmed how gorgeous she was, a petite Irish girl who'd grown up in South Buffalo and had moved home after graduating from Ithaca College. Duff started talking to her after he watched her slide a dollar in the slot and select U2's "Trip Through Your Wires." She said the song was her soundtrack, and played in her head as she walked down the sidewalks around her parents' house on McKinley Avenue. He said they had a date later in the week. I was happy for my friend, but it gave me one of my many opportunities in that first few weeks of work to think about Johanna Darcy. Duff had met a girl with her own soundtrack. With this consideration, my reminiscing about the past didn't seem wasteful.

When I reached adulthood, I thought my days would be swimming in relevance, spent efficiently, not wastefully. I never thought I'd spend my weekday mornings scanning ESPN.com, the *Boston Globe, New York Times, Buffalo Gazette, Boston Herald, Chicago Tribune* and the *San Francisco Chronicle*—all before lunchtime. At twenty-two, I didn't think the highlight of my day would be an e-mail forward from my old roommate Vince Petrocelli, detailing the "25 Ways You Know You're Not In College Anymore." I assumed I would be such a vital cog wherever I was working that I wouldn't have any time for such waffling. Maybe there were young professionals yearning for a fast-forward button through their days, but I wasn't one of them. Even though I had zero interest in the long-term benefits of being a financial advisor, I still wanted to be a valued employee while securing my graduate degree. Instead, most of my time was spent absorbing complaints about student fees and meal plans as I watched minutes fly off my computer clock.

So this was post-college adulthood? I guess I expected more after watching my father operate throughout my existence. I never wondered once what he felt like every morning when he arrived at school, and I never questioned whether setting his briefcase down on his desk made him feel like an adult. I never asked if he counted down the minutes on the classroom clock until the end of his day. He never wore a watch, so I assumed it wasn't an issue. Even when he pulled the Miss Buffalo into dock at the Erie Basin Marina at the end of his night, I never speculated whether he felt a sense of accomplishment. He never gave me a reason to. He never came home from work complaining about how he had to grade the stack of test papers that sat in front of him on the kitchen table. He never once whined about a rowdy Hot Singles Night on the boat, how it was so out of control that at least a dozen drunken passengers puked all over the front deck. He'd simply walk in the door with a smile on his face, take care of his family, and then maybe pour a can of Genesee into a tall pilsner glass before correcting those papers or telling us how long it took him to help hose off the vomit. I never asked him if he felt fulfilled in his job because he never let on that he was yearning for fulfillment through his employment. He never gave us a reason to suspect he was unsatisfied in any other faction of his life either.

I wished I had an answer to these questions. I got to work every morning before nine and walked out nights after five. I rarely left the Student Accounting office feeling more adult-like than I did in college months before. I felt like I was wasting time, but I'd taken the job for the reasons Lou and I had talked about. People who want to delve into a creative field have to earn a living while they try to get paid for what will truly fulfill them. But I had grown up with my father. After watching his life unfold, I'd assumed my life would be as seamless as his. Maybe even easier.

As I struggled through office monotony, I tried to stay positive and patient. I'd take my GRE and apply for graduate school soon, so that process would divert some of my stresses. I stockpiled alternative weeklies from my daily commute, and I'd soon query their editors with some column ideas. These side commitments helped me tolerate the gray walls around my mornings.

Maybe simpler pleasures were what kept my father

perpetually positive. The sight of my mother's smiling face in our kitchen mashing potatoes might have sustained him during the mundane professional periods. Throwing a football to his two sons on our front lawn might have made him forget about the test papers, hot singles and endless vomit. I wanted to call the old man for answers, but since our standoff continued, I held firm. Instead, I tried a shot at self-improvement to take my mind off those questions through the end of August and into the beginning of September. I decided to quit smoking after Lou told me how it would expedite the Irish hairline I feared I'd be inheriting from the Cahans or McNamaras, and I relieved the oral fixation by chewing sunflower seeds. As I spent my days spitting seed shells into an empty Gatorade bottle, I decided to continue my makeover and purchase a cell phone. I used to think cell phones were only for sophisticated businessmen or Zach Morris on *Saved by the Bell*. None of my friends owned one, but near graduation, phones were becoming much more prevalent on the ears of girls walking across the St. Francis campus. Vince Petrocelli was the first person I knew to buy one, and he predictably called me to brag about it.

In Boston, I watched college girls, businessmen and even Lou on their phones. It was cheaper than having a phone in our apartment and, since Eli smoked a joint and fell asleep most nights he was around, it was a more reliable answering machine than he was. I missed countless messages from home during my first few weeks in town, so I bought the cell Lou recommended and joined the communication revolution.

On most days, I didn't bother bringing my phone to lunch when Lou and I would go grab a pizza at DiMarzio's, a cheap dive on Commonwealth Avenue. I tried to explain how Boston pizza couldn't contend with the slices I had grown up with, but Lou had never had a thick and perfectly greasy piece of Buffalo pizza. A large pizza at DeMarzio's cost only ten dollars, so I accepted his unfamiliarity and enjoyed saving some money on some decent slices. When we ordered, we'd talk with their lanky cashier named Dell. He wore a DiMarzio's mesh hat off to the side, a grease-stained green polo, and always sidled up to the register with the same greeting.

"What up, playas?"

Lou would always reply with,

"Living, Dell, living."

"Ah-right, ah-right. You keep living, Louie."

Dell was always the happiest and most laid-back guy we'd encounter on any given day. His greeting would make us feel at ease. He was working as a cashier at a sweaty pizza joint, but he seemed to be delighted with his position. We worked and whined in an air-conditioned office all day, so his demeanor gave us some perspective—if only for the duration of our lunch. When our pie came up one day, we slid into a booth before Lou bounced around a story idea he'd been working on for an upcoming film class.

"What do you think of this one: There's this guy, Tommy,

and he's an out-of-work actor at the end of his rope. Guy's got no money, bills are piling up, and after another unsuccessful audition, he's ready to give up for good."

"Okay," I said, pizza grease dripping down my chin. "Then what?"

"Then, a producer approaches him with an idea. He says he'll pay him twenty grand for the rights to his digital image, so Tommy signs off without even asking what the producer plans on doing with it, man."

"Digital image? What the fuck are you talking about?"

"Oh, uh, yeah," he said. "In the future, Hollywood won't need as many actors as they do today, and they'll be able to use someone's digital image to replace small roles in movies or actors in commercials and will control all their movements with a computer. When Tommy sells his image, he doesn't realize his image will be used as a leading man."

"So what happens?"

"Tommy's image becomes more successful than he ever dreamed he'd be as an actual actor, and he has no choice but to pretend to the public that he's actually been doing the acting. It tears him up inside, so he asks a director for a chance to play it straight for just one role."

"And?"

"He tries, can't do it, and the director ends up replacing him with his digital image. When he ends up winning an Oscar for a role he couldn't play, he finally realizes that the digital him has overtaken the real him."

"So? What does he do?"

"Shoots himself," he said, then shoved a half a slice into his mouth. "Backstage at the Oscars, man. What do you think?"

"Morbid, but it's an ending."

I tried to avoid venting about crazy students or parents when Lou ran out of new script ideas. It was lunchtime away from the office, so we tried to leave the downside of internal operations right where they percolated. Some of the time, this necessitated focusing on of our office's upside—such as attractive female students we helped at the office's front counter.

"Cahan, man. Spanish girl came in for a balance inquiry today," he said. "She was a dead ringer for Salma Hayek, man, but she was wearing a goddamn black beret. Not kidding. Accent, eyes, and this goofy French beret tilted off to the left. Actually gave me this long look before she left. You know, kind of to entice. But, honestly, the beret was kind of a turn-off. Sexy as she was, I just couldn't get past the fact that she actually went into a store and said, 'I'll take that black beret, please.'"

"Was she better looking than Sophia?"

"I don't know if any girl at this school can match Sophia, if you handicap it. How unbelievable she is now, taking into consideration her age? She must have been fucking deadly when she was our age. I can't even imagine."

These conversations would always revert back to Sophia. The bar was always set at her allure when talking about CC's other women. No student would ever clear it. She was in her own category not only in our office, but in the entire school. Her genuine charm and consideration of everyone around her enhanced her value even more. She always offered me help, and with her sultry Spanish accent, I'd sometimes ask her questions just to hear the reply roll off her tongue.

"Oh Joseph, sweetie," she'd say before gently touching my shoulder with her tanned fingers. "You need any help with these parents, you let me know. Some days, they really make me angry too."

When she talked, she'd look into my eyes with her burning Spanish browns. With the continued good health of my family and friends, along with a plea for daily guidance toward opportunities much bigger and better than the ones I was existing through at Commonwealth College, I prayed to God that I'd be fortunate enough to one day wake up next to a woman as breathtaking as Sophia. She didn't necessarily have to be Spanish, but when I'd look into my wife's eyes, I hoped to have the tight feeling in my chest induced by Sophia's stunning glare.

When Lou and I ran out of Sophia opinions, we could always discuss Porsche's Funyon dining over the latest copies of *People* and *US Weekly* while she talked with her boyfriend loud enough for me to hear two cubes away. One morning, she yelled at him for the previous night, when he came home drunk and fell asleep on the couch watching the Celtics' game. On another, she screamed about her birthday and how she didn't care whether his

Jamaican customs prevented him from giving her a big gift or not.

"You in America now, dirty!" she said before hanging up her cell and slamming it on her desk. She came over to my desk and apologized after this argument.

"See, Joe, I'm a Christian woman. I don't like acting like this, but that man! Oh, that man! He make me so crazy!"

If we had to call in sick to work, we'd have to call Porsche's desk. She was responsible for reporting the attendance to Natalie, so if I had to call Porsche's phone in the morning, the following message would play:

Hello. You've reached the voicemail of Porsche Bennett in the Student Accounts office of Commonwealth College. I'm either on another line or away from my desk at the moment, so if you could please leave a message, I'll get back to you as soon as possible. And remember: If you're happy, tell your face, because the joy of the Lord is your strength!

While listening to daily verbal beatings of her passive boyfriend, I always wondered how the joy of the Lord factored into her calling him, "dirty."

When Lou and I had absolutely run out of anything to talk about, we'd reluctantly discuss Natalie, who seemed to be toeing a complete emotional meltdown. If she heard me debating with a student or parent over tuition or fees, she'd race into my cube, frantically waving her hands.

"Joseph! Joseph!" she'd say in a stern whisper. "Don't raise your voice! Calm! Calm!"

There wasn't any real argument taking place, but she'd still stand over me, motioning for me to lower my voice to a veritable hush. She always ended her exchanges with this forced smile, exposing remnants of red lipstick on tightly clenched teeth. It always seemed she'd collapse from the mere effort exerted to hold those choppers in place.

I once asked Lou if he'd ever seen her ex-fiancé. When he asked why, I said,

"Because, the way she acts toward me, I'm convinced I must look like the guy."

Finally, on the odd day or two per week Mr. Davis and I crossed paths, I got to laugh about how he still called me "Cagan." Lou and I bitched about how he only communicated with the staff through e-mail, even though his office door was so close, each of us could hit it with one of Porsche's empty orange soda bottles. I'd see him waddle past my desk in a wrinkled white dress shirt and a tie knotted tight around his protruding neck, but he rarely stopped to say anything.

I told Lou about my most uncomfortable encounter with Mr. Davis over one of our lunches. I entered the men's bathroom one day and opened the door to a putrid and ungodly stench coming from the single stall. The smell joined groans and splashes, forcing me to grab my shirttail with my free hand to cover my mouth and nose as I stood at an empty urinal. I tried to finish quickly, but as I stood at the sink feverishly washing my hands, the stall door swung open. Out came Mr. Davis, giving a thankful sigh while tucking in his shirttail and fastening his belt.

"Mr. Cagan," he said, apparently unaware of the cataclysmic pollution he'd subjected me to. "Another sunny day out there today, huh? You must be relieved to be away from Buffalo, right?"

"You bet," I said, rushed. To save myself from suffocation, I spared Mr. Davis of delivering another meteorology lesson. In return, he had stripped himself of any sort of intimidation he'd ever have over me as an employee. I'd never look at him the same again.

"Man," Lou said with a grimace. "Don't ever tell me a story like that again when there's food in my hand, or soda in my mouth. Chances are I'll drop the pizza 'cause I'm not hungry anymore, or shoot the drink out of my nose because the story's so hilarious."

Still, I remained an optimist throughout the monotony, uncertainty and general unpleasantness of my first month of salaried employment. If things didn't become tolerable, at least I'd found a place in Boston that had decent pizza. Maybe there were catalytic events that evened out my father's life that would soon even out mine, events even more important than finding good pizza. Before I was born, maybe my father dealt with annoyances and discouragements before he acquired the disposition I hoped to one day duplicate or augment. It was only August, and maybe things would change in September.

16

I walked into my cube on a September morning and set my shoulder bag and a folded newspaper on my desk. It was just after nine o'clock, and as I sifted through my pockets to find some quarters for coffee, I turned around to see Natalie.

"Um, uh, Joseph? You're two minutes late. Do you think you could try to be on time tomorrow, please?" She smiled to reveal a small smudge of lipstick on her teeth.

"I'm sorry, Natalie. Train was a little late. It won't happen again."

"Thank you."

I dismissively shook my head once she was a safe distance away. I was two minutes late. Before I walked to the kitchen for coffee, I was stopped by Sophia's voice over my cube wall.

"Um, they just said on the radio that a plane flew into one of the Twin Towers in New York City," she said. "It's on fire, but they're not too sure what's going on."

"That's strange. Do you want a cup of coffee?"

"No thanks, sweetie. I want to stay here and find out what's going on."

I walked out the door to find Lou, who pulled his headphones off as I told him the news.

"Did you hear a plane flew into one of the Twin Towers in New York? Just happened."

"How could a pilot's flight pattern be so messed up that he doesn't notice those towers right in front of him?"

"No clue, but I have to go grab a coffee. Let me know if you hear of anything else."

I filled my St. Francis University mug and stirred in two sugars and one cream before the kitchen door flung open with Lou on the other side. Out of breath from sprinting down the hallway, he exclaimed,

"Man, you gotta get back to your desk. Some crazy shit's going on and everyone's freaking out. Eli called from our apartment and said a second plane just bombed into the other tower. They're saying on television that this isn't an accident; they think these fucking planes were hi-jacked."

With my coffee spilling over my mug's rim, I ran down the hallway and into our office to see everyone standing at Sophia's desk, listening to her radio. Porsche and Sophia held their mouths as Porsche slipped in an "Oh Jesus, oh Jesus" every few seconds. Natalie stood with her hands folded at her waist, eyes even wider now than they'd been in past weeks. There was no television in our office, so Lou and I leaned against the entrance of Sophia's cube, focused on the radio anchor's surreal description emanating from small desktop speakers. The anchor's frantic tone caused my thoughts to wander back to my parents' living room on Halloweens when I was a kid.

Every year, Buffalo news personalities would do a local radio show to reenact the Orson Wells classic, *War of the Worlds*. The anchors would do an entire fake news report on how the city of Buffalo was under attack by aliens, and each was trapped in the battle. City Hall in Niagara Square was on fire and aliens had flown space ships into Memorial Auditorium, trapping the Sabres inside. It was so scary that my mother had to reassure Molly and me.

"It's all make-believe," she'd say as we sat shaken in front of the stereo speakers, with local news anchor Irv Weinstein screaming about our city's alien invasion.

Lou and I stood stoic. The news coming out of Sophia's speakers was so sensational and unbelievable, it had to be a joke. This isn't really happening, I thought. But the anchor's voice was so panic-stricken that, if he was acting, he was doing an Oscar-worthy job.

My hands began to shake with each new detail. My stomach was so tight I clenched it with my right hand. My mind was dazed, unable to grasp the situation's magnitude. I had gotten off the train a half hour earlier, a newspaper folded underneath my left arm. My main concern was Natalie and her lipstick-stained teeth, waiting to scold me for catching the creeping Green Line so late. That insignificant issue would be the last annoyance I'd fear before every American's life would change drastically.

I continued to stand in a mental haze until the sound of my desk phone ringing shook me back to coherence.

"Joseph Cahan."

"Joseph, it's your mother," she said. "Are you okay? They said on the news that one of the planes came from Boston."

"I think, I, I don't know. What's going on now? We don't have a television here."

"It's horrible, Joseph," she said, her voice noticeably shaking. "They're saying another plane was flown into the Pentagon as well. The Twin Towers are on fire; smoke's streaming from their windows. I was watching as they reported on the first plane, and as the camera focused on the first tower, another plane flew right into the second. I haven't been able to get the picture out of my head, and they keep showing it over and over again."

"Are you okay?"

"I'll be fine, hon. I've been praying the rosary in the kitchen ever since it happened. Do you have those rosary beads I gave you, or are they in your car?"

"The car."

"Well, pray just the same, Joseph. I don't know what's going on right now, but a lot of people need our prayers."

"Where's dad?"

"School. They're all pretty shaken up over there. The teachers are watching the television news with their students as this all unfolds. Have you called your friends in New York?

Vince? What about Johanna? She probably knows some people in all of this."

"Yeah, Mom. Yeah."

I couldn't think clearly about anything. As I drifted, I heard my mother screaming.

"Oh my God! Oh my God!"

"Mom! Mom, are you okay? What's going on?"

"Joseph, people are jumping from the tower windows. They're jumping to get out of the building. Oh my God, why is this happening?" she said, then began to cry.

"Mom, it's okay. Settle down, please."

I wasn't sure if I'd ever heard my mother this startled before. She was usually the steady head of our family, but I could envision her at our house as she sat on the other line, tears slipping reluctantly down her face, her lips clenched tight as she shook her head in disbelief at the television with her extra set of green rosary beads held tight in her folded hands. These thoughts rolled and a tear snuck out of my eye. I was stunned any emotion could sneak through in my shocked state.

"Mom, please calm down. Are you sitting down?"

"Yes, yes. I'm sitting."

"Can you call Grandpa to come over there?"

"He's on the way over right now. He was coming over for lunch anyway, so," she said, then stopped talking. "Oh, that's your grandfather at the door. I'm gonna let you go, okay?"

"Okay. I'll call later to check on you, alright?"

"Alright, honey. Just pray, and call your friends in New York right away. I love you, Joseph."

"Love you too, Ma."

I tried to remain calm while settling my mother. I didn't let the shudder down my spine affect the tone of my voice after she mentioned Vince. I knew he worked in the Financial District, but I didn't know how close to the towers. As soon as I hung up with my mother, I dialed Vince's cell phone, but got his voicemail. I dialed again, but got the voicemail for a second time. I wanted to hear his voice to know he was alive, so I didn't bother to leave a message. If he wasn't, he'd never hear it anyway.

My heart dropped when my mother mentioned Johanna. The thought of her being there never crossed my mind; I didn't know if she was teaching in Manhattan. She could have been with students on a field trip around the towers. What if she was within the general vicinity of those buildings as that explosion happened? I had no idea, nor was my head ready to contemplate such a scenario.

I hadn't talked with Johanna since graduation, but I called her anyway. I had to know immediately if she was okay so the grim reality being broadcast wasn't about to decimate me. My mind raced toward pessimism; when Johanna didn't pick up her phone, my thoughts stayed there. Three rings took me to her voicemail, but I felt compelled to leave a message. The thoughts of never seeing her again were too dominating not to stammer through something.

"Johanna, Johanna, it's Joe. Cahan. God, um, please call me when you get this, if you get this. Jesus. I don't know where you are, what you're doing. I should've called you weeks ago, months ago. God, please be okay, please be okay. I need to hear you're all right, wherever you are, so please call me when you get this. 617-555-1283. Bye."

After I hung up, I turned around in my chair to see Lou at my cube entrance.

"Cahan, you okay, man?"

"Yeah, yeah," I said.

"You hear about the Pentagon, man? They hit that too. This is the most fucked up day of my life, and it's not even noon yet."

I got up from my chair to walk toward him.

"Lou, I know you don't, but I need a smoke."

"To be honest, man, I could use one myself right about now."

We walked to a convenience store across the street from our offices. Once inside, you could hear the local news blaring from the radio behind the counter. The reports echoed throughout the store. The few people there wandered the aisles aimlessly, looking as helpless and confused as Lou and I felt. They picked items off shelves, shook their heads or stared at the ceiling and walls, sighing with worry as every new detail unfolded. After we glanced around at this scene, we went right to the counter to find an elderly woman with white hair and a red apron. She looked as vulnerable as her customers.

"Camel Lights, please," I said.

"Hard or soft pack, dear?"

"Lady," I said, then paused. I put both hands on the counter and leaned forward to look directly into her weathered eyes. "I'll take whatever you have by your hand."

I felt a hand on my right shoulder. When it stayed there, I was so numb I didn't even flinch. I slowly turned around to look down and see another older woman, short with white hair and large, plastic glasses.

"Did you know someone in New York or Washington, hon?" she said.

"My friend from college and this girl. Neither is answering their phone. I figure the cigarettes will keep my hands from shaking for a few minutes. They haven't stopped since I was sent into their voicemail."

"Take these, dear," said the cashier, holding out a hard pack of Camel Lights. "The box is better for packing the tobacco. Here are some matches too."

"How much?"

"No charge. Just take them and keep calling your friends. I'm sure they'll answer soon, dear."

"Of course they will," said the small woman behind me, her hand still placed sympathetically on my shoulder. "I'm sure they're fine."

Once outside, I packed the box and pulled out two smokes for us. Lighting each, I sucked on mine with my eyes fixed to the sky. I had a view of both the Prudential and John Hancock buildings down Commonwealth Avenue. I looked toward their tops and feared I'd soon see the Manhattan scene my mother described. They were Boston's tallest buildings, and with news growing more ominous on the radio, it sounded like every major U.S. city with a large building may be a target. If two planes could crash through New York skyscrapers, they could easily coast into two unobstructed towers like the Hancock or Pru.

"I've never been so shook up in my life, man," said Lou. "This reminds me of the time I was at this Phish show in Maine, with like over a hundred-thousand people, and the crowd started caving in on me. I couldn't move, couldn't breathe, and then I realized I was in the middle of a hundred-thousand fucking people and there was no way out. Nothing I could do."

"So what did you do?"

"Completely flipped out, man. I started hyper-ventilating, and my fucking heart was thumping out of my chest. I got down on all fours in the middle of the crowd and stuck my finger down my throat so I could throw up. Thought it would give me some clarity, but it just made me dehydrated and freaked me out more."

"So how did you escape?"

"The guy whose room you took, Sniff. He pulled me out. I hate the guy now, but he saved my life that day. He dragged me through the whole crowd yelling that I was having an acid flashback. I was fine once I got some space and fresh air, but

I've been claustrophobic ever since, man."

"I feel like my chest is caving in right now, and this smoke isn't helping matters. But I definitely see your correlation. I feel trapped, too."

Lou's example was appropriate. We exchanged troubled looks with every person who passed, expressions of confusion between individuals who had no answer for what was happening. A young college student walked past in jeans and a green t-shirt, talking frantically into her cell phone. Another girl walked behind her in a similar conversation, tears streaming from beneath her sunglasses. As I looked toward the sky between drags, I noticed drivers doing the same, rolling along with their heads out the window to look skyward for the next piece to fall. At that time, on that day, everyone's words and thoughts were on the same topic. We were individuals figuring out our own ways of dealing with news so distressing that we were longing for someone, anyone, to come along and drag us to open space for air.

I still hadn't heard back from Vince or Johanna, so negative thoughts kept strangling any positive ones. For every thought I had of Vince on his other line, there was another of him in a nearby building, engulfed in fire and begging for his life. No matter how hard I fought them, the thoughts kept seeping in with the nicotine.

For every thought I had of Johanna's phone turned off or buried in her purse, there was another more alarming fear that made my hand holding the cigarette shake. I thought of her standing near the explosions, gone before I could ever speak with her again, before I could apologize for never helping her the way I wished I could have. I couldn't stop my head from projecting this possibility, no matter how unlikely it was.

I got back to my cube to see my cell phone vibrate with a message. When I heard the message's voice, I could dismiss one of my feared outcomes.

Cahan, dude, it's Vince. Saw your number on my caller ID, so I wanted to tell you I'm okay. My alarm never went off this morning, woke up late, and I wasn't even out my door before this shit started. If you believe this, I had a meeting with a client in the first tower this morning. If I didn't oversleep, we might not be talking right now. If you need to get hold of me, I'll be at St. Patrick's Cathedral, thanking God. Later.

"Was that the girl?" said Lou.

"Naw; my buddy Vince. He slept in and missed a meeting in the first tower."

"Holy fuck. Is he on his way to church right now? If that was me, I would've dropped to my knees right then and there, man, saying novena after novena."

"That makes two of us. I just wish Johanna would call me so this torture could end."

"Tell you what, man. I'll go talk with Natalie, tell her you're losing your mind and I'll get you out of here. She should understand that."

"Thanks, Lou."

Natalie surprisingly understood and let us leave for the day. I called Johanna on our way home and got her voicemail again. I didn't leave another message, but instead walked into our apartment and stretched out on our living room couch. Lou walked over to Sagliano's and got us a large pizza and a six-pack of Budweiser as I lay there, phone clutched in my hand.

"It's not DiMarzio's," he said. "But, with the beers, it'll do."

The pizza was terrible, but my stomach was so anxious that nothing would have felt good sitting in it anyway. The beer went down slowly as my phone remained silent. The television was on for updates, as every station was showing coverage of the disaster. Each station had a different reporter on the scene in New York, Washington, and on the site where another plane went down in Pennsylvania. Each relayed the same unbelievable information and images we'd been hearing about all day.

Lou and I stared in disbelief when we saw footage of each tower go from a billowing inferno to a cloud of rubble. The scene caused me to put my phone down on our coffee table and pace our hallway. My stomach was a wreck, and sitting on the couch simply folded the anxiety inside. I stepped into the kitchen to find a cigarette and solace away from the television—until

Lou yelled to me from the living room.

"Cahan, your phone's vibrating. Number on the ID says unavailable."

I left my cigarette in the ashtray by the window and ran down the hallway to answer my moving phone. The respondent voice quelled what I had feared most.

"Cahan?" she said. "I got your message. Are you okay?"

"Thank God. Where are you?"

"Brooklyn. I'm teaching third graders at a small charter school here, but they've all been sent home for the day because of this. It's just, um, it's, um." She paused for a few seconds. "I can't even describe what I've seen here today."

"Are you okay? God, I've been worried sick all morning."

"I could see the whole thing from my classroom window. Everything. When the first tower was hit, we could see the smoke. The poor kids were looking out the window when the second plane hit, and that's when parents started calling and coming to school to pick them up. When the towers began to fall, I started to cry with some other teachers in my classroom. Some of them have family working over there they can't find or contact. One woman's husband is a firefighter, and when she called the firehouse, they said he was down there. It's just, my God—"

She burst out crying, sniffing and wailing worse than I pictured my mother sobbing earlier. I felt helpless to everything going on around us that entire day. I was helpless to stop

Johanna's tears from streaming down her face in Brooklyn. All I could do was hang on the line with her and try to console with whatever faith or hope I had.

And, that amount of hope increased once I heard her voice.

17

The dream was different.

I wasn't chasing the buffalo around my Southtowns neighborhood, and I didn't hear the stampede off in the distance. I saw the streets void of passing cars or walking students as I stepped off the Green Line, the same way I stepped off it every other morning. I scanned the closed storefronts and empty sidewalks, and walked up a vacant and barren Commonwealth Avenue. I expected the beast to be there, waiting for a chase up the avenue and past the creeping rail cars. But there was nothing. There was no buffalo to chase, and as I stood alone in the middle of the street, an outbound bus sped toward me beeping its horn rhythmically,

BEEP. BEEP. BEEP. BEEP.

I slapped the snooze alarm and awoke to another morning of confusion. Since this dream was void of the reoccurring attraction, the puzzlement multiplied. I was running late for work. It would be another day of fascinating financial advising, but after the events of that horrific September morning, every day had added anxiety. There was the ever-present chance that every morning's Green Line ride would be my last. The nonchalant looks on T riders' faces had been replaced with worry. There was the omnipresent possibility that someone on our train was riding with a bomb strapped to their chest or tucked in their bag, and there wasn't anything anyone could do about it. There was a chance our lives were being sacrificed to jobs or classes we didn't need or want, and the opportunity to lead an ideal life was gone because our assumed security had vanished. Those thoughts would simmer every day right after the T doors closed. Concern was revealed with a bitten lip or wandering eye.

But, with the worry was also camaraderie. We were all united in something for the first time. I saw a young lawyer with a cell phone at his ear show compassion toward an older woman in a Red Sox cap, offering her his seat even though he needed to sit and scribble notes. He'd write later—maybe. I watched a snobbish-looking Harvard librarian put down her Ayn Rand novel for three stops to talk to a weary, yet gregarious construction worker holding his hard hat in the seat next to her. They led different lives, but in those weeks, each of theirs might expire on the same ride.

When the train would stop, passengers who exited together continued their conversations. They'd talk about something as banal as the weather or as intricate as the Red Sox on-base percentage. Each conversation was a sigh of relief, a second chance for so many self-absorbed and narcissistic people to realize the companionable nature inside themselves. What once was considered mindless chatter was treated as essential banter between complete strangers. They might never speak again, but they continued speaking anyway. They were alive, and each stashed their interest in investigating the relevance of selfless kindness.

I treated every day after those attacks as a second chance, too. Grudges needed to be squashed; relationships needed to be rehabilitated. Regret was something I'd have to live with, but I wanted to limit it. I never wanted to be on a train with thoughts of what I should have done or said rolling through my head as I breathed my last breath. With this in mind, I made two calls following that September morning.

First, I called Norton Drive to talk to Patrick Cahan. I didn't care if he said a word. I didn't care if he hated the idea of me being in Boston, New York City, or anywhere outside Greater Buffalo. I didn't care if he thought I was abandoning my family, my city and my roots by taking my life to another area code. And I wasn't interested in making him understand the reasons for what I was doing. I wanted to break the Cahan code for once and step into sappy, emotional territory. I wanted to tell my father, "thank you."

I wanted to thank him for everything he ever gave me, including my strong, Irish name. I wanted to thank him for taking me to my first Bills game when I was six years old and for lending me his first Beatles album when I was eight. I wanted to thank him for his advice and the advice passed down from my

Grandpa Cahan. I wanted to thank him for Friday fish fries, beach days on Lake Erie, and teaching me to throw my first tight spiral in our front yard. I wanted to thank him for "Positively 4th Street." I wanted to thank him for being my father. And, when I did, I may have even said I loved him. Under any other circumstances, the expression would have induced mutual laughter. That day, it induced reluctant compromise.

"Do what you have to do," he said. "Finish school in Boston, go to California, go to—."

"Yeah? Go where?"

"Go to New York—if you have to. But then come back, dammit. Come home to Buffalo."

"Thanks, Dad."

"But if I ever see a Yankees hat in this house, so help me God."

"Deal, Dad. Deal."

I dialed Johanna Darcy for the second call. We still had our issues, but they needed to be cleared up. Our past turmoil wasn't enough to extinguish my feelings for her. As I wrote earlier, relationships are easy when life rolls smoothly. If one can continue while times are rough, there might be something there. During the worst day either of us had ever been through, we needed a faction of that relationship. In the days that followed, we needed our friendship.

She was involved with mothers, fathers and children directly affected that morning every day, and she needed someone to talk to who understood her disposition. She needed someone who knew how she always put others before herself, how she cared too much about her students. When they were hurting, she was hurting. I understood this, so in the hours we talked on the phone, I listened to her concerns.

I was subjected to afflicted faces every day in Boston, and I needed someone to talk to who understood my tendencies of over-analyzing every experience. I needed someone who knew how I was wired, how a self-proclaimed idealist would deal with this new pessimistic fear. I needed someone besides Lou to tell me why I was working in a student accounting office instead of covering local bands for the *Boston Phoenix* newspaper. I needed affirmation, clarity, and confidence. The sound of Johanna's voice gave these to me in abundance.

Family relationships were restored and a friend was recovered, but working inside my cubicle became increasingly constrictive. With my doubts about life being magnified every day, those walls around me grew grayer and taller. The carpet shaded darker, and the daily tasks became so meaningless, I needed constant reassurance from Lou at lunch or Johanna over the phone. Parent and student questions became so frustrating that, when my phone rang, I sometimes refused to answer it. Other times, I'd pick up the receiver and immediately hang up. I even figured out a way to pick up the phone and transfer the call into the Commonwealth switchboard so it would go to another phone in the office. On the rare occasion I was caught, it chipped away at the tentative relationships I was developing with my co-workers. With Porsche so close to my desk, she'd hear a call come in, my fingers press some buttons, then her phone would ring. I'd hear her adjust herself in her seat, put down a copy of *People* focused on J Lo's sexy exploits, and then mumble under her breath before picking it up.

The effect of added pressures and fears on any of our coworkers couldn't remotely compare to what they did to Natalie. Instead of taking the opportunity to reevaluate her life like many were doing, she absorbed the tragedy into her already loaded emotional psyche—exorcised her frustrations on me.

"Joseph, I just got a call from a parent who said he was treated very rudely by a man in this office who identified himself as George Styles. You wouldn't have given someone a fake name on a phone call, would you?"

I'd sit in my chair as she stood before me with those stained front teeth, clenched to magnify the meaninglessness of my position. I should have been doing something else, something more. This couldn't be what life was about, with bosses yelling and pointing and every bit of daily labor chipping away at my body's overflow of ambition. It wasn't, and with a piece of DiMarzio pizza once again flopping greasily in my hand on a cool day in October, I sat across from Lou with these revelations.

"Don't you think our lives would be more fulfilling if we were helping sick kids read or working for a non-profit? I mean, how does this job not make you feel absolutely empty inside?"

Lou looked at me for a second, then shoved half his piece of pizza into his mouth.

"I don't get you, man," he said. "I know this job is soulless, but you'll be going to classes in the spring to satisfy this emptiness. Don't you believe we're all meant to do something?"

"Sure I do, but—"

"Do you know how Harrison Ford became an actor?"

"What? No."

"I read that when George Lucas approached him to be in American Graffiti, Ford turned him down because he was making more money as a construction worker than he would have made to act in that movie."

"So?"

"So?" He threw down his slice. "So if Ford would have stayed a construction worker, who plays Han Solo? Who plays Indiana Jones? Jack Ryan? Henry, in Regarding Henry?"

"What's your point, Lou?"

"My point is that people do things every day to bide their time before their opportunity to do what they were meant to do comes around. You think yours is writing, right?"

"You know I do."

"Well, you have to have some patience, man. Have some patience with this scum job until you can do what you were meant to do. Ford was meant to act, you're meant to write."

I pulled a sip off my sixteen-ounce paper cup of cola.

"And what if I'm not?" I said. "What if I wake up tomorrow

and I'm Mr. Davis, wearing wrinkled short-sleeved shirts to work, calling people by the wrong name and annihilating the bathroom?"

"Would you rather wake up tomorrow and regret giving up? Regret not giving grad school a shot? C'mon, man. I know we've only known each other for a few months, but in that short time, I've seen you tie up these loose ends with your family and friends to avoid the same regret that would be gnawing at you if you quit this. You called your old man to thank him for everything he's ever given you, and that made you feel good, right?"

"Yeah."

"Then you called this girl of yours after not knowing where she was during the attacks freaked the shit out of you. You eliminated the chance of regret with those two. Don't give regret a chance to seep in with this because it will. It will."

He shoved the rest of the slice into his mouth and stored the chewed pizza in the left side of his mouth so he could talk without dough remnants flying into my face.

"You have to learn," he said. "Work to live, man; don't live to work. Like Dell back there. He's living, seven days-a-week."

"Maybe I should get a job with him. Guy always seems stress-free."

"Slinging pizzas isn't gonna get you any closer to where you want to be, man. When you get through school, you'll see. Your life will be your work."

"And we'll enjoy it."

"Right on, man," he said, then raised his beverage. "We'll love what we do while the Natalies and Mr. Davises of the world continue their stroll down the road you fear. Let them go their way and you go yours. You'll be fine."

As a third grade school teacher, Johanna had a different perspective than Lou. She had cohesion in her life, as all hours of her days and nights were spent as a good teacher trying to be a great teacher. My days were spent waiting out Commonwealth shifts so I could go home to write, so I lacked this balance. Unlike the idealism Lou and I explored at DiMarzio's, Johanna was more practical. She suggested I look for another job if mine was mentally debilitating. She confirmed how my unfocused daily routine was probably causing my torment. She also stressed patience, but said patience would only be purposeful if I continued to focus on writing, even if I might never become a writer. In her first year as the teacher she always wanted to be, she doubted whether she could ever embark on such a path of uncertainty.

When we talked, she'd tell me about the papers she graded and the students she reprimanded. She had already devised and organized her lesson plans for the entire year. She seemed a stable guide for these impressionable third graders, and when we talked, I envied her position. I wished I had something else to offer her besides complaints about Natalie or struggles with a story I was editing.

"So what's the story about?" she said one night.

"Well, it's about this guy in his early twenties who's confused about his station in life. He struggles with the loss of past relationships, and he struggles adapting to his new surroundings until he finds the key to dealing with it all."

"So, it's about you?"

"What makes you say that? Because the guy's in his early twenties?"

"Cahan, what would you expect me to think? The topic of this story seems to encapsulate everything we've been talking about for the past few weeks on the phone. How dim do you think I am?"

"Well, maybe it's based on certain events, but it's not some sort of autobiography. I borrow from my own experiences, but this character is not me. Honest."

"So who's the girl from past relationships? Based on someone you know?"

"Maybe."

"Let me guess: red hair, fair skin, kind of crazy?"

I laughed.

"Hey, I have to write what I know, right?"

I gave another small laugh to match hers before we stopped, simultaneously. Five seconds passed with nothing said, but it wasn't an uncomfortable silence as much as a comfortable pause between two people who had things to say. I could feel her desire to speak almost a little more strongly than my own to disclose everything in my head, like thoughts about her, thoughts about a past that had put us on that phone call. I could only offer a brief line to properly consolidate my sentiments.

"I've missed this."

One. Two. Three. Four. Five.

"Me too," she said. "Me too."

"Remember senior year when you were student teaching? Getting up at six o'clock every day? I miss that feeling."

"What feeling?"

"The feeling of watching you leave—and knowing you'd be back."

I could only think of the days from a year earlier. I remembered the mornings with her, the ones I envisioned her as the girl who would leave me at home to write with the kids, drinking my Costa Rican coffee as the sun shines over Lake Erie and the city. Johanna Darcy was that girl at the start of senior year.

She was given her first semester student teaching assignment in a small town in Northern Pennsylvania, just south of Cuba. It was a twenty-five-minute drive for her in the morning, so with school starting at eight o'clock, she had to get up early to make it on time. I didn't have class until noon. Most of my required courses were completed by the time junior year had ended, so at noon, I had to breeze through classes like British and American Media, which required students to analyze and dissect such exotic fare as *Monty Python's Flying Circus*. It obviously wasn't that important. In contrast, Johanna's work was important. That semester, the two of us were on opposite schedules, doing completely different things while finding time to make it work.

We stayed at her place most nights. We'd fall asleep together, talking about her day at school. She would rest her elbow on the bed, red hair against her hand, and tell me how there was a little boy in her class, Malcolm, who wanted to be a professional dancer. When she tried to describe the dance, she'd break up laughing before apologizing for joking about Malcolm's passion behind his back. She'd tell me about Madeline, whose mother came into school to have a private conference with her and her supervising teacher. Madeline's father had been diagnosed with cancer, and as Johanna tried to explain the situation to me, she burst out crying. She had just begun a relationship with some of these children, but as with her job later in Brooklyn, she was taking on their problems and passions as her own.

When her alarm went off at six, I would grab a pillow to hold over my face. Her bedroom lights would come on, and the sun would start to slowly creep under her window shades. I would try to fall back asleep as she'd get ready for her day at school. She'd dry her hair, pull on a skirt and top, and gather all her books and binders into her shoulder bag before coming to the side of the bed. When she tapped me on the shoulder, I would pretend she was waking me up from a sound sleep, though I'd silently watched her whole routine.

She'd say, "I'm leaving now."

I'd say, "Have a nice day at school, dear."

And then we'd kiss. I'd rest my head back on the pillow, put my hands behind my head and watch her walk out of the room. A little wave and a bright smile and she'd close the door behind her to leave me with an unmistakable feeling warming my chest. It was like we were married. I felt like I was saying goodbye to my wife, and I loved it.

Those days waiting for Maureen O'Hara to walk off a movie screen and onto my doorstep were drifting away. I wasn't as interested in emulating the feelings interpreted by the Bogarts, Brandos or Beatles. I no longer hoped Bono wrote "Hawkmoon 269" specifically about the feelings I'd one day feel. That unrealistic idealism was replaced with actual emotion and scenery presented to me every morning before eight. An actual woman, beautiful and charming, alluring and electric, loved me. I experienced a lot of uncertainties in my daily life back then. How I felt about Johanna Darcy wasn't among them.

And I could never convince her of that.

But, when we started talking again in the months following that September morning, hope dawned for a second chance.

18

My desk calendar showed two weeks before Thanksgiving, and I still hadn't heard from Commonwealth College's Admissions Office.

I had submitted a large application packet of recommendations, short stories, poems, and my epic review of Sticky Fingers' St. Francis show a month earlier. According to Lou's friend in admissions, the office was buried and digging out was going to take some time. Since September eleventh, enrollment in creative graduate courses had dramatically increased, thus weakening my previous certainty I'd easily slide into my first classes spring semester. Art, music, film and creative writing classes were targeted by individuals who wanted to love their professional paths, no matter the monetary implications. Those people I'd seen on the train, ones afraid of wasting their time in jobs they hated, had done something about it. As I checked my e-mail that afternoon to see if I'd received a response from admissions, I was greeted by Natalie, who hung over the side of my cubicle holding the holiday vacation request I had left on her desk earlier that day.

Besides Christmas and Easter, Thanksgiving was the only day of the year Ann Cahan deviated from her six-item menu. Visions of her turkey, homemade stuffing, carrots, green beans, homemade gravy and the Cahan hand-mashed potatoes had sustained me through my nightly servings of macaroni and cheese. Since Commonwealth was closed for the holiday, I planned to drive home Wednesday afternoon, enjoy the feast on Thursday, then stay through the weekend to recover.

Aside from the meal, the annual Wednesday night before Thanksgiving was known to Buffalonians as Black Wednesday for the monumental drinking binges that ensued. It was a homecoming for everyone who'd left, back to be together under Springsteen's "Tenth Avenue Freeze Out" or the Allman Brother's "Ain't Wasting Time No More." In a given hour, I could see the first girl I'd ever kissed and the first guy I'd ever punched. I'd see the valedictorian of my St. Augustine senior class drinking the same crappy two-dollar Genesee pounder as a kid arrested junior year for stealing a teacher's car and smashing it into a light post in our school parking lot. It would also be my first time out with Duff and Terry since I left for Boston. We'd toast with Guinness, rotate rounds from Eddie the Bartender at Fitzgerald's, and probably finish the night off with chilled shots of Jameson.

Natalie had other ideas.

"Um, Joseph, this day you're asking off? I can't give it to you."

"Why?"

"Well, you have to be here for five months for your personal days to kick in, and you're only approaching your fourth."

"So I can't go home for Thanksgiving?"

"You can, but if you call in sick on Friday, I'll recommend to Mr. Davis that you be fired. I don't mean to be a—"

"That's fine, Natalie," I said before transitioning to a rude, sarcastic tone. "I didn't have any interest in seeing my family or friends this Thanksgiving anyway. I'll just get a pizza and a six-pack. Should be a night to remember, but I'll be sure it doesn't go too late. I wouldn't want to be two minutes late to sit here on Friday morning."

Natalie looked at me for a second before storming away toward the door. She didn't respond; she didn't gleam that fractured, fake smile. I was starting to get to her, and I wish that would've been consolation for having to miss Thanksgiving in Buffalo for the first time in my life.

On my walk home through Jamaica Plain after work that day, I strolled through the same types of empty Goya bottles, discarded Dorito bags and full bags of McDonald's garbage that greeted my walk every other day. Passing cars blasted bass-driven stereos, and parked cars' alarms activated as beats boomed from trunks of souped-up Accords and Civics. My festering stress and anger rose higher with every step.

I needed to hear something positive so I wouldn't snap. Thankfully, Eli called to tell me he and Lou were down at the Jeanie Johnston, ordering some chicken fingers and getting comfortable for Rockabilly Night with a few two-dollar bottles of High Life. Lou had told him about my day, so he knew I wasn't going home for Thanksgiving or Black Wednesday. He knew I needed a night out to keep my sanity.

I walked into the dank, dark interiors of the Jeanie Johnston to see the bar wasn't even half-full. The band hadn't even shown up yet, but I could see the empty performance space cleared in the corner. The faded oak bar and leather-cushioned stools were in the center of the barroom, with glasses hung upside-down above the taps. On the rear wall hung a framed and signed Carlton Fisk jersey, along with a framed picture of Larry Bird, Carl Yastremski and Bobby Orr. There was also a picture of Boston College legend Doug Flutie, scrambling as a Buffalo Bill to contrast all the locally-uniformed legends. Eli was at the bar with a pint of Guinness as Lou fed the juke's dollar slot. Eli waved when he saw me, but since he was the only one at the right side of the bar, the wave wasn't needed. When I found the empty stool he'd saved, I also found a full pint.

"Figured I'd order it early for you and let it settle at room temperature," he said with a smile and a slap to my back. I saddled up on the stool to clutch the pint, then took a healthy drink before putting it back on its coaster.

"How you feeling?" said Eli. "Lou said he thought you were

going to kill that woman in your office. Just strangle her and be done with it. But, I see you restrained yourself."

"Barely," I said. "Today was your classic bad day. I don't believe I'm going to be here for Thanksgiving with no one but you and Lou. No offense, but it's not what I had in mind."

"Um, about that. I'm going home for that weekend. So is Lou, but if you wanted to you could—"

"Unbelievable," I said. "I really am going to be eating a goddamn pizza from Sagliano's on Thanksgiving."

"I'm sorry, dude. I really am. But, hey, that pint's on me. I'll even buy you the next one, too."

I hadn't seen Eli in a while. His job installing medical software had kept him inside hospitals out of town, and weeks would go by where he wasn't around. He'd be across the country in Portland, over in Chicago, or down in Philadelphia and Washington, D.C. while Lou and I sat in Commonwealth cubes. Eli graduated with a history degree, so as I questioned my own situation, I wondered whether he was happy in his. If he wasn't, he never said so.

When he was home, he would either be asleep on the couch or in his room with the door locked. When I would knock to see if he was awake, I'd hear the song "Ripple" by the Grateful Dead and smell the same scent that penetrated our senior year apartment. Maybe that numbed him to the doubt that dominated me and occurred to Lou. Maybe he was just working to live. Whatever it was, his demeanor was always calmer than mine, his expectations more rational. When Lou told him about "that girl from school" I was talking to again, Eli was concerned. Since we hadn't talked for a while, he hadn't given his opinion about my revisiting possibilities with Johanna. He was there for everything that happened between us at St. Francis so, over pints of Guinness, he inquired.

"So you and Johanna are talking again?"

"Yeah, yeah. But no big deal. Just as friends."

"Friends?" He turned to face me. "Dude, I'm going to ask this as nice as I can, but did you forget senior year? If you didn't, I'm gonna have to ask you if you've lost your mind."

"Eli, look," I said, then turned left to face him. "I know what you're thinking, but—"

"Do you? Do you really?" He stood stern and confrontational, not exactly Eli's style. "What am I thinking?"

"That was just an expression. I really don't know what the fuck you're thinking."

"Well, here's what I'm thinking. I'm thinking of a friend of mine who had his mind screwed by a girl whose insecurities went batty senior year. I'm thinking of a friend of mine who tried everything imaginable to make her understand how he felt, and I'm thinking of a friend who was crushed when he couldn't convince her."

He paused for a moment, then continued.

"Now, I'm looking at this friend and thinking he must be some sort of a masochist, taking another shot in a game he's destined to lose."

One. Two. Three. Four. Five.

"Can I ask you something?" he said.

"Sure."

"You still think it's your fault, don't you? You still think all the drinking, all the drugs, all the problems she had senior year were your fault, don't you?"

"Why?"

"Because after what you went through with her, there'd be no reason to go back except guilt."

I took a large sip off my pint.

"What if it's not guilt?" I said. "What if it's regret?"

"Regret? Regret about what? About not doing everything you could to get her head straight? If that's it, stash it. I was there, dude, and you did everything you could. You were twenty-one years old. Unless your name is Doogie, that's too young to be a doctor. The girl had problems, and every single person at school seemed to realize that except for you."

"I guess I still don't. When I think of her, I don't think of the end. I don't think of the problems. I remember the beginning and the middle, the best parts."

"Hindsight is always twenty-twenty, Cahan."

"And that's how I've been looking at this. It's the only way I've been able to."

"Look, I'm your friend," he said. "As your friend, it's my duty to try to stop you from making a mistake."

"I appreciate that."

"But that's all I can do: try. As of now, I've done my job and my conscience is clean, dude. If you think you know better, go for it. Keep talking to her to exorcise this regret you fear will set in."

"I appreciate your concern, but I'd also appreciate if you could do me another favor."

"What's that?"

"Get me another pint," I said, then shook my empty glass at him. "I have to go make sure Lou's not playing all Willie Nelson songs."

And that was that. Eli said his piece, but he knew there was no use pushing things I was more than conscious of. Friends don't always listen to friends when it comes to relationships. He knew he'd be more useful buying me a beer and punching in some good tunes on the juke. Eli wasted four bucks playing the entire *Born to Run* album, then followed it up with most of *The Joshua Tree* while we waited for the Speed Demons to play their live set. He skipped over "With or Without You" because he knew better, but Edge's blistering intro on "In God's Country" kept our energy going until we switched over to the two-dollar bottles of High Life before the band came on. The Speed Demons played a cover of Santo & Johnny's "Sleepwalk" toward the end of their set, which encouraged Lou to balance himself on the steps of his stool and drunkenly yell out "Richie!" at the song's end to imitate Bob Valenzuela's dramatic cry to the heavens for his dead brother in the movie *La Bamba*. The band got the joke, as did a few of the laughing patrons in chairs and tables around the bar, but the bartender still threw us out. It was approaching closing time anyway. We really didn't mind.

I also didn't mind kicking trash while stumbling back to 3048 Washington Street. I didn't care about the honking horns or the bass-driven salsa music blasted from trunks of low-riding Nissan Sentras with tinted windows. I wouldn't care about Rocky the Barking Dog when I lay down to sleep and I wouldn't care if our upstairs neighbors tried to kill each other over another man. I had a good night out.

In my newfound euphoric state, even the thin piece of mail from Commonwealth College's Admissions Office on our coffee table couldn't turn me sour.

After I opened and read the letter, I calmly crumpled it up and threw it across the living room. I didn't get angry or upset, and I wasn't overcome with depression. I simply walked down the hallway and knocked on Eli's locked bedroom door. "Ripple" and smoke soon danced around my face.

"Mind if I join you?" I said. "I could go for a little Dead."

19

Detroit took on Green Bay in their usual Thanksgiving throwdown as a half-eaten Sagliano's pepperoni pizza idled on my coffee table. Watching the Lions run around the Silverdome was the only indication to me that it was actually Thanksgiving. I was lounging on my Jamaica Plain couch in boxer shorts and my faded blue Buffalo Bisons t-shirt instead of sitting at my parents' kitchen table with Claire, Molly and Frank. Next to the remaining four pieces of coffee table pizza sat three cans of Budweiser, still attached to plastic rings that held six. I probably should have put them in the refrigerator, but there was no point; they were going to go down eventually. Warm or cold, I needed something to wash down the terrible pizza.

Earlier in the afternoon, my mother called to wish me a happy Thanksgiving. After we talked, she passed the phone around the room. I could visualize everyone in the kitchen, the turkey and potatoes, the homemade stuffing, gravy and the fresh cut green beans simmering all around them. My mother told me she'd made an apple pie to go along with a chocolate cream Claire brought. I swore I could smell the sprinkled cinnamon through the receiver.

I still hadn't told my mother or father about the letter from Commonwealth College. My recommendations from St. Francis, my transcripts and my thick stack of writing samples were good for nothing. With this rejection now fact in my fourth month of residency, it was growing obvious that I had no reason to be in Boston anymore. I had no patience left, and no ability to euphemize the time I'd spent. Every week, I would send out reviews of new albums or rock shows to the *Globe, Boston Herald, The Improper Bostonian, Boston Phoenix, Weekly Dig* and *Boston Magazine*. I never got so much as an e-mail in return. I would even offer to work for free if they could offer future freelance opportunities. Still, nothing. I left messages for editors of other crumpled rags I'd find on the Green Line or in the small, colored paper boxes that lined the streets. No response. I even combed Jamaica Plain, Roslindale and West Roxbury to find their local neighborhood publications. I called each to volunteer to cover a town meeting, a political race or a Little League game played by area youngsters. Not interested. With these defeats on my mind, the only people I had to talk to were the commentators of that afternoon's football game. I angrily questioned their predictions out loud as they ran through their banter.

"A pass on third-and-fifteen? You think so, you shithead? Christ, they haven't had a running play for more than five yards all day, so are you sure they should pass here? Hope you get paid millions for that insight, you prick!"

I finished off my beer and whipped the empty can at the monitor before going back to the kitchen for a cigarette. November wind was seeping through the window as I shivered a little, lit the tip and inhaled my first drag. Along with the wind, the sound of Rocky incessantly barking flowed into the kitchen to break my peaceful moment. His barking was soon accompanied by Black Velvet, drunkenly singing Etta James' "At Last" as she shuffled toward our neighborhood park. Then a car alarm went off, followed by another before I was treated to a large crash from the apartment above. More stomping, banging and yelling followed the crash, so I guess I wasn't the only one enjoying the holiday at 3048 Washington Street. If that was their version of togetherness, I was momentarily appreciative to be by myself. During my life, I had never been good at being alone. As I sat in my Jamaica Plain kitchen on Thanksgiving, enjoying a cigarette in place of my mother's mashed potatoes, I realized I still wasn't.

Terry had called the previous night to tell me how he was gearing up to be the third wheel with Duff and Kiley on Black Wednesday. His courses had been so strenuous in his first semester of law school at UB, so he didn't care. Plus, he hadn't had a beer with our friend in weeks. Duff was still working late shifts at the stamping plant and spent all his free time with Kiley. By the sound of Terry's voice, it seemed he was going to appreciate the taste of those beers at Fitzgerald's as much as I would have.

"Hopefully, Kiley will finally hook me up with one of her friends so I don't have to be tagging along for the show again," he said. "Hanging out with those two is nauseating, Cahan. They're always finishing each other's sentences, hugging or even bar-necking. It's shameless. They really seem to be getting serious."

I would have gladly been a wingman for Terry on that night. My Black Wednesday was spent with a bag of tortilla chips, a pack of Camel Lights, and The Clash documentary *Westway to the World* in my VCR. I woke up in the middle of the night with the bag spilt all over me on the couch, so, by comparison, the bar-necking would have been an upgrade.

I sat smoking and staring out the screen of my kitchen window. I couldn't recall a time I'd felt so void of anything to be optimistic about. I felt so beaten and battered and didn't feel like getting up. The discouragement I'd ingested was threatening to be terminal, and I didn't want that to happen. Not on Thanksgiving; not on any other night, either.

I took the remains of my cigarette and extinguished it in my kitchen sink. I stomped down to my bathroom and jumped in the shower to clean off a day's worth of brooding filth. I wanted to get out of my apartment; I wanted to stop feeling sorry for myself. I threw on my cleanest pair of dirty jeans, my least-wrinkled white dress shirt, and headed out the door to the Jeanie Johnston.

I walked through the same darkened, dim doorway I'd

stepped through weeks earlier at a few minutes after five. The bar was surprisingly busy with young singles and middle-aged couples, out for a drink after their small dinners together away from their families or hometowns. Groups of young men and women stood together at high-top tables laughing under Van Morrison tunes, and older couples sat at barstools to smoke cigarettes with a good, stiff scotch or brandy. Once I saddled up on one of the empty leather stools, I was greeted by a short, stout and balding bartender with bar towel tossed over the left shoulder of his solid gray t-shirt.

"Pint of Guinness, please."

He walked to the tap, placed my pint glass underneath, grabbed the spoon hanging on the Guinness lever and placed it over my pint glass before he pulled the handle. The dreaded straight pour. With that, I assumed this guy was as happy to be working at the Jeanie Johnston on a busy Thanksgiving as I was to be sitting there.

"Thanks," I said as he set the pint in front of me. "By the way, that's a great picture you guys have of Doug Flutie over there. That was a good season for him."

"Yeah, but shame it had to be in a purgatory like Buffalo. He would've been better off staying in Canada."

I thought about replying, but bit my lip instead. No sense in playing defense against this pissed-off bartender when he'd never understand. But then he continued.

"If he was going to take another shot at the pros, he

should've come home to the Pats. We never would've cast him off like a piece of garbage the way Buffalo did."

I put my pint down, frustrated.

"What are you talking about? The Patriots released him, remember? That's why he went to Canada in the first place."

"And it never should've happened," he said, then slapped his soiled bar towel on the ice vat below the bar. "The Pats would've won at least three titles by now if Flutie was under center. He would've been a Hall of Famer."

I remained calm.

"He threw *two* touchdown passes his entire last season in New England. Two."

He slapped the ice vat again for emphasis.

"Flutie was a winner, plain and simple. Fuck Buffalo."

And away he went to the other side of the bar as I shook my head in disbelief. Eddie the Bartender would've never lost his cool like that with a customer. Eddie also had intelligent, objective opinions about topics brought up at the bar; he would never stand behind some asinine assertion he couldn't defend. This bartender wasn't Eddie and, after our little conversation, I knew I'd be getting the straight pour for the rest of the night.

These thoughts made me feel even lonelier than I did on the couch in my apartment. Eddie the Bartender—or lack thereof— was only part of the problem. It was the barstool I sat on. Its leather padding was more comfortable than those creaky, wooden stools Duff, Terry and I would pull up to the bar at

Fitzgerald's. It was the bar patrons, talking with people I didn't know about topics I wasn't familiar with. They weren't talking about their days at St. Theresa's, or the days they watched high school football games at St. Auggie's. They weren't talking about the Bills' chances of pulling out of their annual tailspin, and they weren't wondering if the Sabres had a chance to make another Stanley Cup run. They talked about Boston things, and as I sat there listening, I was certain of one thing: I'd never care about Boston things because I was just a kid from the Southtowns of Buffalo.

I slowly brought my pint slowly to my mouth and hoped so badly that one Buffalonian, just one, would walk through the Jeanie Johnston's doors. I'd inadvertently adopted this practice over the first month I was in Boston, and there was nothing I could do to stop it. I'd be having a beer after work around Fenway with Lou, sitting in front of the bartender who looked like Lou Gossett Jr., and I'd case the place for someone I knew. When I walked to the bathroom, I'd search the floor for one person I'd recognized from home, but I could never accept that I knew no one. You always knew somebody in Buffalo. At Doherty's and Fitzgerald's, anywhere on the streets of Elmwood, Allen, Delaware, Chippewa, or down at The Cobblestone after a Sabres game, you always knew someone.

At the Jeanie Johnston or any other bar in Boston I'd walk into, though, I knew no one.

Once this realization shone brightly, the only thing I could do was reach into my jean pocket for my cigarettes and singles. Out of the pack I pulled one smoke, lit the tip and inhaled before counting the folded money. Eight bills to burn, and with them in hand, I let my pint be and walked to the juke. I found the J Geils Band, the Beatles and U2 while flipping through the pages with the arrowed dial. I found *The River* by Springsteen, but I kept flipping the pages until I found *Exile on Main Street*.

Each song was fifty cents, so I put in five bucks to play ten. *Exile on Main Street*. Track One. "Rocks Off." I knew Terry wouldn't be busting through the door to strum the air guitar intro, but for that night, it would have to substitute for the arbitrary conversation I hoped to have with one patron who knew where I came from. Somehow, the Buffalo longing the song would provoke seemed more enticing than the loneliness I'd share with my pint, a cigarette and the biggest Doug Flutie fan in all of Boston.

20

I didn't take any more chances with Natalie as weeks approached Christmas. Instead of filling out one request for a personal day on the Monday following the holiday, I filled out two, putting one on her desk and another in an e-mail.

"Just so you know, you get two vacation days from the university around Christmas: the day before and the day after," she said. "You might not need this extra day."

"But I want it," I said, stone-faced and assured. "I want to use it that day, the day I requested."

"Well, I'm just saying. What if something comes up in January or February? You don't get full vacation time for a few months."

I crossed my arms and leaned back in my chair.

"Natalie, I could be dead in a few months, run over by a bus right outside this door before Valentine's Day. What good would saving those days do then?"

"Look," she said, then crossed her arms. "You want to be a smartass, fine. Be a smartass. But don't come begging when you need a day off you don't have."

The fake smile was stashed again and replaced with a stomping walk out of my cubicle. I didn't care. Since I didn't get into graduate classes, there was no reason to be in that desk except for a paycheck. Rent, student loans, and the minimum amount of hot dogs or macaroni needed to be paid for.

I was sick and tired of every inch of the Student Accounting office. Every morning, I'd walk past a glare from Natalie and back to the kitchen for a hot cup of thin, limp coffee. I would stir in the appropriate amount of cheap cream and sugar needed to improve the taste, then walk back to my cube to hear Porsche screaming into her cell phone at her boyfriend as she crunched away at another morning's Frito Lay breakfast.

"If I come home from choir practice tonight and you sleeping on that couch with no job, you best believe me and Tre' is out, dirty!"

I'd sit and sip the deplorable coffee under my nose. I'd let out a sneeze, only to get no "God Bless You" from the devout Christian woman threatening her boyfriend. I'd sigh and turn to my computer monitor to see a message waiting in my e-mail box from Mr. Davis. When I walked past him in the office, I wouldn't even hear him mutter a basic pleasantry anymore. For this, I was thankful.

After reading through Davis's weekly suggestions, I'd move on to another forward from my old college roommate, Vince Petrocelli, containing a *Good Fellas* drinking game you could play while watching the movie. "Take one drink every time Joe

Pesci says, 'fuck,'" was listed as rule number three. Getting mails from Vince did nothing to stifle the wanderlust I reveled in between calls from students and parents at my desk. The more nauseating the Commonwealth days became, the less I restricted myself from thoughts of departure. Since I cleared up everything with my father, maybe it was time to give New York a shot. Maybe it was time to take the chance I should've taken after graduation. And, since my conversations with Johanna were happening daily, the time had come to seriously consider it. But as I thought of leaving, I could hear my father's words.

"If you're going to move, you better have a job lined up. It's always easier to get another job when you still have one."

I always respected his advice, but I had no immediate opportunity in New York except for change. When I thought about what he had said, I also considered he'd never worked with Natalie or Mr. Davis, never been ridiculed by rich parents from Maine or Michigan, never been lectured by pretentious students about how their father pays his salary. If he was sitting in my chair that December after months of journalistic and scholastic rejection exacerbated by a longing for anything familiar, he might have considered walking without a plan, too.

When I scrolled down my e-mails a little further, another gleamed with the subject heading "Job Opportunity" from some publication called *Prime Cut Magazine*:

Dear Joe,

My name is Ricky Reynolds, and I'm the assistant editor of
an up and coming magazine in Boston called Prime Cut.
We're interested in covering all the "PRIME" trends in the
city, including lifestyle, fashion, and the hottest music in the
clubs and on the streets. I've been forwarded your resume'
and writing samples from an associate of mine, and I think
your writing style would fit nice up in here. I'd like you to
stop in for a meeting, so when you get a moment, drop me a
mail or call me at Prime Cut, 617-555-1383. Talk to you.
Sincerely,
R&R

I felt so vulnerable I paused before even questioning the
source. What the hell was *Prime Cut Magazine*? Did I even care?
And why did this guy sign his name R&R? After about five
seconds spent bouncing these legitimate questions around in my
head, I smacked myself across the face—literally. I'd spent
months whining about how I needed an opportunity to write
something for a magazine, newspaper or website. I was ready to
cover a town meeting at a Spanish Iglesia for the *Jamaica Plain
Gazette*, submit a review of the newest U2 album to the *Boston
Phoenix*, or recount my own experience of Rockabilly Night at
the Jeanie Johnston for weeklydig.com. Someone from a
magazine was finally contacting me and, for some reason, I was
hesitating to reply for more than a half-second. I picked up my
phone and dialed Ricky Reynolds's number with the same hand I

slapped myself with. I'd cover fashion, lifestyle or wear a tight black t-shirt to fit in at the clubs if I needed to. I was ready to do whatever they told me to fit nice up in there with R&R and *Prime Cut*.

A week before Christmas, I was in a waiting room for the offices of *Prime Cut Magazine*, located in the center of Downtown Crossing on Washington Street in downtown Boston. I sat wearing the gray suit my parents bought me for my twenty-first birthday and holding a brown leather binder with my resume and writing samples enclosed. The office's secretary was snapping her gum as her radio quietly emitted rap music. She bopped her tightly braided hair to the beat, and I sat and watched her with a satisfied smirk. I was finally waiting to be interviewed for a writing job. I wasn't sure what to expect from this Ricky and, due to my complete ignorance of his publication, I wasn't sure what he expected of me. I'd walked the streets of Boston searching for a *Prime Cut Magazine* box, but I couldn't find one anywhere. I walked into a few music shops and a Borders Books, whose magazine racks seemed to hold every magazine in the entire country. Publications for blacks, whites, gays, Hispanics, Asians, fathers, mothers, sportsmen, musicians, meatheads and perverts lined their shelves. Unfortunately, not one of those shelves contained a copy of *Prime Cut Magazine*.

But, they did have an office. Ricky Reynolds' answering machine said, "Thank you for calling *Prime Cut Magazine*." They had to publish something or this guy wouldn't have scheduled the meeting, so I stashed my doubts. Instead, I watched the secretary's braids bounce to the bass beat.

When the door opened to my left, a short, young white man styling closely cropped black hair and a trimmed goatee walked toward my chair in oversized blue jeans, an un-tucked baggy red t-shirt, and a large silver medallion hanging far from his neck.

"You Cahan?"

"Yes, sir," I said, though this guy wasn't any more than two or three years older than me.

"I'm Ricky Reynolds of Prime Cut Magazine," he said, then extended his hand. "Nice to meet you."

"You too."

"C'mon, let's go in the conference room over here and get to business. Janita," he said to the secretary behind the desk. "Hold all my calls for the next twenty minutes, ah-ite?"

We walked down a hallway to a small conference room hosting windows facing a brick wall. Ricky and I took seats across from each other at a large mahogany table before I placed my binder between us.

"What'd you bring me in that leather? Anything good?"

"An extra copy of my résumé and some writing samples."

"Nice, nice. I needed more copies for our files," he said, then reached across the table for the copies. "So, about your resume and samples, I thought they displayed the kind of creativity and articulation I'd like to present on our pages."

"Thank you."

"Yeah, yeah. Now, do you know our magazine at all? What we all about?"

"To be honest, I don't. I tried to find a copy of the magazine or a website for you guys, but I couldn't find anything."

"Well, we're currently developing the site, and we haven't dropped our first issue yet; we working on it. What we're looking for right now is a fresh voice to reach our target demographic."

"And what's your target demographic?"

"Erotic urban. Don't necessarily have to be black or Hispanic, but we'd like to tap into the sexually active and explicit market of today's young adults with a mix of mature fashion, lifestyle, and music coverage to arouse their erotic interests."

"So this is a porn mag?"

"Naw, naw, naw. There ain't gonna be no pictures of naked bitches or nothing in these pages. But, we'd like to have the coverage sexually driven, like hot tracks for banging or what pleasing position you should be in when sexing to these joints. Maybe some true erotic stories from the streets, or the best places in the city to pick up a man or a woman for a one-night-stand. Shit like that."

I loosened my necktie. I assumed he hadn't read my review of Sticky Fingers' stellar show in Cuba, NY. I didn't have any erotic lines or intense sex tales in that whole piece. I inquired as my confusion brewed.

"So, do you mind if I ask you a question?"

"Shoot."

"You read my samples, right? You've seen what I've done?"

"Yeah."

"Well, after looking at those, why would you think I could ever do this?"

"You're a writer, right?"

"Sure."

"Well, how hard would it be for you to toss some hot shit in those lines? You like sex, don't you?"

"Yeah, but—"

"Well, what's the problem? You'd be writing about something you like doing, right?"

"I guess, sure."

He set his palms on the top of the conference table and leaned forward with frustrated look on his bearded face.

"Look, Joe, you seem like a good guy, ah-ite. You got good samples here, you can write, and I'm giving you a chance to get some pieces published. If you want in, fine. We can do this. But you know what we're looking for before we drop our first issue."

"Erotic urban?"

"That's right," he said. "If you're down, give me a call. Janita will give you a card with my personal celly number on the way out."

Ricky Reynolds shook my hand before exiting in search of

the hottest erotic urban trends. I loosened my necktie again after he left, then found Janita again for one of R&R's business cards. She continued to rock her head back and forth, not bothering to pause her groove as she handed me a business card and wished me a good day. In the elevator, I was still disoriented and perplexed with the whole encounter. I knew I was no sexual virtuoso, but I certainly wasn't a prude. Still, it seemed like I was interviewing for a job in porn, which felt as dirty as it was comical. Did that interview really happen? If it did, was it really as awkward as I perceived it to be?

When the elevator doors opened at the exit, I walked out into the lobby and through another set of doors onto Washington Street. Once outside, I felt the cold December breeze whip across the side of my face. With the chill came a few snowflakes, and as I held Ricky Reynolds business card firm in my right hand, Boston's first snowfall of the season began. I moved toward the side of the door and under the concrete overhang to light a cigarette before my walk to the T. I lit the tip, inhaled, then exhaled as I held the card below my face.

Ricky Reynolds, Editor

The snow fell around me as I took long drags and considered what Ricky said. Why couldn't I do it? I talked about sex all the time. I'd never written about it, but I could learn. If I could write columns in my own style yet intersperse some sexual content within the development I'd crafted so many times before, I could get published in *Prime Cut Magazine*. When I went to

Borders, I found the shelves swarmed with magazine covers featuring half-naked men and women. Topics on the front pages included, "30 Easiest Ways to Drive Your Woman to Orgasm," and "10 Tricks for the Bedroom Your Man Doesn't Think You Know!" Sex was no longer tame on television either, with casual encounters and random hook-ups the lifeblood of most shows in the prime time schedule. It was right there in front of me every day, every night. It was reality, so why couldn't I detail the stories from the streets? Why couldn't I write articles about gratuitous humping, insatiable desires and coital interlude?

Because if I knew anything, I knew the look that would take shape on Ann and Patrick Cahan's faces as they held my first published piece for *Prime Cut Magazine*.

I knew the awkwardness and general embarrassment that would encompass their kitchen table as they squeamishly told friends about what their son was writing in Boston. Unfortunately, the Buffalonians seated wouldn't be as concerned about the erotic urban demographic as Ricky Reynolds was. I knew the lack of understanding they'd show, and I couldn't blame them. Frank, my sisters, and I may have been aware of the intense contradictions we lived within our lives and our religious faith, but we never talked about them with our parents. We never discussed why sex was such an unapproachable subject in Catholicism with our parents because they never brought it up with their parents either. I could only imagine what my Grandpa Cahan's response would've been if my father ever approached a sexual subject with him in high school. Ol' Patrick wouldn't have made it out alive. Thoughts of their exchange made my father's suggestion of "don't do it" to my teenage sexual query seem liberal.

Sex and sexuality might have been considered a beautiful thing by my parents. After all, they did have four of us through the act, but I've obviously never thought about that until this sentence. We didn't discuss it, didn't bring it up, so if I decided to take my first writing gig glamorizing sex as nothing but a frivolous act between women drinking pink-colored martinis and men who ordered Red Bull and vodka while they waited for their favorite trip-hop track to burst through a specific club's sound system, I was certain the two of them would never speak with me again.

I was warming to the idea of writing for anybody about anything over the months I'd sent out résumés and writing samples to Boston publications. Didn't matter what it was; I was ready to do it. But as I stood underneath the concrete overhang, taking heavy drags off my cigarette as a few snowflakes found their way under to wet the right side of my face, I concluded that the opportunity to inscriptively entice the erotic urban demographic of Boston, Massachusetts wouldn't be worth disrespecting my upbringing in Buffalo, New York.

I took one last drag off my smoke and dropped it to the brick-lined sidewalk. I watched the final remnants of tobacco burn, then took one last look at the business card in my hand before I crumpled it up and dropped it to the ground as well.

21

I kept two hands on the steering wheel as I pushed through falling Christmas Eve snow and New York Interstate slush at a conservative forty-five miles per hour.

I was confident I could drive under any sort of calamitous precipitation after years of driving through Buffalo's infamous lake-effect snowstorms. People bought SUVs and large pick-up trucks with four-wheel drive solely for driving through the harsh and harrowing winters on the shores of Lake Erie. The problem with some of these buyers was how they assumed the truck would drive itself through these treacherous storms. Every year, I'd cruise by SUVs and pick-up trucks, plowed into snow piles or entrenched in ditches as my two hands remained steady on the wheel of a much smaller vehicle. I was prepared for this scene on the I-90 as I puttered home in the Bomber for another Cahan Christmas.

The roads were extremely icy, so I strayed from the usual lakeside drive and took an earlier exit to travel some finely plowed and salted roads to Norton Drive. Driving down my street for the first time since I'd left for Boston, I saw the houses along our street decorated appropriately for the holiday, with extravagant multi-colored lights and manger scenes featuring an illuminated baby Jesus displayed on front lawns. Some houses dressed their pine trees with white lights and a large flashing star at the top; some dressed their entire houses in green lights, bright enough to illuminate the entire block. I drove up to our house to find Patrick Cahan, standing at the end of our driveway in snow-soaked green corduroy pants, a large red ski jacket and an old Buffalo Bills ski hat pulled down close to his eyebrows as he held a large metal snow shovel with his gloved left hand. He still cleared snow with his archaic shovel and refused to buy a snow blower. Slower and arduous, but old school.

"Welcome home, son," he said through the wind, then stashed his shovel in a mound of snow before approaching for a hug.

"Good to be home, Pops. Good to be home."

"Looks like this car's the best dollar you ever spent, huh? I don't believe you made it through this storm in one piece. You took it slow, right?"

"With two hands on the wheel, prepared to turn the car into the slide, not against it. With my foot ready to pump the brake, not slam it."

"Sounds like you've mastered the suicide snow drive, boy. Grab your stuff and get inside. Your mother's making Irish spaghetti tonight, and I bought you a four-pack of Guinness. It's in the fridge, but save one for me when I'm done out here."

"You want any help?"

"I have all the help I need here," he said, hoisting the beaten scooper high. "I'm the master of the snow shovel."

"I doubt you have much competition. You may be the only guy still breathing who owns one."

"Funny," he said, then plunged the shovel into another snow pile. "Go see your mother."

When I walked into our kitchen, I found my mother leaning over the stove opening a jar of Ragu spaghetti sauce as ground beef simmered in a frying pan below her. The whole room smelled like ground beef, and when she drenched it with the sauce, the aroma was of the two slowly cooking in the beef's existing grease. I stood in the doorway with my old red hockey bag draped over my left shoulder, a bag of gifts held at my side and a frozen grin on my face as I kicked snow off my Doc Martens and onto the doormat. Ann Cahan swung around before setting the empty sauce jar in the sink.

"Leave your shoes on the mat, hon," she said, standing before me in a white turtleneck, red sweater, jeans, and woolen socks on her feet. "Don't even think about walking through this kitchen with those wet boots. Your tracks will give us all the wet foot."

I laughed and shook my head.

"Nice to see you too, Ma."

"Honey, you know how I hate to walk around with wet socks. It would ruin my night, so take off the boots and give me a hug."

I gave her the mother-size hug my father never got.

"You're making the Irish spaghetti?"

"Is that okay? Molly, Claire and Frank all voted for spaghetti for their Christmas Eve feast, so if you have a problem with it, you can take it up with them when they get home from the mall."

"Last minute shopping?"

"Of course. Your sisters haven't done a thing on time in their lives, and your brother went to pick up more beer for tonight. You should grab a beer and go relax downstairs. Dinner should be ready in a bit."

The pasta only took eight minutes to boil, so my mother didn't put it on until everyone was back in the house. I sat downstairs in our family room with a fresh pint of Guinness and watched *It's a Wonderful Life* on television. Minutes later, I could hear her yelling at each one of them as they finally walked in the house, clothes covered in snow and boots caked in slush.

"Off! Shoes off at the door! Right there! Leave 'em or you're not getting past me, so help me God!"

I heard their feet stomp and coats shaking clean before each shuffled downstairs while I watched a young George Bailey sprinkled coconut on scoops of ice cream. First one down the stairs was Claire, who jokingly made a scene once she saw me on the couch.

"Oh, brother," she yelled, flailing her arms then

dramatically running toward me. "You're home! Oh, thank God you're home!"

"Funny, Claire. Get all your shopping done?"

"All of it but yours, boy. I couldn't find anything for you, so Frank and I chipped in for that four-pack you're drinking. Hope it's enough," she said with fake laughter as Frank punched me in my right arm.

"You're on a roll," I said, then returned a punch to Frank's left arm. "I hope you didn't already drink all the wrapping party beer. You seem drunk."

"Who do you think I am? Molly?"

Molly slapped Clare in the back, then did it again for good measure.

"Hey! Hey!" said my mother from upstairs. "Knock it off down there! Dinner's almost ready, so come up here and sit at the table."

My mother loved having us all under the same roof again so she could reclaim her post as disciplinarian. It didn't matter how old we were or whether we were joking; she'd still yell at us like we were ten years old. This was strangely endearing.

We took our places at the table. My mother set the large silver bowl of pasta in the middle of the table, with a set of metal tongs placed on top to dish it out onto our cheap Irish china. Empty glasses were set in front of all our plates, and we each poured either water or milk to fill each glass. When the glasses were filled, we all joined hands for one of my father's elongated saying of grace.

"Dear Lord, thank you for bringing us together for this meal and for your glorious birthday tomorrow. Bless all of those on the streets of Buffalo and elsewhere who need a hand this holiday season, and bless all of us at this table in our current and future endeavors, particularly Joseph in his approaching first semester of graduate school this January. In the name of the father, and of the son and of the holy spirit."

"Amen."

I swallowed the lump in my throat, then passed the basket of Italian bread around the table, followed by the pasta, then the sauce. Frank sat on my right as we began to eat. With his mouth full of pasta, he stored it in his right cheek so he could have some semblance of conversation.

"Are you excited about starting classes in January or what? Ma tells me your job is really creasing you."

"Yeah, about that," I said, then put my fork down on the table. "I didn't get into school."

There was no uncomfortable silence needed to hear what I said. They all heard it as they buttered their bread or twirled the strands of spaghetti onto their forks. When they did, they stopped and looked down the table at me, my fork still down as I prepped my explanation.

"You didn't get in?" said my mother. "When did you find out about this?"

"Thanksgiving."

"And you didn't tell us then *why*?"

"Embarrassed, I guess. And I didn't want to tell you over the phone."

"I don't get it," said my father. "I thought by working there you were assured classes or at least a chance to matriculate in, right?"

"Right, right, but the class sizes boomed after nine-eleven, so certain majors were booked solid with students paying full tuition."

"And yours was booked?"

"Solid. Not even a shot on the waiting list."

He leaned back in his chair and folded his arms expectantly.

"Well, what's next?"

"I think you know the answer to that question."

"New York?"

"I'm not sure what other sensible choice I have."

"Nothing's come back from any writing samples you've been sending around Boston? Not a thing?" said my mother.

"Not a thing." I decided I should keep the Ricky Reynolds meeting to myself. No need to mention the erotic urban demographic at Christmas.

"When was the last time you sent something to the Gazette?" said my father. "I know they're still having layoffs, but who knows? Maybe your grandfather knows someone over there. The old man knows someone in everything in this city, so maybe you could ask him when he comes over tomorrow. I know you might not want to come back yet, but it's a thought."

"I'll ask," I said. "But, if I have to move to New York to get something going, are you going to be okay with it?"

He leaned forward over his plate of spaghetti and laid his palms flat on the kitchen table.

"You really feel that strongly? It's something you have to do?"

"I think so, yes."

One. Two. Three. Four. Five.

"Well, if you have to do it, you have to do it. But ask your grandfather about a contact tomorrow, just in case."

"I will. And Pops?" I said. "You have sauce all over the front of your shirt."

"Son of a—"

"Watch your mouth, Patrick!" said my mother as she handed him a wet dishtowel.

On Christmas morning, we slowly staggered out of our beds with a lot less enthusiasm than we had as young children, back when we were a thundering herd from our bedrooms to the living room below. We were tired from the droning midnight mass at St. Theresa's and the post-mass drinking in our kitchen, but we each slowly rose from bed as the smell of my father cooking breakfast whipped through the house and up to our rooms. Christmas was the only day of the year my father usurped the stove from my mother, as he'd make a feast of eggs, bacon, sausage, toast, pancakes, and a full pot of coffee to go with my mother's freshly baked coffee cake.

After the feast, we gathered in the living room around our decorated tree, surrounded by mounds of presents. While some families only bought gifts for one or two people, our family went absolutely overboard. We bought each other multiple presents, though quantity always won out over quality. We never gave each other extravagant gifts like electronics or expensive jewelry, so creativity was the key. Whether it was my mother wrapping up our favorite pretzels, or my father rolling up a copy of *People* magazine's annual "50 Most Beautiful People" for my mother, the thought was always more important. For example, if Molly bought my father *The Clancy Brothers, Live in Dublin* cassette because she heard him mention how he enjoyed their rendition of "Finnegan's Wake" over dinner months earlier, that was huge. The tape might have cost five bucks, but the fact she remembered their conversation would be worth much more. Sounds hokey, but it wasn't sincere as it was competitive. We all wanted to give the most imaginative gifts, so every year, the base of our trimmed tree was buried under small boxes, big boxes, little bags and large packages we all hoped would be the talk of that year's Christmas dinner.

That morning, the gifts were as hilarious as they were clever. Since Claire knew how Molly spent her summer nights down at the lake drinking cans of Genny Light with her underage friends, she bought her a twelve-dollar Genny Light t-shirt from our local beverage center. The look of embarrassment on Molly's face when she opened it in front of my parents, both still in perpetual denial that their youngest slung back a few beers from time to time, was worth much more. And, because of the Cahan Christmas rule concerning any clothing gift, the value increased. New clothes had to be immediately modeled for a picture, snapped by my father. He started the rule with my mother on their first Christmas when he made her pose in her new O.J. Simpson t-shirt that read "The Juice Is Loose" on the front, and the rule's stuck ever since. All our baby pictures had us wearing that season's clothes, my mother responsible for pulling on each piece one at a time.

But, Molly's embarrassment was short-lived. In the hours following my announcement about a possible move to New York, she'd managed to sneak out and get me a special gift to wear. After posing in her new shirt, she passed me a small box to open. I tore off the wrapping paper, popped the top and pulled out a navy blue New York Yankees hat from under a mound of tissue paper. Molly laughed as I held it and sported a mocking smile.

"Timely," I said.

"I don't think so," said my father before he jumped out of his chair and grabbed the hat from my hand, whipped open the front door and tossed the hat out into the falling snow. He pulled the door shut, clapped his hands clean and calmly walked back to his chair as all of us laughed hysterically. The guy hated the

Yankees, and he wasn't real subtle about it.

"Whatever," said Molly and nonchalantly shrugged her shoulders. "It cost four dollars up at the gas station. It was worth the joke."

And on it went, one gift at a time as we'd joke back and forth in the same way we had the year before and the year before that. The next gift couldn't be opened until the previous was reacted to, modeled or shown gratitude for. We weren't allowed to be distracted by anything except my mother's Christmas cassettes. We also weren't allowed to touch the phone if it rang while we opened our gifts. If anyone got up to grab it, my mother would tell the guilty to let the machine answer it. Toward the end of that Christmas day, the machine picked up a call and broadcast a smoky voice into the living room. I knew who it was. Everyone knew who it was.

Cahan, er, Joseph. Merry Christmas, it's Johanna. I couldn't get hold of you on your cell, so I wanted to try to find you there. It's, like, three in the afternoon, and I really needed to talk to you when you get a chance, so when you get one, please, um, give me a call back. I should be around most of the day, and tell your family I say Merry Christmas as well. Talk to you soon.

Everyone's eyes focused on me as I opened my last present from Frank. Always the boldest, Molly was the first to speak up.

"Well? What's going on? Are you and Johanna dating again?"

"Yeah, Joe," said Frank. "What other skeletons are gonna come tumbling out of your closet this weekend?"

"Shut up, shut up; nothing's going on. We're just talking, so can you let me open your present or what?"

"Sure, sure," said Frank. "But I've talked to a lot of girls, and I never got a call from one to wish my family Merry Christmas."

After I ripped off the wrapping paper, I opened the box to find a royal blue hooded sweatshirt with white letters spelling "BUFFALO" across the chest. I pulled it out and immediately pulled it over my head before giving Frank a friendly slap in his left arm.

"Thanks, bro."

"Thought you might need it in Boston to prove the existence of another city in New York State," he said. "Now that you might go to NYC, it should serve the same purpose there."

I got more comfortable in the sweatshirt as my mother started picking up the discarded paper and torn boxes.

"Looks like that's it," she said. "No more gifts, so I'll start cleaning up in the kitchen. As for the rest of you, pick up your things and take them where they need to go."

"I'll help you bring some of these things in the kitchen," I said, then began picking up some empty beer bottles, used glasses and dirty plates scattered on the living room tables.

When I walked into the kitchen, she stood at the sink, ignoring each dirty piece she rinsed as she gazed out the window and into the falling snow. I set some glasses next to her and sighed. I was ready to stare at my bedroom ceiling again before my mother's words intervened.

"Why are you still talking to her? If you don't want to be with her, you need to tell the poor girl you don't want to. I don't know what happened with the two of you back at school, but no one deserves to be strung along like this."

"Strung along? What do you mean?"

"Joseph, you don't date a girl for over three years then reduce your affections for each other to talking. What's up?"

"I don't know," I said and sighed. "It's complicated."

She turned around and leaned her back against the sink. She took a deep breath and folded her arms across her chest. She was my mother, and she knew more than I did. Nothing was too complicated for her to understand.

"Complicated? Joseph Patrick Cahan, it's simple. Either you care for the girl or you don't. Either you know you love her or you don't. What's so complicated about that?"

"Ma, trust me; it is. With Johanna and me, there's more to it."

My eyes wandered, and maybe she wondered whether I wasn't as certain as I thought I was. It was more than a question of love or affection, but maybe not. Maybe it was a simple yes or no between two young adults who had reached the end of their relationship. She was my mother, and maybe she was right.

"Joseph, do you know how long your father and I dated before we knew we wanted to be together for the rest of our lives?"

"Ma, Ma, I know," I said, exhausted from hearing the story again and again. "A year. You and dad only dated for a year before you knew you wanted to get married."

"No, we were married after dating for a year. It was only five months before we got engaged."

"Five months? You only dated for five months before you knew you wanted to cash it in?"

She smiled.

"That's right. And do you know why we knew we wanted to, quote, 'cash it in' after five months?"

"Why?"

"Because we knew we loved each other. We didn't worry about any of the things you worry about today, like whether the city you live in has enough promise, if the job you're working will make you the most happy, or if the person you're with satisfies your every need and desire. It was simple. It wasn't complicated; it was love. Still is."

"But it's not perfect. I've seen the two of you fight about the macaroni salad from Fitzgerald's before."

She laughed.

"Joseph, arguments happen. It's not perfect, but your father and I made a commitment to each other when we decided to get married after that year, a commitment to stick to the choices we made for the rest of our lives. To abandon our commitment because of petty complications would be contradictory of the feeling love is supposed to be. It's forgiving, selfless and focused on being there for the other at all times. If these complications you speak of are that serious, then the two of you must not really love each other. Otherwise, you wouldn't be conflicted over whether to be with her. Make sense?"

"I guess, but I'm still not sure why our issues can't be worked out. It's just confusing."

"But it shouldn't be. Give her a call. You might want to get these things answered before deciding to move within thirty minutes of this girl."

"I know, I know. I'll call her in a few minutes."

I walked through the living room and up the stairs to my bedroom. My mother made sense, but at the same time, didn't. When my father wooed her out of her teller window and into marrying him, love wasn't the only thing that was simpler. Life was simpler. Finishing high school and getting a decent job was possible, if not the norm in an industry-fueled landscape like Buffalo. At eighteen years old, one could find a career on the assembly line at the Ford stamping plant or in the coke ovens at Bethlehem Steel, and our neighborhood was full of people who did just that. The blueprint of a wife, house and family was the normal progression for average adults in their early twenties. These adults didn't plan their lives around having two kids, a two-car garage, a summer home, and a fulfilling job they really, truly loved. They worked, made love and hoped for the best.

There wasn't the accessibility to hundreds of professional paths, nor was there an option to gain entrance with a right-click atop a mouse pad. Magazine pages or television shows that dictated what the perfect man or woman should look like didn't form the foundation of society. It didn't serve as a catalyst for doubts that would surface about the person one lay down with at night. Now, one article in *Esquire* could sway thousands toward the notion that the one they're dating isn't quite sexy or emotionally available enough to travel these paths with. It wasn't commonplace to become debilitated by the stresses that came with making those professional and personal choices, nor was the devastating depression that could set in when one made the wrong choice. If that depression did set in, it wasn't standard to immediately run to the drug store or neighborhood psychiatrist for treatment of this depression instead of taking a deep breath and rationally evaluating one's problems and priorities. When my parents were married, I doubt it was this complicated.

But it was with Johanna Darcy.

The delicate relationship between confidence and self-esteem planted the seeds for the first problems Johanna and I had. The two could be interchanged as synonyms, but in a relationship, each work independently to strengthen the union. I was confident about our relationship, at times to a fault. I was so comfortable, I didn't feel the need to fall over myself for

Johanna the way I did when we first started dating. The occasional flowers or spontaneous romantic act were shelved until birthdays, holidays or when I absolutely needed to unearth such a gesture. When we went out to the Moose Nose, I would go hours mingling with friends, secure enough in my relationship not to keep a perpetual eye on it. As the year progressed, the conflicts in our schedule became unaccommodating to me. It was our senior year in college, and I knew I'd never have such a level of irresponsibility again. I also knew I wanted to be with Johanna even after this irresponsibility passed. I assumed she understood this, so I started to spend more time on barstools with classmates I'd never see again. When these drunken nights started to outnumber the days we spent together, Johanna began to voice her concerns.

"Why can't we stay in and watch a movie together? Are these nights out with people you'll never see again more important to you than me?"

Then she'd suspect I was going out to see other girls.

"So I heard you were sitting at the Moose Nose talking to Susan for, like, two hours last night. You like her, don't you? Think she's better looking than me?"

Susan Kofler was Johanna's best friend and the girl who introduced the two of us. She was also extremely attractive. With brown hair, blue eyes and an unbelievable figure for her small stature, she had plenty of eyes on her. I'd be lying if I said I didn't find her good-looking, but I never would've cheated on

Johanna, let alone with her best friend. On that particular night in question, I talked with Susan about a mix CD I was making for Johanna. Over about a dozen beers and a pack of smokes, we argued over which songs should be included. When she disagreed with my inclusion of "Roll Me Away" by Bob Seger, I spent the better part of an hour detailing the vinyl triumphs of the American Everyman. But, as her self-esteem dipped, Johanna didn't want to hear this. She wanted me to tell her how I was romantically interested in Susan Kofler, how I did want to sleep with her, and if she was outside the room at that very moment, I'd take her to the kitchen floor and do it right there. Johanna wanted to hear all this, but it would've been a lie. Still, she continued and continued throughout the semester.

"Why don't you call me every night and why do I have to call you? Don't you love me anymore? I'm so fat and ugly. Aren't I fat? I'm going to be a horrible teacher. Why am I even doing this? I'm going to fail and be horrible, and all the kids are going to think I suck. Do you think I'll be good? Why? You don't mean that. Why do you like me? You don't seem like you love me anymore. Why don't you say you love me every time we talk? Do you love me? Do you? Do you? Do you?"

This is the delicate relationship between confidence and self-esteem. When I became too confident with our relationship, I started taking it for granted. The assurance eased my affection, which Johanna needed. While she longed for such expression during hectic times, her self-esteem started to wane. Johanna stopped believing in herself to the point that she spent time trying to get me not to believe in her as well, affecting my previous belief in the strength of our relationship. This became our problem, and with time, her deteriorating belief in herself started to affect the confidence I had in us.

I remembered the first time I met Johanna and my shortage of breath when I saw her shimmering blues. I stared at her skin and crimson locks and was taken back in a way I thought only existed on movie screens. I remembered the feeling of our first kiss, accompanied with the awkwardness of my foiled attempt to be slick with Bob Dylan. I remembered when my grandmother passed away, and how Johanna's consoling compassion got me through what was, at the time, a new experience of grieving loss. I remembered the calming certainty that came over me when I prayed to God by the foot of her bed, thinking we were going to have a child together. And simply, I knew who Johanna Darcy was: Intelligent. Beautiful. Personable. Congenial. Loving. Giving. Selfless.

Maybe that last trait was the one she didn't realize, the thing I didn't let her know enough that set her apart from the rest. She cared for everyone more than she cared for herself, and maybe she should have cared a little bit more about herself. If she had, I wouldn't have started doubting if I could ever convince her of how much I loved her.

But feelings can be questioned only so many times before one tires of proclaiming them. I became worn down by Johanna, worn to the point that I became proud and offended. Didn't she realize who she was for me? It was a tremendous deal for me to find my first love, and with her continuous questioning of my actual feelings, it was starting to seem insincere. I shouldn't have to say I love you in defense of how I feel; I wanted to say it as a proclamation of how I felt. Say it too much and it loses its meaning. Before I met Johanna, I'd never said it to any girl. After, I'd only said it to one. She knew this, yet she badgered.

"Do you love me? Do you? Do you? Do you?"

After one of these arguments, she left her house to go to the store and grab a pack of cigarettes. While she was gone, I decided to make up for my recent romantic lapses. I took pieces of her class construction paper and a large black marker, then wrote statements of what I loved about her on each sheet and hung them up around her bedroom. From then on, every time she questioned whether I loved her eyes, heart, face or soul, the answers would surround her. They acted as obnoxious reminders, taped on the wall to alleviate the swirling doubts that were crippling us.

When she came back to see alliteration like, "beautiful blues" and "breathtaking beauty," she laughed and smiled. She knew she was acting ridiculous, so she apologized and enjoyed the spontaneous gesture. And she appreciated it—until the next week. The next week, she questioned my feelings on Monday, Tuesday and Wednesday. On that Wednesday, she began to get absurd.

"Why do you hate me?"

There are questions I've heard women ask to purposely trap men. Am I fat? Do I look pretty in this? If these women were confident of the answer, they'd have never asked the question. But, I realize our insecurities – for both men and women – trigger these reluctant questions. When I get up to look at myself in the mirror every day, I don't see a muscle-bound Adonis. No one is going to mistake me for George Clooney or Leonardo DiCaprio in the facial department either; I've accepted this. I've also accepted that, in a relationship, there are going to be doubts. But amid these doubts, I couldn't accept the word hate being frivolously tossed around. The girl I loved actually had the word hate seep into her depiction of our relationship. Hate being used to describe my feelings for her was insulting; too insulting. At twenty-one, we were on two different levels of certainty: I was certain I loved Johanna Darcy, and Johanna Darcy was certain I didn't.

Could it have been a simple misuse of a word? In the past, I had tossed around hate pretty liberally. Though he had never done anything to me personally, I told Vince I hated Jim Morrison almost daily at St. Francis. The term is laced with venom, and looking back at it, I guess Morrison wrote some decent songs after all. ("Peace Frog" was pretty catchy.) But, unless Johanna caught me in bed with her sister, found out I'd killed her grandmother, or realized that I wrote the four verses of the Doors' "Crystal Ship" for her, hate seemed to be a rough word to assign to your boyfriend's feelings. I gave her a chance to clarify.

"Hate? You want to take a mulligan on that one?"

"I don't need a mulligan," she said. "You must *really* hate me."

Understanding becomes necessity once a relationship matures. With comfort and assurance comes understanding, and Johanna wasn't able to achieve either. No amount of flowers, romantic sentiments or construction paper could remind her of how certain I was about her. I could have held her hand and looked into those eyes every morning to pledge my desire to be with her forever, but the doubts she had about herself could never be remedied by the love I felt. She didn't understand what I thought we had: magnetic attraction, resilient unity and undeniable purity. Instead of appreciating these certainties, she wondered aloud how long it would be until my feelings for her would match the disparaging ones she had about herself.

Did I love Johanna Darcy? Yes. Was there any doubt? No. Did her incessant doubts about herself and our relationship serve as the first steps toward the end for us?

Absolutely.

22

I hung up after the fourth ring. I thought about leaving a message on her voicemail, but I didn't feel like talking into the machine. Before I could dial again, I heard my mother's voice up the stairs.

"Joseph! Joseph! Your grandpa is down here. Please come down and talk with him! Now! Let's goooo!"

I was out of my room and down the stairs as quickly as she called. When I walked into the kitchen, there was Grandpa Cahan, seated at the table in navy blue slacks and a green and white plaid flannel button-down, the top button undone for his white t-shirt collar to peek out. Taking his red, white and blue Bills mesh hat off of his white hair, he scratched the back of his head as he smiled.

"Your mother tells me you're having girl troubles," he said with a strange sense of pride. "Johanna, right?"

"Right."

"What did I tell you about the redheads, kid? Fiery and unpredictable. You never know if they're gonna give you a smooch or a sock to the kisser." He flashed a smirk. "I'm just kidding, kid. Only having some fun with you. But sit down; I want to talk with you."

He pointed to the chair across from him and gave a glance over to my mother.

"Ann, would you put the kettle on and leave us be for a while. I'd like to have a few minutes with my grandson."

My mother nodded and placed the tea kettle atop the burner before walking down the hallway. Placing his hat on the table, he looked sternly across the table. He seemed more certain of the image he wanted to project than assured of the advice he wanted to deliver, but he started talking to me anyway.

"Now, Joseph, I've talked with your mother about what's been going on lately. She tells me school didn't work out and you're thinking again about moving to New York."

"Maybe."

"Why? For a job, money, or do you want to root for the goddamned Jets now?"

"All of those things, except for the Jets," I said. "I'm thinking about moving to New York, not New Jersey."

"Good man." He always hated Joe Namath and the Jets. "So you think there's more waiting for you in New York than you've found in Boston?"

"Has to be. Since I've been in Boston, I've had zero opportunities to write anything, so I think I'd have a better chance getting an opportunity in New York to write on the side while I work another pointless job like the one I'm working right now."

"You think? You mean you don't have anything lined up?"

"No, not yet."

"Well, what about medical insurance? What if you get sick or injured? Those bastards will leave you for dead on the streets up there!" He was agitated. "Guy I was in the service with was mugged, beaten and stabbed right in broad daylight in midtown. He just wanted to grab a beer. Survived, but still. They don't care who you are up there."

Then he paused to collect himself. Leaning back in his chair, he put his right hand through his white hair and folded his arms across his chest as a revelation seemed to come over him.

"Is it this girl, Johanna? In White Plains, right? You want to be closer to her, don't you?"

"No, well, no." I struggled. Of course I did, even though I knew it might be a bad idea. Still, I tried to stay guarded. "I don't know, maybe. But that's not the only reason. I don't want to move just for this girl."

"You sure about that? I mean, this plan of yours seems awfully convenient."

I struggled again. Some mornings in Boston, I woke up with certainty that I wanted out of town as quickly as possible. A ride to the Mass Pike and I'd hitchhike out of the city if I had to. But there were other days I doubted that anything worthy waited for me anywhere, thinking I'd run into the same stonewall with magazines or newspapers in New York, Los Angeles, Chicago or even at home in Buffalo. I'd already been rejected by the *Buffalo Gazette* multiple times, but in my wanderlust, everywhere seemed like a better place to be than Boston. And maybe Johanna was the subliminal reason I felt New York was my best option. If I was bound to fail professionally, at least I could give my love life a final shot. I attempted to deliver a relevant explanation to my grandfather with these thoughts bouncing through my head. But, before I could explain, he started up again.

"Joseph, do you know what it is to be certain about anything?"

My hesitancy to respond answered his question. I thought about reacting petulantly toward his insinuation, but it would have only dragged things deeper into the stubborn traditions I'd learned from him and my father. We all hated to admit we were wrong, but I was. He was right.

"No, I'm not sure that I do."

"Not sure if you're sure, eh boy?" He got comfortable in his chair, prepping for another one of his long and detailed stories. "Well, let me tell you something about being certain: Cherish the times when you can find certainty, Joseph. In seventy-five years of my life, there hasn't been many of them."

"What about when you were my age? Did you know anything?"

"Kid, when I was your age, I knew I was happy to be alive. I was happy to have my arms and legs after the war. Happy to have a job. Happy to be married. Happy to be a father. Happy to be loved. Happy to be in love."

He paused briefly for a smile, with memories of his youth running through his head.

"You know what that's like, Joseph?"

"To be happy?"

"No," he said. "To be in love?"

"I think with Johanna, yeah."

He smiled.

"Still thinking, eh kid? But you're still not sure?"

"How'd you know for certain you loved Grandma? Do you remember when the two of you met?"

"Of course I remember, dammit. How old do you think I am, kid?"

"Sorry, Gramps."

The tea kettle started to whistle, prompting him to rise from his seat to turn off the burner. He answered my question while pouring water over the tea bag dangling in his cup.

"July 26th, 1946. Up at Crystal Beach in Canada for a Friday night dance."

He clutched his steaming cup and walked back over to sit down. He leaned back and got comfortable again, dipping the tea bag in and out of his cup, then straining all the tea out of the bag by wrapping the string around the bag and pulling it against the spoon. He dropped in a teaspoon of sugar and a shot of cream, then stirred as it settled.

"They used to have these dances up at the beach, with an eighteen-piece orchestra playing to all of us up there to meet girls and do the bunny hop," he said, then laughed. "I'd just come back from the war, and as I walked into this dance hall, I remember seeing your grandmother, sitting against the wall with her hair up and wearing a white dress. As I walked over to where she was seated, I noticed she was seated next to this other guy."

"So what did you do?"

"Well, I walked right up to her and said, 'Are you with him?' You know what she said?"

"What?"

He grinned, ear to ear.

"*Not anymore.*"

"Then what happened?"

"Well, we danced and danced the whole night until we were the last two on the floor. When they eventually threw us out of the joint, we walked down the beach to where your grandmother was staying. We sat on the beach and talked under the moon until the sun started to come up. If I can remember correctly, it was a harvest moon, orange in color."

"You remember the color of the moon?"

"The moon, the reflection on the lake, the way the moonlight shined on your grandmother's face. All of it, and that's what it's like."

"What what's like?"

He slowly took another sip from his tea, then pressed his

lips together to enjoy the taste before he answered. He leaned back and looked as sure now as he must have felt on July 26th, 1946. He was just a kid, but he felt something that had eluded me for most of my young days; it was still fresh. He took a deep breath, enjoying the tea and the warm feeling in his chest, and answered my question.

"Certainty," he said. "It's a feeling that seeps deep inside your head and heart, kid. What do you know in your heart to be true?"

At twenty-two, what didn't I question? After that September morning, I began to question everything I took for granted. I began to doubt my security, and I analyzed how I was spending precious minutes of a life that could end in a blink. I questioned whether the rest of my life would be full of the rejection and frustration my time away from home was already saturated in. I knew my grandfather had faced decades much tougher than any of my own, but my questioning still seemed relevant. I knew I'd never voluntarily serve in the military like he had, and I hoped I'd never be forced into action as a result of a war. The thought of war made my worries seem petty, so I didn't mention them to my Grandpa Cahan. Instead, I tried to focus on different certainties as they flickered through my head like a lightning storm, providing small sparks and departing as soon as they flashed their identity.

Amid all my new cynicism, what did I know to be true? What did I believe? I believed in God. I still believed in love, even if I wasn't sure whether the kind I'd felt was strong enough. I knew I was smart, but not so smart that I'd never be perceived as stupid. I believed in the Cahans. I knew Duff and Terry would be my friends for life, whether in Buffalo or elsewhere. I believed that, even though Jack Kemp led the Bills to two AFL titles in '64 and '65, Jim Kelly was the greatest quarterback in Buffalo Bills history. I believed that, someday, the Bills would win the Super Bowl. I believed that *Exile on Main Street* was a better album than *Sgt. Pepper's Lonely Hearts Club Band.* I believed the E Street Band should be in the Rock and Roll Hall Of Fame with Bruce Springsteen, and I knew The Clash would always remain the most underappreciated band in rock history. I believed the first sip of Guinness to be the best. I believed the city of Buffalo would, one day, rise to prominence. I believed the most important part of a woman is her eyes, and I didn't say that just to get laid. I knew Johanna Darcy had unbelievable eyes. I believed I loved her, but I knew I'd never appreciate how much with how badly things ended. Finally, I knew that my Grandpa Cahan knew much more about life than I ever would.

"How about what I don't know?" I said. "It'd probably be easier for me to tell you those things."

"Okay, okay. What don't you know?"

"Well, with no school or career prospects, I don't know the point of being in Boston anymore. That's why I'm thinking of moving to New York."

"Okay. What else?"

"I don't know if I made the right decision with Johanna, so moving to New York would give me a chance to be certain, one way or the other."

"Anything else?"

"When this is all said and done, I don't know if I'll regret the decisions I've made, or whether I'll be able to live with those regrets."

My grandfather put his hand through his thinning white hair again. I couldn't tell whether he was thinking of a response or frustrated with my petty concerns. He scratched the back of his head with a drawn look on his face, then glanced up to the ceiling. It was only for a second, but I still caught it. It acted as a look to the heavens, almost attempting to summon divine guidance for his delivery. After that brief look skyward, he looked back down at me, his grandson.

"You want me to go one at a time with those, or do you want me to answer all of them with one answer?"

"Your call."

"Well, one answer to all your problems?" he said. "You worry too much. You worry about things you can't do anything about, like regret. Regrets are realized in hindsight, not foresight, so why waste your time anticipating? Give life a go, kid. With that thought, I'll try to go one by one with the rest. You comfortable? We Cahans like to talk."

I smiled.

"Yeah, I know."

"First, if where you move for a career doesn't work out, you still have a home, right here. Your parents will be here. Your sisters, Frank, they'll be here. And, God willing, I'll be here.

"Second, you're not doing yourself any favors being someplace you don't need to be. At this point in your life, you'd only be betraying yourself if you stay. Move on, see new things, but listen to your father. When you've made your millions and you're a big-time writer, come back to Buffalo. This is and always will be your home."

"I know, Gramps."

"But don't take it for granted, dammit. Don't treat this city and this community like a weigh station. You respect your home because it raised you. It made you who you are, sitting right there across from me."

He paused for a sip of his tea.

"Lastly, this girl," he said. "Do you really think you have to move close to her to see if you made a mistake?"

"Well, what do you think I should do? We've been talking on the phone, things have gone well, but I'm afraid to see her again after the way things ended. It would bring things back together too fast. If we lived closer, like at school, we could give it time and take it slow. Weekend visits tend to be rushed, and I'd feel like everything had to be fit into that time frame instead of being brought about gently. I don't want this to be condensed."

He looked at me, confused.

"And you think uprooting your life for her is a better idea? How far is Boston from New York?"

"Three or four hours, I think. Why?"

He leaned forward, hot cup in his hand.

"Well, call me old fashioned, but when I was dating your grandmother, she lived in Syracuse and I had to take the train to see her. Since we were still developing feelings for each other, it would've been a little rash if I picked up my things and moved to Syracuse so our visits weren't so condensed, don't you think?"

"So you think I should risk it? Go see her for a weekend?"

"Sure. Go meet her in New York for the weekend, even a week if you have to. Spend some time together and talk before you dive into even more uncertainty."

I didn't need more doubts or questions. When I considered going to New York, a second chance with Johanna always existed as an added bonus that could flourish into an ultimate incentive to stay. If it ever seemed risky, I always balanced it with the city's potential professional opportunities. My Grandpa Cahan knew better. He knew love should never be an extra incentive. If I were thinking of it as such, it would never work. Not with Johanna, not with anyone. If I was going to bring her into my already unstable life, I'd better feel the rare certainty in my head and heart my grandfather described. There were few certainties in life, but there was a way to eliminate some of the anomalies in my daily life. Johanna, unfortunately, had become one of them.

"Can I ask you another question, kid?" he said. "Have you written this girl anything since the two of you started talking again?"

"Like a letter?"

"Sure. Letters, poems, whatever kinds of creative stuff you do."

"I've tried, but it's been too hard to put any rational thoughts together about us, about her. Talking on the phone has been easier."

He leaned down to his left, picked up a wrapped box next to his feet and set it on the table.

"Well, see what you can do with this."

I took off the wrapping paper and opened the cardboard top to find an old, beaten up black typewriter inside. The keys looked in decent shape, but the ribbon was unfurled and worn. As I removed it from the box and held it in front of me, I tried to put on a grateful face, though I had no idea why my grandfather was packaging up old things from his house and giving them to me for Christmas.

"Thanks. So where's this from?"

"It was mine when I was around your age. I used it to type letters to your grandmother when we started dating that summer. They'd read better than my terrible handwriting. Since you're the writer, I thought you might get some use out of it. Now that I know you're having these difficulties with your girl, it might stand to serve two purposes."

"You typed all your letters to Grandma on this typewriter?"

"Every one. When I sat down in front of it, it always inspired me to write my best for her. It worked for me, so hopefully, it will work for you. Put all the confusion you're feeling through that ribbon, kid."

"Thanks, Gramps," I said, then walked over to give him a firm handshake.

"Merry Christmas, Joseph." He pulled me in for the hug. "Now go get to work."

He had one last sip of his tea, and then popped his cap back atop his white strands. Like a doctor making a house call, his job was done and he was ready to move on. I watched him get up from his chair slowly, then head into the living room to talk with Claire and Molly, still organizing their gifts into piles. He'd addressed my problems, but his years gave him wisdom to go around. Maybe Molly had met a boy at school, or maybe Claire had a problem with one of her advertising clients. I stood in the kitchen holding an old typewriter and could see empty chairs in the living room. If he planned on handing out more life lessons that Christmas, he'd have to get comfortable in one of them.

After all, as I'd found out over the years, the eldest Cahan liked to talk.

23

Terry wasn't happy as we sat at Fitzgerald's, watching the Bills-Jets game on the television attached to the wall.

"I still don't believe we kept Rob Johnson to play quarterback over Flutie," he said. "He's fucking injured again while lil' Dougie has started every game for San Diego this year. How many games did Johnson finish on two legs this season? Five? Six?"

Doug Flutie had been released by the Bills the previous offseason amid a quarterback controversy, but Terry's loyalty kept Flutie's royal blue jersey on his back. He sipped his Budweisers in denial as we sat at the bar watching that Sunday's game, waiting for Duff and Kiley to join us. Duff, according to Terry, did everything with Kiley. He'd work an early shift at the stamping plant, then take her out to dinner or stay in and rent a movie. On the weekends, they'd meet up with Terry around the University of Buffalo campus, head down to Elmwood and monopolize the Doherty's jukebox. Terry couldn't find anything bad to say about the girl, except that she still hadn't hooked him up with one of her friends. It was a wonder that she'd refused to toss someone she cared for into the arms of Buffalo's biggest Doug Flutie fan. I continued with him on that topic.

"The defense propped up Flutie when he was here and you know it. The whole league had him figured out in ninety-nine by week nine. The Bills had no choice."

"You're a fucking traitor, Cahan," he said, feebly pointing at me. "Bag on him now, but in his first year here, I remember how you ate Flutie Flakes before every Bills game out of superstition. Did you think I'd forget that shit?"

I grabbed his finger in front of my face.

"Would you settle down? I'm not saying he wasn't good; I'm just saying it was his time to go. Chemistry with the team took a nosedive with him at the helm, and you know that too."

"Well, I'm not sure if you've seen a newspaper in Boston lately, but we've won two goddamn games all season, with two left to play." He grabbed his beer bottle and swigged. "Now it's up to Van Pelt to get us number three. I'm sure Flutie could've gotten us more than three fucking wins."

"Why?" I turned away from the television to look right at him. I knew exactly what he was going to say. "Because he's a winner? Is that what you're going to say?"

"Well, he—"

"Save it," I said. "Just drink your beer and hope AVP can find a receiver for a touchdown or two today."

I took a swig and felt a slap on my back.

"What's the score?" Duff said, staring at the television

while taking off his coat and draping it over the top of an empty barstool.

"Nothing-nothing," I said, "but it's only the first, and we've gone three-and-out our first two possessions. Beer?"

"Two. Kiley dropped me off at the door so she could park. My yelling at the radio was driving her nuts, so she made me get out."

I stood waiting to get Eddie's attention as Kiley walked in the door, brushing the snow off the sleeves of her camel pea coat as she pulled a light blue and white striped ski hat off her dark hair. She held a smile but alternated looks between the television and us before she reached Duff, draped her arms over his shoulders and looked toward me with rich brown eyes.

"You must be Cahan."

"And you must be Kiley. Nice to finally have a face to go with secondhand stories."

"Likewise," she said, then looked to the television. "So what's the score? Still zero-zero?"

"Yup."

"At two and twelve, you would think they'd turn Van Pelt loose and pass on every down. Guy did break every one of Dan Marino's college passing records at Pittsburgh."

"You see?" said Terry. "I told you this girl's impressive."

"Do you have any sisters?" I said, smiling.

She popped her head back and laughed.

"Two," she said. "But one's fourteen and one's two hundred

fifty pounds. Which one do you want to wait out?"

I looked to Duff and shook my head.

"Where in God's name did you find this girl?"

"Doherty's," he said, then clanked his bottle against mine. "After all our years picking songs on that juke, I finally found a girl who was picking the same ones."

"And that's it? That's all you needed to find this aberration?"

"Music says a lot, dude. What can I say? Girl's got a soundtrack," he said, then shrugged before taking Kiley's kiss on his left cheek. She glanced up at the game again, then let go of Duff so she could step away to the bathroom. I turned to Duff and shook my head again in disbelief once she was a safe distance away.

"Are you kidding me? Did you feed her that Van Pelt shit to impress us or what?"

"Cahan, girl grew up in the end zone at Rich Stadium with the Section A drunks. Her father had season tickets there. Now, he works the turnstiles at every home game. He actually let Terry and I pass through free for the Carolina and Miami games. She knows her stuff."

"So what are your intentions with this girl?"

"Go ahead, dude," Terry said. "Tell him what you told me last week at Doherty's."

"Well." He took a quick swig of his bottle. "I think this is it for me, Cahan. I really do."

"What do you mean *it*? Marriage?"

"She's the one, Cahan. She's got to be the one."

I kept in mind that Duff had never been in a serious relationship throughout our irresponsible lives. It's not that he had trouble finding girls either; quite the opposite. Girls outside of high school, at parties on the weekend, or at Doherty's and Fitzgerald's would always approach him, but he never committed himself. On a Sunday after Christmas, sitting next to me at that same bar he'd picked up one-nighters and backseat make-outs, he said he was through with his indecision. He wasn't even twenty-three years old, and on that day, he told me he was ready to cash it in with a girl from South Buffalo named Kiley Donlan.

"And you'd say that with her standing right next to you?"

"It's come up, and she feels the same. I can't explain it. Makes you wonder what the hell you're doing with yourself, doesn't it?" he said, then delivered another lighthearted slap to the back.

"All right, all right," said Terry. "No more of this. Game's back on. Let's watch and leave the life decisions until the next commercial."

We stared intently at the television above as Alex Van Pelt hit running back Larry Centers with a screen pass for a first down, causing the whole bar to enthusiastically clap or slap the bar top. Terry smacked the bar top before pointing at the television to yell,

"Every fucking time, AVP! Every fucking time!"

Eddie stood tall behind the bar, arms crossed with his bar towel slung over his left shoulder.

"Terry, keep the language down or I'll toss you out onto the lake with the ice fishermen," he said.

Kiley took a seat next to Duff as the Bills broke their huddle. I leaned over to Duff before the snap.

"I'm thinking about calling it quits in Boston and moving to New York."

"You're going there for Johanna, aren't you?" he said, still focused on the game.

"Not yet, no. But, I'm thinking about taking one more shot to see if I should. I might take a train down to the city in a couple of weeks."

Van Pelt took a sack behind the line.

"Come on, Alex," said Kiley. "You have to dump that to Centers in the flat!"

"What's stopping you from going?" he said. "Shit doesn't seem to be happening in Boston except unneeded stress from your job and that crazy boss of yours."

"I'm still not sure if it's a good idea. What if it doesn't work out again? What if it's another waste of time?"

"And you think it's more constructive to keep asking yourself the same damn questions about this girl, wasting your time wondering while we should be focused on the game here with a couple of beers?"

Terry jumped up off his stool again.

"That's pass interference, ref! That's pass interference!" It was, and it gave the Bills the ball with first and goal on the three.

"Look, Cahan," said Duff. "We had this conversation back at Doherty's over the summer, remember?"

"Sure."

"You said you were finished with this girl, but something keeps bringing you back. Something in her is making you ignore all the reasons you shouldn't be together, and that something is preventing you from moving on with your life. Christ, Maria was all over you that night, and you couldn't seal it with her because of Johanna."

"Don't forget the whiskey."

He laughed.

"Right. And the whiskey."

The Bills lined up at the three.

"Three yards, Alex," said Kiley. "You know the Jets are expecting the halfback dive, so go with the play-action. You know a receiver will break free in the right corner."

"I understand your hesitation, Cahan, but you have to bag it to see if this is your real chance at this," he said, then motioned to his left with his bottleneck. "If it is, God bless you because it's fucking great."

Van Pelt relaxed in the pocket and found wide receiver Eric Moulds in the back right corner of the end zone on a beautifully executed play-action pass. Terry jumped from his stool and threw his arms up for the signal.

"Touchdown! You called it, Kiley! You called it!"

Duff turned and looked at me with a smile of satisfaction, as if Kiley's call exhibited his entire point. He held out the neck of his beer for a cheers and gave me another slap to the back.

"See what I mean, pal? Get on the train and find out so we can both celebrate our good fortune."

"Merry Christmas, Duff," I said. "And, go Bills."

"You got it pal. Go Bills."

24

Penn Station in New York City always had a smell to it. I always took the train from Exchange Street Station in Buffalo right into the bowels of Penn whenever I'd visited Johanna on semester breaks. I would emerge each time from the musty smell of an Amtrak rail car to be hit directly in the face with Penn Station's thick smell: boiling hot dogs and buttered popcorn amid an aroma of sweat.

It wasn't necessarily a bad smell; it was just familiar. The humidity that filled the air off the tracks worked to accentuate the smell to such strength that, when I thought of Penn Station, I could bring the scent under my nose. The smell was in my head even before I removed my old red hockey bag from the luggage rack above my seat as my train slowly crept toward Penn. I took the train to New York from Boston after work on a Friday to meet up with Johanna for the first time since we graduated. My head was flooded with rational and irrational thoughts of what was going to happen. Both dueled for most of the trip, so thinking about something different, even if it was the aroma of hot dogs, popcorn, and sweat, was releasing.

The train came to a complete stop on a cold night in the middle of January without many passengers on my train. I appreciated the space when I reached up to grab my oversized bag. The length and girth of the thing wasn't very accommodating, so if there were a crowd, it would've been hard for me to not hit people with it as I turned corners. I'd only be in town for the weekend, but the bag appeared to be packed for a week.

I exited the train into Penn Station, walked past the entrance to Madison Square Garden and up the escalator and came up out onto 7th Avenue to hail a ride across town to Grand Central Station. I had to grab the Harlem Line train out of Grand Central to get to Johanna's place in White Plains. The ride would take another half an hour, but waiting for a cab in front of Penn gave me a chance to stretch my legs, still cramped from sitting and staring out the window through Massachusetts and Connecticut for four hours. When the next one pulled up, I opened up the passenger door, tossed my bag onto the leather upholstered back seat, and followed it in.

"Grand Central Station, please," I said.

We pulled away from Penn and I looked out the taxi window to see buildings and billboards lining the streets. Being in New York City always provided me with a surreal feeling, its surroundings so sensational they made me feel like I was in a movie. The scene was the backdrop for so many stories and, as I rode along, I hoped it would play a role in my life that weekend.

The doubts about whether a life with Johanna would be ideal were shelved. But, my idealism was always more fantasy than reality, always much simpler in my head than in the situation that would unfold. It wouldn't be easy to straighten things out with her, nor would it be easy to slip into a New York City existence like slipping into my Doc Martens. Still, my movie-scenario mindset intervened, and these minimal reservations were quelled by the urban playground passing my cab.

I needed to call Johanna and let her know where I was. My cell had died on the train, so I asked the driver to pull over at a pay phone in front of Connolly's Pub on 45th Street, right down the street from Grand Central. While I sifted through my pockets for change on my walk to the phone, I was approached by a bearded man in a tattered, blackened overcoat and a New York Rangers ski cap from across the street. He began to proposition me before reaching me.

"Sa-sa-sa-sa-sir, sa-sa-sa-sa-sir? Du-du-du-du-du-du-du-do ya-ya-ya-ya-yu . . . uh, uh," he said, becoming frustrated with his dramatic stutter.

I would have assumed this guy was insane if not for my sister Molly's childhood stuttering problem. I accepted his hitch and was patient while guarded. Just because he had a major speech impediment didn't mean he wasn't about to rob me blind of my red bag and everything in my pockets. I had Black Velvet milling around my apartment every night, so for all I knew, this guy might have been approaching me for fifteen dollars or more.

I let him finish while standing defensively, my left hand grasping my bag.

"Ah-ah-ah-ah-ah-ah-enie ch-ch-ch-ch-enge, pu-pu-pu-pu-leez?" he said.

"Sure," I said. I felt around my right leg for a single, but didn't want to pull out the wrong bill. If I pulled out a twenty, I'd have to give the guy a twenty. I knew my cash was in a roll, so I tried to pull from the inside where the ones were. When I saw I'd grabbed a five, I hesitated—then forked it over.

"Here you go. Go grab yourself a drink inside, take a load off."

"Yeah, yeah," he said, shaking his head in agreement. "Tha-tha-tha-tha-thank you, sir."

I watched him limp into Connolly's for a drink, then set my bag down on the sidewalk and straddled it with the inside of my left and right ankles; there was less of a chance to be tackled for my belongings than to have them grabbed. I looked to the left and right one last time, then picked up the phone to dial Johanna's cell. She picked up after two rings.

"Hello?"

"Hey, I'm outside Grand Central and about to go in to grab a ticket for the next train to White Plains."

"Don't bother," she said. "I'm at Grand Central right now. I wanted to come into the city to meet you."

"Perfect. So, you want to meet me at Connolly's on 45th, between Madison and 5th?"

312

"I'll be there in a minute," she said. "Go to the bar and order me a Guinness."

I hung up the phone and had a warm, anticipatory feeling come over me. Maybe it was hearing her smoky voice. Maybe it was a feeling of excitement at the chance to get things between the two of us right, a chance to grab what I saw Duff had, what I thought I once had. I wanted to make amends with Johanna and continue toward the serendipitous movie scenario that crossed my mind on hundred thirty two times during the train ride from South Station. The ride in the cab, passing busy pedestrians, towering buildings, and the huge advertisements which symbolized New York's streets on a national stage seemed to be inviting an ideal encounter between the two of us. Maybe we could get back to a time we smiled more than we argued, back to the days when we appreciated the significance of our feelings. Back to the nights when the sincerity of my words wasn't constantly questioned, and back to a place when I didn't question whether my feelings made sense. I stood outside Connolly's Pub in midtown Manhattan and enjoyed thinking of the possibilities.

I walked into the dim bar to see a framed picture of John F. Kennedy displayed proudly behind the bar. An isolated light shined brightly on his visage, magnifying his prominence. The room was scattered with people dressed in business attire, their woolen hats and winter coats resting on stools and chairs around them. Most men were sitting on barstools or standing at high-top tables, with suit pants, dress shirts and loosened neckties. They laughed in conversation, holding their beer bottles and pint glasses under the Knicks-Bulls game on television. The women were interspersed in pantsuits and skirts, sipping from martini glasses or milking half-empty bottles of Amstel Light. It was obviously a professional crowd, so when I came through the door wearing a blue car coat, an unbuttoned yellow dress shirt over a Ramones t-shirt, faded jeans and an oversized red bag tossed over my shoulder, I looked out of place—almost more so than the tattered-clothes guy, who'd found himself a private spot in the back corner. He was standing discreetly under one of the elevated televisions. He spotted me and raised his rocks glass full of brown booze. I gave him a small head nod and smile, then continued to an empty high-top across from the closest corner of the bar.

I settled myself into one of the heightened seats. I set my bag underneath, and the cocktail waitress immediately approached.

"What can I getcha?" she said, alternating uncomfortable looks between the awkwardly large bag and me.

"Two pints of Guinness, please."

"For who? You and the stiff?" She cracked a smirk through her heavy lipstick. "What the Christ you got in that sack, or shouldn't I even ask?"

"It's just clothes and books. I'm here visiting for a few days from Boston."

"Boston, huh? Too bad the Sox couldn't beat the Yankees

for the division again this season, huh?"

"I'm actually not from Boston. I'm from Buffalo."

She laughed.

"Buffalo? Bills fan?"

"Of course."

"Oh boy, you know who the coach of my kid's Pop Warner football team is?"

"Who?"

"Otis Anderson. The Giants running back? Remember him from the Super Bowl against the Bills? That uppercut?" She mimicked how Anderson's forearm swung under Mark Kelso's chinstrap during one of his debilitating runs in Super Bowl twenty-five.

"I remember."

"Too bad you guys couldn't make that short kick at the end. It would have been exciting."

"It was forty-seven yards, on grass. It wasn't short or easy."

Her brown eyes perked with interest.

"Forty-seven? Really? I always thought it was way shorter. Well, at least you're out of those Buffalo blizzard conditions. Welcome to the city," she said, then set down two bar napkins and walked off to the bar.

I shook my head dismissively and reached into my shirt pocket to pull out a crumpled soft pack of Camel Lights. I pulled out the one cigarette poking out of the pack, lit it and took a long drag before placing it in the ashtray to burn. The smoke wafted

315

off its tip as the door opened to the right of me. Johanna Darcy.

The memories gushed forth in a three second rush. The sparkle of her eyes right before we'd kiss; the way her red locks would toss to the side when she turned; the sound of her voice when she'd say my name; the smell of her skin as she'd lay next me on a lazy winter morning. When you miss someone, you never think about the bad times. You edit out the calamity and only let the angelic experiences exist as history. Right there at the door of Connolly's Pub on 45th Street, between 5th and Madison, my heart pounded thinking about that past.

I walked over to Johanna and pulled her close to me. My hands touched her waist and slid across her lower back to meet in the middle. Her arms wrapped around the back of my neck. At first, it was a very friendly hug. After about three seconds, we started to hold tighter, pull closer. It was as if we each had a preconceived line we didn't want to cross, but halfway through, decided to blur or eradicate that line. The seconds continued to pass as she buried her head deeper into my shoulder, and I pulled her closer to my chest. I brushed her red hair behind her ear and whispered into it softly.

"I missed you."

"You mean it?" she said, letting out a small giggle before pulling back a bit to look at me. Blues soft and deep. We were lost in a small stare, only to be broken up by our waitress.

"Ah, a third wheel for you and the toe tag, huh? This one seems a bit more mobile, handsome," she said, then set the two pints down on our table. "You want to pay for these, or do you two want to run a tab?"

"Tab, please," said Johanna, then handed her credit card to the waitress. "You don't mind if we hang out for a few, do you, Joseph?"

"Joseph?" It was the first time she didn't call me Cahan. It sounded nice. "No, I don't mind."

We sat at the high-top, looking over our pints at each other; exhibiting embarrassing smiles you try to control, but they control you. My smile widened as I raised my pint toward Johanna.

"I would think a toast is in order here, right?"

She smiled.

"What are we toasting tonight?"

"How about to what could be the start of a great weekend together?"

"Don't be so pessimistic there, buddy. It will be a great weekend. I promise."

"I'm going to hold you to that on Sunday."

"I hope you do."

We raised our pints to each other, and then lightly clanked them together before taking our first sips. Mine had such a good taste that I leaned back to enjoy it. I reached toward the ashtray to have a drag off my still burning cigarette, but continued to admire her as she fiddled through her purse on the table.

"You look beautiful."

"As do you—in a manly sort of way. That Ramones shirt does wonders for your complexion."

"I forgot how hilarious you are in person," I said, smiling as she placed an unopened pack of cigarettes on the table. "Still smoking I see."

"I'm committed."

One. Two. Three. Four. Five.

"And what about the pills?"

I went right after it. I didn't want to interrupt the moment, but I needed to know before I started fooling myself again. If she was still taking them, then there'd be little room for compromise. The weekend's imagined movie ending would crash into the pavement before my Guinness was gone.

"Well, it's taken you long enough to ask," she said. "What's it been? Three minutes?"

"How about three months? It's taken me this long to bring this up because I didn't want to know; I didn't think I'd be able to take the wrong answer. But, now that we're here, I need to know. Are you off of them?"

"I'm off them, yes. I didn't want to bring this up over the phone, but I've been going to counseling once-a-week to talk out some of the stuff that was taking me down, taking us down. I think it's been going well. This doctor's better than the one at school."

"You only went to two sessions with him."

"But, I felt comfortable with this one from the first meeting.

No bad vibes. Sometimes, you can just feel them right away."

"And the drinking?"

"You're looking at it. A few beers here and there. No more shots, no more liquor. I left that stuff at school. I'm not the same girl you left in May, Joseph."

I leaned toward her and placed my elbows on the table.

"What about the girl I fell in love with? The girl I've been talking with for the last few months. Am I sitting with her or what?"

She looked at me, put her elbows up on the table and pushed her pint to her right. She leaned forward, her head upon her hands and eyes sparkling with sincerity.

"I hope so."

I moved closer to her, as she did toward me. We met for a kiss over the table top, over our Guinnesses and over my still burning cigarette. It felt like the first time again. It felt like we were back in my dorm room kissing over cans of Busch. I felt nervous again, like I was fiddling around with the remote, trying to play Dylan. It's a crazy feeling to be able to unintentionally reinvent a moment. It happened when I was in my car, a bar or a record shop and I'd hear a familiar song coming through the surrounding speakers. I'd hear the first notes and think back to the time and place I first heard those notes. A rush of feelings associated with the track would follow those thoughts. And these experiences remained forever, like the feeling of my first kiss with a woman who floored me with the touch of her lips.

I noticed a jukebox on the wall once we broke apart. I motioned to Johanna that I was going over to play a few songs, then went over to find a stacked selection: The Clash, tons of Stones, and even a little Dylan lined the juke's pages. It was three songs for a dollar, so I put in a buck for "Stay Free" by The Clash, "Loving Cup" by the Stones, and Dylan's "Abandoned Love." Going with "Visions of Johanna" would have been too sentimental, so I decided to lighten the mood after our intimate sincerity. The Clash started to storm through the pub as I walked over to the table and reached out my hand.

"Wanna dance?"

"In here?"

"Sure, why not? I don't know any of these people. Do you?"

"Guess not. Let us dance, young Joseph," she said, then stepped off her chair, curtsied and grabbed my hand. I twirled her into me and we shuffled around in an open bar section not meant for dancing. Mick Jones's vocals pumped over us as I sang along to Johanna,

"We met when we were at school. Never took no shit from no one. We were fools!"

She laughed as I spun her around like we were in an old swing club. The music didn't call for it, but that's how we felt like dancing. While we continued to bop around, the tattered-clothes guy came over and tapped me on the shoulder. I was surprised, but not as guarded as before.

"Hey, how's your drink?" I said.

"It's gu-gu-gu-gu-good. Th-th-th-th-thanks again!"

"Say, what's your name, anyway?"

"Tom. Tom De-sa-sa-sa-sa-Sarlo."

"Well, Tom, this is Johanna. Johanna, Tom DeSarlo. We met outside before you got here."

"Hi, Tom," she said, then extended her hand without a hint of apprehension. "It's nice to meet you."

I stood and admired as she talked to Tom, asking him questions and patiently listening to each one of his labored responses. Gratitude beamed across his face, causing me to wonder when was the last time anyone gave Tom DeSarlo this kind of humane attention. I assumed it wasn't recently. But there stood Johanna, ignoring what this guy looked like, enjoying every word he stuttered.

And, as I watched Tom talk with her, I could see his drink was down to the cubes.

"So, Tom," I said, "how about another drink?"

"Sh-sh-sh-sh-sure. I'd lu-lu-lu-lu-love one."

"What are you having?"

"Wild Tu-tu-tu-tu-turkey, please. On the ru-ru-ru-ru-ruocks."

"Johanna?"

"Another Guinness, please."

I stepped back to our high-top to see if our waitress was milling around in the area. As I stood with palms on the tabletop,

I noticed her across the room talking to a large bouncer at the door. He stood well over six feet tall in a black polo shirt with arms crossed, and she spoke toward his ear, tilted down so her voice could reach it. She seemed to be motioning over to our table with her eyes, but she didn't notice me tapping my fingers, waiting for drinks. After I noticed her eye movement, I saw her hand motion toward my table. She tried to be subtle about it the first time, but the second time was a deliberate point, left index finger extended. Her eyes followed her finger, and she saw me standing. I raised my hand to get her attention, and she cut off her conversation and proceeded to walk over. The bouncer stood up straight again, chest puffed out and arms folded as he followed her path for a second, then panned across the room to stare at Johanna and Tom, standing and laughing in the middle of our makeshift dance floor. When the waitress reached our high-top, she gave a good-natured rhythmic tabletop tap.

"Sorry 'bout that," she said. "You weren't waiting long, were you?"

"No, no problem. Can we get two more pints of Guinness and one Wild Turkey on the rocks, please?"

She stepped back from the table. She shifted her eyes from side to side, folded her hands uncomfortably and rocked back on the balls of her feet. When she saw my confusion, she stood flat-footed and put her palms back on the tabletop.

"Is there some sort of problem?"

"Um, yeah" she said in a very low tone. "Do you know the

gentleman speaking with your girl over there?"

"I just met him. Why?"

"Well, he usually sleeps in the alleyway out back and, somehow, he got in here for a drink. We have a new bartender on tonight, and Nick over there on the door wasn't here earlier, so he got in and was served. I didn't notice him until a minute ago, but we really can't have him in here."

"Why? Has he gotten out of hand or something? I've been standing with him most of the time, and he hasn't done a thing except drink his drink. What am I missing here?"

She stood up straight and glared at me, visibly agitated.

"Look," she said. "We can't have dirty, Oscar the Grouch street bums sipping drinks in here. It makes our clientele uncomfortable. Maybe upstate, you can drink beers with homeless tramps without the threat of one of them stabbing someone, but things are a little different here in the city."

"But I live in Boston. Not significant enough of a city for you?"

"It's not New York, sweetie. Nowhere is."

I looked at her, waiting for her to crack a smile and say she was kidding, but she didn't. I looked back at Johanna as she talked to Tom, who didn't seem violent or crazy, but appeared to be a guy who hadn't encountered one person with the patience to listen to a word he had said for years. What I saw as a positive was being condemned as negative. All I could do was shake my head and laugh before responding.

"You're right. Being raised upstate, I was too busy fighting through ten-month snowstorms and Super Bowl agony to be stabbed by a street bum. Christ, this is the first time I've ever seen one.

She crossed her arms and rolled her eyes.

"If I had any idea that Tom over there was a calculating lunatic, waiting to go insane on this whole bar, I wouldn't have bought him his first drink. The last thing I wanted to do was threaten your clientele while you rape them for seven dollar beers."

She put her palms back on the tabletop.

"Look, I don't have time for some liberal lesson in humanitarianism. Do you want the two pints or not?"

"No," I said. "Here's the money for the first two, close out her tab, and we'll let you get back to your misconceptions."

"Funny."

She took my bills and stormed off to the bouncer, his arms still crossed. When she reached him, she talked into his ear again before pointing right at us, nothing subtle or secret about it. He lumbered over to our dance floor and grabbed Tom's arm as my Dylan song played out of the juke. I could see the surprised look on Johanna's face, so I made my way over for an explanation.

"What's going on?" she said.

"This guy's gotta go. The two of you are out too."

His voice was deep and almost purposely intimidating.

"What, why? Joseph, what the hell is going on?"

324

"C'mon, we got to go," I said. "Grab your card from the waitress. I paid for the drinks."

But Johanna was never passive; she wasn't stupid either. She could sense something cold was going down. I could sense her getting angry as the seconds passed and the reasons tumbled to set themselves inside her head. Johanna was friendly, excessively compassionate, humble, and always tried to lend a hand toward the unfortunate. Sometimes, her biggest fault was her inability to understand why anyone would think differently, especially since that September morning. She could sense the bouncer didn't share her opinion as he led Tom DeSarlo out the bar by his coat sleeve.

"No, I want to know why the hell that guy's throwing Tom out," she said. "He wasn't bothering anybody."

"The waitress told me they didn't want him in here because he sleeps in a back alley around here. She said he's making people uncomfortable."

"Who? Who's he making uncomfortable?"

"She didn't really give me the specifics."

She couldn't believe what had happened—even if it was quite believable. She'd just met Tom, but she seemed prepared to swing at a gargantuan bouncer named Nick in his defense. She panned across the bar and high-tops, then cupped the sides of her mouth to speak to the bar crowd.

"Excuse me!" she said. I jumped, surprised at the announcement, then muffled my mouth with my hand.

"What the hell are you doing?"

"Don't worry. I just want some answers," she said, then reared back for another announcement. "Excuse me, please! Were any of you uncomfortable with the guy I was talking with? The waitress seems to think it was a huge problem."

The bar become remarkably quiet, focused on this small redhead addressing an entire pub of strangers in midtown Manhattan. The waitress stood embarrassed at the corner of the bar as perplexed looks cascaded over the silent crowd. Johanna waited for a response, but the only comments were mumbled under people's breath, wondering who the lunatic at the front of the pub was.

"Anyone?" she said.

I approached her and whispered into her ear,

"Can we please get out of here, now?"

While a hushed confusion encompassed the place, someone in the back shouted, "Shut up, you crazy bitch!"

This broke the silence, causing most of the young men in ties and young women in pant suits to let out a laugh and go on with their martinis and Knicks basketball. Just another crazy person in New York. With that, I grabbed my red bag from under the table and led a fuming Johanna to the door. The bouncer stood before us again at the exit, leaning up against the wall with his arms folded. We walked past him without saying a word, and stepped outside the door as Johanna noticed Tom walking down the street toward 5th Avenue. When she saw him, she started to yell for him.

"Tom! Tom!"

He stopped, turned around and gave a little wave. We waved back to him before he continued down the street to wherever he'd be sleeping. I knew she wanted to go after him, maybe try to get him something to eat or find him someplace to stay. But we quietly stood there, only to be interrupted by Nick's muffled chuckling. When we looked over at him, he glared back sympathetically, shaking his head like we were the most unfortunate losers he'd ever seen. This officially pushed Johanna to her limit. Although compassionate, she was as fiery as the next redhead, unquestionably fitting any stereotype my grandfather assumed.

Upon hearing the bouncer's laugh, she walked right up, stood before him, and flashed a condescending, mocking smile. When he smiled back, she leaned back, inhaled, and spit right in his face. I was caught completely off guard. The bouncer put one hand on his face before using his other hand to push Johanna to the ground. My eyes widened and my adrenaline surged. I decided to ignore the indisputable advantage this behemoth held over me, take a deep breath and then make a run at him. As he stood there wiping more residue off his face, he noticed my approach just soon enough so he could turn his head toward me. But, before he was able to properly focus, I did the only reasonable thing a five-ten kid of medium build could do to a heaping six foot-plus mound of mass clad in black: I wound up and kicked him in his sack.

Maybe it was dirty, but after pushing a woman to the ground, rules went out the window. I pulled the red bag off my shoulder, swung it around and connected squarely with his left jaw and the rest of his face as he hunched over grabbing his groin. Something in the bag—maybe the books—hit him and sent him to the pavement, out cold. I slung the bag back over my shoulder, grabbed Johanna's hand and started to sprint down 45th to the doors of Grand Central Station. We didn't say a word to each other for the whole run, and as we burst through the station doors, we separated hands and ran individually down the stairs to the Metro North ticket window. When we arrived at the counter out of breath, we found a teller waiting, startled by our fevered arrival.

"Two tickets to White Plains, please," I said.

"Do you want to wait for the next one, or do you want to try to grab the one that's on track twenty five right now?"

"Track twenty five!" Johanna and I said in unison.

The teller passed the two tickets through the window, and I passed her a twenty through the slot. We ran from the window as I yelled "keep the change!"

We sprinted across the station lobby to track twenty five and arrived at the platform as the conductor was getting on the train. We jumped through the doors behind him, surprising him as he moved to the side.

"Lucky, lucky, lucky. Just made it," he said, then flashed a small grin.

Out of breath, we looked for a seat.

"Sir," I said, "you have no idea."

25

We didn't do much talking on the train.

I touched the sides of her face as she grasped the hair on the back of my head. We spent most of the ride with our lips connected, with stray, unused seconds spent catching our breath while cradled in the red pleather seats of a Metro North railcar. When we had to take our moments, we spent them staring into each other's eyes in a dazed glare, fatigued but not finished. I went away from her lips to give her time to inhale, kissing the sides of her face and forehead. I even worked her ears, starting at the tops then flowing down to the lobes. I operated on the left and peeked out my right eye to see a smile accompanying her closed eyes.

There may have been other people in our car as it rumbled to the 125th Street stop in Harlem, but neither of us cared. The stirring emotions from Connolly's internalized on our run to Grand Central, then erupted as reckless passion. I heard a cough or two echo behind us at one point, but it wasn't enough of a distraction to stop us. We only took one intended pause when I pulled back with questions. This session had to stop at some point. She lived with her parents, so going back to her place to advance action was out of the question.

"Wait," I said. "What are we going to do when we get off this train? I don't want this to stop, but with your parents around, where can this, you know, reach its conclusion?"

"It's my parents' twenty-fifth wedding anniversary today."

I paused, confused.

"That's fantastic, I guess, for them. So they're home celebrating?"

A devilish smile curled onto her blushing face.

"No. They have a room uptown at the Park Central Hotel, overlooking Central Park. Real swanky place. Even more romantic than our kitchen in White Plains."

"So they're not coming home tonight to greet me?" I said, sarcastically. Her parents were never too thrilled with me.

"Nope," she whispered, then leaned toward my right ear. "Just you and me until Sunday night. House to ourselves, bed to ourselves, us by ourselves. That's okay, right?"

"It'll have to do."

I gently grasped the back of her neck and brought her lips toward mine. My mind was racing. I thought about my cab ride from Penn, peering out the window to wonder if the city that served as the setting for so many reconciliations would serve as the backdrop for another. I thought about Connolly's door opening with Johanna on the other side, then smiling as the track lighting reflected off her eyes. I remembered wrapping my arms around her waist, wondering if the feeling of warmth that ripped through my chest was anything like the feeling my grandfather once felt. I recalled my admiration as she made an outcast feel like he was, for once, part of a cordial society. My heart raced as the train rolled, and my head replayed how my heart thumped under my Ramones t-shirt as we ran hand in hand down 45th. It all happened so fast, but relaxation gently set in with each kiss.

I grabbed my bag and helped Johanna out of her seat as the train finally pulled into our stop. I followed her off the train, down the platform stairs and through the parking lot to her navy blue Ford Explorer. I opened the back door to throw my bag in, and she called to me from the driver's side.

"I know it's no Blue Bomber, but you want to drive? I don't have my glasses, so I really shouldn't be driving at night."

"Little bigger than the Bomber, but I'll give it a try."

I clapped my hands together to call for the keys, then caught her toss in my right hand. Once we were in. I sped through yellow lights and rolled through side street stop signs, making no secret of wanting to get to her house. When we pulled into her driveway off a residential street lined with white mailboxes, large oak trees and property-separating hedges, Johanna leapt out of the car. She ran up the sidewalk to her front door, laughing as she feverishly reached under her door mat for the key to open the door, like she was running for a game of hide-and-seek. When I got to the front door, it was opened a crack for me to let myself in. I nudged it open and looked down at the carpeted floor see a trail of Johanna's clothing down the hallway toward her bedroom. I followed a light blue top to a white bra a few feet ahead. A right and left brown boot on each side of the hallway preceded a pair of cargo khakis and two gray woolen socks. In front of a slightly opened bathroom door laid a pair of small white panties, kicked off rather than placed neatly. I pushed the door open to hear the shower running amid a cloud of steam.

"Hello?"

"Are you coming in or what?" she said, behind the shower curtain.

"Actually, I washed my face and chest in the Amtrak bathroom sometime around Albany, so I think I'm all set for now."

She whipped the curtain open to show herself, body wet and red hair matted back from the water.

"Joseph," she said, softly. "Don't make me walk over there and take your clothes off myself."

I stripped and stepped over the tub's edge to press my chest up against Johanna's under a steady flow of hot water. We touched and moved across each other under the water. There was nothing awkward, nothing out of rhythm. Over the time we'd spent together, we became good at this. We knew where to kiss, how to move or what to touch, how much or how little. Though there was little surprise in the moves we made, it was still adventurous. The shower had been done before, and the maneuvering needed so we wouldn't break our necks by slipping on a bar of soap was well covered. A leg lifted here, a hand to balance there and we were into it, lost in the kissing and the breathing as the water continued to fall. I watched her full of whatever feeling she was experiencing through the look in her eyes or the curl of her smile. Those eyes gleamed brighter against her pale skin and the white tile behind her. She looked into mine as she moved her hands from around my waist to wrap them around the back of my neck. We started to breathe heavier, and I leaned in to kiss her upper lip. I quickly pulled back to ask a question that, judging by the look on her face, was probably too late.

"Are you sure this is a good idea?"

She turned her head to the right and let out a long, quiet sigh. Her hands gripped the sides of my shoulders, and then slowly moved down toward my waist again to pull me close. After she caught her breath, she slowly turned back to face me, eyes closed before she opened them slowly. She leaned in to kiss my neck and then moved across to my lips, gently kissing them before backing away for an answer.

"Oh, I'm sure it was, Joseph. Positive."

A few seconds later, I couldn't disagree. I slumped down toward the base of the tub to rest against the back wall. My arms were tired from the holding and balancing and the numbing serenity running from my neck to my knees. With the water still streaming down upon us, Johanna slid between my legs to rest her back against my chest, her red hair wet on my left shoulder. I sat motionless, enjoying the shared tranquility as I put my hand on her chest to feel her heart racing. She turned her head around enough to see me out of the corner of her right eye.

"So why aren't we together?" she said.

"You tell me. You know this was never the problem. This has always been right, always been easy."

"But the other thing. That's it, huh? That's all that stands between you and me doing this on a regular basis again?"

"Honestly? I think so, yeah."

"So, honestly, if I'm not taking the pills and continue to work out my issues with the therapist, you could see the two of us getting married at some point? You'd want to be with me for the rest of your life?"

"Johanna, that's what I've always wanted. I've never stopped loving you, and the only obstacles are your doubts and drugs. If they're history, well, yeah, I could see myself with you for the rest of my life. No questions asked."

"And that's why you came here this weekend? To see whether those barriers have crumbled or not?"

"Absolutely," I said, experiencing a brief moment of certainty I was both surprised and appreciative of. "That, and to see if New York City is a place I could actually live."

She got up to sit across from me.

"So how's it going so far? You think you're gonna move here soon or what? Be around me all the time? C'mon, c'mon, c'mon," she plead jokingly while grabbing my knees and shaking them from side to side.

"Well, I wasn't given too spectacular of an intro to New York hospitality over at Connolly's tonight, but the verdict's still out on the other issue."

"Me?"

"Bingo."

"But, how am I doing so far? Say good, c'mon. Say I'm so cute and adorable and you can't live without me, little Cahan."

And she was so cute, so adorable and so beautiful. It was all so easy, so simple. When all the complications of our relationship were stripped away, I was left with one question: Is *it* there? What it is, I guess, is left for each individual to figure out for themselves. But for Johanna and me, it was there in abundance. It was delivered with a look in the eyes or a slight touch of the face, or maybe with the anticipation in our stomachs when in each other's company. It could even temper unsettled youthful curiosity of what things might be like with someone else. And those thoughts would come up, even during our best of times. Could things be as good, even better with someone else? Could there be deeper looks, transcendent sex, and conversation more enlightening and engaging with another? Was there a girl out there with Nicole Kidman's eyes, Madonna's sexual acumen—and a genuine interest in defending the Buffalo Bills place in NFL history, albeit saddled with four Super Bowl losses? Perhaps. Maybe. Possibly. But, even at twenty-two years old, I appreciated how *it* didn't fall into every man's lap. I appreciated what was important, what lasted and what would get very old, very fast. I understood the irrelevance of fantasizing about someone better when the woman in front of me may have been as good as it gets.

As I watched her smile and giggle across from me, I also appreciated "it" was too important to shove to the side because of what happened in the past, like the arguments and addictions that left me apprehensive in Buffalo and Boston. Sitting in that tub, I appreciated it all—even if I didn't understand why something so easy had been so hard.

26

The next morning, I rolled over in bed to see Johanna asleep. My slight movement caused her eyes to flutter open. She stretched her arms down under the sheets and let out a sigh.

"What time is it?"

"Nine-thirty," I said. "Do you want to go grab breakfast somewhere or eat here? Personally, I wouldn't mind sticking around if we're going into the city later to meet up with Vince."

"We're going into the city to see Vince?" She seemed slightly disappointed.

"Well, yeah, I told him we'd go out for the night so he could talk me into moving here. Why, what did you have in mind?"

"I thought we could catch a movie around here. There's a special screening of *An Affair to Remember* at midnight tonight over at this small theater in Greenwich. Thought it would be appropriate since you were in town to woo the redhead, right?" she said, smiled.

"I'll tell you what: How about I call and tell him we'll shoot in there for dinner, have a few beers, and then take the train back here in time for the movie? That's a decent compromise, right?"

She crossed her arms.

"And that's what we're going for these days, is it? Compromise?"

"Absolutely."

"Fine, fine," she said. "Let's do it."

Later that day, we took the train back into Grand Central Station, conveniently avoided walking past Connolly's Pub and grabbed a cab to McFadden's Pub and Restaurant on 2nd Avenue to meet up with my college roommate. Vince and Johanna's relationship was always pretty tepid, so her apprehension toward meeting him was understandable. He was around for our good times, but he was also there for the shit. He was respectful of my hopes with Johanna, but he also had the right to be pessimistic. She thought he didn't like her, which wasn't the case. He just wanted me to be with the girl he endorsed freshman year, the girl with the soundtrack.

Vince was now living uptown with two guys he met on a summer internship at LMN Advertising, nestled in the lower east side of Manhattan. They all accepted intro positions with the agency, with Vince landing a spot in the sales department. The minute he became involved in pitching ad specs for prospective clients, he knew he was born to do the job. When informed of the salary and possible commission, he was convinced. He lived in a moderately priced section of midtown Manhattan, but that didn't say much. For a three-bedroom apartment at the corner of East 51st and 2nd, each tenant forked over fourteen hundred-a-month, utilities not included.

"But the view!" he said. "It's fucking awesome. I feel like goddamn Bud Fox in Wall Street, Cahan!"

Knowing Vince, I assumed "fucking awesome" was a view of the top of the Chrysler Building, some tenement rooftops and peeping Tom's sight of some nimble co-ed in gym shorts and a red sports bra doing Tae-Bo on her living room carpet. He wanted to sell me on moving to the city and, over the summer, he even proposed that I crash at his place until he could break his lease on his Bud Fox-ian pad. I appreciated his loyalty.

When we walked through the front door of McFadden's, I could see Vince at the corner of the bar with his back to us. He looked engaged in an intense conversation, waving his hands about in a typically animated Italian way. I crept behind, wound up and gave him a hard slap to his back, which interrupted and startled him.

"Sorry to intervene, but what girl from college are you telling them about?"

"Casey," he said, not even breaking away from his story to introduce Johanna and me. "You remember her, right?"

"The girl you dumped when you found out she listened to Yanni?"

He popped out a loud laugh.

"Yes. But she was dope, right?"

"Whatever you say, pal," I said, then brought him in for a handshake hug.

He greeted Johanna with subtle trepidation, then introduced us to his two roommates, Aldo and Jack. They both offered friendly, firm handshakes before Jack ordered Johanna and me bottles of Budweiser. Aldo was a tanned-skin Italian of slim build whose parents moved from Sicily to Edison, New Jersey when he was two years old. One look at his collared tan Polo shirt on over gray slacks and I assumed Vince regularly raided his closet. Jack was a short and stout guy who, with freckles and red hair, could have been Johanna's brother. He grew up outside Cleveland as a diehard Indians and Browns fan. After I told him I was from Buffalo, we knew we'd have a lot of pain to discuss. When Jack handed Johanna and me our beers, the five of us went over and settled at an empty table, one with an unimpeded view of a big screen television showing the New York Giants-Minnesota Vikings divisional playoff.

"So, Johanna," said Aldo in a thick Jersey accent. "Are you a Giants or Jets fan?"

"Giants, definitely," she said. "I used to have a Phil Simms jersey when I was a little girl. Morehead State's finest, right?"

"Definitely, definitely," he said. "How about you, Joe?

"Neither."

"Not a football fan?"

"No, I am. Just not a fan of teams from New Jersey. I'm a Buffalo fan, born, raised and suffering."

Aldo looked offended.

"The *Bills*? Why the fuck would you do that to yourself after they blew that Super Bowl to my Giants? Are you some sort of a masochist?"

"It's not like I wanted them to lose four Super Bowls in a row. Like I said, I was born into it. There's no getting out, even if I wanted to."

"And you don't?" he said. "Wouldn't you rather follow a team that isn't a perennial choker?"

"What's the point if they're not my team?"

"Right on," said Jack.

"Point of being a fan is to stick around during the bad times so you can claim your place in the parade when it turns around. And, when you follow a team who the rest of the country expects to lose, you're not only cheering for a win; you're cheering for a chance to tell the whole country to stuff it as their perceptions vanish. Figure when that day comes, I'll be overcome with an orgasmic joy that made sticking through those cataclysmic losses worthwhile. I'll also get credit from guys like you for being a so-called masochistic fan for simply remaining faithful to my birthright."

"Wait a second," said Aldo. "Are you the old roommate who's hoping to be the poet or writer or something like that?"

"Was it that obvious?" said Johanna.

We all had a laugh, then Aldo capped the debate.

"Whatever. Root for your Bills and whatever other tragic

franchise you want to empathize with. Your girl and I will enjoy our Giants in the playoffs today and, despite the outcome of last season, we'll enjoy our third Super Bowl championship this winter," he said, then raised his Long Island iced tea toward Johanna.

Our waitress came over and handed us menus, but we didn't plan on eating for a while. Vince and I led the conversation with stories from college as the others laughed in amusement or out of politeness. Inside stories elicited these responses from Aldo and Jack, and earned a smile and dismissive head shake from Johanna. After one of these stories, she took a sip of her beer and got up from the table.

"Where you going?" I said.

"Bathroom. Have to take a break from all the laughs," she said, sarcasm evident as I watched her walk to the bathroom. Dressed in a soft white blouse over a white t-shirt and faded jeans, she turned a few heads as she passed the bar into the bathroom corridor. Aldo and Jack both turned their chairs around to easier watch the game. With their attention on the Giants and Johanna a safe distance away, Vince leaned over with some questions.

"So how was last night? You guys seem to be getting along, so it must have gone well, huh?"

"Yeah, it did, it did. After last night, it would be easy to go back to Boston and pack it up, but we'll see. I still have to find a job."

"Like I told you before, we'll work that shit out when you get here. A buddy of mine over at LMN, his father owns this bar uptown by Columbia called the Bear's Den. I'm sure I could get you in there bartending until you get something at a paper or magazine around here. Gotta come here if you still want to do that, right?"

"You're right. But like I told you, I have to get this Johanna thing straightened out before I go diving into another exhausting situation, like finding a writing job."

He raised his glass.

"Well, it's good to see you here, no matter. Just relax and let what happens happen. If you're meant to be with this girl, you will be."

I noticed Johanna walking back from the bathroom, so I quickly raised my bottle to his.

"Here she comes, but thanks. We'll see what happens. Cheers."

"Cheers."

She reached our table as our bottles clanked together, placed her palms on the tabletop and leaned toward us, playfully suspicious.

"You two were talking about me, weren't you? Weren't you?" she said, smiling.

Vince and I kept our bottles to our mouths, but I flashed her a suggestive eyebrow raise before offering a wink. She shook it off as Aldo jumped up out of his seat to scream, "Go! Go!" at the screen, showing New York's tailback streaking down the sideline of the Metrodome in Minneapolis. The tailback dove past the last defender and over the goal line, causing the entire bar to start clapping and cheering. When Aldo moved to the right, I could see the player in the end zone taunting the Minnesota fans before Aldo turned around to taunt me.

"That's New York football, Buffalo Joe!" He flung his hand up for to slap. "A Kerry Collins spiral flows smooth under the dome, baby, and he's about to make amends for last season. What are your Bills doing? Waiting for the draft?"

I sat there, flashed a fake smile and drank my beer. I'd only met this guy an hour earlier, before he was getting in my face about my home team and assuming I'd let him. If Duff ever overheard Buffalo taunting like this in a bar, he'd cold-cock the perpetrator out of principle. If Terry met this guy and endured the first Super Bowl crack, even he would have covered Aldo in beer and bar nuts. I started to think that Vince's roommate wasn't a real Giants fan; he was just a real asshole. I was thankful when he excused himself to go to the bathroom so I could stop feigning amusement, but as I turned to Vince, Johanna was getting up again, too.

"Where are you going this time?" I said.

"To the bathroom and up to the bar for another round. Is that all right?"

"Sorry, but you do remember we have a waitress for the drinks, right? Can't you wait until she gets back?"

"She just jumped behind the bar to get a cigarette from her purse, so she's not coming back for at least ten minutes. I don't feel like waiting ten minutes for another beer, do you?"

"Fine, but you sure you're okay?"

"Joseph, I'm fine. Don't worry about me. See?" She pointed to an exaggerated smile, one with all teeth.

"All right, I'll take another beer, but grab one for Vince and Jack too."

I watched her turn and walk into the bathroom corridor. Jack turned away from the screen during a commercial break to talk with us.

"Joe, don't worry about him," he said. "He's a token New York prick who'll start something with any opposing fan who doesn't bow down before him. Once he gets it out of his system, he leaves you alone. Hasn't said shit to me about the Browns in months, even though they finished in the cellar this season."

"Kind of a front-runner too, but don't say anything to him about it," said Vince. "When we first met, I asked him where his Rodney Hampton jersey was and he didn't have a fucking clue who I was talking about. Not sure if they existed to him before he counted their Super Bowl trophies, and I was surprised he even knew who Phil Simms was earlier. Just let him talk; he's a good guy."

I gave Jack and Vince the benefit of the doubt, then watched the Giants continue to blow out the Vikings. A swing pass to the right, a ten-yard sweep to the left and they were rolling toward another score. The entire bar waited for an inevitable Giants touchdown as I was still waiting for Johanna. It had been a good fifteen minutes, and as I looked toward the bathroom area, there was still no sign of her. When I stood up to look around, I saw New York quarterback Kerry Collins find Amani Toomer in the back of the end zone for another six points. Amid the booming televised commentary, I heard a shout from the bar that sounded like Johanna's voice, followed with the start of a "Let's go, Giants!" chant in the voice of Aldo. When I turned around, I saw the two of them, shots raised at the corner of the bar before taking down the booze with a whip of their necks. I stared, but she didn't see me. If she had, she wouldn't have let a swaying and slurring Aldo, his right arm draped over her neck and shoulders, summon the bartender for two more with two fingers over their heads.

She was off the pills, but she had told me this behavior was behind her. She supposedly realized that liquor didn't mix well within her, yet there she was at the corner of the bar, ripping shots with this guy from Jersey. He'd acted like a complete prick since I'd taken my seat. With every glimpse of him, the closer I inched toward a re-enactment of my Connolly's performance. I didn't have my red bag, but as I watched this skinny Italian prepare to shoot down another shot with Johanna, I knew I wouldn't need it. I could've beaten the shit out of him with my right arm in a sling. I pushed my chair out, but Vince saw what was going on and grabbed my right shoulder.

"Whoa, whoa, what are you doing?"

"What do you think I'm doing? I'm going over to the bar to get Johanna away from her new buddy. You know she shouldn't be doing that shit, Vince."

"I'm sorry." He shrugged his shoulders. "What do you want me to do?"

"Tell you what," I said. "Either you go over there and straighten him out, or I beat the living shit out of him in front of this whole fucking bar."

"Cahan, he's a little drunk, I guess," said Vince, standing over me. "Guy has three or four drinks and starts feeling it. He doesn't know any better. Let me go talk to him. You stay here with Jack. Smoke a butt; I'll be right back."

Jack shook his head to apologize as much as he could. We'd just met, so he didn't owe me anything. But Vince did. He owed me an explanation for why he was living with this douche, and an apology later for not letting me straighten said douche out.

Johanna didn't owe me an explanation as much as she'd owe me a confession. Was a regression going on right in front of me? Around the bar, people were eating sandwiches and steaks, fish and French fries while they watched their hometown Giants stomp all over the hapless Vikings. It was dinnertime for them, or even a night out for a few game time drinks. They had no clue that the Johanna Darcy I walked away from after graduation— the one who'd get up for strange reasons and appear later to do shots of Jack Daniels or Southern Comfort that would make her crazy enough to start fights with me or others around her—had reappeared. The empty accusations of what I'd done or hadn't done would follow, and within our arguments, she became so delirious that she'd threaten me with suicide. When I would try to calm her down, she would grab something sharp to magnify how serious the mix of alcohol and prescription pills in her body had made her believe she was. I'd wrestle the object out of her hand, throw it to the ground and try to make her understand what was going on. I'd put her to bed, lie there next to her in disbelief, and then wake up in the middle of the night from an anxiety attack, worrying that this girl I loved would kill herself one night when I wasn't there to stop her. It all came rushing back to me.

This is what happened to Johanna Darcy when she ingested what her doctor described as harmless anti-depressants, prescribed to a girl who didn't have a chemical imbalance, but a dire need for reassurance from a trained professional that her problems and pressures were normal. When these pills didn't react as intended with her body, she would drink to chase away the heightened anxiety. When the two mixed in her stomach, it would influence an imbalance that often turned cataclysmic.

I brought myself back down as these thoughts passed. She was just shooting shots of liquor, shots we had done a hundred times when we first met. She didn't pop pills then; she wasn't depressed, either. When school and life grew more complicated years later, she didn't know how to handle it, and didn't feel she had an empathetic ear to vent her concerns to. She didn't want to bother her family and, as I found out too late, she never wanted to bother me. Instead, she went to her primary care physician. When she explained problems common to every young adult of her age, this doctor passed her a slip of paper instead of suggesting the counseling she actually needed. He prescribed medication without explanation, never cautioning her of the damage it could do to her. These meds were becoming as common as aspirin, a quicker fix than the ear of a sympathetic specialist. Take one a day with water; wait a little while, problems solved. Happy Johanna, happy little world. All smiles and teeth while taking down a prescription that made her problems worse. She told me she was done with these. She was in counseling for the issues that would come up, making the medication as unnecessary for her as it was from the beginning. Hopefully, I thought, she had finally understood this.

Maybe she was trying to be nice. Maybe she was stuck in an uncomfortable situation and Vince was going to rescue her. I gritted my teeth and tried to stop my heart from beating furiously. Then, I noticed Johanna's small tan purse was still on the table. Suspicious, I opened the purse to find a pack of Parliament Lights, a pink disposable lighter, and a pack of Wrigley's spearmint gum. There was a black protective case for the blue-rimmed glasses she wore when she drove at night, and tucked underneath rested an orange cylinder with a white cap attached. I pulled it out to read the prescription label: DARCY, Johanna. Alprazolam. 2 mg.

Now past her Paroxetine Hydrochloride-soaked days at St. Francis, she had decided to advance to high-octane anti-anxiety tranquilizers. Since our previous escapades led me to research, I knew these were used to treat individuals with unrealistic worries or concern. They provided more of an immediate jolt than her anti-depressants ever would have and, with overuse, were highly addictive, caused blackouts and encouraged suicidal thoughts. The date on the bottle was from two days previous, but already, the bottle was over a third light. Since Johanna was still chasing prescription meds with copious amounts of liquor, these pills must have worked as well as the old ones.

At the corner of the bar, Vince had Aldo's tan shirt clenched in his hand and jawed on aggressively as Aldo drunkenly brushed him off. Johanna had slipped back to the bathroom again, but as I still held the bottle, I saw her walking back through the corridor to the bar to grab the beers she never came back with. I put the bottle in my pocket and pushed the purse back to where it was before she reached our table. When she handed me my beer, she looked mildly apologetic as Vince and Aldo continued to argue behind her.

"Sorry," she whispered. "He kept buying them, so what was I supposed to do?"

"How about say, no, I don't do shots. Simple enough," I said. "How many did you take?"

"Five."

"In fifteen minutes? You're kidding, right?"

"Well, it was more like twenty minutes, actually." It was an attempt to joke, but the look in her eyes had turned glazed and reminiscent of past nights. My eyes were now wide and almost twitching.

"You're joking now? This problem is funny to you?"

"Joseph, these are your friends, not mine. I didn't bring us here."

I confusedly looked at her. It was now my fault she excused herself to down five shots in fifteen minutes with this prick we'd met an hour ago. Looking into her eyes, I didn't need to see that prescription. I knew, but I still wanted to reach down into my pants pocket and pull out that bottle. I wanted to show her the even bigger problem we had in my hand, but it wasn't the time. I was so emotionally steamrolled, I couldn't have delivered a coherent argument. It would have been all emotion, no thought or reason to any words that would jump out. It wouldn't sound good, and it definitely wouldn't look good in a bar full of celebratory patrons. An hour before, I was talking to Vince about how everything was working out the way I wanted. At that moment, I found myself staring at my ex-girlfriend who had lied to me. I felt so duped, so stupid that anything that happened in the next five minutes would have set me off. Just as I hoped nothing like that would occur, I was greeted at the table by Vince and Aldo.

As Vince passed behind me to get to his seat, he patted me on the back; he'd taken care of it. I had nothing to worry about now except everything with Johanna, so as Aldo sat down across from me, I assumed he would apologize. When he turned around, his eyes looked mildly glazed and his nostrils were red with white residue visible on the left one. I assumed he slipped back into the bathroom to do coke off the back of his right hand; the residue on his hand placed atop the table made me positive. I decided not to hold out for an apology. But, if he did open his mouth, I hoped to hear something cordial, something nice. Anything even mildly sarcastic or aggressive and I'd jump across the table. Two altercations in two days would surpass the amount I had had in the previous five years. My heart was pounding; my hands were shaking along, rhythmically. The pounding and shaking accelerated after he opened his mouth.

"Sorry about the shots, Joe. Just thought they'd make your girl feel better about banging someone from Buffalo."

As soon as his mouth closed, my fist re-opened it. When Vince failed to grab my shirt, I jumped over the table and cracked Aldo's teeth and nose with one swing. I got a hold of his shirt collar and rained about three more blows to the left side of his head before Vince and Jack grabbed both of my arms and led me outside and away from any bouncer. Johanna ran after the three of us as Aldo lay on his back in front of the television, smothering the blood from his mouth and nose across his face as Kerry Collins found Amani Toomer with a forty-two-yard touchdown pass down the left sideline.

When we got outside, Jack let us be and went back inside to

check on Aldo. Vince threw me up against the pub's brick exterior by my shirt collar, eyes bulging and yelling at me within four inches of my face.

"What the fuck is wrong with you? Are you nuts?"

"Why couldn't he keep his mouth shut? You really hang around and live with cokehead pricks like this guy? You're the one who's gotta be fucking nuts!"

Johanna stood to the side of us, sifting through her small tan purse for a cigarette as I noticed her sift more frantically. With a frozen look on her face, she stared into it, seemingly waiting for the pills in my pocket to appear. They didn't, and when she put it all together, my attitude toward the shots with Aldo, the look on my face when she returned from the bar, then the explosion I unleashed on this unfortunate Giant fan, she looked up at me with her wide blues, ashamed.

Vince saw our eyes. He let go of my shirt and let me lean against the wall. When he saw tears start to come down Johanna's face, he got the hint.

"I'm, uh, gonna go inside and check on Aldo. I'll be back in a minute."

Johanna continued to stare at me. I turned away and reached into my pocket for a cigarette. The one I pulled out of the crumpled pack was cracked near the filter, so I ripped the filter off, wet the end together with my lips, lit it and took a deep, deep drag. I could feel her eyes burning into the left side of my head, but I couldn't look at her. Smoking a non-filtered cigarette

354

seemed like a better idea than listening to any half-hearted excuses.

"You don't understand. You don't," she said, standing in front of me on the sidewalk, her arms crossed as traffic passed behind her.

"Don't understand what? Why you now need to pop tranquilizers like Tic Tacs? When you started taking those anti-depressants, your life became worse, yet you didn't learn a thing. Instead, you've decided to kick it up a notch. And these ones work so good that you chase them with booze, even when you know what will happen. Do you honestly think these help you?"

"Sometimes. You're not here to see the terrible weeks I go through. I can't imagine how bad the days would be without them."

"So you're not going to counseling?"

"Oh, Joseph, it doesn't do any good. You wouldn't understand."

"Understand why you won't give it a fair shot, and instead, abuse medication and lie to me about it? No, I don't fucking understand."

"Joseph, school is so hard, so frustrating. The kids, the lessons. I'm a horrible teacher and I'll never be any good at it. You know it."

"Why would I know it? Have I ever said you're going to be a failure as a teacher? Have I ever said you're no good?"

"You're thinking it."

"No, no I'm not." I took a long drag off my smoke. "You are. This is all in your head, nothing more. Look at yourself and how amazing you are, appreciate it and your doubts will evaporate. How many of these conversations are we going to have before you realize it's the truth?"

"And then there's you," she said.

"What about me?"

"What are we doing?"

"We're standing outside this restaurant so I don't go back in there and smash that guy's face in."

"No, I mean, are we going to end up together? Can you really see it happening?"

"Together? Didn't you hear me yesterday? Why do you think I'm here? You're chasing tranquilizers with booze because you're unsure about a truth that's obvious every time I'm around you?"

I held my cigarette, took a deep breath of air and looked up at the darkened sky, silently praying for patience and an explanation of the unexplained, unsure or unknown.

"I hate to tell you this, Jo, but there's people crazed with uncertainty and doubt all over this city tonight who aren't popping meds to temper their expectations of the unknown."

"You don't know what my head's like. You don't know what it's like to pass hours ignoring the negative thoughts that pop into your head, spending your nights in bed praying to God you'll wake up with an answer, with the faith that everything is going to work out. And you don't know what it's like to awake the next morning with tears streaming down your face when you realize it's going to be another day of that same agonizing worry and crippled self-esteem you begged and prayed to be alleviated the night before. You'll never get it, no matter how hard you try. You won't."

"You don't think the time I've spent in Boston, away from friends and family, away from you, hasn't had rough patches? With days I didn't want to face because I was so sick of failure? Everyone has, and they're not all popping meds and shots. You may think you need this shit in your system to coax your fears, but it strips you of everything else you already had. It strips you of your personality and your sanity. The side-effects of the last meds and your reluctance to quit them stripped you of me. Do you remember your senior year?" I took the last drag from my smoke, flicked it to the ground and waited for her response.

"It wasn't that long ago, Joseph. I remember."

"Good. Then you'll remember the nights when you would pop those pills secretly after promising me you stopped taking them. I wouldn't see you until the end of the night at the Moose Nose, and you'd be violently drunk and refuse to go home. When I finally got you home to lay you down, you'd say you wanted to kill yourself. You remember that?"

"Are you done?"

"Remember the night when you took your dosage, drank a fifth of vodka, and then I had to call the police because I found you locked in your bathroom with a knife?"

"Stop it!"

"And do you remember the mornings when you'd wake up after doing all of this shit, not remember a thing because you blacked out and then plead with me not to call your parents for help?"

"Fine, Joseph! Fine!" She started to cry, with tears flowing down her face as she began to shake. "You're right! So what am I supposed to do? What do you think I need to do for my problems?!"

I paused, looked to the sky then back to Johanna.

"Look in a mirror."

"What?"

"Look into a mirror, because everything you need is right in front of you, Johanna. If you could only see what I do."

"Forget it," she said before quickly walking down the street. I jogged after her, caught her about a block away and grabbed her arm. As people passed us on the street, they turned to see what was going on, with some briefly stopping. We stepped to the side of a building and I put my hands on her shoulders, trying to calm her down as she continued to cry and shake.

"Johanna, there's nothing I can say or do any more to make you understand how amazing you are. How blessed and fortunate and beautiful and kind and—goddammit!"

A buzz came up my spine and to my head. I could feel the chill gathering behind my eyes, and as I turned my head, tears began streaming down. Standing with her in the middle of New York City, I had no clue what I was doing with my life. Twenty four hours earlier, I had no new job opportunities, and my trip to New York was an attempt to find out if moving there would move me closer to some. There was a girl in White Plains I loved once, was reluctantly still in love with, and I knew my feelings for her were the one certainty I might have had in my life. I stood on the sidewalk as that certainty was evaporating.

She couldn't appreciate all she was, and no one could make her understand that except for herself. She refused to do this, refused to talk about her problems with someone trained to break through apprehension, and she refused to realize that the medication she was abusing to assuage her concerns about the future was dismantling her chances at having the future she wanted. Standing before each other, we failed to appreciate the irony.

The next morning, I woke up early from another dream of chasing the buffalo. This one didn't frighten me or inspire me or get me to jump on another train to brazenly capture what was gone. In the dream, the buffalo ran so far out of my reach that I stopped running and let it gallop away. Since I had this dream on the same night I realized how far away Johanna had gotten from me, my morning conclusion was simple: The evening's buffalo symbolized Johanna.

I carried her to bed once she passed out the night before. I stayed up writing pages and pages at her kitchen table until I fell asleep on a placemat, pen in hand. When the morning came, I left a long letter on her nightstand, along with a shorter one on her parents'. Their letter detailed what I couldn't explain over the phone to her father, who I called at the Park Central Hotel after sealing the letter. He wasn't especially pleased I was calling from his house, but he appreciated my honesty and agreed to meet me at the house with Johanna's mother by nine o'clock. His daughter wouldn't listen to me, but I hoped she would listen to the concerns of her own family. When I heard their car pull into the driveway, I grabbed my bag and stood in her bedroom doorway.

She slept soundly as her woolen sweaters sat folded in the corner. U2 albums were stacked by her stereo, and her S.E. Hinton classics stood crammed amidst the countless literary standards lining her oak book shelves. The faded jeans she wore the day we met might have been packed away in her closet, but the Johanna Darcy who once filled them was long gone. Her blue eyes were still as mesmerizing, her touch still soothing, but the girl behind these had diminished with the help of emotional chaos and chemical remedy. She was gone, and as I quietly snuck out of her house and into my cab to the train station, I knew it.

There would be no morning give-and-take full of the same pleas and excuses we'd exchanged before. Even with the unbelievable fortune we had, finding the kind of unattainable love people comb over bars, coffee shops and dating services for, we couldn't make it work. The more I tried to help her understand what she had and how what she was doing was destroying her, the more I felt like a failure. At twenty-two, I couldn't handle failing with Johanna Darcy.

I got off the train in Grand Central at ten and walked across the station's marble floors, dazed. With my red bag flung over my shoulder, I walked through crowds in the concourse, accidentally hitting a few people with my bag as I bobbed and weaved through them. I had to get across the city to Penn Station and see if Amtrak would allow me to slip onto the eleven o'clock train back to Boston instead of the later seven o'clock one I had a ticket for.

Walking by the ticket booths, newspaper stands, and central information kiosk, I knew I wouldn't be coming back any time soon. At the Hudson News stand, there were reasons upon reasons on shelves and racks for me to shun all that happened that weekend and come to New York anyway. There were magazines, newspapers and little information rags full of stories and columns I would've killed to write, but I didn't care. I was getting out of there and going back to Boston. There had to be an alternative to throwing myself into this mess. Once I accepted losing Johanna, I could try again at casting myself into the lead role of that Robert Frost poem, willing to take the road less traveled. As I stood atop the main stairwell at Grand Central to see the entire concourse below, I knew I'd have to.

I walked out the station doors to find thousands of men, women and children on the street, holding large signs and stretched banners to jam taxi cabs and sedans behind one another. The cars blared their horns loudly, trying to drown out the chanting protests booming a block in front of them. I walked further down the sidewalk to see people lining both sides of 6th Avenue accompanied with traffic trying to cross over on 48th Street. When I stopped on the sidewalk to watch, a young man holding a picket sign bumped into me, then spun around to reveal a large peace sign drawn onto his hoisted white poster board. I then noticed a policeman standing a few steps ahead of me, so I went up to him to get some answers.

"What's all this?"

"Protest calling for peace," he said. "Tree huggers think we're not going to find those terrorists overseas and execute them on sight. Fucking unbelievable. If I had my way, we'd drop the bomb over there and be done with it."

I nodded, then turned toward a set of subway stairs, its entrance blocked with yellow police tape. Looking at my watch, I only had thirty minutes to make it across town, so I went back to the cop for more answers.

"Why's the subway closed?"

"Protest, kid. Didn't I just tell you about it? Whole fucking area's shut down for security purposes."

"I have to get over to Penn Station in thirty minutes. What am I supposed to do?"

"Hoof it. Ain't no way you'll be getting through this cram in a cab, kid."

I gave him another quick nod before I started walking quickly toward the thick of the march. Before I was too far away, I heard him yell,

"And hey, at least you got that big friggin' hippie sack. You'll blend right in!"

I took the white handles of my bag and wore it like a backpack. I had half an hour to get down fifteen blocks, ten of which would be packed with chanting protesters calling for world peace. A block through, I bumped into a bearded man in a ski hat who shoved a Libertarian brochure into my chest. I threw my shoulder into two peace sign-flashing college students so I could get through quicker. When I grazed past others, I heard angry shouting directed at me, but I was going so quickly I doubt they would have ever bothered chasing.

I broke through the protest at 35th and 6th and went into a dead sprint over to 7th and down the front stairwell of Penn Station. I ran down three steps then jumped down five, repeating this rhythm down the succession of steps. When I reached the ground level, I scampered to the first open ticket window and ignored the long line of people waiting to buy tickets. At seven minutes before eleven, I looked up at the departures board to see the eleven to Boston had already been boarding for fifteen minutes. The people who I'd cut in line yelled and swore at me as I stood pounding at the ticket window with my fist, trying to catch my breath while getting the ticket attendant's attention. When an elderly woman finally approached the glass, she wasn't very polite either.

"Sir. Excuse me, sir." Her smoker's voice echoed through the speaker holes. "You can't cut everyone in this line. You have to go to the back and wait your turn."

"Lady, please," I said, desperate. "I have to make the train to Boston that leaves in five minutes, but my ticket's for tonight's train. Can I please get an exchange?"

"Absolutely not. If the ticket's for tonight, you have to either go tonight or buy a new one. Now if you'll please—"

I took a deep breath, then let loose.

"Look, lady, in the last forty-eight hours, I've knocked out an ape of a bouncer, fallen in love again, made plans for the future, broke a guy's nose, probably lost a friend, and lost that found love for good. I just ran, rammed and bobbed my way through a peace protest that wasn't very peaceful, and then hauled ass another few blocks to get here in time to leave it all behind. I'm asking you, begging you, pleading with you, please. Let me on this goddamn train so I can get the fuck out of here."

No reply. She studied the desperate look on my face as I still panted. She looked at me the way an elementary school teacher would inspect a possibly lying child, waiting for him or her to crack. Finally, she motioned with her right hand for me to slide the ticket through the window. She gave it a punch, click and a stamp, then slid the ticket back to me. I grabbed it and flashed a grateful smile.

"Thank you."

"You better run," she said. "And thanks for visiting New York."

27

The calendar read late February. Sitting in my brown leather recliner, I wore red flannel pajama pants, my faded blue Bisons t-shirt and had grown a full brown beard to drink ample amounts of evening whiskey through. The facial hair was itchy and scraggly, with small patches of red scattered throughout the brown. The whiskey soothed the irritation at three o'clock on a Saturday morning. With half a bottle down and melting ice in the rocks glass in front of me, I watched Scorsese's concert film, *The Last Waltz* alone. Again.

I refused to go out with Eli and Lou to the Jeanie Johnston or the bars downtown for the fifth straight weekend. On Fridays, I would get home from work and change into my flannel pants and a t-shirt. I'd curl up in a blanket and sit in front of the television or next to my stereo, glass in hand and bottle at the ready. I would never shower, and I'd only move from the recliner or floor to change the music, refill my ice, or to grab a bag of pretzels for dinner. In my darkened and drafty bedroom, I'd rotate such sunny favorites as "So Cruel" off U2's *Achtung Baby*, "Hawkmoon 269" off *Rattle and Hum*, Dylan's entire

Blood on the Tracks album, or the last three songs off the Stones' *Sticky Fingers*. Sometimes, I'd play "Moonlight Mile" on repeat five or six times until I regained coherency during Mick Jagger's impassioned wails.

Like I told Johanna, I did feel depressed at times. Whether it was when my grandmother passed away or working at Commonwealth, depression seeped in. When it would strike, I'd tolerate each attack before brushing it off. But, in the month following the last meeting I'd ever have with Johanna Darcy, the depression didn't go away.

I'd wake up for work and contemplate calling in sick before I'd smash the snooze alarm, roll onto the floor and will myself into the shower. I'd want to throw up from the depression and anxiety as the warm water fell over me. I couldn't form one positive thought inside my numbed brain, and I'd only get out of the shower when Lou or Eli screamed for their turn. Even then, I'd still take another five minutes to gather myself. Every morning, I'd open the curtain into the thick cloud of steam, step to the mirror and wipe it clear to see my reflection. I'd look past the beard and into my brown eyes to see nothing but hopelessness, nothing but surrender from a thin-faced twenty-two-year-old. When I looked into a sink sprinkled with shed hair, I'd feel nothing but worry about a future murkier than ever. I finally knew what real depression felt like while looking into that mirror. If there were any doubts, the darkened, torturous nights full of tears falling into my beard as I listened to Dylan's somber vocals and harmonica on "Visions of Johanna" confirmed it.

I was drunk and powerless every weekend, unable to see how great my life still was, unable to appreciate my paycheck, my health. I didn't care about my parents, my sisters, brother or grandfather, even though many people had no family. I didn't revisit Duff's theory of how happy I should be to have two good friends, let alone the others I had. Johanna was gone for good. I was languishing in professional oblivion. I was too empty to be positive about anything.

I'd walk from the Green Line past countless beautiful college girls and young professionals, bundled in overcoats, winter caps over their ears. But with each stunner who passed, another reminder of Johanna inserted itself into my head. Brown hair, blonde and red escaped from each cotton cap, but instead of appreciating the bevy of available women who walked past me every day, I could only think of the one who was missing. I walked the chilled streets of Boston on my lunch, surrounded by the city's classic architecture and brick sidewalks that first lured me. I'd walk through Boston Common and Copley Square, then through the venerable shadows of Fenway Park. I was working in one of the most beautiful cities in the world, living among a youthful, vibrant population. As I'd walk those streets, I didn't think of what I could be experiencing; I could only obsess about what I wasn't.

Feeling sorry for myself was the only thing that took no effort at all. This state seemed natural during the month after

New York.

At the end of every night since I started at St. Theresa's elementary school, I said a quick prayer to ask God for a hand in the next day. That month, I never folded my hands once; it was pointless. I also stopped sending out resumes and writing samples. I stopped writing. I couldn't even will my fingers at a time I absolutely needed to vent onto the pages of a notebook, a computer keypad, or on the weathered keys of my grandfather's typewriter. Creative thoughts that used to consume my head morning, noon and night were now replaced with black, and the inspiration from the lyrics or rhythms of Springsteen and Dylan had evaporated. Usually, the intro percussions of the E Street Band's "Candy's Room" would send a chill down my spine and ignite a passionate energy. That month, its beat elicited nothing.

And maybe this was how Johanna felt. Maybe when she'd look in the mirror, she saw nothing but despair even amid so much promise. When she felt lost, maybe she spun her own copy of *Achtung Baby*, switched to track nine, but couldn't stop her tears when she felt nothing from the beat of Larry Mullen Jr.'s bass drum in front of Edge's prosaic synth work. Maybe this was the feeling I could never understand. I knew I couldn't call her to ask. I simply had to assume that now, I understood.

Eli came through the door that morning to find me reclined and watching *The Last Waltz*. He nodded hello as he stood in the doorway, staring at me.

"Have you been in that chair all night again?"

"All night."

"How many times have you watched this movie tonight?"

"Four times. The more I watch it, the better Robbie Robertson's guitar playing gets—and the more flamboyant Van Morrison's stage presence gets. What the fuck is with the purple-sequined suit anyway?"

"You want to go in the kitchen and have a smoke?"

I hauled myself up out of the chair and walked down the hallway. Eli and I took a seat at the kitchen table before he rolled me a Camel Light over the tabletop. After he lit his, he opened the window and let in a chilling breeze.

"Go grab that blanket you got in your room," he said. "I'm surprised you weren't wrapped in it when I walked in."

"The whiskey really lights up my insides," I said, then took a long drag off my smoke.

"Cahan, you really have to clean yourself up." He exhaled out the open window. "You look like hell, you smell like shit, and this place is starting to look worse than it ever did when Sniff was here. The guy left his shit scattered everywhere, but your empty pretzel bags and bottles are making me long for the past."

"What do you want me to tell you?

"I want you to tell me you'll think about getting some goddamn help. I can find a trusted doctor through work if you want."

"A shrink? You think I should see a therapist?"

"Well, unless you think this whiskey intervention is going to sort things out, yeah," he said. "I think you should see a shrink."

"What about the yoga Lou does? Why does he do that again?"

"Meditation, I think. He says the breathing releases toxins and helps one to transcend human stress and worry."

"Well? What about that?"

He disposed of his cigarette in a Busch Light can on the windowsill.

"Cahan, I think your worries are a little more intense than Lou's. You're consumed and debilitated. He's functional."

"So what do you think talking to a doctor's going to do for me?"

"The same thing it would have done for Johanna. I know you don't want to talk about her, but here's your chance to practice what you preached. Maybe it's too late to save that relationship, but it's not too late to save yourself."

"And what if she was right? What if it doesn't work?"

"If it doesn't work, then you can go back to medicating your self-loathing however you please. Deal?"

I stuffed my cigarette butt into that same beer can.

"Deal. Anything else?"

"Well, I know it's three in the morning, but can you please take a shower?" he said. "You smell like my St. Francis gym locker."

Two weeks later, I found myself reading an old *People* magazine in the drab waiting room of Eli's referral, Dr. Kenneth Thompson. His business card advertised that he specialized in "mental health and sexual dysfunction." I panned across the room to judge the other patients, wondering silently what their issues might be while I waited.

For the middle-aged overweight gentleman wearing glasses two seats to my right, his clothes, demeanor and fidgetiness made me assume his mother sent him. His khaki pants were pulled up to the chest of his short-sleeved white poplin. The top button was buttoned, absent of a tie. Maybe he yelled at the old bag a little too loud when she told him to clean his room. Since he was over forty, maybe he didn't want to listen to her anymore.

For the teenage girl sitting across from me, her headphones were turned up loud as she painted her fingernails black. Her hair matched the polish, and it all assimilated with her manner as she sat with a scowl. I assumed her parents had sent her in as well, but for what I didn't know. Since Goth had gone mainstream a few years prior, it couldn't have been for acting abnormal. Maybe they were concerned with how much she hated them. If my parents had shipped me into a shrink when I was a teenager, they wouldn't have been too popular with me either.

I looked at myself in the mirror above the magazine table and wondered what they thought of me. A guy in his early twenties in a shirt and tie, blue car coat, a shoulder bag full of notepads, and an ambitious attempt at a full beard? Was it obvious I was there to talk about my apparent quarter-life crisis, or did they wonder if I had a sexual dysfunction? The elderly receptionist called my name before I had the chance to worry about their thoughts.

"Joseph? The doctor's ready for you."

I entered his office and didn't see the long couch usually featured in movies or television shows; just a black leather desk chair adjacent to Dr. Thompson's seat.

"Joseph?" he said, then got up to shake my hand. "Ken Thompson, pleasure to meet you. Can Lucille get you a coffee or anything?"

"No thanks. I'm all set."

I took my seat in the leather chair, and Dr. Thompson grabbed a pen and a yellow legal pad off the top of his desk. He looked no older than forty, wearing a gray cashmere v-neck sweater, black slacks and a tanned complexion behind wire-rimmed glasses. His dark hair was receding in the alleys like my father's, and as he turned to face me, he crossed his right leg over his left.

"So Joseph, let's get right at it. Why are you here?"

"Well, I wanted to talk to someone about remedying my recent depression," I said. "Over the past month or so, I've lost the will to do so myself."

"That's a good start. Now, have you lost the will to live?"

I paused, taken aback by his bluntness.

"The will to live? You mean do I want to kill myself?"

"Precisely."

"No."

"Never thought about it?"

"Never," I said. "I just want to live my life and appreciate how fortunate I am. Lately, all I've been able to do is dwell on the things I don't have or haven't achieved."

"And this attitude is preventing you from living?"

"Yes."

He scribbled on his yellow pad as we talked, writing more after some comments than he did after others.

"Now, how about odd visions or dreams, Joseph? Any specific topic that's been repetitive?"

"Well, I have had these dreams of chasing a buffalo for years. Ever since I started college. That's something, right?"

"That's something," he said, then scribbled onto his legal pad. "Ever been on medication for your problems before, Joseph?"

"No. You're the first doctor I've ever seen about anything like this."

"Do you want to be?"

"On meds? No," I said. "I don't need to. I just need to talk with someone."

"Well, if you've never been on meds, how do you know you don't need them? Many people do."

"But I don't. There are old men with war flashbacks or

women with child molestation experiences that might need meds to coax them through their troubled past. For my whiny, minor-by-comparison issues? I don't. I need to get some answers from a pro. That's why I'm here."

"So you know what your problems are already?"

"Of course."

"Most people who come in here try to explore their past for underlying experiences that may be affecting their daily routine. For those depressed about the current events of their lives, I prescribe medication to shake free from their doldrums so they can better attack their situation. You're saying you're not interested in doing either?"

"I know what my problems are, where they come from, and I don't want to shove down medication to treat them. I need to know how I, Joseph Cahan, can use what I already have to persevere in my life."

Dr. Thompson took off his wire-rimmed glasses and dangled the frames between his right index and middle fingers. He set down his pad and pen on his desk, and then looked across the room at me.

"Joseph, can I call you Joe?"

"Sure."

"Okay. So, Joe, when people find out what their problems are in here, we figure out how to attack them. What are your problems?"

"You mean besides the dreams of the buffalo?"

"Yes, besides those."

"Well, my job and uncertain future, to start." I sat up straight. "Then there's the girl I let go of."

"So, let's attack these one at a time. Ready?"

"Sure."

"The job. Do you like it?"

"Hate it. Every day is worse than the previous."

"Then quit," he said. "Next problem?"

I laughed.

"You get paid for this?"

"Handsomely," he said. "As for your future, see that up there?" He pointed to his doctorate framed on the wall above some obscure painting of a seaside boathouse. "You know what that assures me of?"

"A good job?"

"Sure it does, if I make it in here. I could get run over by the goddamn Green Line on my way to get coffee tomorrow, and the only thing that piece of paper would do is assure me of a decent funeral."

"That's dark."

"But it's the truth. The only thing I can do is get up in the morning and, after all I've worked for in my life, keep working and hope for the best. I can't spend every day fearing for all the terrible things that could happen before they do. If I did that, I would have never moved out of my mother's house, become a doctor or made it here for this session."

"I appreciate that, Doc."

"Now the girl." he said. "How long did the two of you date?"

"A little over three years."

"It's said that it takes a year to get over someone for every two years you've dated. Think you can wait it out?"

"But doctor, it's so much more," I said. "She was so much more."

"Look, Joe." He leaned forward in his chair. "How old are you?"

"Twenty-two."

"Good. Twenty-two. It's a nice age to start trying to accept what you do and do not have control over. With your job, did you take it with the best intentions and, despite them, you still sit here today?"

"Yes."

"Then it's time to move on to something else," he said. "With your future, that's easy. You have little to no control over what happens. The only thing you can do is get up, give your all, and hope for the best in what you're striving to accomplish."

"Stripped down, but I'll take it."

"Now, with the girl, do you feel you did and said everything you could've to make it work? You're the only one who can answer that."

"Yeah," I said. "I think I did."

"But you're still here to talk about it. Why?"

"Because I failed. I guess that's a hard thing for me to accept."

"Joe, relationships are full of variables, much like life. You don't have control over a lot of these variables, so you have to go back to what I told you about the future."

"And that was?"

"That effort is the only thing you have control over. If you did everything you could to make it work, you have to walk away knowing you didn't fail. You simply fell victim to variables out of your control."

"Makes sense, but my acceptance of this won't happen overnight."

"And it shouldn't. The only things that happen overnight are your dreams. Speaking of which, the dreams of the buffalo? Those are easy," he said. "You're chasing something you long for."

"But what?"

"Once again, Joe, you're twenty-two years old. You know what I was searching for at twenty two?"

"What?"

"Everything," he said. "Eventually, I found what I needed and left the trivial concerns behind. Give yourself some time, and you will too. "

When he noticed my pensive look creep toward clarity, he leaned back in his chair, folded his arms across his cashmere sweater and flashed me a grin. After he turned to see the clock above the door, he turned back to me.

"Joe, I want to thank you for the most relaxed and efficient first session I've ever had as a doctor. You still have about ten more minutes left, but if you want to call it a day, you're more than welcome to."

I stretched my arms out, scratched the side of my scraggly beard and reached out to shake Dr. Thompson's hand.

"I appreciate your time, Doc, so I'm not going to take any more of it. Instead, I'm going to try and get started on your suggestions."

"Sounds like a good first step. Until next time, here's my card if you have any questions."

I stopped and turned around with a last concern before heading out his door.

"Dr. Thompson, one more question."

"Sure."

"Where's the closest pharmacy around here?" I scratched the right side of my face again. "I need to grab a razor and some shaving cream for this beard. Thing itches like you read about."

My shoulders felt loose once I left the office. The cloud in my head started to thin. I still had issues to handle, but remedies were presented in the same simple terms my parents, grandfather and even Duff had offered earlier. I don't know whether Dr. Thompson's words held more clout because of his mounted degree but, for the first time, it made me accept how the complicated answers and solutions I was looking for might not be that complex after all.

Though I was born into Generation X, I walked the streets as a member of Generation What's Next. Every day, I was bombarded with so many more answers, possibilities and options that I ignored the simplest solutions. Laptops, cell phones, MP3 players, text messengers, and portable DVD players filled lonely hands on the Green Line, but a casual conversation with the person next to them might have provided more comfort than any combination of technological toys. Online dating services seemed like a streamlined way to deliver the perfect spouse or companion, but a friendly "hello" at the Soul racks of a local record store might ignite a meaningful relationship, free of charge. That catastrophic September morning delivered a fact each of these new amenities would never change: When life is saturated with fear and doubt, we'll all retreat to the simplest truths and reevaluate. Values like hard work, trust and faith still soothed the tough questions, causing people to reprioritize their lives on the foundation they assumed crumbled with their parents' generation. After I left the doctor's office to shave off my scraggly beard, I realized it was time to accept some things as they were. Like my parents had done, I could only live, work and hope for the best.

I knew I was finished at Commonwealth College and, as soon as I could afford to, I needed to quit. I didn't know what was going to happen over the next week, let alone the next year. Johanna was gone, and it was time to move on.

Walking toward that pharmacy, I had my whole life ahead of me with no obstructions that couldn't be overcome. I wasn't sick or dying. I was far from rich, but I wasn't poor. I thought about how much worse off I could be and, in the early March breeze off Boston Harbor, this assurance made me feel even better—until I answered my vibrating cell. I heard Terry's voice on the other end and quickly grasped how much more burdensome my life could be.

"And then there were two, Cahan," he said. "Kiley's pregnant."

28

I got an excited call from my mother in the weeks before my first St. Patrick's Day in Boston. She wanted to relay the best news my family had heard in years.

My Grandpa Cahan, loyal member of the South Buffalo Knights of Columbus for over forty years, was finally rewarded for his undying patronage to the club. On Sunday, March 17th, he would lead the Buffalo St. Patrick's Day Parade down Delaware Avenue as its grand marshal. My mother couldn't explain how he earned this honor, but my father told me that any man who enjoyed as many pints of Genesee Cream Ale as my grandfather did at the K of C deserved some sort of award. The opportunity to lead the illustrious St. Patrick's Day parade through downtown would have to do.

My mother knew I wanted to experience the holiday in Boston, but if I could sacrifice, she wanted me home. The parade usually took place on the Sunday before the 17th, but since the holiday fell on a Sunday that year, the parade was scheduled for the actual feast day. My whole family planned to stand on the corner of Delaware and Allen, right in the middle of the parade route to properly greet my grandfather in all his glory. He'd wear a black suit, top hat and a green grand marshal sash over his long black overcoat, and he'd want to show off my great-grandfather's blackthorn walking stick by the time he reached Allen. My mother said it would be a nice surprise if he saw his grandson home from Boston, so I told her I'd throw my red bag in the Blue Bomber and head home. I didn't tell her about Duff, so she didn't know I had already promised Terry I'd be home that weekend anyway.

According to Terry, Duff called him on a Tuesday night around seven-thirty. He'd be over to pick Terry up in ten minutes, but didn't say why. When Terry came out to Duff's car, he found a six-pack of Bud cans in the passenger's seat; two were missing, and one was opened in Duff's hand. When he asked him what was up, Duff didn't answer; he just drove them down to the Southtowns pier near where we grew up. There was a numbing breeze off of the lake, but Duff still got out of the car to sit on its hood. Holding the four cans by their empty plastic holster, he ripped off a beer, threw it to Terry and asked, "Will you be one of my best men?"

When Terry asked him what the hell he was talking about, Duff told him that he and Kiley were getting married at the end of April in a small ceremony at St. Theresa's. After Terry asked him why the rush, Duff simply said, "If we wait any longer, she'll look too pregnant."

When he finished that sentence, he chugged the rest of his

beer, then walked to the end of the pier and launched the empty can into Lake Erie. Terry was so shocked with the news that he took down his whole beer, too. He didn't know how to react, so he stood there in the freezing cold with Duff and finished the six-pack. Terry let him be, chaperoning more than supporting, but he knew I should come home as soon as possible. If I could make the trip, we could get together the morning of the parade to let Duff be petrified in front of the both of us. Duff always said that a man is a lucky man if he has one good friend. According to Terry, Duff needed to feel lucky.

On the morning of St. Patrick's Day, I put on my cream-colored Irish-knit sweater with a pair of jeans, along with my gray Irish cap handed down to me by my grandfather. March in Buffalo was usually cold, but with the sun shining through my front windshield on the drive downtown, it made an unusually mild day even warmer. Bars off Delaware Avenue opened at nine on the morning of the parade. At five after nine, I found myself driving to meet Terry and Duff at a place off Delaware called Founding Fathers, a clandestine dive with a brick façade and Ireland's tri-colors flying from its flagpole twelve months per year. Terry drank beers there on Thursdays with his law school classmates and, with its proximity to the parade route, it was a perfect spot to start before watching the festivities outside.

When I opened the bar's door, I saw an enthusiastic and thick crowd, with men and women hoisting pints of stout and shots of liquor under the songs of The Clancy Brothers. The celebratory atmosphere made it easy to find Terry and Duff, both slumped on stools at the far corner with full pints and shots placed on napkins in front of them. I spotted the empty stool next to them, cut through the crowd and found my place.

"Another round," I said to the bartender, cleaning a glass near the taps. I saw Duff's long face and knew his drinks wouldn't last long.

"Well, you're home," said Duff. "I wanted to wait until you got here to ask you to be my other best man. Well?"

"I'd be honored. It might be the only wedding I wear a tux to in some time."

"Yeah, I heard." He slapped my back. "Terry told me about Johanna, pal. You okay or what?"

"I'm home to be at a bar with you at nine in the morning, so I think we have bigger problems to address than mine. I'll make it. What about you?"

He took down half his pint in one swig.

"Cahan, I was serious at Christmas when I said I wanted to marry this girl. Still do. But now with a kid in the picture?" He let out a long sigh, staring at his pint. "I don't know shit about being a father."

"But that's love," I said. "Sometimes it's about real commitment in the face of total uncertainty. You don't know what's going to happen, but you know you want to find out together, right?"

"Sure, but do I want to be stuck working at the stamping plant while I wait? No. For now, I don't have much of a choice. Up to this point, this whole ride with Kiley has been like a fucking Springsteen song. Every day has been full of this crazy optimism, this reckless passion."

"Maybe too reckless," said Terry, then hid his mouth in his pint.

"I mean, my life has been like Bruce's lyrics for Out in the Street, but now? Now it's like, like—"

"I Wanna Marry You," said Terry. Duff and I looked at him for a second, and then confirmed his Springsteen reference before moving on to another pint. Still, with his identification close enough, Terry continued.

"Look, a life could never be defined by one song. A song can define a moment, but an album could describe a life. Life has different moods, highs and lows, and the inevitable mistakes, just like an album. If you're looking for a defining album, look at The River. Like life, it's a delicate balance of idealism and realism, with the classic Bruce rebellious optimism of Out in the Street on one end and the youthful burden of the title track on the other. In the middle, he mixes in the brazen profession of love on Crush on You, the somber admission of Independence Day and the rescuing anthem of I'm a Rocker. This pregnancy? It's one track that changes the mood of the album, one experience to change the course of your life. But, there are more songs to get to, so let the album play. In the end, you might like what you hear."

After we digested this ambitious metaphorical rant, Duff and I turned to look at Terry. Slowly but surely, our confusion turned to affirmation. Terry Ford, aspiring attorney, decided to bench his limited knowledge of litigation and, instead, simplify the intense complexities grasping Duff's life with the music our friendships were built on. His life was about to change earlier than anticipated, but Duff still nodded in appreciation. An exhale gave way to a satisfied grin, and he raised his chilled shot of whiskey for a St. Pat's toast.

"To my two best friends in celebration of this holiest of holy occasions: May the road rise to meet you, may the wind be always at your backs and such. May you both be there through my marriage, my eventual fatherhood, and the rest of our long and prosperous lives—"

"Amen," yelled Terry.

We raised our glasses, inhaled the shots and let the whiskey burn in our chests. A wider grin came to Duff's face as he grabbed Terry and me by the backs of our necks and gave us a shake. Though Terry's Springsteen reference may have been the clincher, our mere presence gave him confidence toward his next step. If he put forth all he had, he knew we'd never let him fail. With this support in hand, he raised his pint in front of him and shouted over the rest of the bar.

"Happy St. Patrick's Day, Buffalo! I'm in love, and I'm getting married!"

He was greeted with cheers and hoots, and finished his stout before "The Wild Rover" emanated out the juke to serenade the congratulatory patrons. Duff was in love. He shouted it out like he knew the feeling wasn't induced by the liquor flowing through his veins. It was real, it was thrilling, and the responsibilities that came with it were daunting. When the refrain of the song demanded a sing-a-long, we obliged with the rest of the bar.

"*And it's no, nay, never*," we sang, then stomped four times on the bar floor. "*No, nay, never, no more. Well, I played the wild rover. No, never, no more.*"

When the song ended, we all cheered as Duff fell back onto his stool. His smile grew stronger as he turned to me, looking for answers.

"So I'm getting married. Gonna have a kid," he said. "And what are you doing with yourself? What's next?"

"For the first time in my life, I think I'm okay saying I have no clue," I said. "I'm taking a break from finding all the answers, but I do have a few."

"Johanna?"

"Gone."

"Boston?"

"Still there."

"Job?"

"Need to find a new one."

"I have a job for you," he said. "How about being the

godfather to my child?"

"Pencil me in," I said, then raised my new pint to his.

"But you'll have to be around. My kid can't have some fucking deadbeat godfather. Think you could be coaxed back to town?"

I was where I wanted to be, on that stool with who I wanted to be with. It wasn't these friends or this setting that kept me from being home; it was fear of me on the streets of Buffalo, with no professional reason to be there. When Johanna Darcy was clutching my romantic expectancies, there was no reason to be looking for love on Elmwood or Delaware. Those feelings were tied to White Plains, not Buffalo. The next girl I found could be anywhere.

"I'm just looking for a reason," I said. "If you could find one that would pay my student loans or another who would like to have a drink, let me know. I'll be the best godfather you and Kiley could hope for."

He glanced toward the door and noticed someone who could provide one answer.

"Well, I don't think she'll pay your student loans, but she'll let you buy her a drink."

I turned to the door to see Maria Santoro and a friend heading toward us, waving while beaming a smile. Her brown hair hung straight to the shoulders of her black car coat, and her eyes were dark and wide as she worked through the crowd. She wore a Kelly green v-neck sweater underneath her coat, modeling the day's color over her tanned skin. There wasn't another girl in Founding Fathers who looked less likely to own a Kelly green v-neck sweater. I stepped off my stool to give her a hug when she reached us. The side of my face touched hers long enough to notice something different.

"Lost the hoops for little shamrocks, huh?" I said, admiring the small green earrings peeking out from underneath her hair.

"To represent my Irish ancestors, Joey. The Santoro clan moved from Sicily to Ireland before coming to Buffalo."

I smiled.

"Yeah, so did the Cahans. Are you going to introduce us to this other Celtic princess or not?"

"Guys, this is my friend from work, Tracy." She presented us with a bronzed female, dark hair pulled back in a ponytail while she flashed emerald eyes and whitened teeth.

"This is Joe, that's Duffy, and over there is Terry." She placed extra emphasis on Terry. "Terry's in his first year of UB law school, Trace."

"Really?" she said. "I'm starting there next semester. Have any advice?"

Terry's eyes widened.

"Plenty," he said. "Take a seat and I'll start at the beginning."

Duff and I laughed as Tracy walked behind us and over to Terry. His time spent engrossed in law classes would be useful earlier than expected, but this girl wasn't the dim Fitzgerald's talent Terry had hoped his degree would lure; Tracy looked savvy, schooled. Still, Duff and I were thankful for Terry's chance to break out his old bullshit for someone new. My chance revealed more of her Kelly green v-neck by removing her coat and hanging it on the back of my stool.

"So how did you know we were here?"

"Your mother," she said. "I passed her on the corner of Allen a little while ago. She's down there with Claire staking out spots for your grandfather's big day, and told me you were starting here before coming up there."

"That's all she told you?"

"Well, no. She told me about the girl, too."

"And?"

"I'm really sorry, Joey. It's too bad it didn't work out."

"Serious?"

"Well, you want the truth? Or, do you want the appropriate, albeit fake, sincerity?"

I let out a pop laugh.

"Truth. But, let me buy you a drink and then we can talk all about it."

Smiling, she grazed my left hand with her fingertips.

"I'd like that, Joey. I'd like that a lot."

I was letting it all come to me. The times with my friends. The joy of a St. Patrick's morning. The feeling that crept up my arm when Maria touched my hand. It didn't have the sinking feeling of a rebound; it simply presented the chance to buy a girl a drink. Since this girl happened to have her own apartment off Allen, even better. If my day advanced to a tour of her living room, I'd be grateful when her parents were nowhere to be found.

We left Founding Fathers at eleven to join my mother and Claire at the corner of Allen and Delaware. My father, Frank and Molly were supposed to be there as well, and Frank was bringing the beer for us to drink as the parade marched up Delaware. The St. Patrick's Day Parade created an environment of peaceful anarchy downtown. People stood on the streets with four-packs of Guinness, twelve-packs of Budweiser and bottles of Bailey's, passing drinks back and forth as the police would stand by idly and chaperone. As long as chaos didn't ensue, the police remained reserved and friendly, enjoying the day as much as we did. They made sure families were allowed to enjoy the festivities without drunken Italian and Polish buffoons in green top hats disrupting their day. Most of us afforded the day's ancestral birthright applauded the Buffalo Police Department's efforts, albeit with a full beer in hand.

We reached our spot to see my mother and Claire had lawn chairs set up off the curb, four opened arm-to-arm, and two others with coats draped over their seats.

"Joseph, sit in one of these seats here," said my mother. "People keep trying to sit in them, and I've had to fight them off for the last twenty minutes. Everyone wants to be up front for this, you know that."

"Where's everyone else?"

"Well, Frank went over to the market to get the beers, your sister is talking to some of her friends in the parking lot over there, and your father's behind us with that older gentleman," she said, then motioned through the sidewalk crowd. When I saw him, I let Duff, Terry, and the girls talk with my mother and sister. I weaved through the crowd and patted my father's shoulder as he talked with this man. After he felt my hand, he turned to introduce me.

"Joseph, I want you to meet Ed Devaney, friend of your grandfather and fellow Knights of Columbus member. Ed, this is my son, Joseph Cahan."

"Pleasure to meet you, sir," I said, extended my hand to feel his firm, salesman-like grip. But the name: Devaney. Ed Devaney. Where had I heard it before?

"Likewise, Joseph," he said. "Your father tells me you're an aspiring writer in Boston."

"Trying to be, sir. Trying to be."

"What beat have you been trying to cover?"

"Music, mostly. Concerts, albums, that sort of thing. But at this point, sir, I'd really write about anything for anybody. Any topic, any beat. Anytime, anywhere."

"What about Buffalo?"

"Of course," I said. "Unfortunately, the powers that be at the Gazette haven't found my desire that, well, desirable. I've sent the paper inquiries, résumés, and samples almost every month since I graduated, but I've never gotten a response. I've been wondering whether I should be mad at the paper or the U.S. Postal Service."

"Well, none of these letters has ever come across my desk. I think I would've remembered."

I stood confused as my father intervened.

"Mr. Devaney is the editor-in-chief of the Gazette, Joseph. Along with the content, he's responsible for most of the hiring, firing, you name it. Right, Ed?"

"Don't like to talk about the firings or the layoffs these days. It's been a real shame," he said. "But I would like to talk to you more about where you could fit in with us at the paper. Would be an entry-level position, but I'd love to consider giving a kid with your ambition a start."

I wanted to hug this old man, but I instead politely nodded.

"Here's my card," he said. "After you celebrate your grandfather being the mightiest man in town, get back to Boston and give me a call."

"You got it, Mr. Devaney." Numbing excitement flowed down my arms and legs. "I'll call you first thing on Tuesday morning, sir."

I looked to my father. A subtle laugh crept out his mouth as he shook his head at the stunned look on my face. All those nights spent worrying about my future, all those days spent frustrated at my professional prospects were momentarily alleviated by a two-minute conversation with my grandfather's drinking buddy. I didn't know what would come of the card in my pocket, but I knew my whole year was spent looking for a connection who, the entire time, was down at the K of C, sipping Genny Cream Ale with the grand marshal of the city of Buffalo's St. Patrick's Day Parade.

My father always had advice to pass on, whether on the way home from St. Francis, in Fitzgerald's, or on that morning at the corner of Allen and Delaware. Even when I thought some of his theories were antiquated, there he was to prove how little things have changed. To him, a great résumé would never beat a firm handshake and a look in the eye, and the lessons he taught in the classroom could never top earned experience. What I knew was great for conversations over coffee, but who I knew paid for the coffee. This was the friendship and loyalty the best of Buffalo was built on. My father believed this; I understood this. I looked to him again, still grinning, arms crossed in affirmation.

"You set this all up, didn't you?" I said.

"It's the parade, Joseph. Every responsible Irishman in the city is down here. Ed happens to be one of them."

"So he just happened to pick you out of a crowd of thousands, ironically milling around this specific corner?"

"Allen and Delaware's a hot corner, son. What can I tell you? And sometimes, you know, things happen for a reason."

"And the reason for this?"

"Maybe it's to show you this is where you belong, in this city, with these people. Go grab a beer from your brother, cheer for the grand marshal and think about it, okay?"

"Thanks, old man," I said with a firm pat on his upper back. "Now let's go wait for the other old man."

We cut back through the crowd. I grabbed two cans of Budweiser from Frank and passed one to my father. I found Maria talking to Duff in the front row along Delaware and draped my right arm over her shoulder. She felt my hand graze the top of her arm, turned and flashed me a smile.

"Happy St. Patrick's Day, Joey," she said, then leaned in to kiss my right cheek.

As I enjoyed it, I saw my mother out of the corner of my eye, spying and approving with Claire. When I caught her, she gave me a quick wink before looking down the street for the oncoming Buffalo Fire Department's column of pipes and drums. They walked in file with their cadence while a small elderly gentleman in a top hat and overcoat led them past the cheering and singing masses.

Tapping the pavement with his blackthorn walking stick in his white-gloved hand, my Grandpa Cahan waved to the crowds lining both sides of the street. He wore a Kelly green tie to complement the sash angled across his proud chest. He had waited his whole life for this day, and as his black loafers moved slowly beneath him, he was taking his sweet old time with his grand marshal duties. He wanted to patiently soak in every smiling face and every bellowed salutation he had rightfully earned with his service to the city. He had made it his home, like his Ireland-born father before him; like my father after him. He cherished his roots, and the cheers from some were in appreciation of that. He was the definition of a Buffalonian, and as he led the cavalcade of thumping drums and squealing pipes toward our position on Delaware, he knew it—and loved it.

Before he reached Allen, he saw us waving and screaming on the right side of the avenue. His steps quickened as he pointed his walking stick at us, momentarily abandoning the lead of the parade to join us. He approached his clan and assembled supporters with open arms, holding up the entire troupe behind him. He found my mother for a kiss, then grabbed both my sisters and pulled them toward the shoulders of his black overcoat. He hauled in Frank for a handshake hug, and then, with his blue eyes wide with surprise, he pulled me in for one as well.

"You made it home, huh, kid?"

"I wouldn't miss this, Gramps."

"Make me a promise, Joseph. Promise you'll lead this parade someday when I'm gone."

I laughed and smiled.

"You got it, Gramps. Count on it."

He pulled away and grabbed my father. The pipes pumped out a repetitive melody in place behind him as he led him into the street.

"Walk with me, son. This is a proud day for the Cahans."

My father left the crowd and walked up Delaware Avenue with his own father. My mother sniffled before welling up as we all cheered. This was the most sentimental thing our family had been part of in years; caught up in the moment, she let some tears slip. We usually celebrated our Cahan connection through loving mockery, appreciating that the larger the laughs, the stronger the bond.

On that Sunday, together with his family and thousands of drunken revelers he considered neighbors, my grandfather let our familial bond lead the St. Patrick's Day parade through the sun-drenched streets of Buffalo, New York.

29

At the beginning of every winter, a string of logs known as the Ice Boom are placed across the eastern end of Lake Erie near the mouth of the Buffalo River.

The logs keep large chunks of ice from moving down the Niagara River during the winter and early spring, which prevents major damage to docks and the intakes of power plants downstream. However, many experts suspect the Boom is directly responsible for Buffalo's non-existent spring, as we usually skip right from the snow of winter into a cold rain, then a beautiful summer. The apparatus is usually removed in the early weeks of April, and around two weeks later, the remaining ice melts and flows down the river. This signals the end of winter and, every year, its extraction from Lake Erie acts as an annual renewal.

But 2002 hosted Buffalo's warmest in seventy-two years. Only minimal ice formed on the lake during the unusually temperate months, so the Ice Boom was pulled in and stored on March 4th. I was sitting in my parents' kitchen two weeks later, letting a mild breeze through the window soothe a headache sustained from the spirits of St. Patrick's Day. I sipped a cup of Tim Horton's coffee at eleven as my father walked unexpectedly in the side door behind me. He'd usually be at school, but with an early spring break scheduled, this was the first day off in his vacation week. When he saw my red bag packed and in the middle of the kitchen floor, he knew I was minutes from a trip back to Boston.

"Planning on leaving soon?"

"Hoping," I said. "But I'm not looking forward to the drive."

"What time did you get in this morning? Your mother said you weren't in bed when she checked at eight."

"I stayed downtown last night. With a friend."

"A friend? What friend of yours lives downtown?"

I held back my answer, but only for a moment.

"Maria. And I was asleep on her couch at midnight, I swear. Please don't tell Mom; I'm not really sure how she'd react to that."

"You know exactly how she would react to it—and that's why we're not going to tell her," he said. "So what's with Maria?"

"Honestly," I said before taking another moment. Maybe I was thinking, but maybe I was enjoying a realization. "I don't know, and I don't need to. We'll see what happens."

"Things happen, Joseph. Things happen for a reason all the time—like today. I'm home, you're home, and you're dreading this drive back. Do you want to take a little ride before you leave?"

"Where?"

"You'll see. It'll only take an hour or so, and then I'll let you zone out down the ninety. What do you say?"

"Can I finish my coffee first?"

"Bring it. It'll be nice to enjoy with the view."

We drove along the lake in his Buick, over the Skyway into downtown Buffalo; past the closed Memorial Auditorium and on toward the Erie Basin Marina. The sun shone upon the lake. A refreshing breeze blew into my half-opened window as we approached the parking lot of the marina. The Miss Buffalo was docked in its slip, and as he put his car into park, my father turned to me and said, "I have to take her out for her annual test run. Ready?"

We climbed aboard for departure, the ice melted and the waters of the Buffalo River inlet flowing freely below. Revving an engine that had been inactive since September, my father let her warm up before backing out of the marina to head down the river along the shores of the city. I opened a window to enjoy the season's abnormal warmth while my father stood at the helm inside the wheelhouse. Steering steadily, he started his questioning as I sipped silently.

"So yesterday was fun, right?"

"Absolutely," I said. "I haven't had a time like that in a while."

"Did you learn anything from the day?"

"I think so. When I saw Grandpa walking up Delaware, with everyone waving and cheering, it made me appreciate his role. He's been able to affect so many lives by rooting himself here."

"Anything else?"

"I appreciated the opportunity you had to share in his moment. It really means something to represent your family like the two of you did. I'm not sure I ever fully understood that until yesterday."

"What you saw yesterday was the reason I couldn't watch you leave Buffalo. You have choices I've never had, opportunities I never dreamed of. But the feeling I had walking with my father up Delaware Avenue, past people we've known for years, people I grew up with? It was a feeling you'll never experience until you understand that the one thing these kids in Boston and New York are searching for is what you already have right here."

"And what's that?"

"A life," he said. "Yesterday, you had a front row seat to see what one looks like."

Eyes ahead, he watched the Niagara River flow away from him as we continued down toward the Peace Bridge and the Black Rock Locks. The city passed on our right, some of its structures neglected and battered. Even with the mild winter, brick and stone exteriors had been whipped with wind and snow.

But, interspersed, there were others, buildings shimmering in the sun, beacons of hope for area residents. They gave a glimpse of Buffalo's preserved past and potential future, just off in the distance. Considering this history, I thought of its representation from the day before.

My grandfather had seen a war. Friends died at his feet on a battlefield, and he was grateful for every day he lived after. He romanced a stunning brunette under a harvest moon on Crystal Beach. Decades later, he reluctantly watched that woman pass on to heaven. He toiled in a career with bad days and good, but he never let the bad ones make him forget who he was working for. He fathered a son, became a father-in-law to that son's wife, and blessed the four kids their union produced. His life's only certainties were where he needed to be and why. Buffalo was his home and the Cahans were his family. He led his parade, and his loyalty to each was on display for all to see.

I drove back into Boston later that night, and this reality still dominated my thoughts the way it had on the Miss Buffalo, the way it had as I watched my father walk with his father. The next day would be Tuesday, and in my left pocket sat a possible ticket home. I pushed the Bomber past Fenway, down the Pike and toward the Pru. I wasn't concerned with working in New York or Boston, begging to write for a public I had no connection with. I didn't wonder where I could find a life, because I already had one waiting. The morning was hours away, but I needed to dial. When I reached my apartment, I grabbed my red bag from the back seat and went inside to use my phone.

It was late but, hopefully, someone would answer.

I pulled my cell phone from my jeans pocket and dialed while pacing across my bedroom floor. Another car alarm went off outside my open window as a variety of considerations careened through my head.

RING.

I thought about my St. Francis classmates. We stood together at graduation, enthusiastic to effortlessly find the answers; all of them. What would we do for work? Where would we live? Who would we live with? Would we be successful in any of these pursuits? Still in our college utopia, we had the privilege to assume, not yet hobbled by the rejections from corporate officers and copy editors who could cripple us or breed resiliency. Nine months out, I wondered how many graduates had come to my conclusions. I wondered how many were sickened by life's uncertainties, and how many of them questioned their purpose after that catastrophic September morning. How many were left aimlessly searching for answers we assumed would come from our diplomas, not from our faith or quiet confidence? How many had decided to inhale anti-depressants or other drugs to eliminate the questions, to coax the emptiness our culture was feeding us? Finally, how many decided to walk away from the wrong answers toward something of substance? Approaching my twenty-third birthday, I was ready to walk toward the fulfillment I saw on my father's and grandfather's face.

RING.

I thought about Johanna. I wondered how many other men and women my age were coming to the same crossroads in their relationships. How many of them were approaching a point where marriage was the next step? At such a young age, how many really knew what love was? If they did, did any ever question whether, in some cases, love was enough? How many were with someone they thought they could change, but would unfortunately find out that only people who want to change can? If any had tried to help a love and failed, I know their pain. If any had spent time praying for things to get better only to see them get worse, I understand. And, if the relationship had to end, I can assuredly say the pain associated doesn't dissipate quickly. It still hurts whenever I think of Johanna Darcy. I sometimes slip into thoughts of how I could've saved things, how I should've helped her. Regret gnaws at so many memories, but I don't regret falling in love with Johanna—and I'll never regret how far I fell. I now know what the certainty of love feels like in my heart, in my head. Hopefully, I'll feel that sensation again. Someday.

RING.

I thought about my professional dreams. I wondered how many other young adults were having their aspirations squelched as they slogged inside cubicle America to pay the bills their lives and education accumulated. How many were walking into their first day of a job they'd rationalize as "just a job," but could never subscribe to Lou's French theory of "working to live"? In the midst of failed rationalizations, how many had a Natalie who brought her baggage to work and emptied it on anyone to make her own fragile days more sustainable? How many had a Mr. Davis who made no attempt to know anyone as a person? When they thought about their professional prospects, how many woke up at night in a cold sweat fearing that, one day, they'd become what they despised? But how many would make it out the door with their soul intact, their dreams still visible, and their confidence blossoming with every step to the exit? After being broken down by the gray walls of Commonwealth College, I thankfully still had my ambition. I knew I'd never let myself become a frazzled mess like Natalie or a short-sleeved social introvert like Mr. Davis. I had seen the worst of cubicle monotony on their watch, and later that night, I'd prepare my two weeks' notice for the two of them. After months searching for inspiration, I finally had something to type on my grandfather's typewriter.

RING.

Finally, I questioned if anyone would be led back home not by fear or failure, but by their dreams and experiences. When I thought about the buffalo, I always had a sense that when I was close to catching it, it would trigger a realization. If I ever encountered the beast, the look I'd see in its eye would tell me why I was having this recurring dream since I started college at

St. Francis.

The morning after St. Patrick's Day, I awoke on Maria's couch from another dream. This time, I was running right alongside of the buffalo, somehow keeping up. It thundered ahead, up Norton Drive and toward my parents' house on the right side of the street. When we reached the house, the buffalo turned into our driveway and stopped as my family stood on the front lawn clapping for my arrival. The goofing duo of Claire and Molly stood there pointing at me, holding their umbrella message from graduation of "We love you, Cahan." Frank smiled devilishly as he cracked his knuckles and readied a punch hello for my left arm. My grandfather stood with his blackthorn walking stick, tipping his red, white and blue Buffalo Bills mesh hat in my direction. My mother and father stood side by side, Ann holding her wedding day blue rosary beads in her right hand, and Patrick with his arms folded across his chest, nodding his head in satisfaction. His advice was correct again.

Out of their side door emerged Duff and Terry, each holding cans of Budweiser from my parents' refrigerator. Smiling and pointing, they raised their beers toward me before the door opened again behind them. Out of the kitchen came Duff's new wife, Kiley, cradling a beautiful baby boy as I stared in amazement. Smiling at my reaction, she waved before hoisting up the giggling baby for me to see. Handsome and jovial, it was my newborn godson. He was the godson I would take to Bills football games, the godson who'd absorb the importance of Springsteen's passion, Dylan's lyrics, and The Clash's melodic aggression. Drooling and gurgling with his whole life ahead of him, he was the most beautiful thing I'd ever seen.

I had finally run with the buffalo. And, when Maria adjusted herself inside my arms, I woke up to see I was home. My dreams had taken me there. Soon, my life would as well.

RING.

"Hello?"

"Ma. I'm coming home."

"Again?"

"Yes," I said. "For good."

Born in Buffalo, New York and raised in nearby Hamburg, **Michael Farrell** held jobs as a paperboy, landscaper, busboy, caddie, dishwasher, pro shop attendant, house painter, cashier, stock boy, salesman, fundraiser, factory worker, office drone, waiter, bartender, NBC intern, and Capitol Records intern before having his first piece published in 2002. Since then, his work has appeared in the *Buffalo News*, *Buffalo Spree Magazine* and the *Boston Herald*, where he worked as a reporter from 2004 to 2011. He earned an MFA from Pine Manor College's Solstice Program in 2010, and now serves as an adjunct professor at SUNY Erie Community College in Buffalo.

This is his first novel.